RALLY

WALL STREET JOURNAL & USA TODAY BESTSELLING AUTHOR

DEVNEY PERRY

Editing:

Elizabeth Nover, Razor Sharp Editing

Proofreading:

Julie Deaton, Deaton Author Services

Judy Zweifel, Judy's Proofreading

Logan Chisholm

Cover:

Sarah Hansen © Okay Creations

OTHER TITLES

The Edens Series

Indigo Ridge

Juniper Hill

Garnet Flats

Jasper Vale

Crimson River

Sable Peak

Christmas in Quincy - Prequel

The Edens: A Legacy Short Story

Treasure State Wildcats Series

Coach

Blitz

Rally

Haven River Ranch Series

Crossroads

Sunlight

Standalones

Clarence Manor

Rifts and Refrains

A Little Too Wild

CONTENTS

CHAPTER ONE

FAYE

Camping. It had seemed like such a good idea when I'd left Mission an hour ago to spend a weekend in the woods. I'd planned to enjoy the mountains. Breathe in some fresh air. Clear my head and disconnect.

Camping.

I was such a freaking idiot.

"I hate you." I kicked the tire on my old Ford Explorer.

The flat tire.

"Ugh." I closed my eyes and groaned. And because I was stranded and alone, always alone, I tilted my head to the lovely blue sky and screamed. "Gah!"

I was in the middle of nowhere. I barely had cell service, and even if I could manage a call, it wasn't like I could afford a tow truck. Not this far from town.

Why couldn't anything come easy? Why was it that whenever I did something spontaneous, it always ended in disaster? Why did life have to be so . . . hard?

"I should have stayed at work." I sneered at my tire and kicked it again.

Tears pricked my eyes, but crying wouldn't get me off of this lonely gravel road, so I blew out a long breath, then pulled my phone from the back pocket of my jeans.

"If there's an angel nearby who feels like lending a wing," I said, tipping my face to the tops of the towering evergreens and the heavens above, "I'd be forever grateful if you could send me enough data to let a single YouTube video load onto my phone."

I typed in a quick search.

how to change a flat tire

Thirty minutes later, the last part of the video was still buffering, but I'd managed to get out the jack, tire iron and spare.

"I can do this," I told myself, fitting the tire iron in place. I wasn't a helpless waif. I could change a flat tire, right? I'd changed Gloria's flat bike tire once. This couldn't be too hard. "Lug nuts. Here goes."

With all my might, I torqued on the tire iron. It didn't budge. The lug nut wouldn't turn. It was supposed to come loose. According to the video, it should have turned. I tried again. And again. And again. Except no matter how hard I pushed or pulled, it didn't move.

"No," I groaned. "Please don't do this to me. Please."

With my teeth gritted, I pulled on the tool, hoping for just a tiny bit of movement.

Nothing.

"Oh my God." The iron clattered on the gravel as I buried my face in my filthy hands. They smelled like grease and dirt and metal. Maybe I was helpless after all. "Fuck."

I let my hands drop and stared down the road. "Now what?"

As I'd driven into the mountains this afternoon, I'd

passed a few ranches. How far back were they? One mile? Two? Five? If I started walking now, would I make it out of the forest before dark? Or should I camp out here, on the side of this gravel road, then walk in the morning?

I really, *really* didn't want to get eaten by a grizzly bear or mauled by a mountain lion. Which meant this was my campsite.

Spinning in a slow circle, I surveyed the surrounding evergreens and thick underbrush. It certainly wasn't the camping area I'd found on Google this morning. There was no charming mountain lake. No picnic table or firepit. After nightfall, once I was locked in the car, regretting all of my life's choices, I wouldn't be able to see the stars through all the trees.

"Worst. Idea. Ever."

A bird flew overhead, mocking me with a cheerful tweet.

"Stupid bird." I bent and picked up the tire iron. "Stupid lug nut. Stupid flat tire."

Dusty had told me it was time for me to get new tires. She'd warned me that mine were bald and overdue for a change. This car was overdue for a lot of things.

I'd had my 1992 Explorer since my senior year in high school. It had cost me an entire summer's worth of wages and tips, but it had never failed to take me from home to school to work, bald tires and all.

I guess camping was just too much for it to handle. The two-tone green and tan paint looked faded and dingy under the bright summer sunshine. The back window was coated with a sheen of dust. And this flat tire was as sad and pathetic as me.

If I called Justin, would he come out to get me? Probably.

He'd undoubtedly bring Alexa along, and she was the reason I'd decided on this camping trip in the first place.

What did that say about our relationship that I didn't want to call my boyfriend for help? That I'd rather sleep in the Explorer on the side of the road? That I'd hike however many miles tomorrow in order to beg help from a stranger?

That was another day's problem after I sorted this mess.

At least I had snacks.

I opened the Explorer's back door and reached for the plastic bag of foodstuffs I'd bought at the grocery store earlier. The box of s'more granola bars had seemed fitting for camping. So had the bag of generic-brand potato chips. And my splurge, a king-sized bag of Skittles.

As I reached for the candy, the sound of an engine ricocheted through the air. My breath caught in my throat as the noise of tires crunching on gravel grew louder and louder. My gaze stayed glued to the road, waiting. Hoping.

A black SUV with a shiny, silver grill emerged from a bend in the road, a cloud of dust billowing in its wake.

"Oh, thank God." My hand slapped over my heart. Maybe I wouldn't have to hike out after all. If I could get this tire changed, if this person could help me loosen the lug nuts, I'd be able to turn around and go home.

Screw camping.

I was sleeping in my own bed tonight. After a stop at Tire-Rama.

The money I'd been saving for a new apartment would be allocated to tires instead. But if I had to live in Justin's trailer for a few more months to ensure this flat situation *never* happened again, so be it.

I raised a hand, about to wave so the driver knew to slow, except my hand froze midair.

Wait. I was a woman in the woods alone. What if the person barreling down the road was a serial killer or rapist? What if I was easy prey? As much as I wanted to get the hell out of here, maybe flagging down a stranger wasn't the best idea. I had zero desire to be abducted or brutalized today.

There was a chance I'd been reading too many thrillers. But just in case, I whirled for the back seat, throwing Skittles and chips and granola bars aside for the other plastic bag on the floor. This one from Bucky's Sporting Goods.

Dusty had made me promise not to leave Mission without bear spray, and the clerk at the store had been nice enough to show me how the canister worked.

Pull away the safety. Press the trigger. Spray at a slightly downward angle toward the bear's feet.

What about people? Did you aim for their feet too? Or straight in the face? Should I try to get downwind? Which way was downwind?

"Shit," I hissed, clutching the can as the SUV began to slow, the dust blowing into the trees with the breeze.

Okay, I guess that way was downwind.

The vehicle came to a stop about ten feet behind the Explorer.

I gulped as the driver's side door opened and a tall man stepped outside. His eyes and most of his face were shielded by a royal-blue hat with a curved brim. His faded jeans hung low on his narrow hips, and his long legs ate up the distance from his SUV to the Explorer.

He was tall. Really tall. I was only five three, and he had to be at least a foot taller. His broad shoulders were testing the elasticity of his plain, gray T-shirt. It stretched tight across his chest and the sleeves strained around muscled biceps.

5

The Treasure State Wildcats logo was stitched in gray on the front of his hat. Was he a fellow student? It wasn't exactly a comfort. Crime was a concern on college campuses across the country, and one of the most commonly reported crimes among college students was sexual assault.

Not that we were on campus. This wasn't a raucous party or downtown bar. Still, I clutched the can tighter, ready to yank off the safety at the first hint this guy had ill intentions.

"Hey." He jerked up his chin and grinned. It was crooked, higher on the left than the right. Charming, actually.

Serial killers were charming. In every true-crime documentary I'd ever watched, they were always, always described as charming.

I was dead meat.

"Flat tire?" he asked.

My gaze flicked to the flat tire.

"Right." He chuckled. "Dumb question."

He shifted his hat, spinning it backward, and my entire body lurched at the sight of his face.

His granite jaw was dusted with stubble. The corners were sharp and defined. His dark blond hair was long enough to escape the band of his hat, the ends curling at his ears. And his eyes were a rich, chocolate brown.

Straight nose. Soft lips. He was, well . . . hot. Scorching hot. So hot that a flush crept into my cheeks.

Seriously, Faye? Was I really blushing for a stranger who may or may not want to tie me to a tree and leave me as coyote food?

"Need a hand?" he asked, reaching for the tire iron on

the ground. A tire iron that a man with that much muscle could easily turn into a weapon.

"Stop." I lifted the silver can.

He held up both hands. "Whoa. Easy. Don't spray me. Please. I'm just trying to help."

"I, um . . . who are you?" At the very least, I'd know my murderer's name.

"Rush."

That sounded like a fake name. I narrowed my eyes. "Do you go to Treasure State?"

"Yes," he drawled, confusion mixing into his expression like me asking if he was a Wildcat was the stupidest question in the world. Probably because of the hat.

Except those hats were sold all over Mission. Grocery stores. Gas stations. Grant's General Hardware.

"What's your major?" I asked.

"Business finance. Minor in economics."

I opened my mouth, about to ask the name of his favorite professor, but I didn't know any of the business professors. "What's your student ID number?"

Rush blinked. "Huh?"

I raised the bear spray a little higher. "Your student ID number. Prove you go to Treasure State."

"How will that prove I go to Treasure State?"

"Just tell me."

He stared at me for a long moment then, with a slight head shake, rattled off, "38-19037."

Seven digits. With the dash. And every student who'd started in the same year had a number starting with the same two digits. My ID started with 38 too.

So he was, in fact, a student. And so far, I didn't think he was a liar. I let the canister drop to my side again.

"Can I change this tire now?" He pointed to the wheel. "Or do you have more questions?"

"Um . . ." Did I have more questions?

He gave me a sideways glance, then spun his hat forward again, the brim once more shielding his eyes before he bent and picked up the tire iron. He moved so fast, so gracefully, I startled, jumping back a foot and smacking into the Explorer's open door.

"Easy," he said, holding up his free hand.

"I'm a woman half your size stranded in the middle of the woods alone. Switch places with me. Wouldn't you be a little jumpy?"

Rush's gaze traveled down my body, head to toe, maybe because I'd just called out our height difference. "You can trust me."

"Said all serial killers in history."

Apparently, my fear was amusing because he flashed me that crooked grin again as he rubbed a hand over his jaw. "Okay, I'll tell you what. I'm going to change your tire. While I do that, take your bear spray and go stand by that tree over there to watch."

"We're in the middle of a forest. We're surrounded by trees. You're going to have to be more specific."

That grin widened. "Any tree you want."

"Fine," I muttered, sidestepping away from the Explorer and into the grass and brush that bordered the road.

I picked a pine tree that was closest to the car, standing next to its boughs. Then I watched as Rush—if that was his real name—got to work on my tire.

With barely a flick of his wrist, the nut I'd been wrenching on earlier turned. It took him only a minute to loosen them all.

I gritted my teeth. "Stupid lug nuts."

The fear subsided as annoyance took its place. Here I was, being rescued by a big, strong man. Did I want to change a tire today? Definitely not. But it irked me that I hadn't been able to do it myself.

"So you go to Treasure State?" Rush asked, glancing over his shoulder from where he was crouched.

"Yes."

"What's your major?"

"Human development and family science."

He nodded, trading the tire iron for the jack I'd hauled out earlier. He positioned it under the axle, exactly like the video had shown, and began to crank. "Do you want to do this? I kind of took over, but if you want to change this yourself, I'll get out of the way."

That was actually . . . nice. Really nice. "Um, no. I'm good."

Sure, it would be empowering to change a tire myself. But I doubted he'd leave until it was done, and I didn't feel like fumbling through it, referencing my YouTube video with an audience.

This strong, strapping guy could rescue me from the side of the road.

No one rescued me. I usually rescued myself.

Except today.

There was an odd mix of relief and disappointment as he went back to work. I wasn't great at asking for help or giving up control. I also couldn't seem to walk away from this tree.

"What's your name?" Rush asked as the Explorer lifted off the ground.

"Faye Gannon."

"Nice to meet you, Faye Gannon. I'm Rush Ramsey."

Rush Ramsey? "Is that really your name?"

He paused the jack, resting his elbows on his knees as he looked at me. There was that confused expression again, almost like he expected his name to mean something. "Yes. That's really my name."

"Okay." Still sounded fake.

"Are you sure *you* go to Treasure State?"

"Yes, I go there." I scoffed. My ID was 38-20183.

"You've never heard of me?" It should have been an arrogant question, but it was genuine curiosity.

"Why would I have heard of you?"

He blinked. "Seriously?"

"Seriously," I said. "Have you heard of *me*?"

He worked his jaw, almost like he was fighting a smile. "No."

"Then there you go."

"There I go." Rush went back to work like he'd done this countless times, unscrewing the lug nuts entirely before yanking my flat tire free.

The muscles of his arms flexed as he moved. That T-shirt molded to the honed strength in his back.

Who had muscles like that? A model? An athlete? Was that why he'd expected me to recognize his name?

"You never answered my question," I said. "Why would I have heard of you?"

He paused and faced me, turning his hat around backward again. It was like being hit with a wave of raw sex appeal.

My pulse boomed as heat spread across my face. Rush might be the most attractive man I'd ever laid eyes on in real life. Probably not something I should be thinking, considering I was in a relationship.

I stared at the pine needles beneath my shoes.

"I'm on the football team," he said.

"Ah." So he was an athlete. "I'm not really a football person."

"Kind of figured that," he said as he took out the spare. He carried it like it weighed nothing and fitted it on the wheel hub with ease, shifting and angling it into place. Then he began refastening those blasted lug nuts. "Are you camping?"

"That was my plan. I was on my way to the lake."

With the spare in place, Rush lowered the jack until the Explorer was on four wheels again. Then he quickly tightened the tire, standing to brush his hands on his jeans when he was finished. "All set. This is an actual tire, not a donut, so you should be good."

"For how long?"

He shrugged. "I'd be more worried about your other three tires than this one."

"I'll be getting new tires." Even if I couldn't afford it.

I really should have stayed home to work this weekend.

Rush opened the back hatch, putting the flat inside along with the tools. "I'm heading to the lake myself. My parents bring their camper up every year for a couple weeks. They had a wedding to go to this weekend, so I'm going to stay up here while they're gone. My campfire is always open if you stick around."

"Oh, um . . . I think I'll probably just go back to town."

There were tires to buy. My own bed to sleep in, though the last place I wanted to be with Alexa visiting was home.

"All right. Drive safe." He nodded, then strode for his SUV. He was gone as quickly as he'd appeared, his engine rumbling as he pulled onto the road, leaving a fresh cloud of dust in his wake.

I waited until the sound of his car was gone before I walked to the Explorer, tapping the freshly changed tire with the toe of my tennis shoe.

"Rush Ramsey." Had I heard that name before? No. But I liked it. I liked that it was real.

The bear spray in my hand felt ridiculous now that he was gone. "Nice, Faye."

I huffed a laugh and tossed it in the back seat, closing the door and rear hatch. Then I walked to the driver's side door.

Time to forget about this ridiculous idea of camping. Time to go home.

Something I could do now, thanks to Rush Ramsey.

"Damn it." I kicked a rock. "I didn't say thank you."

CHAPTER TWO

RUSH

The phone that kept vibrating in my pocket, over and over and over again, was ruining camping.

"For fuck's sake, Halsey." I dug it from my jeans. Another missed call.

That made fourteen. Fourteen missed calls since I'd left Mission this afternoon.

Three of the fourteen had come while I'd been changing Faye's tire.

Another notification popped up on the screen, a voice-mail. Halsey would fill my mailbox before the night was over if I didn't answer, but I was done playing this game. I was done letting her push and push and push until I caved.

She could call all she wanted. I was taking this weekend for myself. To stop. To think. To breathe. To figure out my next steps so that when I went home, I'd have a plan.

We weren't in a good spot. We hadn't been in a long damn time.

I'd asked her to leave me alone this weekend. To give me

a break to decide where we went next. If she couldn't stop calling, well . . . I guess I knew what had to happen next.

We'd been together for over two years. After all the shit that we'd gone through, especially in the beginning, ending this relationship felt a lot like quitting.

I fucking hated quitting.

But somewhere along the way, we'd fallen apart.

My phone buzzed again, her name appearing along with a picture of us on the screen.

Halsey was standing on her toes, kissing my cheek after a game last year. My helmet was pushed up on my head, my cheeks sweaty and my smile wide after a win. A whisp of her brown hair was blowing into my face as I looked at the camera.

It was a good picture. Halsey was a beautiful woman at any angle. Except the longer I stared at it, the more it seemed . . . staged. Shallow.

Instead of coming up to congratulate me on the game, she'd had her phone armed and ready on its selfie stick. This was one of at least twenty shots she'd taken. Before she'd texted it to me, she'd made sure it was edited and cropped.

Was there anything real between us anymore? Had we always been this fake?

In my gut, I knew the answer. Admitting it to myself wasn't easy. Ending it with Halsey was going to be brutal.

I declined her call and set my phone on the cooler I was using as my makeshift table beside the campfire ring.

Maybe I should just shut the damn thing off. Everyone important knew exactly where I was this weekend. Mom and Dad would be back Sunday to pick up the camper. Maverick, my best friend and roommate, was at home. If there was an emergency, he knew where to find me. He'd come up here last summer for a couple nights to go fishing.

Except as my phone vibrated again, call number sixteen, I didn't trust myself to touch it. Not when Halsey would likely say something to piss me off and there was a chance I'd snap.

We'd been together a long time. If—when—I broke it off, I owed it to her to do it in person.

So I let it ring through to voicemail as I reclined in my collapsible camp chair and stretched my legs closer to the fire crackling in the pit.

The scents of smoke and forest mingled in the air, and I breathed them in, holding every inhale until it burned. My vision blurred as I stared unfocused at the dancing orange and red flames.

They reminded me of the woman I'd met today.

Faye Gannon.

Her strawberry-blond hair was shades lighter, but damn, she had fire.

The way she'd clutched that can of bear spray. The tilt of her chin, stubborn and defiant, when she'd asked for my student ID number. The complete lack of recognition when I'd told her my name.

All I'd been to her was a stranger. I was fairly recognizable on campus, but it was refreshing to be just another student at Treasure State.

I glanced over my shoulder, past my Yukon parked beside the camper, toward the road that looped around Gray Rock Lake.

Had Faye turned around? Driven back to Mission?

There was a chance she'd slipped past my campsite while I'd been unloading my bag in the camper. I'd brought a cooler to refill the fridge. But I hadn't heard her drive by, and since this was the first turnout on the road, she would have had to pass by.

Hopefully, those bald tires would make it back to town.

Gray Rock was over an hour from Mission. There were campgrounds closer, minutes away from city limits, and some with lakes and rivers. But they were always packed. Too noisy for my tastes, Mom and Dad's too. And Gray Rock was a nice halfway spot between my place in Mission and my parents' ranch.

It was beautiful. Peaceful. Quiet, with plenty of space between sites. Its only downfall was the damn gravel road.

Every year, Dad swore the narrow dirt track got worse. He wasn't wrong. Where it wasn't covered in washboard, it was riddled with potholes.

Not the place to be with shitty, old tires.

Maybe I'd bump into Faye again on campus this fall. Though considering I didn't cross paths with many human development and family science majors, chances were slim. Besides that, I found myself wandering campus less and less these days.

If I wasn't in class, I was at the fieldhouse or stadium for practice and meetings. The Wildcats would have a new head coach this year and it was yet to be seen what he'd expect from his players.

No, I probably wouldn't see Faye again. And that was probably for the best.

She was intriguing. I wasn't in a place to be interested in any woman but Halsey, so I pushed Faye from my mind and tilted my head to the sky.

A cloud drifted past an opening in the treetops. The wind rustled branches and leaves.

While Gray Rock Lake was a quiet spot, I wasn't the only guy camping this weekend. Across the lake, a drift boat floated. The girl inside wore a neon pink lifejacket as she cast a fishing line off the bow.

I watched her until she reeled in a fish, then after releasing it back into the water, she took the oars and rowed away to the opposite shoreline.

There wasn't much to do out here, the beauty of camping. Mom loved Gray Rock because she could sleep in and read. Dad loved to fish and hike, and being out here forced him to disconnect from the ranch.

No chores or office work. No phone calls or emails. No cattle to move or fences to fix.

Other than the weekends when they came to watch me play, they worked all year without much of a break. But camping at Gray Rock was an activity they never missed.

I sagged deeper into my chair, crossed an ankle over the other and let the fresh air fill my lungs. Out here, it was easier to breathe. This year and next might be my last at Gray Rock for a while. If everything went according to plan, I'd be leaving Montana after college, so I soaked in the sounds of the forest and let them chase away the noise in my head.

My stomach growled. I'd been too angry after that fight with Halsey to eat lunch, and breakfast had been early this morning.

I stood, tossed another log on the fire and was almost through the camper's door when the sounds of an engine and tires on gravel pulled my gaze to the road.

From beyond the thicket of tree trunks that bordered the lane, an old two-tone Explorer emerged, bouncing and swaying as it avoided one pothole just to hit another.

Faye. She hadn't left after all.

It shouldn't have made me smile. But it did.

She parked beside my truck, shut off her car and hopped out, hesitating before she slammed the driver's side door closed, like maybe she wasn't so sure about coming here yet.

"Hey."

Faye jumped at the sound of my voice, her eyes whipping to where I stood beside the camper. Her hair was in the same messy knot it had been earlier, though more of the strands had slipped free. She brushed a lock behind an ear. "H-hi."

"I almost didn't recognize you without your bear spray."

The corner of her mouth turned up. She twisted, turning sideways, to reveal the can tucked into the waistband of her jeans.

"There it is." I chuckled. "Figured you'd be halfway home by now."

"I was, actually. I drove all the way to the highway before I turned around."

So she'd been driving on this shitty road for hours. I swallowed a comment about her tires. It would only send her away. "Why?"

"I forgot to say thank you."

"You came all the way back here to say thanks."

"Well, yeah. I was rude." She shrugged. "Thank you, Rush Ramsey. I appreciate your help with my tire."

"You're welcome, Faye Gannon."

She looked around the area as she rocked from her toes to her heels. Back and forth a couple times, like she wasn't sure if she wanted to take a step forward or backward. "I'll, um, let you get back to camping. Thanks again."

"Wait." I jerked my chin toward my chair and the fire. "Want to stick around?"

"Uh . . . that's okay. I need to find a camping spot."

"You're staying?"

She nodded. "I think so."

Good for her. She hadn't let the flat ruin her plans. "Way to rally."

"Thanks. Anyway, I'd better go."

"Just to warn you, the best spots beside the lake are probably already taken since it's Saturday. Most campers come up midweek to claim the good sites. You're welcome to stick around. Set up your tent over there." I pointed to a clearing between two large fir trees on the opposite side of my site. "That's where I always set up my tent when I was a teenager."

"Oh, that's okay."

I held up both hands. "If you're set on finding your own place, I get it. But if my mother was here, she'd kick my ass for not offering. She wouldn't like the idea of you being out here alone."

"I'm not actually excited about it either." Faye worried her bottom lip between her teeth, her gaze darting from me to the camper to me to the fire to me to the chair.

Was it me? She had to know she'd be safer here than in some isolated corner of the woods, right? Or was she seconds away from taking out that bear spray?

"What's it going to take to convince you that I'm not a bad guy? I'm just trying to do the right thing."

Her shoulders sagged as she exhaled. "I finished a book the other day where the villain kidnapped a woman and plucked out her fingernails but gave her a pedicure because he had a foot fetish."

What the fuck? What the hell kind of book was that? "I don't have a foot fetish."

Faye let out a dry laugh. "I'm a bit paranoid today. Or every day."

"Understandable. Though I think maybe your reading material isn't doing you any favors."

"Probably not." She sighed, then took a step forward, followed by another. Both were slow but it was forward progress.

"How about a hot dog?" I asked. "I was just going to make a couple. I'm hungry."

"Oh, I've got my own snacks."

"Or you can save them for the drive home and eat a hot dog. I even brought relish." Before she could tell me no, I snagged another chair that was collapsed beside the camper's door. I shook it out as I walked to the fire, setting it down. Then I smacked the Wildcats logo printed on its back. "Have a seat."

Faye stared at the royal-blue canvas, unmoving.

"It's just a hot dog, Faye."

She thought about it for a moment, then walked to the chair and lowered herself into the seat, testing it out. Except before her spine touched the back, she stood again, reaching behind her.

Out came the bear spray.

Faye studied the silver can for a moment, and I was sure she'd leave it on her lap. But when she sat back down, this time all the way, she put the can on the ground beside her feet. "I don't like relish."

I grinned. "More for me."

CHAPTER THREE

FAYE

Rush's phone buzzed—again—from its spot on top of the cooler between our chairs.

Someone had called him while he'd been inside the camper gathering everything for dinner. Someone had called him while we'd scarfed hot dogs, mine plain, his loaded with ketchup, mustard and relish. Someone had called while we'd roasted marshmallows and made s'mores.

Buzz. Buzz. Buzz.

"Do you need to get that?" I asked, amazed that he even had service.

He must have Verizon. I couldn't afford Verizon, and my discount provider clearly wasn't as reliable in the Montana wilderness. Though I'd give it credit for that YouTube video, even if it had taken forever to load.

"Nope." Rush swept up his phone, gave the screen a withering glare and declined this call like he had the last.

A heavy silence settled over the campsite, as palpable as the fire's smoke. Every time his phone vibrated, Rush tensed. He'd frown and grit his teeth. By the time he relaxed and stopped glaring at the fire, it would ring again and we'd start this loop of *super awkward* all over again.

Someone really wanted to get ahold of Rush and he was really not interested in being gotten ahold of.

If not for the insistent calls, it might have been enjoyable to sit here tonight. Well, as enjoyable as it could be sitting beside a stranger. But now I'd started to feel like an intruder.

Maybe he wanted to answer the phone. Maybe he wasn't taking those calls because he felt some sort of obligation to entertain me since he'd invited me to stay in the first place.

"I should go." I'd claim the first empty campsite I came to along the road, lock myself in the car and sleep until dawn.

Not a chance I'd drive home in the dark with my tires on that gravel road. I'd wait until morning, then never, ever go camping again.

"Thanks again."

"Don't go. Please." He stopped me before I could push out of the chair. Then he shut off his phone and slid it into a pocket of his jeans. "It's my girlfriend."

He had a girlfriend? Good. That made all of this easier. I didn't have to worry about dodging a lame pickup line. Not that Rush would ever try to pick me up.

The idea of him hitting on me was, well . . . ridiculous. Guys who looked like Rush Ramsey, who played college football and drove a new Yukon and slept in a fifth-wheel camper with those fancy pop-outs, did not go for girls like me.

I bet his girlfriend was stunning. Supermodel beautiful. She probably wore designer-label jeans and had her nails done each week.

Rush and I were from two very different worlds. No, he wouldn't hit on me.

And now I felt a little sleazy for checking him out while he'd been cooking our hot dogs. In my defense, it was hard not to stare at a guy like Rush. He was the kind of good-looking that didn't seem real.

"Is everything okay?" I asked.

"She's not very happy with me at the moment." He turned his hat backward, then forward. A nervous habit? "We got into a fight before I left."

"Oh. I can go if you want to call her back. Talk it out."

He shook his head, brown eyes glued to the flames. "Don't go."

There was a plea in that request. Like if I was here, he wouldn't *have* to call her back.

And if I stayed, out here in the mountains with questionable service, I wouldn't *have* to call and check in with Justin. Had he tried to call me? I didn't want that answer.

So I stayed in my seat because he'd done me a favor with my tire and if he wanted company for a while longer, I could do that. And because I didn't want to go, not really.

I'd been sitting here for almost two hours, and with every passing minute, I found myself relaxing. Breathing. That's why I'd come up here, right? For an escape?

For a chance to take a break, even if it was only for one night.

The evening light was slowly fading, the bright blue growing darker overhead as the sun inched closer to the jagged mountain horizon in the distance. The lake was so calm that the water was an exact mirror to the forest and sky. Dark evergreens and a brilliant swath of yellow and gold from the sun.

"I've never watched a sunset," I said. "You know how

you catch pieces of it if you're driving or something. But I've never sat in one spot and watched the sun set."

"The only time I do is when I come up here camping."

Camping. Maybe it hadn't been the worst idea after all.

I gave him a small smile, studying his gaze in the fading light. His chocolate irises were flecked with gold and ringed in charcoal. His eyelashes were long and sooty. No man should be blessed with such nice eyelashes.

"Thanks, Rush. For the tire. And the hot dog. And the s'mores."

"You don't have to keep thanking me, Faye."

Very few people did me favors, so yes, I would keep thanking him. "I want to make sure I have it covered so when I leave, I don't feel guilty and drive back."

He grinned, his eyes crinkling at the sides before he sighed and returned his gaze to the fire.

Rush stretched out his legs, crossing them at his ankles. "Halsey, my girlfriend, doesn't like camping. She wanted me to stay home and go with her to this party her friend is hosting. But I'd already told Mom and Dad I'd come up and stay in the camper tonight. And I like it up here. She doesn't understand why I wouldn't cancel, and I don't understand what's so important about a party. It shouldn't have become a fight, but it feels like everything . . . escalates. So I told her I wanted some space for a few days."

And instead of giving him that space, she'd been bombarding his phone.

"Sorry." He pulled off his hat, dragging a hand through his dirty-blond hair. He put it on facing backward, then turned it forward. "I don't know why I unloaded that on you."

"It's all right."

24

He slouched even deeper into his chair, until his nape was against the back and his face was aimed toward the darkening sky overhead. He yawned.

It was contagious. A yawn stretched my mouth as I sagged into my chair. Weeks, months, years of exhaustion seemed to crash forward.

"What's it going to take to convince you to camp here instead of trekking around the lake?"

"Not much," I murmured.

"Good. I don't want you out there alone."

The protective tone in his deep voice made my chest feel tight. I wasn't used to anyone other than Dusty being protective. Justin certainly hadn't worried about me spending the night out here alone.

I stared at the flames, drawing my knees into the chair as I hugged them to my chest, trying to ignore the strange flutter in my heart. "Thanks, Rush."

"That's the last one, okay?"

"No promises."

He chuckled, a sound so natural it felt like I'd heard it a thousand times. The *super awkward* was gone, disappearing more quickly than I'd expected. But without that phone buzzing constantly, the air cleared.

It was comfortable. I still had a can of bear spray on the ground by my chair, but I dropped my guard because this felt . . . easy.

I liked easy.

I liked that Rush didn't feel the need to fill every waking second with noise or conversation. I liked sitting in the peace and quiet, watching a fire crackle and a sunset.

I needed more easy in my life, even if that meant making some changes. Big changes.

Starting with Justin. Was it weird that he was so close to Alexa? Or was I being paranoid?

"Can I ask you something?" I asked, waiting for Rush to nod. "My boyfriend's best friend from high school is visiting this weekend. She's, um . . . affectionate."

Rush looked over and arched an eyebrow. "Affectionate?"

"They touch a lot. I'll be holding his hand, and she'll take the other one. She kisses his cheek when she comes into the room, and her hugs linger a long time. Is that strange?"

"The fuck? Yeah, that's strange."

The air rushed from my lungs. "Thank you. That was the validation I needed."

"What does *he* do?" Rush asked.

"He holds her hand. He hugs her back."

And it broke my heart every time.

When she'd slide into his side, he'd tuck her close. While they watched a movie, they'd curl up with each other on the end of the couch, and I might as well not exist.

"She's visiting this weekend," I told Rush.

"Hence why you're camping."

"Yep. I needed to get out of the house."

"You live together?"

I nodded. "Yeah. For about six months."

And after I bought new tires, it would probably be another six by the time I'd saved a deposit and first month's rent to leave. But I would leave. "I'm moving out of Justin's place as soon as I can afford it."

"I'm going to break up with Halsey," Rush murmured, more to himself than to me. Like he'd finally come to a decision and the only way to cement it was to say it aloud. "Sorry. I shouldn't have told you that. Not before Halsey."

"Yeah. Same here." There was a twinge of guilt, but I'd needed to say it out loud too. I'd needed to tell someone so that when I returned home, I didn't lose my nerve. "I won't say anything."

"Neither will I." He sat up straight, standing from his chair to tend the fire. As he tossed on another piece of wood, a surge of embers burst above the flames. "Want help setting up your tent?"

"No tent," I said. "I'm just sleeping in my car."

"Oh." He looked to the Explorer and his smile faded. "The table in the camper turns into a bed. It's yours if you want it. You can keep your bear spray tucked under your pillow."

"That's okay. But thanks."

"Figured you'd say that." He returned to his seat, and we fell into more of that easy silence.

We stared into the fire, not talking, just breathing and thinking and watching the sun until it touched the jagged mountain horizon, casting the sky in a kaleidoscope of pink and gold and blue.

"Camping," I whispered.

"Not bad, right?" He smiled, flashing me straight, white teeth and a dimple on his left cheek.

Something strange fluttered in my chest, a feeling I'd never had before. I rubbed at my sternum until it was gone. Then I smiled back. "Not bad at all."

Rush leaned forward, dropping his elbows to his knees as he twisted to look at me. "You really haven't heard of me before?"

I laughed so loud it startled me. When was the last time a laugh had taken me by surprise? Too long. "This again?"

The firelight limned his face, accentuating the sharp

corners of his jaw. The straight line of his nose. The soft pout of his lips. He grinned and spun his hat backward, and damn if I didn't feel that flutter again.

He was so handsome it was dangerous.

Good thing I had a boyfriend. And he had a girlfriend.

"Your ego needed me," I teased.

His arrogant smirk shouldn't have been so attractive. "Probably."

"I'm not into sports."

"Then what are you into?"

I shrugged. "School. Work."

"Hobbies?"

Hobbies were expensive. They cost money and time, both of which were a luxury for me at the moment. "Someday, I'll have hobbies. I work a lot."

"Where?"

"Dolly's Diner."

His forehead furrowed. "Is that in Mission?"

No surprise he hadn't heard of it before. Dolly's wasn't exactly where people like Rush spent time. But that was something I was trying to change.

Dolly's might not be fancy or new. It wasn't even all that convenient for students. It was fading, slowly, but I refused to let it die.

"It's on the outskirts of town," I told him. And not the best part of town.

"Favorite item on the menu?"

"Pancakes." Dusty made them with a special batter that had been her mom's recipe. They were light and fluffy and sweet. Whenever I had a bad day, she'd make me pancakes.

"I'll have to try it out," he said, and for the first time today, it sounded like a lie.

We wouldn't see each other again, would we? I'd return to my life in Mission and he'd return to his, our paths unlikely to cross. Rush wouldn't come eat pancakes at Dolly's, and I'd never watch his football games.

Two people from two different worlds.

The easy vanished, snuffed out with pleasantries and politeness.

I missed it immediately.

"I think I'll call it a night." I bent and picked up my bear spray, and when I made a move to stand, he didn't stop me this time. "Good night, Rush."

"Night, Faye."

With a wave, I left the fire, the chill from the night air biting into my skin. I climbed into the back of the Explorer, shifting the seats so they lay flat. Then I unfolded the blankets I'd brought from home, forming a makeshift bed, and traded out my jeans for a pair of loose sweats and a hoodie.

My hair smelled like campfire smoke. I wanted to brush my teeth, and sooner rather than later, I'd need to pee. There was no way I'd fall asleep. It was too quiet without noise from neighbors or traffic. I was too aware of Rush still outside.

So I stared out the window, snug in my makeshift bed, through the glass and past the treetops to a sliver of sky that changed from blue to black.

And spent a sleepless night camping beneath the stars.

Alone.

CHAPTER FOUR

RUSH

Sunlight streamed through the camper's bedroom window, so bright I couldn't ignore it any longer.

I lifted off my pillow and whipped the covers off my legs as I swung up to a seat. A yawn stretched my mouth as I rubbed both palms over my face. Then I stood, raising my arms until my hands pressed flat on the fifth wheel's roof.

Damn, I'd slept hard. What time was it? The last time I'd crashed like that had been over Christmas break when I'd gone home to the ranch. I always slept better when I was in the middle of nowhere, without the noise from neighbors or traffic.

I shuffled into the kitchen, swiping my phone from the counter to turn it on.

Ten thirty. My stomach growled as I opened the fridge, taking out eggs and sausage. Except before I could get to work on cooking, my screen flooded with message notifications.

Voicemails from Halsey. Texts from Halsey.

And a text from Maverick.

dude call your girlfriend she's freaking out and annoying the fuck outta me

"Shit," I muttered.

I hit Halsey's name and pressed the phone to my ear.

"Hey." She sniffled. "Sorry."

I exhaled, leaning against the counter. "Hey."

"Did you listen to my messages?"

"No."

"Don't. Please. I, um . . . just don't."

Which meant she'd said some stuff she couldn't take back. It wasn't the first time we'd gotten into a fight. It wasn't the first time she'd asked me not to listen to her messages.

Other times, I'd deleted them. But maybe I needed to listen for a change. Maybe it was time to hear what she said in the heat of the moment.

"I'll be back later and we can talk, okay?"

"Okay." Her voice trembled. "I don't want to fight."

"Me neither," I murmured.

"I love you."

I opened my mouth but couldn't bring myself to say it back. Not anymore.

This was over. It wasn't fair to either of us to drag this out any longer.

"I'll come over when I get back to town, okay?"

"Don't hang up," she said.

"I'm hanging up."

"No." The sound of her crying was a gut punch.

"Halsey."

"Rush," she sobbed. "I don't want to break up."

Either she guessed that's where I was at. Or she'd broken up with me on a voicemail message that I hadn't listened to yet. "Later, all right?"

Another sniffle, then a clipped, "Fine."

Frustration mixed with sadness. Yeah, that's where I was at too.

Before I could say goodbye, she was gone.

I set the phone aside, my appetite gone, so I put the food back in the fridge and walked to the duffel bag on the table, rifling through it for a pair of jeans and a T-shirt that didn't smell like campfire smoke.

Maybe I'd take a hike this morning before breakfast. Maybe Faye would be up to tag along.

Faye.

My eyes flew to the far wall of the camper, like if I could see through the metal and siding I'd find her car parked outside.

Strange how I'd forgotten about her, but hadn't, all at the same time.

I pulled on my boots and walked to the door. It opened with a pop, the metal stairs creaking as I stepped down to the dirt.

The air was cool this morning, fresh and clean as it filled my lungs.

I breathed it in as I stared at the space where Faye's Explorer should have been parked.

The empty space.

Damn.

CHAPTER FIVE

RUSH

O ne month later . . .

"Stop pouting," Maverick huffed. "You're killing my buzz."

"I'm not pouting."

"Tell your face." He clinked his pint glass against mine. "Come on. This is our last night of freedom. Drink up, buttercup."

As I took a sip from my beer, he lifted his own to his lips and chugged until it was empty.

"Dude. Probably not the smartest move, getting drunk before practice starts tomorrow."

He pressed a fist to his heart as he belched. "I'm going to miss beer."

Our football season officially started tomorrow, and until our final game, Maverick, Erik and I wouldn't drink much, if at all. The beer at our house was already gone. We'd finished it off over the last month and no one had bought more. So tonight, to celebrate this last night of freedom, we'd come to a sports bar downtown.

"Get off your phone." Maverick shot a scowl at Erik, on the stool beside mine. "She can go one night without you."

Erik grinned, his fingers still flying over his screen. "She said she misses me already. How much longer is this going to take?"

"For fuck's sake." Maverick rolled his eyes, lifting a hand to flag down our waitress.

"Seriously, though." Erik tucked his phone away, running a hand over his braids. "Can I go now?"

Maverick groaned. "I need new roommates. You both hate fun."

"I love fun." Erik stood from his seat, taking out a five-dollar bill and tossing it on the table. "Which is why I'm leaving."

"See ya." I knocked my fist against his.

"Bye."

Like he did most nights, Erik would stay at his girl-friend's house. Maybe he'd swing home before practice tomorrow, but I was guessing he'd meet us at the fieldhouse for practice.

We hardly saw him these days. When the three of us had moved in together sophomore year, we'd been inseparable. If we weren't in class, we were studying or working out or watching a game together. But a lot had changed since those early days.

About a year ago, Erik had met Kalindi. They were nearly inseparable and his free time was spent with her. Before graduation next year, I suspected they'd be engaged.

Halsey and I had been together longer, but we'd never been like Erik and Kalindi. A night like this, I would have chosen beers with Maverick and Erik over a quiet night on the couch with my girlfriend.

Probably why she was no longer my girlfriend.

We'd broken up after I'd gotten home from camping last month. I'd listened to all twenty-one of her voicemail messages. A few were rather hard to forget.

My friends all warned me that you'd eventually cheat. Once a cheater, always a cheater. What's her name? This girl you're fucking in your parents' camper.

All you care about is football. All you've ever cared about is football. I am so tired of taking second place to a game and your team. Your precious fucking team.

We're over. Done. I never want to see you again, Rush.

I'd listened to her call me a fucking asshole. I'd listened to her spew venom. I'd listened to her cry and sob and, in her last message, beg me to forget everything she'd said when she was angry.

The breakup had been messy. I'd never seen a person cry so hard.

But after a week, the dust had settled. She'd called to apologize for the dramatics and asked if we could be friends. Maybe we could have been friends. I didn't mind the random texts and funny memes she'd find online and send over. But earlier tonight, she'd crossed the line.

She'd come to the house and told me it was time we got back together.

Apparently, she'd thought this was a break, not a break*up*.

Which meant tonight, I had to do it all over again. Break it off. Watch her cry. Say goodbye.

"You're still pouting," Mav said.

Maybe so. I'd had better evenings. But when it came to Halsey, I couldn't confide in Maverick. He wouldn't understand. Not with their history.

"Sorry." I took another sip of my beer.

"I saw Coach Ellis when I was coming out of the weight room this afternoon," Maverick said. "He was in his office setting up some stuff. He had his daughter along."

"Did you talk to him?" I asked.

"No. I figured I'd just meet him tomorrow at practice."

The Wildcats had a new head coach this year. Our previous coach had gotten his ass fired this spring for hosting underage parties like a fucking moron.

It hadn't really come as a surprise to hear the news. Most of us had wondered how long it would be until he got caught.

Too long.

And the hell of it was, it had taken a bad situation to finally bring it all to light.

One of the younger players this past spring had landed in the emergency room with alcohol poisoning and a baggie of Adderall in his pocket. He'd been drinking at Coach's house.

Coach had invited me to his place a few times my freshman year. Erik, Maverick and I had gone once and only once. It hadn't been uncomfortable, but it hadn't exactly been fun either. Coach had told us he wanted us to have a safe place to go and unwind. He hadn't given us alcohol but the fridge and the liquor cabinet in his basement had been stocked. We'd watched a game on his massive TV while some of the other guys took a few tequila shots. Then some girls had come over to hang.

Coach hadn't been with us that night. He'd been some-where else in the house doing whatever it was that he did during the parties. But the whole encounter had given me a strange vibe. He hadn't asked us not to talk about it, but we all just knew to keep it quiet.

It had been fairly tame, but odd enough that Maverick, Erik and I had never gone back.

Apparently, over the last three years, things had escalated. This spring, one of the parties had been busted and Coach had lost his job.

I hadn't minded playing for him, but I also wasn't heartbroken to see him go.

And considering Ford Ellis's experience and reputation, we'd traded up. Way the fuck up.

"What do you think it will be like?" I asked Mav. "With Ellis?"

He shrugged. "I don't know. I hope he's not an arrogant prick."

"Same."

Ford Ellis was an NFL superstar with the Super Bowl ring to prove it. He'd retired from the Seahawks as a player after an injury and taken an assistant coaching position with their franchise.

Now he was in Montana to lead the Wildcats, which to some might seem like a step backward, except Ford had played at Treasure State in college. I understood that desire to lead your former team.

Personally, I was going to soak up as much as that man could teach. He'd played for the Wildcats, been drafted and had a successful career in the NFL. He'd paved the road I was hoping to walk myself.

Graduate, then God willing, go pro.

That was the plan. The dream. The goal I'd been working toward for years.

It was never a guarantee I'd get drafted. There were quarterbacks across the country playing at bigger, better colleges. But it was possible. With a lot of hard work and luck.

Maybe Coach Ellis would bring me a bit of his luck.

That, or he'd be a cocky bastard who bragged about his own accomplishments and treated us all like we were beneath him.

Guess we'd find out tomorrow.

"This job isn't as prestigious as an NFL coaching job," I said. "Makes me think he's not here for the money or glory. That's gotta be a good sign."

"I hope you're right." Maverick slid Erik's full pint glass across the table and took a gulp. "We'll know soon enough."

"Yep." I took another drink, glancing around the bar.

Legends was one of the less popular hangout spots in Mission. It was at the end of Main Street, blocks away from the cluster of bars that were most popular with other college students. We came here because beers at Legends were two dollars cheaper than anywhere else, and they had TVs on every wall, each tuned to a baseball game.

Beside us was a group of guys each dressed in slacks and button-down shirts. They'd probably come for a beer after work. A few other tables were taken, but for the most part, Legends was quiet for a Saturday night.

The front door swung open and a cluster of girls dressed in argyle socks, plaid skirts and polo shirts shuffled inside. A blond in the middle of the pack was wearing a tiara and feather boa.

"Bachelorette party?" Maverick mused.

"I bet they're bar hopping."

One of the girls was wearing a necklace of miniature dicks. I recognized her from school, and before she noticed me, I pulled the brim on my hat lower, shielding my face.

Maverick smirked as he watched them all pile in close to the bar and order a round of shots. "So now that you and Halsey are finally done, are you going to be my wingman tonight?"

I scoffed. "Absolutely not. You're on your own. I'm about to head home."

"The hell you are," he said, but there was no threat to his words. He was too busy gawking at the girls, probably picking his target. Mav raised his beer but before he took another drink, he froze, glass halfway to his mouth, his gaze glued across the bar. "Damn, she's hot."

Which meant I could go home. He'd ditch me the second that beer glass was empty.

In all the years we'd been friends, not once had I ever seen him get serious about a woman. Maverick was content to play football, go to school and hook up with every single, beautiful woman in Mission.

It was curiosity for whoever had snagged his attention tonight that made me turn and glance over my shoulder. And it was a flash of red hair that made me do a double take.

Faye.

I hadn't expected to see her again after camping, but she'd crossed my mind a few times. I'd wondered if I'd see her on campus after school started.

Guess I wouldn't have to wait.

Maverick smacked his glass down on the table, stealing my focus. "Okay, you can leave."

Absolutely fucking not. I had no idea if he'd zeroed in on Faye, but I wasn't letting him within an inch of her body.

He rose from his stool, but before he could fully stand, I stretched across the table and clamped a hand over his shoulder.

Mav looked at my hand. "What the hell?"

"The redhead. Don't even think about it." I stood, pushing harder on his shoulder until his ass was back on the stool. "She's mine."

"She's yours?" He blinked, then a slow grin stretched across his mouth. "Ah. Rebound. About damn time."

"That's not . . . I know her. I met her camping this summer."

"Whatever, man." He held up his hands, that shit-eating grin stretching wider. "I was going for the petite brunette in the peach polo anyway. Have a good time."

I shot him a glare before walking away, his chuckle following me as I weaved past tables toward the bar.

Faye was standing at the edge of the group, not removed but not in the mix either. Her hands were clasped together in front of her as she looked up at the TV above her head on the nearest wall.

She looked . . . bored. Beautiful.

Her strawberry-blond hair cascaded in loose waves over her shoulders. It was longer than I'd realized, since she'd had it piled in a messy knot when we'd met by Gray Rock.

She was dressed for the party in a lime-green and white argyle sweater-vest over a tee. Instead of a skirt like the other girls, she was in a pair of denim shorts that showcased her toned, lean legs. Her blue socks came up to her knees.

I stopped in front of her, waiting until she noticed me.

When she did, it was her turn for a double take. "Rush?"

"Hi, Faye."

"H-hi." A pretty flush crept into her cheeks as she stared up at me.

"Do me a favor? Spin around."

"Huh?"

I twirled a finger in the air. "Spin around."

"Okay," she drawled, her eyebrows coming together as she obeyed. Her hair tickled the middle of her back as she turned in a complete circle, stopping when she faced me again with her hands planted on her hips. "Why did I just do that?"

"I'm trying to figure out where you're hiding the bear spray."

A giggle burst from her lips, so loud and carefree it seemed to surprise her because she clamped a hand over her mouth.

I chuckled. "Good to see you, Faye."

She was wearing a breathtaking smile when her hand dropped. "You too, Rush."

"Can I buy you a drink?"

She glanced past my arm to her friends. "We're supposed to leave soon for the next bar."

"Bachelorette party?"

"Yeah. We're doing a bar crawl. My friend Hannah is getting married in two weeks. This isn't really my thing but we've been friends since high school so here I am."

"Here you are." My gaze roved over her face, taking in the details I hadn't let myself appreciate when we'd been sitting at that campfire last month. The straight, cute nose. The delicate chin and pink lips. The caramel eyes with striations of copper and gold.

"Faye." One of the girls thrust a shot into her hand.

She lifted it to her mouth and threw it back, nose scrunching as she swallowed.

Fuck, she was pretty.

Had she broken up with her boyfriend? Maybe I'd find out if I could convince her to stay for a little while longer.

"On to the next bar," the bride-to-be announced.

Damn.

Faye sighed and set her empty shot glass aside. "Guess we're taking off."

"Where to?"

She pulled a card from her back pocket and scanned the list of bars they'd lined up for the crawl. "The Eagles."

"Mind if I tag along?"

"If you must," she teased, a smile toying on those sweet lips.

Yeah. I must.

———

"RUSH." Faye's breath hitched as I slid inside her body.

"Fuck." She was tight. So damn tight.

The world was spinning too fast. The edges were blurry.

But Faye. God, she was incredible.

Her fingertips dug into my shoulders as her eyelids fluttered closed. She pulled that pink bottom lip between her teeth and moaned.

Nah. She didn't get to bite that lip. Tonight, it was mine.

I sealed my lips over hers, swallowing a moan as I eased out of her body. Then I drove home, deep, in a single, deliberate thrust.

Her gasp mingled with my own.

"You feel so fucking good." I set a steady rhythm, my hips cradled in hers and her legs widening with every stroke.

"Yes," she hissed when I moved, her calves wrapping

around my hips and her heels digging into the small of my back.

Her pebbled nipples dragged across my chest as I rocked in and out, over and over and over.

Each time I kissed a part of her smooth, perfect skin, she'd mewl.

She moved her hands into my hair, tugging at the strands. Tugging hard. Faye clung to me as I locked my gaze with hers.

I was drunk. On the booze. On this woman.

When I crushed my mouth to hers, giving her everything I had, she gave it right back. Her sounds filled the room, mingling with my own.

We fucked for what felt like hours, without restraint or pause. I lost myself inside her body, and no matter how many times I drove to the hilt, it wasn't enough.

It was the best sex I'd ever had in my life.

She ignited under my touch. My whole body was on fire, and I never wanted those flames to stop. When we finally came together, it was in a tangle of sweaty limbs and raging heartbeats.

"That was . . ." Magic. Fucking magic.

"Yeah," she panted.

Tomorrow, we'd do this again. Then the day after that and the day after that and the day after that.

"Faye," I murmured her name, not sure what else I was going to say. So I buried my face in her hair, my mouth stretched in a smile, and passed the hell out.

———

THE SOUND of a car door shutting jolted me awake.

Moonlight cast my bedroom in rays of silver and gray. I lifted up on an elbow, blinking the sleep and whiskey haze away.

Where the fuck was my pillow? Or my blankets?

My vision swam as I glanced to the empty space beside me.

Where the fuck was Faye?

CHAPTER SIX

FAYE

O*ne month later* . . .
Was there a limit to how much a person could cry and vomit in an hour?

Every time I thought I was done, the nausea and hopelessness surged like there was an infinite well of tears and retching and no matter how long I sat on the diner's bathroom floor, there was no end.

I flushed the toilet and leaned away from the porcelain bowl, sitting back against the wall as I swiped at my mouth and cheeks.

"Oh my God."

A fresh wave of tears flooded my eyes. A sob escaped.

I'd had a lot of bad days in my life. More than seemed fair. But I'd always managed to keep going. Keep walking, step by step, knowing that if I just didn't quit, there'd be better days ahead.

That belief, that blind faith, had been the only thing keeping me afloat on days when I'd felt like I was drowning.

Today, I wasn't sure how to stand up off the floor. I wasn't sure how to keep going forward.

I wasn't sure I wanted to anymore.

It was so hard. Everything was just too hard. And I was tired of fighting. Tired of struggling to just breathe.

Now this?

Now what?

Another sob choked free as I buried my face in my hands, bringing my knees to my chest.

Now what?

"Faye?" Dusty knocked on the door. "You all right, sugar?"

No. No, I wasn't all right. A hiccup was the only reply I could manage. Considering the door to this bathroom was about as thick as paper, I was sure she'd heard me puking and crying.

"Oh, honey. Are you sick? Come on out so I can give you a hug."

Dusty's firm hugs had soothed a lot of my heartaches over the years, but even they wouldn't be enough, not today. Not for this.

She knocked again. "I'm getting worried, Faye Marie. And I'm about to pick this lock if you don't say something."

I choked back another sob. "I-I'm o-okay."

"Little liar, you are not okay."

I sniffled, sucking in a sharp inhale that burned my raw throat. "G-give me five."

"Sure. You've also got a visitor but that asshole can wait."

Which meant Justin was here. I groaned, so loud it made Dusty snicker.

She'd never liked Justin much, but after what he'd done

this summer, she loathed him with every bone in her fifty-seven-year-old body.

It took all of my strength to force myself to my feet. Even then I leaned against the wall, letting it hold me steady until the wave of dizziness passed and I found my balance.

When I flipped the lock and opened the bathroom door, Dusty was there, arms wide open.

I fell into her chest, fighting another wash of tears as she ran a hand up and down my spine.

"I hate him for breaking your heart."

She thought Justin was the reason for these tears? Oh, shit. To be fair, he'd been the cause of plenty. But today, it was something else entirely.

Something I'd tell her after Justin was gone.

"Where is he?" I asked, standing tall and wiping my eyes dry.

Dusty hooked a thumb over her shoulder. "In a booth. He asked for a menu. I told him to drop dead."

I didn't have the energy to laugh. "I'll go talk to him."

"Or I can kick him out."

"No." Someday, I'd let her ban Justin from the diner, but not until I was out from living under his roof.

She scowled but didn't stop me as I made my way from the bathroom through the kitchen.

Mike was at the flattop, flipping pancakes. I hadn't seen him for a while, but he and Dusty must be on again because he'd been here when I arrived.

A good thing too. I'd been a useless waitress tonight.

I was still lightheaded, probably because I hadn't eaten anything today and the idea of food made my stomach roil, and when I rounded the prep table, my hip clipped its corner. The pointy steel dug into my flesh, making me wince.

"Ouch," Mike hissed. "You okay?"

When would people stop asking if I was okay? Clearly, not.

"Fine," I said past gritted teeth, then walked to the swinging door that separated the dining room from the kitchen.

Justin rose from the vinyl-backed booth as I walked past empty tables. It wasn't late, not quite seven, but Sunday was our slowest night of the week, and I doubted we'd see another customer before we closed at eight. From the smell of ammonia clinging to the air, Dusty had already started cleaning the tables for closing.

"Hey." Justin had the audacity to look sorry as he took in my splotchy face and red-rimmed eyes.

Did he think he was the cause of my tears?

Cheating asshole.

"What's up?" I asked, crossing my arms over my chest as I stopped in front of him.

"Nothing. Just thought I could hang out until you were off. Maybe we could go out or something."

"Out?" Was he serious? He wanted to go out? "Like a date?"

He shrugged. "Why not?"

"Why not?" My head began to throb. Well, throb harder. I didn't have it in me to deal with Justin. Not tonight. "I'll see you later. Bye."

He blew out a long breath, dragging a hand through his shoulder-length brown hair before plucking an elastic band off his wrist to tie it up.

Once upon a time, I'd loved watching him put up his hair

into a man bun. It used to be sexy. It used to make me feel like I was special, the woman who saw him in all ways, hair up or down or messy on a pillow.

But then he'd taught me I wasn't special.

Honestly, it was my fault. Hadn't Mom told me that for years? *You're not special, Faye.*

Silly me for forgetting.

"Please, Faye?" Justin clasped his hands together. "I'm sorry. I'll keep saying it until you believe me. Give me another chance."

"You cheated on me."

With Alexa.

Maybe if it had been with a faceless stranger from a bar, it would have been easier to swallow. Probably not, but maybe. Except he'd cheated with his best friend. He'd known about my insecurities with their relationship, that I hated how they touched, and proved them accurate.

He'd slept with her this summer while I'd been camping. He'd fucked her in our bed.

His bed now.

When he'd confessed to cheating with Alexa, I'd started sleeping in the other room at his trailer.

I still couldn't afford to move out, not when I'd spent my deposit savings on four new tires. Not when I'd already paid this month's rent.

So I was stuck living with my ex-boyfriend in the house where he'd betrayed me and broken my trust. I was trapped with him, pandering to these visits and humoring his attempts to win me back until I was able to leave.

Awkward didn't even begin to cover it. But I was biding my time until I could escape. I'd endured worse than uncomfortable silence in the kitchen each morning. I'd had plenty of practice hiding in my room thanks to years spent living with my mother.

Now I'd have to expedite my plan, wouldn't I? Somehow, I'd have to scrape together enough money for a deposit and rent and utilities. My plan had been to live alone, find a cheap studio where I could have some privacy, but was that even an option? Studios were more expensive than simply finding an available room for rent.

But I'd never lived alone before. Not having to share a bathroom or write my name on a gallon of milk seemed like a dream.

Except I couldn't afford it, could I? Not anymore. I'd have to expand my search for rooms available. I'd get to live with strangers for a while.

Who the hell would want me as a roommate?

Who'd want to live with a poor, pregnant waitress whose life was imploding?

My insides knotted, and I nearly gave in to the urge to vomit on Justin's shoes.

"I need to get back to work," I muttered, not waiting for his reply as I turned and scurried out of the dining room, through the kitchen and right into the bathroom, where I dropped to my knees and dry heaved into the toilet. Again.

"I'm taking you to the hospital," Dusty said, coming up behind me to hold my hair because I'd forgotten to lock the door.

"I'm fine."

She tsked. "I'm about done with your lies tonight, baby-cakes. You're not fine."

"Okay, I'm not fine," I whispered, shifting away from the toilet. There wasn't anything left inside to vomit. I was empty. The pit inside my soul, bottomless.

Tears pricked and my nose stung. Empty, yet apparently there was still enough left to cry.

"Faye." Dusty crouched in front of me, concern filling her blue eyes as her forehead furrowed. She hated to frown because it made her wrinkles look deeper.

Most days, I tried my hardest not to make her worry. Plenty of her silver-gray hairs were my doing.

She worried about me the way a mother worried about her daughter.

And for a solid chunk of my life, I'd wished Dusty would have been my mom.

I wished so much was different.

I wished, down to my weary bones, that I'd never met Rush Ramsey.

But wishing was pointless. Not a single wish of mine had ever come true.

"Sick? Heartsick? Or both?"

This was no flu. "Heartsick."

"He's not worth your tears," Dusty said.

"It's not that." My voice was raw and cracked.

"Then what?"

I swallowed hard. "I'm pregnant."

Dusty gasped like I'd slapped her. Then the shock faded and the sheer devastation on her face was a knife to my heart.

The tears streamed down my face as I watched her heart break.

"Oh, baby. Are you sure?"

"There are two tests in the garbage can if you want to triple check." I'd grabbed them on my way to the diner today. I hadn't been feeling well all week. My boobs hurt and my period was late.

The sinking feeling that I might be pregnant had finally gotten so deep that it couldn't be ignored.

"Oh, God." This wasn't happening. This couldn't be happening.

Except it was. Without a doubt.

This time when I cried, I didn't bother trying to hide or muffle the noise. I cried as Dusty pulled me into her arms, rocking me back and forth as I soaked the shoulder of her teal Dolly's Diner T-shirt.

"It'll be okay," she murmured.

"Now who's the liar?"

She hugged me so tight it made my ribs ache. "It will. I promise."

"Don't make promises you can't keep."

Dusty let me go, taking my face in her weathered hands. "We'll figure it out."

I gave her a sad smile as she brushed the tears from my cheeks. "I'm such an idiot."

"Yep."

My nose scrunched. "Ouch."

"I'm not gentle, you know this."

I forced air into my lungs, holding it as I reined in the tears. Then I exhaled as Dusty let me go to sit in the space on the floor beside me.

She stretched her jean-clad legs out long as I rested my head against her bony shoulder. The smell of her perfume covered up the scent of smoke from her latest cigarette break.

I hated how cigarettes smelled. How the secondhand smoke would cling to my clothes and hair. As a kid, I'd earned more than one sneer from someone at school because I'd smelled. But over the years, Dusty's scent had become a comfort, smoke and all.

I closed my eyes, drawing it in as we sat in silence, letting the reality of this situation hover like fog in this tiny bathroom.

"When will you tell Justin?" she asked.

"Who cares? It's not his."

Dusty's jaw dropped. "Excuse me?"

"Remember Hannah's bachelorette party? I bumped into a guy from school." Not that I'd known him from school, but I hadn't told Dusty about the flat-tire incident.

No one knew how I'd met Rush.

"We had a lot to drink that night," I admitted. "He was sweet and made me feel wanted and he was such a good kisser."

"A good kiss is no reason not to use a condom," she scolded.

I cringed. "I know."

"What happened to your birth control?" she asked.

More tears blurred my vision. God, I was so sick of the tears, and I wiped at them with angry strokes. "It didn't work."

That shot I'd been getting for years had failed me completely.

Yes, we should have used a condom too, just to be safe. But I'd lost my freaking mind the moment Rush had kissed me. I'd never felt that way before, and I'd gotten swept up in the feel of his hands and mouth and body.

The alcohol was most definitely partly to blame. It had made me forget that we were from two different worlds. It had given me the courage to flirt and say yes when he'd invited me home.

When reality had slapped me in the face late that night, I'd snuck out of his bed, head pounding from the shots, and tiptoed out of his house before it got awkward. Then I'd spent money I didn't have on an Uber home.

It hadn't even occurred to me to use extra protection. The drunken haze, the Rush haze, had chased away all logic. I'd wanted to feel him, only him. All of him.

His hands. His tongue. His limbs tangled with mine. The strength of his arms when he'd held me like I was precious.

No one, ever, had made me feel precious.

Not Justin. Not my mother. Not even Dusty.

She loved me, but like she always said, she wasn't gentle.

"What am I going to do?" I whispered.

"You've got options," Dusty said.

Two. I had exactly two options. Give this baby up for adoption. Or become a mother. Those were the only options I'd consider for reasons I hadn't even told Dusty.

The idea of giving up a child made me want to move to the toilet again.

Which meant I had one option.

Get my shit together because I was about to be a mom.

I buried my face in my hands. "Fuck."

"Yep."

I was never going to grad school, was I? Hell, it would be hard enough to finish undergrad. To afford to finish this year. Was I going to have to drop out? That possibility made me want to scream.

There was no way I could afford rent and food and tuition and a baby. I was already drowning, living from one paycheck to the next, pinching every penny until it was pressed so flat it was like those souvenir machines that turned your coin into a pressed keepsake.

My heart hurt so badly I pressed a hand to my sternum as it cracked into pieces.

How many years had I fooled myself into believing I could be more than a waitress making minimum wage? I'd sacrificed so much to get this far. To get to my senior year.

My credits wouldn't go anywhere, but with every passing second, my dreams slipped through my fingers like grains of sand.

How many single mothers could balance school and work and childcare? I'd watched my own mother struggle for years. I'd lived with her resentment, her hostility that I'd come along and ruined her life.

"I won't be like my mom," I said.

"No, sugar." Dusty slipped her arm around my shoulders. "No, you won't."

Maybe I'd be poor for the rest of my life, but I'd move every mountain surrounding Mission to make sure this baby never felt the animosity and bitterness I'd lived with for so long.

"Okay." I inhaled, holding the air in my lungs until it burned.

Okay.

There were choices to make, paths to choose. But they could wait. First, I had to find the strength to stand up off this bathroom floor. Then, I had to tell Rush.

"I don't know how to tell him. Rush."

"His name is Rush? Is that a real name?"

I nodded. "Yeah."

Dusty hummed. "Do you at least have his number?"

"Yep." I groaned, shifting to dig my phone from my pocket.

We'd been on the third or fourth bar after Legends when

we'd drunkenly exchanged numbers. He'd given me his so I could call him if I ever needed a tire changed. And I'd given him my number in case he ever wanted to borrow my bear spray.

"How do I do this?"

Dusty shrugged. "Fess up. The sooner the better."

My stomach churned as I unlocked the screen. "Do it for me?"

I'd meant it as a joke, expecting her to laugh, but she plucked the phone from my grip and shot to her feet before I could steal it back. "Dusty, I was kidding."

Her fingers flew across the screen.

"You can't text—"

"Sent."

My eyes bugged out as I scrambled to my feet. "You didn't."

"You asked me to do it for you."

"I didn't think you'd do it." I swept the phone from her grip to read what she'd written.

There was a single message to Rush.

A single, devastating text.

I'm pregnant

"Oh my God."

No *hello*. No *could we talk?* No *call me*.

Nope.

I'm pregnant

My knees wobbled as I shuffled toward the toilet, the nausea returning with a vengeance. "Dusty."

She shrugged. "I'm not gentle, you know this."

Yes. Yes, I did.

Shit.

CHAPTER SEVEN

RUSH

I nside the football stadium at Treasure State, lying on the fifty-yard line, a guy could see a perfect oval of midnight and stars.

Strange how I'd spent countless hours on this field but I'd never noticed the stars. The few night games we played each year were done beneath the bright lights. The stars didn't stand a chance competing with those blinders. And otherwise, my time playing and practicing here had been under the sun, not the moon.

It was so beautiful I didn't want to blink. And if I stared at the stars, if I traced imaginary lines with my fingertip, connecting them into random shapes, then I could keep ignoring the phone in my pocket.

I could pretend like I hadn't gotten that text from Faye.

I'm pregnant

Thinking about it made my head spin, so I locked my eyes with a star and let the others swirl around it until they blurred to white circles.

For a month, I'd been staring at Faye's number,

wondering if I should call or text. But every time I started a message, I'd delete it just as quickly.

She had slipped out of my bed last month. *She* had walked away in the middle of the night. If *she* wanted to hear from me, she would have stayed until dawn.

So I hadn't texted or called. Instead, I'd dwelled on our night together for a month.

That had been one of the best nights of my life. And she'd walked out on me. Maybe she didn't want to get involved with a football player. Some of the guys, like Maverick, had reputations for getting around. I wasn't like that, but maybe she thought she was just another one-night stand. Maybe she hadn't enjoyed the sex? That seemed impossible considering the way she'd clung to me, but what the fuck did I know?

Faye was pregnant.

That, I knew.

"Fuck." I rubbed both hands over my face, swallowing the scream that clawed at the back of my throat.

What did this mean? What the hell did I do now?

Should I text her back?

I hated texting.

That one message had just changed my life. Flipped everything on its head.

And to think, my day had been going so well. I'd woken up early and made breakfast. I'd tossed a load of laundry in the washer and hung out with Maverick before we'd come to campus for the day. Practices had been hard but fun. My two workouts had been solid.

Then after a shower, I'd gone shopping to get Mom a birthday present. She wanted thermal underwear, so I'd gone downtown to Bucky's Sporting Goods. The cashier had flirted with me shamelessly.

Maybe I could have gotten her number, taken her home, except I had no desire for casual hookups. The only one-night stand I'd had since my freshman year had been with Faye.

I'd been telling myself for a month that my lack of interest in other women wasn't because of Faye. I'd refused to admit how often I'd thought about her—constantly.

So I'd brushed off the cashier's attempts to score a date and left with Mom's gift. An hour later, while I'd been shoveling my favorite fried rice and mushroom chicken into my mouth at the Chinese restaurant in town, I'd gotten a text from Faye.

The hours after that were fuzzy. There'd been driving. Disbelief. More driving. Then somehow, I'd found myself at the stadium. I'd had to climb over the fence since the gate was padlocked, but I just . . . needed to be here.

In this place, I could think. On the field, I was in control.

I'm pregnant

The stars seemed to rearrange themselves in the heavens until they spelled out those two words with their white dots.

Was this a joke? Faye didn't seem like the kind of person who'd joke about that. Granted, I didn't know her very well, but she wouldn't joke about this, right?

My phone chimed in my pocket again. The sound was terrifying. Faye had made me scared of my own damn phone.

It had been ringing for hours, and I hadn't once looked at the screen. Was it her calling? If it was, she'd have to wait. I wasn't ready to talk. Not yet. Not to anyone. Not until I could breathe through the tightness in my chest. Until I could think through the haze of shock and panic.

Pregnant.

My phone dinged with a voicemail message.

"Fuck," I hissed.

Couldn't she leave me alone? Couldn't she stop calling until I had a minute to think this through? Fucking hell, was it too much to ask that I have a few hours to myself to contemplate fatherhood?

The noise stopped. I braced, waiting for it to start again, but the only sound was my thundering heart.

My exhale was deflating, my limbs and spine sinking deeper into the turf.

What did I do? How did I manage this? What the actual fuck had we been thinking that night?

Faye and I hadn't used a condom. I'd assumed she was on birth control, but I didn't remember asking because I'd been drunk.

My hangover the next morning had been a motherfucker and that first practice had kicked my ass. A month ago, I'd thought that hangover had been worth it. Now?

My head throbbed like my brain cells were being stretched to the max as they tried to fit this in.

I'm pregnant

"No." I pounded a fist at my side.

This wasn't happening. This wasn't part of the plan. Faye couldn't be pregnant because I wasn't ready to be a . . . dad.

My insides churned, my fried rice threatening to come up. I breathed through my nose, letting the night air cool the sweat beading on my temples as I stared at that oval of stars.

Was it real? Was this really happening?

My phone rang in my pocket. Again.

"For fuck's sake." I dug into my jeans, expecting to see Faye's name on the screen. Instead, it was a missed call from Maverick. Behind that notification were ten others. Three texts, a missed call and a voice text from Mav. A text from Erik. A missed call from Dad. A missed call and voicemail from Halsey.

I sat up, then bent over my phone and opened my texts and calls.

Maverick. Erik. Dad. Halsey.

Nothing from Faye.

Seriously? So she hadn't even tried to call me since she'd sent that text?

"What the fuck?"

I clutched the phone in my hand and raised my arm, about to throw it as far and long as possible, but stopped myself before I launched it across the field.

Shattering my phone wasn't going to solve anything. It wasn't going to make this better.

That was really all Faye was going to say? *I'm pregnant* and then silence?

No. "No fucking way."

Maybe she'd gone to the house. Maybe that was why Maverick had called and texted.

I pulled up his messages.

Where are you

I'm bored

Tell me you're not with Halsey

I hit play on his voice text.

"Stop ignoring my texts. Also your ex is annoying the fuck out of me. Tell her to forget our address."

What? I pulled up my voicemails and hit play on Halsey's.

"Hey, Rush. I, um . . . I wanted to say hi. And I miss you. A lot. I stopped by your place but Maverick said you weren't home. I don't know if he was lying to me or not, but if you're around this week, maybe we could talk. Call me. If you want. I heard you last month. I know you said it was over. I just . . . I miss you. Bye."

My finger hovered over the delete icon for a long moment before I tapped the glass.

Halsey hadn't spoken to me much over the past month. We'd bumped into each other at the grocery store. She'd had a couple of my hoodies at her place from before we'd broken up, and she'd dropped them off at the house a couple weeks ago. But otherwise, we were done. We'd been done since the breakup after my camping trip.

Except tonight, a part of me wanted to call her. Not because I missed her, but because she was familiar. But that would be a dick move and I wasn't going to lead her on. It wasn't easy with Halsey, but it was a hell of a lot simpler than anything with Faye.

I ignored the text from Erik and the call from Dad, moving back to Faye's text from earlier.

My hand felt heavy, my fingers sluggish, as I tapped her name and typed a reply.

Is this a joke?

I cringed as I added the question mark, then deleted every letter.

Are you sure?

After an eye roll, I deleted that text too. Of course she was fucking sure.

Is it mine?

Another cringe. Another hard press on the delete key until the reply was gone, and I was staring at a blank text box.

What did I say? Why hadn't she called? She wasn't scared of me, was she? I hadn't done anything wrong the night of the bachelorette party, right?

I racked my brain, replaying every moment, some clear and some fuzzy. I remembered dragging my knuckles across her arm. I remembered her touching my lower lip with the pad of her thumb. I remembered nibbling on her earlobe with my teeth.

I remembered our first kiss.

A hundred years could pass by, and I'd still remember that kiss.

It had been a thunderbolt. Lightning had zinged through my body the moment her soft lips had brushed mine. The flick of her tongue had ignited an inferno that had raged through my veins.

My arms had locked around her automatically, intent on never letting go.

Maybe that was the problem. Maybe I'd come on too strong and freaked her out.

Except she'd been as into me as I had been into her. When I'd asked her if she wanted to come to my place, she hadn't hesitated, not even a millisecond. On that cab ride to my place, she'd all but crawled into my lap to make out the entire drive.

And damn it, she'd been the one to start undressing first. The moment we'd crossed the threshold of my house, she'd whipped that argyle sweater-vest over her head.

"Fuck." I tossed my phone aside and let my head fall back to the turf as I stared into the stars.

I'm pregnant

Now what?

No matter how many times I asked myself that question, I couldn't come up with an answer. So I stared up at the oval of stars and spent the worst night of my life in the place where I was normally my best.

Come sunrise, she still hadn't called.

———

THE FIELDHOUSE HAD a keypad for student athletes to access the weight room. We could come and go as needed to work out and train. Coaches didn't want us paying for gym memberships or using equipment that wasn't top-of-the line, so we all had codes to get in at odd hours.

Six o'clock in the morning wasn't exactly an odd hour, but the doors had been locked when I'd walked over from the stadium after spending the night on the fifty-yard line.

The building had been quiet, the scents of concrete and floor cleaner thick in the air. Our first practice wasn't until around noon. A workout might clear my head, help me think of a reply to Faye.

Hours spent staring into the night certainly hadn't helped.

The locker room's automatic lights had flickered on when I'd stepped inside. The lingering smell of cologne and sweaty clothes and metal lockers that was as familiar as my own skin should have been a comfort, except after I'd changed into shorts and a T-shirt from my locker, the knot in my gut had only seemed larger.

I'd trudged into the weight room, moving to the far corner of the huge space. The football team had reserved blocks when the entire gym was ours alone, but otherwise, we shared this facility with other student athletes.

I liked seeing friends from the basketball team. There were a few girls on the track and volleyball teams who were in better shape than any male athlete, myself included. Sharing had never bothered me.

And in my years on the Wildcats team, not once had it felt crowded.

Not before today.

I hadn't been able to muster the strength to exercise. Instead, I'd been sitting in the corner, tucked behind a weight rack, staring at nothing for hours. Hoping to avoid notice. So far, I'd been lucky.

There'd been a handful of people who'd come in earlier. One of the assistant athletic directors who worked upstairs. A guy from the golf team. A girl I didn't recognize but who'd been wearing a ski team T-shirt. Two basketball players.

Maybe there'd been others. I hadn't really paid attention. I'd just sat in this corner, staring at a blank spot on the floor, hoping everyone would leave me the fuck alone. If they'd noticed me, no one had approached.

At some point, after everyone had left, the lights had gone off. I couldn't find it in me to move and trigger them on. The dark seemed fitting for my mood.

How long had I been here? I was probably late for practice. I'd get my ass chewed for sure.

Whatever. A lecture from a coach seemed fairly trivial today.

The door opened, the lights flashing bright. My phone,

clutched in my hand, started to ring. The number on the screen read Seattle, Washington.

Not Faye.

She still hadn't called. How could she not call? What the hell was her problem? Why would she have texted me in the first place? Was she really such a coward that she couldn't face me?

Well, she couldn't avoid me forever. I mean . . . maybe she could.

If she didn't want to keep the baby.

Did she want to keep it? Did I?

The phone kept chiming in my hand as a towering figure appeared beside the weight rack.

I didn't need to look up to recognize the man staring down at me. I recognized his Nikes from practice.

Coach Ellis.

"Rush."

He was from Seattle. He'd played for the Seahawks. I should have put that together and realized who was calling.

Yep, I was late for practice. *Shit.* I gulped but kept my eyes glued to the screen.

The ringing finally stopped.

She was going to call me, right? Eventually, if I didn't reply to that fucking text, she'd call.

Coach dropped to his haunches. "Rush."

"Coach." My throat was raw, my voice hoarse.

We had some strict rules this year, either because of all the shit that had gone down in the spring or because it was Coach Ellis's style.

Our curfew was midnight. No drinking. No bars. Practices were mandatory. Don't be late. If you broke the rules, your ass was on the bench. Indefinitely. I couldn't sit on the bench. I had to play.

Move. Stand up. Why the hell couldn't I get up off this floor?

I glanced at Coach Ellis, expecting to see a frown or glare. Instead he looked . . . worried.

"Tell me what's going on." Only an idiot would argue with that tone. It wasn't angry, but it was firm. My dad had that same tone.

Would I have that with my kid?

I swallowed hard, turning back to my phone. At some point, I'd have to admit what was happening. I'd have to tell someone. But if I said it out loud, then it was real. I wasn't ready for it to be real, not yet.

"Are you in trouble?" he asked.

A fuck ton. I nodded.

"Scale of one to ten, how bad is it?"

My throat bobbed as I swallowed a lump. "Eleven."

Coach's exhale was audible as he sat on the mat beside me, mirroring my posture with his forearms draped over his knees.

I tensed, waiting for the lecture I most definitely deserved. The ass chewing I normally got from coaches when I fucked up. Did Coach Ellis know I'd slept on the football field? "Aren't you going to scream at me? Tell me to get off my ass and get to practice?"

"Not really a fan of screaming." His voice was steady and calm. Not exactly gentle, but he wasn't pissed off.

I stared at a concrete wall, still not sure what to say. Would it be easier if Coach yelled? Yes. No. Nothing mattered, not right now.

Coach Ellis didn't move or speak. He simply sat with me

until finally, knowing I couldn't say the words but couldn't keep this to myself any longer, I opened my phone, pulling up Faye's text and shifting the screen for Coach to read.

I'm pregnant

The color drained from Coach Ellis's face.

It took him a few minutes. But then he cleared his throat and told me a story.

The story of his daughter.

———

WE MISSED PRACTICE.

My butt was numb from sitting on the floor in the weight room, but I'd listened to Coach without so much as shifting a millimeter as he'd told me about the girlfriend he'd gotten pregnant in college. How it hadn't been easy, but he'd managed. How he had no regrets because his daughter was the light of his life.

The dread in the pit of my stomach felt never-ending, but at least the panicked fog had begun to clear.

"My life is over," I muttered.

"Your life is different," he corrected. "Not over. Just different."

My life was definitely over. At least the life I'd planned. Goodbye professional football.

I opened my mouth, ready to tell him to stop pandering to me, but before I could say a word, I noticed the design on his white T-shirt.

A Super Bowl championship T-shirt.

He'd had a kid. And he'd still been a champion.

"It'll be all right." He stood, reaching out a hand to help me to my feet. "Call her. Talk it through."

Pins and needles zinged through my legs as he gave me a moment to get my balance. "Thanks, Coach."

"Welcome." He dipped his chin. "You have my number. I'm here, day or night."

I gave him a sad smile. "Sorry about practice. I'll make it up to you."

"We'll talk tomorrow, yeah?"

"Yeah."

Coach Ellis clapped me on the shoulder, then with a strong grip, steered me away from the wall, past the racks and treadmills to the door.

Guess my time in the weight room was over.

"Your car is at the stadium," he said. "Houston found it."

"I, uh . . ." *Damn.* "Sometimes I come to the field. To think. Sorry. That's probably breaking the rules."

Not probably. It was.

But he hadn't gotten mad so far. Maybe today he'd give me the break I needed. Maybe he understood what it was like when a football field was your safe space.

Coach Ellis escorted me not just out of the weight room, but out of the fieldhouse entirely. I felt his gaze on my back as I started across the parking lot toward the stadium beyond.

As much as I wanted to find a new hiding place, I kept walking, one foot in front of the other, until I was behind the wheel in my Yukon.

Then before I could talk myself out of it, I pulled up Faye's number and dialed.

She answered on the first ring. "Hi."

"Hey."

Silence settled between us, a quiet so still and noiseless I lifted the phone from my ear to make sure she was still there.

Then rested my head against the seat, my body sagging as deep as the steering wheel would allow.

"I'm sorry." Her voice cracked.

"I don't know what to do," I murmured.

She sniffled. "Me neither."

"Guess we should talk?"

"I guess so."

CHAPTER EIGHT

FAYE

The Treasure State University campus was lonely in the summers. It was strange to sit on my favorite bench outside Williams Hall and be the only person in sight.

Though considering I looked like death, being alone was a good thing for a change. When I'd gone to Dollar Discount this morning, two people had stopped me in the aisles to ask if I was okay.

Nope.

I'd nodded and forced smiles even though I was definitely not okay.

But at least I'd stopped puking.

At this point, I was reveling in the little wins. The vomiting had stopped last night, either because there was nothing left in my body to retch or because the numbness had finally sunk into my internal organs.

My brain was as eerily quiet as this campus.

A gentle breeze blew hot summer air across my cheek and lifted a tendril of hair that had escaped my ponytail, dragging it across my mouth. It stuck to my lip balm. I hated having hair in my mouth, but I didn't hate it enough to tug it free. That would require moving.

I was too tired to move.

Was this rock bottom?

Everything felt so . . . heavy.

It had been two days since Rush had called me. He'd asked to meet sooner, but yesterday, I'd had a double shift at the diner. He'd offered to come to Dolly's, but I'd lied and told him we were so busy that I wouldn't be able to talk.

We were never busy.

But Dolly's was my safe place. It was bad enough having Justin pop in at random. I didn't need Rush intruding on my sanctuary either, especially if—*when*—this conversation went sideways.

So we'd decided to meet on campus today, on neutral ground, between his football practices and before my shift started at three.

The mid-August sunshine was sweltering this afternoon, and even though I'd found a bench in the shade, sweat beaded at my temples. How did Rush play football in this heat? Wasn't it dangerous? It was forecast to be in the nineties.

I dug the bottle of ice water from my purse, taking a sip as a tall, broad figure rounded the corner of a brick building. His long legs ate up the concrete sidewalk as he walked my way, his hands tucked into the pockets of his black athletic shorts.

Rush's baseball hat was turned backward. His white shirt was sleeveless, his muscled arms on display. The fabric stretched across his chest and hugged his washboard stomach. His shorts were normal athletic shorts that probably would have been baggy on most guys, but they molded to his bulky thighs, barely swishing with each of his long strides.

I hated the way my heart trilled as he came closer.

That stupid fucking trill was the reason I was sitting on this bench in the first place.

Rush's expression was blank, guarded, as he stepped off the sidewalk and onto the freshly cut lawn. His brown eyes flickered to the building at my back before he sat on the bench, leaning forward with his elbows to his knees as he stared forward. "Hey."

The edge to his voice was as sharp as the corners of his jaw.

How long until he asked me to get an abortion? One minute? Two? Three?

The sting of tears pricked my nose as the same burning lump I'd been fighting for days swelled in my throat. It made speaking nearly impossible. Or maybe I just didn't have a clue what to say.

I sat close to one end of the bench while he did the same at the other. The space between us was only a couple of feet but it might as well have been miles for the tension that stretched tighter and tighter and tighter.

The T-shirt I'd worn felt damp with sweat and clung to my spine.

Why was it so hot? Meeting outside had seemed like a good option, giving us air to breathe and space to walk away if things turned sour. But with every passing second, the heat spiked, making me dizzy.

"I don't come on this side of campus very often." Rush broke the silence, still not looking at me as he spoke. "It's nice."

"Yeah," I muttered.

"So . . ." Rush blew out a long breath, his shoulders sagging away from his ears as he spun his hat forward to shade his eyes. He sounded tired. He sounded heavy too.

It should have made it easier knowing I wasn't alone in this. Except it was actually harder.

Why? No clue. That was something I'd figure out after I figured out how to stop crying.

I swiped at my cheeks, the dark circles beneath my eyes raw from being rubbed so much. "So."

"I don't know what to do here, Faye."

"I'm sorry."

He hung his head. "I'm sorry too."

The mutual apologies should have made it easier too. They should have defused the tension.

They didn't.

Maybe nothing about this would ever be easy, and the sooner I made peace with that, the sooner I'd get my emotions under control.

I sniffled, wiping my eyes again and forcing air into my lungs. Then I took another drink, letting the cold water ease the pain in my throat.

"Have you decided what you want to do?" The question was too flat, too practiced, for me to tell if he had an opinion one way or the other.

I dragged in a ragged breath, my heart beginning to race as I clasped my hands in my lap.

Rush deserved to know why I was going to stand firm in this choice. But this explanation wasn't exactly something I liked to broadcast. It wasn't a story that was fun to share, which was probably why Gloria was the only person who knew.

And the only reason my sister had a clue was because she'd lived it too.

"My mother is not a nice woman," I said.

"What do you mean?" For the first time, Rush's gaze met mine. There was a furrow between his eyebrows and a hint of worry.

It seemed like genuine concern. Rush seemed like a good guy.

I guess I'd find out soon enough how deep that goodness went.

"Before she had me, Mom was . . . pregnant." Days had passed and it was still nearly impossible to choke out that word. "Three times. She had three abortions."

Rush stiffened but stayed quiet, probably because that could be taken either way. Or only one way, once he learned the rest.

"She's told me more times than I can remember she wishes she had aborted me too."

"What the fuck?" Rush's nostrils flared as his hands fisted.

"Like I said, she's not a nice woman."

If I spilled a glass of water, she'd remind me of how hard her life had become after she'd become a mother. If I made a mess, she'd curse and yell and say how much she hated living with me. When I was in high school, I'd dropped a plate on accident once. While I'd been sweeping up the broken pieces, she'd come into the kitchen and told me her biggest mistake was bringing me into this world.

Mom hated being a mother, and yet she'd had Gloria too. I'd never understood why she'd had another child when she'd loathed my existence. My sister hadn't escaped Mom's cruelty either, but at least Gloria had been able to count on me as her shield and her father's home as a safe haven. I'd taken the brunt of Mom's insults to spare my sister the pain.

For a long, long time I'd tried to prove myself. To make her love me. To show her I was worth her struggles. Worthy of life.

I'd tried so hard to be a *good* daughter.

And I *had* been a good daughter. Except nothing would ever be enough, not for Brynn Gannon. When I'd finally stopped letting her break my heart, I'd set myself free. But the wounds had been cut deep for too long. Some were knitting together, closing up and becoming old scars. And others would likely bleed for the rest of my life.

"I realize that abortion is the right choice for some women," I said. "I'm glad to have that choice. But I can't be like her. I can't. I won't."

Rush's throat bobbed as he swallowed, staring out across the lawn.

My heart hammered as I waited, and with every passing second, the reality of this, my suspicions, came crashing down.

I was alone in this. I was always alone.

He'd come here hoping for a very different outcome, and I was as much of a disappointment to him as I was my mother.

It was fine. I'd be fine, right? I'd keep telling myself it was okay until I *was* okay.

I did not need Rush Ramsey.

I didn't need anyone.

He smacked his hands on his knees, nodding once as he shot to his feet. "Do you have a doctor's appointment scheduled?"

"Uh." I blinked. "Not yet."

"I'll go."

Huh? "To my doctor's appointment?"

"Yeah." He nodded once, then spun on a heel and walked away, disappearing long before I could figure out what that meant.

CHAPTER NINE

RUSH

"Rush." Maverick smacked me on the arm.

I tore my attention from my phone and the text I'd been attempting to type all morning. "What?"

"You didn't hear a thing I said, did you?"

"You said something? When?"

He rolled his eyes as he rounded the kitchen's bar and took the stool beside mine. He slid my plate and the breakfast burrito that was most definitely cold by now out of the way. Then he sat sideways, one arm braced on the granite as he looked between me and my phone.

"What is wrong?"

"Nothing." I shot him a frown.

"You're the worst liar." He scoffed. "Talk to me, man. You've been off since that night last week. What is it? A girl? You're not back together with Halsey, right?"

I set my phone face down on the counter as he leaned in closer to look at the screen. "Do you mind?"

"It is her, isn't it? You know I can't stand her but if you're with her again, it's just whatever. But don't hide it from me."

"I'm not—" I shook my head. "It's not Halsey."

"Thank fuck." He blew out a long breath. "Then what's up? Is something wrong with your parents?"

"Nah, they're fine."

"Okay," he drawled, stretching out the last syllable like I'd pick it up and tell him everything that was going on.

I stayed quiet.

With the exception of Coach Ellis, I hadn't told anyone about Faye. Instead, I'd spent the past week trying to wrap my own mind around everything rather than bring others into the mix.

Faye and I had texted a few times since we'd met on campus last week. She'd made an appointment with a doctor and had sent me the details. I'd asked if she was feeling all right to which she'd replied *I'm fine.*

She wasn't fine, not if she still looked like she had last week. Pale. Splotchy. On the verge of tears.

For the past ten minutes, I'd been trying to figure out how to invite her out for dinner. To talk, not a date. Except everything I typed sounded shallow or forced or like I was asking her out on a date.

I'd type. Delete. Type. Delete.

Faye wanted to keep the baby. Did that mean she was okay with me being involved? Because I was going to be involved. She knew that, right?

Fuck, I hated texting. We needed to have a real, honest conversation, face-to-face, which was going to be damn hard to arrange if I couldn't even figure out how to invite her out for a cheeseburger. Did she eat cheeseburgers?

I probably should have said more on that bench. Asked more questions. But there were too many emotions swirling, and they'd rendered me useless. The tighter I locked them up inside, the harder they fought to escape.

"Rush, talk to me. I'm worried." There was a softness in his voice I hadn't heard before.

Maverick was crass and direct. What came to his mind usually came out of his mouth. But he was my best friend in the entire world.

Maybe I should tell him the truth.

For all his bluntness, he was one of the most logical people I'd ever met. He was an economics major and in our years at Treasure State, I'd realized he barely had to study. Mav always said it was because economics was basically common sense. That, and he was too smart for his own good.

I sighed, rubbing a hand over my stubbled jaw. I hadn't bothered shaving for a couple days and the coarse hair scraped against my palm. "I need to tell you something."

"No shit," Maverick muttered.

I inhaled, holding it in my lungs until they burned. Then on my exhale, I set the truth free. "I got a girl pregnant."

Oh, fuck that sounded bad. Cheap and sleezy. I was definitely going to need to refine that a bit. Except I couldn't say "Faye's pregnant" because no one knew about Faye.

Mav's jaw was on the floor when I looked over, his eyebrows so high they nearly kissed his hairline. "Say that again."

I gulped. "I'm having a kid."

Better. That didn't sound as dodgy, but it still wasn't a great way to break the news. Now I sounded cold and detached.

Before I told my parents—an idea that made my insides roil—I'd have to find a softer, warmer way to drop this bomb. *Tomorrow's problem.*

"With Halsey." Mav's mouth closed with a click before his lip curled. "I fucking knew she'd trap you. I told you to be careful with her. After all that shit that went down freshman year, I warned you not to trust her. Look what she did to me."

"Whoa." I held up a hand. Okay, so maybe Maverick wasn't going to be the logical one here. "It's not Halsey."

Those eyebrows shot sky-high again. "It's not?"

"No."

"Who?"

"Remember that night we went to Legends?"

Maverick snapped his fingers. "The redhead."

"Faye." He might as well know her name.

"Dude." He blew out a long breath, shaking his head. "Holy fuck."

"Basically," I mumbled.

"You okay?"

I shrugged.

"Of course you're not okay." He slid off his stool, pacing the length of the bar. "That's why you didn't come home that night last week."

"Yeah. That was the night I found out."

"Were you with her?"

"No. I, uh, needed to be alone for a while."

"Damn, Rush. What can I do?"

"I don't know." I picked up my phone, unlocking the screen. My text thread with Faye appeared and the empty text box seemed to jump off the glass, flashing in my face like a strobe light.

What did I say? Why was this so hard?

If I gave my phone to Maverick, could he think of something to text? What if I asked him for a plan? Let him sort this out.

"What are you guys going to do?" he asked.

"She wants to keep the baby."

He nodded, still pacing with his hands on his hips. "All right. You good with that?"

"Yes." After the story Faye had told me about her own mother? Absolutely, yes. I would never ask her to have an abortion.

"Okay." He clapped me on the shoulder, squeezing for a second before he walked back into the kitchen.

Maverick's older sister, Mabel, had gotten pregnant in high school, and while it had thrown their family for a loop, he loved being an uncle. He'd witnessed his sister's struggles but knew each had been well worth it.

His nephew was the center of the Houston family's universe.

And the guy who'd walked away from that kid, from Mabel, was the person who'd missed out. Maverick hadn't even told me the guy's name because it had been all but banned in his family.

"You got this." He stopped on the opposite side of the bar and braced his arms on the speckled, granite countertop. "It won't be easy, but you got this."

"Thanks," I breathed, not realizing just how much I'd needed someone to tell me I could do this.

"When is the paternity test? Or did you already take it?"

"Uh, no."

He narrowed his gaze. "But you're going to get one, right?"

"Hadn't planned on it."

If those eyebrows weren't attached to his forehead, they might have flown away. "Are you serious right now?"

"She's not lying, Mav."

"Oh my God." He raked both hands through his hair. When they dropped, he pointed a finger at my nose. "You're getting a paternity test."

"Mav—"

"No, Rush. You're doing it."

Were there women who'd purposefully get pregnant to manipulate a man? Sure. I imagined it happened with pro athletes and celebrities. Definitely in fiction.

My mom loved daytime soap operas, and she always made sure to schedule a break in their chores at the ranch so she could catch *The Young and the Restless*. She'd summarized more than one "accidental" pregnancy whenever I asked her what was happening on her soaps.

But this really had been an accident.

I could see why Mav would be skeptical. He didn't know Faye. Granted, I didn't really know her either, but she wouldn't do this on purpose. And she had to know this baby was mine, otherwise she never would have texted me.

"I don't need to do a test," I told him. "I believe her. And I didn't use a condom."

He blinked. "You're a fucking idiot."

"Tell me something I don't know."

"Okay. No condom. Not a smart move. But what if she's wrong? What if you weren't the only guy she hooked up with around that time?"

A sour taste spread across my mouth. Definitely didn't like the idea of Faye with another guy. "I'm telling you, Mav. She's not lying."

"Rush." Maverick held up a hand. "Listen. Please. I'm

begging you. This is your life we're talking about here. This girl is a stranger, right? Or have you been dating her on the sly all this time?"

"No."

"Then she's a stranger."

"Yeah," I admitted. Definitely didn't like classifying her as a stranger either. But he wasn't wrong.

"Maybe she's not lying, but what if she's . . . mistaken? A kid will change everything. You have *got* to be sure. You know some of these girls. And I know you like to give people the benefit of the doubt. You're not as cynical as I am. If you want to believe her, great. Trust, but verify."

Damn it. That wasn't bad advice.

Still didn't like it, but it wasn't bad advice.

"She's not a jersey chaser. When I met her this summer, she had no idea who I was."

Maverick laughed. "What?"

"She's not into football."

"But she goes to school here."

"Yes," I drawled.

Maverick's groan was so loud it would have lured Erik out of his room, if Erik ever slept in his room. "You're actually killing me. You are Rush Ramsey."

"Really? I had no idea," I deadpanned.

His look flattened. "Your face and name are on a giant sign outside the student union building. They're also on a billboard off Sixth Avenue, right across from the grocery store."

I hated that billboard. I'd started taking a different route to the store just so I wouldn't have to see my own face on that damn sign.

"Even people who don't go to Treasure State know about

Rush Ramsey," he said. "You were on a commercial this spring, for fuck's sake."

Four of us had been asked to film an ad for a swanky golf course in town. It had been easy money plus a chance to get on a course that was typically for country club members only.

"Maybe she doesn't watch TV. Or pay attention to billboards. She had no idea who I was, okay? Trust me on that."

I'd searched her face for even the slightest hint of recognition. There hadn't been a flicker.

Faye had no clue who I was, and that was part of the appeal.

"Fine." Maverick tossed up his hands. "We'll pretend that she's really that oblivious and didn't know that she was going home with the Wildcats star quarterback and a guy who's got a shot at being drafted into the NFL. We'll suspend reality. But you still need to take a paternity test. Make sure this baby is actually yours."

"I'm not—"

"If it was me, if I was in your place, what would you say?"

Well, fuck. If this was Mav or Erik or any other of my friends, I'd tell them to get the test.

He wasn't wrong, was he? Trust, but verify.

Faye had mentioned a boyfriend while we'd been camping. Maybe she hadn't broken it off as quickly as I'd called it quits with Halsey.

"Gah," I growled. "Fine."

"Thank fuck." The air rushed from Maverick's lungs. "I know you don't want to hear this, but it might be worth asking around the team. See if she's been with any of the other guys."

"The fuck? Why?"

"You, of all people, know that some of the girls move from player to player."

My jaw clenched.

"Or not." He held up a hand. "It was only a suggestion. But shit will get weird if she's been with another guy on the team."

"She hasn't." I shot him a glare.

Okay, I didn't exactly know that she hadn't hooked up with another player. But that uncomfortable twinge came roaring back, the same one I'd had a moment ago thinking of Faye with another man, and I didn't have the headspace for it.

What if she had been with another player? What if I found out in the locker room?

I'd had enough surprises. Maybe it was time for some information.

I picked up my phone, opening up my text thread with Faye, and for the first time knew exactly what to type.

Can you meet me at the fieldhouse in an hour? I need to talk to you about something.

I didn't wait for her reply. I slid off my stool and disappeared upstairs to my bedroom where I took a long, hot shower. Then I stood at the sink and shaved, staring at my reflection for a few long moments.

My body was clean. My hair was shampooed. My face fresh and ready for practice.

So why did I feel so slimy?

CHAPTER TEN

RUSH

P ractice started in ten minutes. If Faye didn't show up soon, I was going to be late.

"Damn it." I checked my phone, making sure I hadn't missed a call or text, but other than her *sure* reply to my request to meet at the fieldhouse, I hadn't heard from her since.

The parking lot that separated the fieldhouse and stadium was massive, but there weren't many cars here today. Once school started, it would be packed, but at the moment, most vehicles belonged to employees or athletes who were on campus to practice.

From where I was standing at the base of the main entrance's stairs, I'd see her when she drove in. Her car was fairly recognizable. She knew where the fieldhouse was, right? The building at my back was huge. Had she gone inside from a different entrance?

I hit her name, pressing my phone to my ear as I started down the sidewalk. As it rang, I glanced over my shoulder, checking the parking lot again.

"Answer the phone," I muttered.

It kept on ringing. Three times. Four.

This is Faye. Leave a message.

"Fuck." I didn't have time for this. After Coach had found me in the weight room last week, I'd been on my best behavior. I'd promised to make it up to him and that's what I'd been doing ever since. I couldn't be late to practice.

I rounded the corner of the building, walking so fast it was almost a jog. Faye was nowhere in sight.

"Hell." Asking her for a paternity test wasn't urgent, but it also wasn't something that I wanted to let drag out. Now that I'd decided to take Maverick's advice, I wanted to get this conversation over with.

Had she gone into the fieldhouse already? I didn't have time to make a lap both inside and out.

The summer sun beat down on my shoulders, soaking into my royal-blue T-shirt. Our first practice would be hot, but the second session, late this afternoon, would be scorching. Maybe Faye had gone inside for the air conditioning.

I jogged to the nearest entrance, a row of steel and glass doors that opened to the first floor. A few of the window-panes were etched with the Wildcats emblem, and past the white logo, I caught a swish of strawberry-blond hair.

Yes. I could still make it to practice on time. I'd already changed into a pair of shorts and my tennis shoes. We'd be doing drills and conditioning most of the day, so I didn't need pads or my helmet. All I had to do was ask Faye for that test, then I'd hustle to the practice field.

With a quick yank on the door, I stepped into the concrete hall. The sound of a sweet, musical laugh hit my ears.

Faye was smiling at Sam, a sophomore on the team.

"She's the worst, right?" He grinned down at her, their eyes locked.

"I had her for an Exceptional Learners class junior year, and she was much better than she was in Relationships and Family Systems. But she was still brutal on my final."

They must be talking about a professor. Was Sam an education major or something? We didn't play much together since I was on offense and he was on special teams, so I wasn't sure what he was studying.

But I really didn't like the fact that he stared at Faye with stars in his eyes. And why the fuck were they standing so close?

Sam inched forward and lifted his hand to the sleeve of her T-shirt. "You've got a piece of lint."

"Oh." She brushed it away. "Thanks."

"Would you ever want to go out for—"

Absolutely fucking not. "Faye."

Her face swung toward my clipped voice as I marched toward them. Good to know she could tear her attention away from Sam. "Hey."

"Ramsey." Sam jerked up his chin when I came to a stop at Faye's side.

"Sam. See you outside at practice." The unspoken "go away" was fairly clear, but this idiot didn't take the hint.

"Yeah. One sec." He gave Faye a shy smile. "Anyway, would you—"

"Go away, Sam." Was that clear enough?

He opened his mouth, but the scowl on my face must have convinced him it was better to stay quiet. With a dip of his head, he retreated down the hall, looking back just once.

Faye frowned as the sound of Sam's footsteps faded. "What was that about?"

"If one of my teammates feels the need to flirt with you, do me a favor and put a stop to it."

She recoiled, her mouth parting. "Excuse me? He was just being friendly."

Friendly? My ass he was just being friendly, but I didn't have time to argue about Sam. "Look, I'm late for practice because I've been waiting for you to—"

"*I've* been here for twenty minutes. Waiting on *you.*" She crossed her arms over her chest, shooting me a glare.

The last time I'd seen her she'd been hollow. Numb. But here was the spitfire I'd met camping.

The doors opened behind us, a few people walking inside. It was one of the track and field coaches with two kids who looked like they were in high school. The coach talked with her hands, pointing around, probably giving a tour.

"Come on." I clasped Faye's elbow to steer her down the hallway, but the moment my fingers wrapped around her arm, she yanked it away, and I earned another glare that was pure venom.

"What am I doing here, Rush?" Faye asked when we were out of earshot.

"I need to talk to you about something."

"Okay," she drawled, coming to a stop.

I gulped, squaring my shoulders. "I'd like a paternity test, and I'd like to know how many guys you've been with on the team."

Phew. It came out in a single breath, barely a blip between words. But it was out there now.

Mav would be proud.

"I'm sorry." Faye's forehead furrowed. "What did you just say?"

Oh, hell. Was she really going to make me repeat it?

I opened my mouth, about to say it all again when she held up a finger.

"You want a paternity test." Never in my life had I heard someone articulate a sentence so clearly.

"Yes, just to be sure that—"

Her index finger sliced through the air, cutting me off. "And you want to know how many guys I've slept with on the team."

Or kissed. Had she kissed any of them? "Yeah, I, uh—"

"You don't believe me."

"What? No. I'm only—"

"Calling me a liar." Her voice got louder, a red flush creeping into her cheeks. "You're only calling me a liar."

"I'm not calling you—"

"Are you calling me a whore?"

"No! Fuck." I dragged a hand through my hair. How the hell did we end up here? Was it really so unreasonable for me to ask for some damn information? "Would you just listen to me?"

Her body began to tremble, as shaky as her voice. "You think I planned this, don't you?"

Seriously? I stretched my arms wide. "That's not what I'm saying, Faye!"

And if she'd listen to me, if she'd stop cutting me off, I'd explain.

"Then what?" Her voice was practically a shriek, so loud I barely heard the throat clear beside us.

I jerked, my eyes widening. Millie Cunningham was in the hallway. Millie was one of the assistant athletic directors. And she'd most definitely heard us fighting.

Not the best person to overhear, but at least she wasn't a coach.

An apology was on the tip of my tongue, except before I could speak, Coach Ellis rounded the corner.

Damn it. I was late for practice and causing a scene in the hall. My ass was getting benched.

"What the hell is going on?" he barked.

Nothing, Coach. Just my life imploding.

Fuck.

———

COACH ELLIS and Millie dragged us into a conference room where I got to summarize how Faye and I had met and how we'd hooked up. How we were going to be parents in the not-so-distant future.

"I didn't mean to insinuate anything in the hallway." I dragged a hand through my hair as I looked at Faye. She was staring anywhere but at my face. That hollowness was back too. It made me feel like I was about three inches tall.

Maybe I'd earned that.

"I'm just . . . I don't know what I'm doing or saying," I told her. "I only asked about other guys so that I wouldn't be surprised. I don't like surprises."

"And the paternity test?" Coach Ellis asked.

Probably not the worst idea, but yeah, my delivery could have been better.

"It's fine," Faye said before I could answer. Her hands were fisted on her lap. Her eyes were full of tears.

I was such an asshole.

"I'll get one," she said.

"You don't have to."

"No." The betrayal in her voice was like a knife through my chest. "I'll get the test. Then there won't be any doubt."

92

There was no doubt. Not now. Not after her reaction. Not with that conviction in her voice.

This baby was mine.

"Bit of advice," Coach Ellis said. "Find a way to talk to each other. In person. Texts. Calls. Emails. Whatever. You're going to get a lot of external input, but at the end of the day, all that matters is what you both decide together."

Faye's chin began to quiver.

Millie had taken the seat beside her. She reached over to put her hand on Faye's. "You'll be okay."

I wished I was that sure.

Faye sniffled, a single tear falling down her cheek. "I'll be okay."

She didn't believe that in the slightest, did she? I wasn't sure I believed it either.

Coach Ellis's gaze was waiting when I glanced over. The set of his jaw spoke volumes.

Yeah, I'd fucked that up.

"Thanks, Coach," I murmured.

"You're late for practice, Rush." As in, time to go. Now.

"Yes, sir." I stood and, even though Faye and I had plenty to discuss, left the conference room.

Damn it. I fisted my hands as I walked down the hall, resisting the urge to slam my knuckles into a concrete wall. I forced my legs to move, one after the next, until I reached an exit and shoved outside into the blazing sunshine. Then I marched to join the team.

Usually, I'd throw myself into practice. I'd let it drown out anything else. Except for the first time in a long, long time, the last thing I wanted to do was play football.

Sam was standing with a couple guys from special teams.

Maybe if he hadn't been flirting with Faye, I would have handled that better. Maybe not.

I resisted the urge to flip him off as I walked by and kept going toward where the offense was gathered.

Coach Parks spotted me and tapped his watch. He hated when players showed up late. He'd make me pay for it before the day was over.

"Rush." Maverick jogged over, falling in step at my side. "So? Did you talk to her?"

"Yeah."

"How'd it go?"

I huffed a dry laugh. "Great. It went fucking great."

———

DOLLY'S DINER was in an area of Mission I hadn't been before. There were no condos or apartment complexes like there were in the blocks that surrounded campus. There were no quaint family homes with manicured lawns. Actually, there didn't seem to be many homes around here at all.

Just like Faye had said, the restaurant was on the outskirts of town, a couple blocks away from a truck stop along the highway.

I'd passed that truck stop a hundred times on my way in and out of Mission, yet I'd never once noticed Dolly's. Probably because it was mostly hidden from view of the highway by a grove of trees and a faded blue steel building.

There weren't offices or businesses nearby. I'd passed a small ranch with a dozen head of cattle in an overgrazed field. And there'd been a few old trailers on the road out that had seen better days.

I parked in a lot that was more pothole than paved

asphalt. My car was the only vehicle in sight. Where was Faye's Explorer? Did she park in the back? Hopefully there were more lights than the single, flickering lamp that lit the front entrance. I didn't like the idea of her walking to her car at night without decent lighting.

The sign for Dolly's Diner was neon red and trimmed in teal. It hung from a rusted post beside the restaurant. In case anyone missed that sign, the word DINER was spelled in white, blocked letters, each mounted on a stand from the roof.

The green siding was weathered and long overdue for a fresh coat of paint. It wasn't big but it was bright, the florescent lights streaming outside to mingle with the evening glow.

A chime dinged as I opened the door and stepped inside. The sound was tinny and lingered in the empty space. The scents of syrup and sausage and cheeseburgers filled my nose and made my stomach growl.

It might not be the fanciest café in Mission, but damn, it smelled good. Maybe Faye worked here for the food. Couldn't fault her for that. I was starving.

After practice and a shower, I'd thought about going home and making myself dinner. But I knew that the moment I walked through my front door, I'd find a reason to stay and avoid Faye.

So I'd forced myself to drive across town to this dingy diner and face the woman who was going to be a part of my life. Indefinitely.

I stood on an industrial doormat next to a sign that read *Please Seat Yourself* and scanned the space.

Teal, vinyl booths, the color the same as the sign outside, lined the windows. Two rows of tables filled the center of the restaurant. Their tops were white laminate and their edges lined with aluminum. Most were chipped to the wood beneath and a few had permanent coffee stains. On each, there was a caddy of red ketchup and yellow mustard bottles stowed beside shakers of salt and pepper.

The diner wasn't long or wide. At most, fifty people could enjoy a meal at Dolly's, and I had a hunch that this place rarely reached capacity.

A silver swing door with an oval window in its face whipped open.

Faye emerged from what I assumed was the kitchen. She had a stack of plastic menus in one hand and a bunch of napkin-rolled silverware in the other. The moment she spotted me, she froze.

"Hey."

She dropped her gaze to the white-and-black-checkered tile floor. "What are you doing here?"

As in, *you weren't invited, Rush.* I deserved that. "I'm sorry, Faye."

She swallowed hard.

Please seat yourself? I took the sign's invitation and walked to the third booth against the windows. The vinyl stretched and creaked as I slid into the bench. My knees whacked the metal post and my chest brushed the table's edge.

This spot clearly wasn't made for a six-three, 220-pound man. But I relaxed into the seat, pretending like I'd never been more comfortable. And I wasn't going anywhere, not yet.

Faye huffed and trudged over, dropping a menu and a set of silverware for me before taking the rest to a waitress station in the corner. She filled a glass with ice water, bringing it over, but rather than set it down, she lifted it higher. "I sort of want to dump this over your head."

"I wouldn't blame you if you did."

She arched an eyebrow, and for three heartbeats, I braced to get soaked. But then she set it on the table, a bit too hard, and the water sloshed over the rim. "What do you want?"

"To start over."

Her eyes narrowed. "No. You don't get to erase what you said."

Wow. She really wasn't going to cut me any slack, was she? But I guess I hadn't earned any. The paternity test was one thing, but the more I'd thought about it, the ask for her roster of past lovers had crossed the line.

Too far. I'd gone way too far.

She hadn't asked me for a list of my ex-girlfriends or hookups. What the hell gave me the right to demand hers?

"Fair enough," I said, my fingers drumming on the table. "Coach said we should figure out how to talk to each other. It's a good idea. Maybe we could start by something other than texting."

"Okay," she drawled.

"I don't like to text. I'd rather call or talk in person."

"Really?" Faye's nose scrunched up at the bridge.

"Blame it on my parents." I shrugged. "They aren't big texters either. My mom never answers them, so if I want to talk to her, I have to call. I kind of got into that habit with everyone else. It's easier. Hearing someone's voice. If it's okay, can I call you?"

"Oh. Um, yeah."

Progress. "I really am sorry about what I said."

Her caramel gaze dropped once more to the floor, like the shame of that moment still weighed on her mind.

Yep, I was an asshole.

"I'll do better," I promised. "We'll figure this out. We'll rally."

Her eyes shot to mine, staring for so long that I fought the urge to squirm. But then her arms uncrossed, falling to her sides. "Can I get you anything to eat?"

I flipped open the menu, breathing a full inhale and exhale for the first time since I'd walked into Dolly's Diner. "Please."

CHAPTER ELEVEN

FAYE

Justin's trailer had two bedrooms, one on each end of the house. When I'd moved in after we'd started dating, I'd put most of my things in the smallest room even though I'd slept in his bed. I didn't have a lot of clothes or belongings. Everything I owned could fit in the back of my Explorer. But the closet in his room was small and cramped and it had just made sense to leave my stuff in another room.

The twin bed I'd been sleeping on since we'd broken up had been his former roommate's bed that she'd left behind when she'd moved out a year and a half ago, right about the time we'd started dating.

Had they dated? I'd always wondered if that's why she'd moved out. Justin didn't really talk about her, and I hadn't asked.

Maybe I'd been the girl he'd cheated with. Maybe I'd been her Alexa.

The idea made my stomach churn, but at least she'd left the bed. I straightened the sage-green comforter, then fluffed the pillow and straightened my throw blanket before grabbing my wallet from the collapsible TV tray that acted as my nightstand. With my keys in hand, I walked to the door, easing it open slowly. It squeaked if you pulled it too fast.

Then, breath held, I tiptoed down the hallway toward the living room.

I hadn't seen Justin in two days. He'd been gone when I'd gotten home from work the past couple of nights, probably at a friend's house playing video games. With any luck, I could avoid him for two more days. Three if I was blessed.

The front door was within reach when I heard the floor creak from the far hallway. "Faye."

Shit. Before I could make my escape, Justin emerged. He walked through the kitchen and into the living room, stopping a few feet away.

"Hey." He took in my jeans and Dolly's Diner tee. "Heading to work?"

"Yeah." I laid my fingers on the door's handle. "See ya."

"Wait." He held up a hand. "I need to talk to you about something."

Oh, God. Not another *let's get back together* chat. "Justin, I really do have to go."

"Look, I'm sorry to do this, but I have to increase your rent."

Every mental wheel spinning in my brain came to a screeching halt. "What?"

"It's getting more expensive."

"What exactly is more expensive?" My hand dropped from the door's handle and balled into a fist. "You own this place free and clear thanks to your parents. And I cover half of the utilities."

"Taxes and insurance and shit is more expensive."

"How much more expensive?"

He lifted a shoulder. "A hundred bucks a month?"

My jaw hit the trampled beige carpet. "An extra hundred dollars?"

I couldn't afford that. Not before I'd found out I was pregnant. Certainly not after.

My apartment hunting had been disastrous at best. School had started, and any available inventory had disappeared. In all of Mission, there were six listings for roommates wanted. All six would mean living with guys. After Justin, I was done with male roommates for a while. I had zero desire to convince my roommates, male or female, how much fun it would be to live with a newborn baby come spring.

And the only available studios were within walking distance to campus. That convenience came with a high price tag.

So where did that leave me? Here. That left me here, paying an extra hundred dollars a month while I waited for something else.

It would come though, eventually, right? Treasure State had brought in a ton of new recruits over the last few years, which had zapped most availability on the rental market. But if I could just wait it out, if I could hold fast, something would eventually pop up.

"Fine," I clipped, yanking the door open.

"There's another option," Justin said, stopping me before I could storm outside. "You could move back into my room. We could get another roommate."

This. Asshole.

There was no increase in property taxes or insurance, was there? No, he was just trying to manipulate me. Begging hadn't worked. So what now? Extortion?

"I'll pay," I said through gritted teeth, then before he could say anything else, I stepped onto the wooden steps and slammed the door at my back.

Shit. I never should have moved in here. I never should have let Justin trap me like this.

My nostrils stung as I marched to my car and my eyes flooded. Damn it, I was so sick of crying. I was so sick of feeling like I was never going to get ahead. Like I was always going to be living from paycheck to paycheck.

I slid into the Explorer, shutting the door and closing out the world beyond. Then I gripped the steering wheel, letting it ground me as I blinked away the unshed tears.

Justin was dreaming if he thought he could force me into a relationship. So I'd come up with the money. Somehow.

A hundred dollars a month.

I had forty-seven dollars and thirty-three cents in my checking account. Last month, I'd had to shell out a chunk of cash for books that my financial aid wouldn't cover. It was the tenth of September. That gave me twenty days to come up with rent money, cash for utilities plus extra for this increase.

Maybe I could cut back on gas. I'd managed to arrange my class schedule so that I could swing home between classes and shifts at the diner to change clothes. But I could start taking my clothes to school and changing in a bathroom on campus. I could probably trim twenty dollars from my grocery budget.

Ramen noodles and instant macaroni weren't exactly healthy for a pregnant woman, but I could survive on peanut butter and honey sandwiches. As a kid, I'd eaten enough of those to last a lifetime. The idea made me gag, but I didn't have much of a choice.

Would Dusty give me a few more hours at the diner? She'd already given me more than she could afford. I wasn't the only one struggling for cash.

And Gloria. I'd have to give Gloria less each month.

Fuck Justin. Fuck him for doing this. I really, *really* needed to move.

But first, I had to get to work. So I fit the key into the ignition and started the engine, then drove to the diner on the tires I shouldn't have bought this summer.

What was it like to be rich? To never have to think about skipping a meal or two to save a few dollars? What would it be like to not know your account balance at all times?

I didn't know any rich people to ask.

The diner was quiet. Dusty's car was parked beside the back door. I eased in beside it and grabbed my backpack from the passenger seat before hurrying inside. Then I snagged an apron from the folded pile of clean linens to tie around my waist.

Dusty was bent over the stainless prep table when I walked into the kitchen. She had a yellow pencil in one hand, its pink eraser worn to the silver metal ferrule. In the other hand, she held a french fry, its tip dipped in her famous homemade ranch dressing. She was focused on the newspaper splayed in front of her, eyes narrowed through her wire-framed reading glasses.

"Hey," I said.

"Hi." Her gaze didn't break from the black print. She drew a circle on the page.

Oh no.

Dusty read the obituaries daily, never missing the local Mission news. She was estranged from her family, every single member. When her mother, Dolly, had died, she'd passed the diner to Dusty instead of to Dolly's twin sister, Diana, as originally promised.

Diana had tried pressuring Dusty into handing it over, but Dusty had refused her aunt, and it had created a rift in their family.

Diana had told lies and forced people to choose a side—hers.

The squabbling and fighting had finally gotten so bad, Dusty had cut off most communication with her family members. It had broken her heart to walk away. But she'd honored her mother's wishes and kept Dolly's open.

Since she wasn't on speaking terms with her family, Dusty read the obituaries every day to make sure that if someone important died, she wasn't left out.

Dusty had read her cousin's obituary in this kitchen. I'd been here when she'd circled his name.

I came to a stop at the table's side, letting my backpack drop to the floor. "Who?"

She set the pencil on the table. "My aunt. Diana."

"I'm sorry."

She stared at her french fry for a long moment, then stood tall and tossed it in a nearby trash can. "It's all right."

"Can I do anything?"

Dusty plucked the glasses from her face, folding them to tuck into her apron pocket. "No, sugar. I'm fine."

I walked to her anyway, arms open.

She let me hug her for more than ten seconds before squirming free. Which meant she wasn't really fine. "You got homework?"

"Yes."

How many times had she asked me that question over the years? She cared more about my education than my own mother. Dusty always made sure my work was done before I left here each night.

The semester had just started, but she'd been even more insistent about study time lately. Maybe because she knew it was probably my last year. And there was a chance I wouldn't get to finish.

We'd know soon enough. My first doctor's appointment was on Tuesday next week.

According to Google, my due date was around April twentieth, but I wanted a doctor to confirm. And once I had an official due date, I'd know if I had a chance at finishing spring semester.

"Get to work." She walked to the dishwasher and began putting away clean mugs and plates. "I'll make you some dinner in a bit."

"Okay." With my backpack slung over a shoulder, I walked through the swinging door to the diner, passing tables and chairs for the booth in the far corner.

It had been hard to muster the motivation to study. Maybe that was because the semester was young, and I hadn't settled into the groove with classes or professors. Or maybe it was because at the moment, it felt . . . sad.

I'd graduate this spring, hopefully. I was crossing all my fingers and all my toes that I wasn't the first pregnant woman at Treasure State and my professors would allow me to finish my last semester early.

Then what? My plan had always been grad school. Leaving Montana to try something new, even if that meant less time with Gloria. But I was ready for a change of scenery. There were three universities I'd been accepted to for next term, one in Washington, another in Idaho and the third in Oregon. I'd have to turn down them all, wouldn't I?

But an undergrad degree was better than no degree, so I spent thirty minutes on an assignment for my Family Law and Public Policy class, then put everything away and took my backpack to Dusty's office, leaving it inside the door as I went to work on the dirty dishes she'd piled in the sink.

The entrance chime echoed through the kitchen as I was scrubbing a bowl.

"I've got it." Dusty held up a finger as she abandoned the celery she'd been chopping for her tuna salad. Then she breezed out, returning before the door had even stopped swinging. "Your boy's here."

"Justin?" Today, after that shit he'd pulled at home, I would let her ban him from Dolly's.

But Dusty shook her head. "No."

I groaned. That meant it was Rush. Again. "He's not my boy."

Dusty arched an eyebrow.

He was not *my* boy. He was just *a* boy. A boy who happened to have gotten me pregnant and had become a regular at Dolly's.

"I'll finish the dishes in a minute," I muttered, drying my hands before walking into the dining room.

Rush was in his usual seat—third booth against the windows, the bench that faced the swinging door. His broad, six-foot-three frame was cramped into the seat like it had been nearly every single weeknight for the past two weeks.

"Hey." His chocolate eyes snared mine as I walked down the aisle, stopping beside his booth.

My stomach fluttered. It was nerves. Not attraction because he seemed to get more and more handsome with every visit. No, it was just nerves.

There was barely an inch between his stomach and the

106

table's edge, and when he shifted, his knees knocked the table enough to rattle the salt and pepper shakers.

"Why don't you sit at a table where you can move the chair away a little?"

He shrugged. "I like sitting beside a window."

"But you barely fit."

"I don't mind." He splayed both hands across the table's surface. "I like this spot."

My heart beat a little faster, like it usually did when he was around. Nerves. It was only nerves. And a healthy dose of self-consciousness.

Rush belonged anywhere else but here. He looked so out of place. This diner was too small, too dingy, for a guy like him.

Textbooks and papers were stacked around him like he was gearing up to stay for a while. Exactly like he had last night and the night before.

Since our fight at the fieldhouse, Rush had come to the diner every evening that I'd been working, without fail. How had he known I would be here tonight?

Normally, I didn't work on Wednesdays, but Mike hadn't been here for a while. He and Dusty must be on one of their off-again moments. So when she'd asked if I wanted another shift, I'd jumped at the chance.

"Did Dusty tell you my schedule?" I asked.

"No." He reclined in the seat, as much as possible, stretching one of those muscled arms across the back of the booth. The size of his arms, those roped biceps, never failed to make me do a double take.

Muscled guys weren't my type. Or they hadn't been before Rush.

"What?" The corner of his mouth turned up.

"Nothing." I ripped my gaze away from the veins that snaked over his forearms. "How did you know I'd be working tonight?"

"I didn't. I came out after practice and saw your car."

"Oh." So he'd driven all this way just to see if I was here. "Why didn't you just text me?"

"I don't like to text."

Apparently not. He'd asked me to stop texting and so after I'd made my appointment with the doctor last week, I'd called and left a message.

"You could have called me to see if I was here." He'd asked me two weeks ago if he could call me but he hadn't. Not once. Instead, he visited the diner.

He lifted a shoulder. "Seemed easier to come out."

"Every night?" Dolly's was twenty minutes from campus. He'd drive for nearly an hour just to see if I was working. "Why?"

Rush's gaze shifted to the window like he didn't know how to answer that question.

The glass was slightly hazy, filmed with a layer of grease and dust that should have been cleaned away months ago.

For the first time in years, I felt as grimy as the glass. Since Rush had started coming here, I'd noticed more about the diner. The coffee stains on the tables. The chipped tile inside the door. The cracked vinyl booths and the neon OPEN sign that no longer flickered on to glow red.

I loved this little diner. It was more like home than work. But I knew what people saw when they walked through the door. I knew the way it looked.

I knew the way *I* looked.

We might not have much, but we could have clean windows.

Dusty hated cleaning windows and she couldn't afford a service. Mike usually cleaned them when he had a few extra minutes, but if he was gone, well . . . I'd do it for her later tonight or tomorrow.

"I like to study here," Rush said, tearing his gaze from the pothole-riddled parking lot. "It's quiet."

Unfortunately quiet. But I was doing my best to change that. Today, I'd tacked up a handful of fliers on various informational boards around campus. Once upon a time, Dusty had told me that Dolly's had been a popular college hangout. Maybe it could be that again.

"The library on campus is quiet too." And the library was in exponentially better condition.

"The food's better." He gave me a crooked grin. "And so is the company."

Me? I was horrible company. I avoided him, hiding in the kitchen because I didn't know what to say or how to act.

Was that why he kept coming? Because he knew we couldn't always have this awkward tension between us. Because he was brave enough to try.

I had to try too, didn't I? I had to figure out a way to be around Rush. And since he was here, I might as well start now.

"How are your classes going?" I asked, sliding into the opposite side of the booth, keeping my legs tucked close so our knees wouldn't touch beneath the table.

"Not bad. You?"

"Good. I've had all of my professors before so I know what to expect."

He nodded. "You feeling okay?"

"The mornings are a little rough." Thankfully, my first

class wasn't until eleven and by then, I was usually done puking.

"So . . . Tuesday." My doctor's appointment.

I nodded. "Tuesday."

"Thanks for letting me tag along."

"Sure."

Part of me wanted to go alone. It was hard to concentrate with Rush in the room. Besides that, I was used to doing things on my own. Alone was easier.

But he'd asked to come, and I wouldn't cut him out.

Rush's phone vibrated on the table. *MOM* looked like *WOW* from this side of the booth. He tapped the button and sent it to voicemail.

"I can go if you need to answer that."

"Nah. I'll call her later to talk."

Talk about what? "Have you, um, told them? Your parents?"

His gaze dropped to the table. His hair fell onto his forehead, so he dragged a hand through it, shoving it away.

Why did that have to be sexy? My core clenched. I needed him to be unsexy. Immediately.

He smoothed his hair again and this time, the scent of his cologne wafted across the table, rich and masculine, but also clean like soap. He smelled good. He smelled so, so good.

Ugh. I *had* to stop thinking about his shampoo or biceps or the way his jaw looked so rugged with that day-old stubble.

"I, um, haven't," he said.

"Haven't what?"

He gave me a sideways glance. "My parents. I haven't told them that you're pregnant."

"Oh." Right. Shit. I'd asked a question, then my brain had been scrambled by sexy hair.

"But I told my roommate," he said. "Sorry."

"It's okay." I looked to the wall that separated the kitchen and dining room. "I told Dusty."

He nodded, tracing a circle on the table with his finger. "I'd like to tell my parents. When you're ready."

I swallowed hard. "Can you wait? At least until after we have a due date?"

"Sure."

It wasn't that this pregnancy didn't feel real. My morning sickness had made sure I knew exactly what was happening with my body. But the idea of announcing it to his parents or to my sister made my palms sweat.

Family, in my experience, only made stressful situations worse. His parents would be disappointed. So would Gloria. I was carrying enough disappointment of my own that I didn't need more at the moment.

I hoped his parents could at least be civil. And kind, if not to me, then to this baby. To their grandchild.

They'd be the only grandparents he or she would have because I sure as hell wasn't letting my mother into the mix.

And Dusty was, well . . . Dusty.

As if she knew I was contemplating the idea of naming her Nana Dusty, a loud crash came from the kitchen, the sound of metal clanging on metal followed by a muted string of curses.

"I'd better go check on her."

Rush nodded as I slid out of the booth. Except before I could walk away, he called my name. "Faye?"

I stopped and turned. "Yeah?"

"Are you working tomorrow?"

Here was my chance to have a night without him around. To not worry about the looks Dusty would give me or the tension that came anytime I was in the dining room. All I had to do was say no. To tell him to come back next week.

But I hated lying.

My father had been a liar.

He'd promised to come back for me.

And I hadn't seen him since I was five.

"Yeah, I'm working," I told Rush. "Three to close."

CHAPTER TWELVE

RUSH

"April twenty-fourth." Faye's voice filled the Yukon's cab even though she spoke in a whisper. Her hands were clasped in her lap, her chin tucked.

"April twenty-fourth," I repeated, gripping the steering wheel like it was the only thing tethering me to reality.

April twenty-fourth.

We were having a baby on or around April twenty-fourth.

"That's draft day," I murmured, staring unblinking out the windshield and across the vehicles parked in the fieldhouse lot.

"What?"

I forced my vision into focus as I looked to the passenger seat. "Draft day. When college players get selected by teams in the NFL."

"Oh." Faye's forehead furrowed. "Are you, um . . . doing that? The draft?"

"No. I still have a year of eligibility left to play at Treasure State. I was a redshirt my freshman year."

She blinked. "Huh?"

I forgot she wasn't ingrained in the world of football like everyone else in my life. "An athlete can only play four seasons within a five-year calendar window. My freshman year, I only played a few games. I practiced and worked out with the team, but because I sat out for most of the games, I didn't have to count it as a full season. So I can play one more year in college."

"Ah." She nodded. "Then you'll do the draft thing?"

"Maybe." That was the plan. To play my ass off at Treasure State, pray I didn't get injured and possibly get picked up by an NFL team. Even if I went in the last round, I didn't care. I just wanted to keep playing.

Except during next year's draft, I'd have a kid. A one-year-old.

How the fuck was that going to work? How was any of this going to work?

My head had been spinning for the past hour and a half. Ever since we'd walked into the doctor's office for Faye's appointment.

I'd done my best to blend into the walls as Faye had answered a litany of health questions and been run through all the standard tests. If not for the stiff chair beside the exam table they'd told me to sit in, I might have passed out when the doctor had used a wand to listen to the baby's heartbeat.

And then she'd dropped that date on us like a bomb.

April twenty-fourth.

Yeah, it was only September, but wasn't April too soon? That would be here in a blink. I wasn't ready to be a father. We needed more time. I needed a better plan.

Except whenever I tried to visualize this new future, it was like staring into a black hole. An abyss.

"April twenty-fourth is two weeks before graduation." Faye tapped her fingers together, like she was counting the days in her head to be sure.

Fuck. While I was freaking out about next year's NFL draft, Faye wasn't sure if she'd be able to finish her last two weeks of her senior year. They had to make exceptions for stuff like this, right? Faye certainly wasn't the first pregnant student at Treasure State.

"Whatever I can do to help, I'll do it," I told her.

She glanced over, almost like she'd forgotten I was here, and gave me a half-hearted attempt at a smile before she opened the door and hopped out.

Last night at the diner, as she'd wiped down tables, I'd asked if I could drive us today. The moment she'd agreed, I'd put my schoolwork away and gotten the hell out of there before she changed her mind.

It felt like I was walking on eggshells and one wrong word would destroy this awkward peace. Faye hadn't mentioned the paternity test again. I sure as fuck hadn't brought it up.

We didn't talk about much when I went to Dolly's. Mostly, I sat in a booth that was too small and uncomfortable, watching as Faye waited on customers. But at the moment, it was all I could come up with.

To just be around her. Be available in case she needed a hand.

I reached into the back seat and grabbed my backpack, locking the car's doors when I was outside. Then I jogged to catch up to Faye, who was already heading toward the fieldhouse.

Shortening my strides, I fell in step beside her. "You have one more class today?"

"Yeah," she said. "In Williams Hall."

"I'm headed to O'Donnell for Supply Chain Analytics."

Her nose scrunched up.

I chuckled. "My thoughts exactly."

When we reached the sidewalk, we skirted the field-house, heading toward the crosswalk that would lead us toward the lecture halls and other campus buildings.

Except before we made it to the intersection, a side door to the fieldhouse blew open and two girls walked outside.

They were both on the volleyball team. Younger by a year or two maybe, I wasn't sure. All I knew was that one of them—Megan?—trailed Maverick around campus like a lost puppy.

I doubted he even knew her name.

She spotted us walking, her eyes blowing wide. Then she leaned in to say something into the other girl's ear as they both stared at Faye. No doubt the rumors were flying through the athletics department. No doubt they knew Faye was having my baby.

Fuck their gossip.

I shifted, moving behind and to Faye's other side in a flash, blocking her view so she wouldn't see them whispering.

"What?" she asked.

"Nothing." I put my hand on the small of her back when we reached the street, not touching but hovering close as we stepped onto the crosswalk.

A quick glance over my shoulder and the volleyball girls were close.

They were still heads bent, whispering.

Fucking girls.

And the real fuck of it all was that the only person I

could blame was myself. Because I'd lost my mind weeks ago and started an argument with Faye in the fieldhouse where everyone could hear.

People had started to talk. The rumors seemed mostly limited to the athletic department, but that wouldn't last. Maverick had probably told Erik. Erik would tell Kalindi.

And while it would be great to keep this under wraps for a while, a pregnancy wasn't something we could hide forever.

Clearly, not even a couple of months if the news had spread to the volleyball team.

Gossip amongst athletes was normal. I'd certainly heard my fair share in the locker room. Hell, I'd even had the gossip be about me. Though that had been a while ago. I'd done my best to fly under the radar since everything had happened with Halsey our freshman year.

Shit. What was Halsey going to do when she found out? Should I tell her? Maybe it would save some drama if she heard it from me. I didn't want to call her, but I would. Later.

The girls behind us laughed, a little too loudly.

"Are you working tonight?" I asked Faye as we crossed the street. If I talked, maybe she wouldn't be able to hear whatever it was they were saying.

Her eyes were aimed forward, her arms wrapped around her middle. "No."

"Oh."

"I'll still be at the diner later."

"Really? Why?"

She glanced up, caramel eyes holding mine for just a moment. "It's easier there."

"With me? Or with everything?"

Faye blew out a breath. "Both."

It *was* easier at Dolly's. Why was that?

Stepping into the restaurant was like entering a bubble. Like nothing else existed except for the smell of cheeseburgers and bacon. Like the future couldn't touch us when we were within the diner's walls. Like we didn't have to have it all figured out, not yet.

"I think I'll change it up tonight. Get the pancakes instead of a burger," I said. "They're your favorite, right?"

"Yes."

"Pancakes it is. Since you're not working, maybe we could eat them together. Sit in that booth and pretend like we're both not freaking out about April twenty-fourth."

The corner of Faye's mouth turned up. It was a barely-there smile I'd seen a handful of times since I'd started visiting Dolly's. And it always made me want more. It made me want a real smile, like the ones she'd given me the night of the bachelorette party. "All right. Pancakes."

I grinned. "Can't wait."

Her smile widened, her cheeks pinkened.

Faye was gorgeous. Completely, intoxicatingly gorgeous. I hadn't really let myself look, truly look, at her these past few weeks. Mostly because I was worried I wouldn't be able to stop staring.

We had enough problems. She didn't need me drooling over her right now.

She glanced up, catching me watching. "What?"

You're beautiful. "Nothing."

The brown brick of O'Donnell Hall came into view. Normally, I liked that it was so close to the fieldhouse. Walking between the two buildings was quick and convenient.

But walking with Faye was nice. It felt like we were two

normal students passing time between classes, enjoying campus on a crisp, fall day.

"What class do you—" My question was cut short when the people outside O'Donnell shifted and a familiar face appeared in the crowd.

Halsey. Storming my way.

The anger on her face meant only one thing. She'd heard the gossip too.

"Oh, fuck." So much for delivering the news myself.

"What?" Faye glanced around.

"You should go," I said, jerking my chin toward the opposite end of campus.

"Huh?"

There was no time to explain and the last thing we needed today was drama. Especially with the volleyball girls still behind us. "Trust me? Please? I'll see you at the diner tonight."

Faye stared at me for two heartbeats before she nodded.

I slowed my steps, letting her continue forward. Then I stopped entirely as Halsey marched closer and closer.

There was no way for me to keep the two women from crossing paths. But Halsey's attention was locked on me, and I hoped that I'd remain her target.

She breezed past Faye, not so much as sparing her a glance, and the air rushed from my lungs.

Good. I'd take whatever wrath was coming. Faye didn't need to get dragged into this bullshit.

Halsey stopped ten feet away, twisting to point at Faye's back. "Is that her?"

Keep walking, Faye. Just keep walking.

She stopped.

Damn it.

"Don't do this," I told Halsey.

There was a blaze in her eyes even though they were swimming with tears. "Is it true?"

"Hals—"

"Is. It. True!" Her voice bounced off the nearby buildings and all other conversations came to a screeching halt.

This was going to get ugly, wasn't it? "We're not talking about this."

"Oh, really?" She crossed her arms over her chest. "We're not talking about how you cheated on me and got *her* pregnant?"

Past Halsey, down the sidewalk, the color drained from Faye's face.

The doctor had told us that it was common for expecting parents to wait until the twelve-week mark before making announcements. Now? There wasn't a chance we'd make it to that three-month mark. I hadn't even told my parents yet.

"We weren't together," I told Halsey. "I didn't cheat on you. And I get why you're upset, but this is not your business."

A tear dripped down her cheek and with an angry swipe, she flicked it away. "So are you together now?"

"I'm not talking about this." I kept my voice as gentle as possible. "Let it go."

"Let it go." Her voice cracked. "I have spent months proving how much I love you. I have never given up on us, even when you did. I have been your number-one cheerleader for years. I would have followed you to the NFL if that's what you wanted, or I would have stayed here, just to be with you. I have tried everything. *Everything*. And you want me to let it go?"

Damn it. "I'm sorry, Hals."

I'd never meant to hurt her like this.

Another tear fell and this time, she didn't bother catching it. "Now I have to hate you."

It didn't hurt. She delivered it, expecting it to be a blow, but it didn't hurt. Probably because it wasn't the first time she'd said she hated me. That camping trip, after we'd gotten into a fight, she'd told me in a voicemail that she'd hated me then too.

Without another word, she walked past me, her shoulder clipping my arm before she disappeared.

The people who'd obviously been watching suddenly found the ground, the clouds, the grass quite interesting as they tore their attention away and pretended not to have eavesdropped on that spectacle.

I didn't have it in me to care that I had an audience, not today.

My focus went to the sidewalk, searching for a woman with strawberry-blond hair.

Faye had already walked away.

So I went to class and did my best to focus on school. I worked my ass off at practice, pouring all of my frustration and irritation into football. And after taking a shower and changing into a pair of clean jeans and a long-sleeved T-shirt, I drove across town to Dolly's Diner, my stomach growling and ready for some pancakes.

I ate them alone.

Faye stood me up.

CHAPTER THIRTEEN

FAYE

My sister jabbed her elbow into mine before she snapped her fingers in front of my face. "Um, hello. Are you going to help me with this or what?"

I jerked, tearing my gaze away from the diner's front door.

Gloria and I were squished together in a booth—Rush's booth. When had this become his booth?

"Sorry," I told her. "I'm distracted tonight."

"You think?" Gloria sneered with an eye roll.

The teenage sass was thicker than Dusty's country gravy. She'd been in a bad mood all evening and the eye rolls were wearing thin.

"Can you dial back the snark?"

"Can you pretend like you actually want to be here?"

"Gloria," I warned.

"Faye," she mimicked, and just to irk me, she rolled her caramel eyes again. Had I been this bratty at fifteen?

"You know what? I think you can figure out algebra on your own tonight." I slid to the edge of the booth, about to stand, when she wrapped her hand around my arm, stopping my escape.

"Wait. Don't. I really need your help."

"Then be nice."

She let me go and sighed. "It just seems like you're not paying attention."

"I've got a lot on my mind," I said, shifting back into the booth. "Give me some grace."

" 'Kay." She gave me a sad smile. "Sorry."

"It's all right." I leaned closer, our shoulders touching, as we both focused on the worksheet in front of us. "Next question. In this expression, what represents the coefficient?"

She groaned as she stared at the four multiple choice options. "I don't know. I suck at math."

"You're good at math." I nodded toward her paper. "Come on."

With a huff, she picked up her Ticonderoga pencil, and as she worked out the problem, my gaze once again drifted toward the door.

It had been a week since I'd seen Rush. A week since my doctor's appointment. A week since we'd agreed to meet for pancakes, and I'd stood him up instead.

Dusty had told me that he'd waited here for two hours that night before finally leaving. He hadn't been back to the diner since.

Eventually, we'd have to talk again. Eventually, I'd have to work up the courage to call him. Eventually, I'd have to figure out exactly what to say.

But what did I say? I'd overheard that argument with his ex-girlfriend last week. I'd heard her accuse him of cheating, that she loved him and also hated him.

I wasn't sure who I felt worse for, Rush or Halsey, but I doubted either would want my pity.

"It's B," Gloria said, circling the answer on her worksheet.

"Good job." I patted her arm as she moved on to the next question.

The swinging door to the kitchen opened and Dusty came out with a basket of chicken strips and fries.

"Oh, thank God. I'm starving." Gloria tossed her pencil aside and shuffled her homework out of the way as Dusty set her dinner on the table.

"I'll get you some ranch," I said, sliding out of the booth.

"I can get it," Dusty offered but I waved her off and stood.

"I'm supposed to be working."

"Because we're so busy?" She glanced around the empty diner and laughed.

A laugh? Really? It used to bother her that business got slower and slower each year. How could it not? Was she actually laughing about it now? Was that how far we'd come?

So far tonight, I'd waited on five tables. Sure, we had our regulars, the people who'd come in once or twice a week. But even those patrons had dwindled lately. Most were older. Dusty had probably read a few of their names in her daily obituary hunt.

It was after seven o'clock. Gloria would likely be the only person here the last hour we were open.

"I can clock out," I said. "There's no point in you paying me."

"No."

I'd learned a long time ago not to argue with that tone.

"I'm going to pop out back for a quick smoke," she said

before disappearing to the kitchen, but not before a long look around the empty room.

The back door slammed closed, and I turned in a slow circle. Guilt weighed heavy on my shoulders as my gaze drifted from table to table.

Should I quit? Find a job at a restaurant where I'd make better tips? Give Dusty a chance to save some money by not paying me each week? I worked for minimum wage, but still, that was a cost she could cut.

She'd never fire me, not unless things were dire. Even then, she'd probably short her own bank account before letting me go.

If I left her alone, she'd be forced to work every shift without a break. Not that she ever took a break. Even when she and Mike were together and he'd come cook, she was here too. Even when I was capable of closing down and locking up, she'd stay so we could walk out the back door together. There were no such thing as vacations for Dusty.

Was that by choice? Or necessity?

Maybe I should quit. Work somewhere else during the day, then visit Dusty at night. I had no idea how that would work with a full class schedule.

Or a baby.

My stomach did a somersault. It seemed to be in a constant state of acrobatics these days. Before noon, it was churning with morning sickness. After lunch, it was spinning with anxiety.

I trudged to the waitress station and filled a glass with ice and Sprite. Then I snagged a bottle of ranch dressing from the fridge and returned to the booth. I slumped beside my sister, who was too busy inhaling her food to notice as I wiped my clammy palms on my jeans.

"Want some?" She pushed the basket closer, her cheeks bulging as she chewed.

"No. And don't talk with your mouth full."

Gloria rolled her eyes.

I was too tired to scold her for it this time. So I sipped my drink and read the next question on her worksheet, mentally going through the math for the answer. "What else do you have to do tonight?"

"This and a take-home quiz for health." She snatched her pencil, tapping the eraser on the table. "I have to answer a bunch of dumb questions so that my teacher knows I understand sex and won't be stupid enough to get pregnant."

I gulped. How was I going to tell her? Gloria wouldn't understand a mistake like this.

Though at least I wouldn't have to explain my choice to keep the baby. We had the same mother who'd used abortion as a way to crush our tender hearts.

I was a carbon copy of Mom. I had to see our face every day in the mirror. Gloria, at least, took after her father. From her olive skin and straight, black hair, people didn't realize we were sisters. The only trait we shared were our caramel eyes. Hers were framed with thick, sooty lashes. I looked like a corpse if I didn't add a few swipes of mascara each day.

My gorgeous, headstrong sister who still saw the world as black and white would not understand how I could have possibly gotten pregnant.

Honestly, there were days when I could hardly believe it myself.

"Do you think I should get on birth control?"

My gaze flew from her algebra worksheet to her profile. "What? Why? Are you, um . . . active?"

Please say no. Please, God, say no.

"Active?" She scrunched up her nose and grimaced. "Faye."

"Well? Are you?"

"No."

Phew. "Then why do you think you should be on birth control?"

"I don't know." She shrugged. "Just in case."

It was too soon for this talk. She was only fifteen. I hadn't lost my virginity until freshman year in college. But Gloria was the most beautiful girl at Mission High School. I didn't need to ask if boys had shown interest. Of course they were chasing her.

It was too soon. But it was time.

"I'll call Planned Parenthood and make an appointment," I said.

She worried her bottom lip between her teeth. "Can we not tell my dad?"

"We don't have to. But at some point, he's probably going to ask." Her dad was not the type to ignore the tough subjects, not when the health and safety of his daughter was on the line.

"He already talked to me about sex and it was the worst, most uncomfortable conversation of my whole life. Forget it. I'll just stay a virgin forever."

"I support this plan."

She giggled. "All the boys at school are dumb anyway."

"Boys are dumb no matter—" Before I could finish agreeing, the front door opened.

As the chime dinged through the empty restaurant, Rush walked inside.

He'd come back.

The instant surge of conflicting emotion was so strong I

nearly choked. Relief and panic and nerves and excitement. I wasn't sure if I should smile or wave or crawl under the table and hide.

"Oh my God," Gloria whispered, tucking her chin. "That guy is *hot*."

"Gloria." I elbowed her in the side.

"Ow." She elbowed me back. "What was that for?"

She wasn't wrong. Obviously, he was drop-dead gorgeous. But it was going to get really weird if she drooled over my—what? Baby daddy?

Eww. Just thinking *baby daddy* made me cringe. We were going to need to come up with something else. Friend? Acquaintance?

Co-parent?

"He's coming over here." She squirmed a little, sitting straighter as she smoothed her hair.

"No." I sliced a finger through the air. "He is too old for you."

"How do you—Wait. You know him?" Her eyes bulged. "Please tell me you dumped Justin and hooked up with this guy instead."

"It's, um . . . complicated. Now shush."

"What's complicated? He's frickin' hot."

"Hey." Rush's deep voice sent a shiver down my spine.

I risked a glance up, up, up to that handsome face. He looked like he was holding back a smile. Which meant he had most definitely heard Gloria call him hot. *Awesome.*

"Hi." I shifted, about to stand and make an escape, but before I could get to my feet, Rush slid into the booth across from us.

"I'm Rush." He extended a hand to Gloria.

Her blush turned fuchsia. "I'm Gloria. Faye's sister."

His gaze flickered between the two of us as he shook her hand. Later, I'd tell him we were half sisters. Not that it made any difference. She was all mine and had been since the day she was born.

Mom had told me once that all I was good for was free babysitting. She'd meant it as an insult, but I'd been more than happy to watch Gloria morning, noon and night.

"Nice to meet you," he said, his attention zeroed in on me. He leaned his elbows on the table, his broad, large frame taking up the entire side of the booth. Even seated, he towered over me. "You okay?"

"I'm okay."

He hummed. "Pancakes?"

"Sorry."

Gloria looked between the two of us, her eyes narrowing. "Why are you apologizing for pancakes?"

"Long story," I said, getting to my feet. "Would you like to order anything?"

"The regular is fine."

A cheeseburger deluxe with waffle fries.

"Wait." Gloria held up a hand before I could leave. "He comes here enough to have a regular? What about Justin?"

"We broke up."

Her jaw dropped. "You didn't tell me that. Did you move out? Who is this?"

This was not a conversation I wanted to have in front of Rush, so I pointed to her worksheet. "No, I didn't move out. This is Rush. And you need to do your homework."

She shot me a glare. It was our mother's.

I ignored it and walked into the kitchen. Dusty was bent over the newspaper, pen in hand as she reviewed the obituaries.

She hadn't mentioned her aunt's passing or the funeral. I'd asked on Monday if she wanted to talk, which she'd ignored, and then she'd gone outside to smoke.

Dusty and I had an unspoken rule. We didn't push each other on the tough topics. But she was here if I needed to talk. She'd be here to give me the hard truths. And if she ever needed a person to hug, I was at the ready.

Quit? I couldn't quit. I wouldn't leave her alone. Besides, I doubted any other restaurant would let me sit beside my sister and help her with homework so often.

"Customer?" Dusty asked.

"Yes. Deluxe cheeseburger and waffle fries."

"Ah." She set her pen aside and stood tall. "So your boy came back."

"He's not my boy."

"Right, sugar." The corner of her mouth twitched before she turned and walked to the flattop.

Rush wasn't *my boy*. This pregnancy wasn't going to lead to some fairy-tale romance. We were simply trying to figure each other out. Figure out how to survive in each other's orbit.

One cheeseburger with waffle fries at a time.

I returned to the dining room, moving to the beverage station to fill a glass of ice water, then grabbing a roll of silverware with a ketchup and mustard caddy and carrying it all to the booth. "Here's—What's going on?"

Gloria stared at Rush, her glare as sharp as a sword, looking like she wanted nothing more than to separate his head from his shoulders.

Rush stared right back at my sister, but he looked . . . curious? Bored? Irritated? I didn't know him well enough to know what that tilt of his head meant.

"Number seven." Gloria didn't shift her gaze as she slid her worksheet across the table to the edge for me to see. "What is the answer?"

I set down the caddy, silverware and Rush's water, then picked up the paper. It took me a minute of mental math, but I worked it out. "B."

Rush's chuckle wasn't loud, but it seemed to fill the room with that deep, sultry noise. That chuckle had no business being attractive.

A shiver rolled over my shoulders. *Crap.*

"Ugh." Gloria snatched the page from my hand so fast I nearly got a papercut. Her lip curled as she scowled at Rush. "Who *are* you?"

"A guy who's good at math." He leaned forward, elbows on the table, then nodded to her worksheet. "Number eight. Let's go."

"Fine," she muttered.

Then together, they worked on number eight.

No one helped Gloria with her homework. No one but me.

I'd been the person who'd gone through her Friday folders in kindergarten and praised her artwork. I'd signed her first- and second-grade reading logs. I'd quizzed her on spelling words in fourth and helped her with science projects in fifth.

Chuck, her dad, simply wasn't around enough. Gloria's grandmother was a nice woman, but she'd always been fairly disconnected from Gloria's education. And our mother, well . . . school was our responsibility. If we succeeded, she was indifferent. If we failed, she lamented her "idiot daughters."

I had yet to let Gloria fail.

Not once had another person stepped in to help me, help her.

Until Rush.

"Nice." He grinned as Gloria picked the correct answer for number eight and immediately moved on to number nine.

He was going to be a good father, wasn't he? Maybe I'd fucked up my life, but at least my kid would have a good dad.

Rush looked up and his eyebrows came together. "You okay?"

All I could manage was a nod.

He'd be a good dad. Would I be a good mom?

I was going to be a mom. Not just an older sister, there to help along the way. This child would rely on me for everything. I was going to be its mother.

When would it stop surprising me? When would it lock into place? My head started spinning so I put my hand on the table to steady my balance.

Rush's hand clasped over mine, his palm warm and firm as his calloused fingers squeezed.

"I'm fine," I whispered, drawing in a deep breath before I slipped my hand out from beneath his. I instantly missed the heat from his skin.

"I got this," he said, nodding to Gloria, scribbling furiously on her sheet to calculate the next answer. "Why don't you sit down?"

In that booth? Nope. I was a bit too frazzled, and given my emotional state, frazzled usually meant tears. If I started crying, Gloria would ask questions, and I wasn't ready to give answers, not yet.

"I'll be back." I slipped away on wobbling knees.

Dusty was busy cooking Rush's burger, so she didn't notice as I shut myself in the bathroom.

I slumped against the door, closing my eyes as my heart stopped hammering against my sternum. "Get a grip, Faye."

It was just algebra homework. It was sweet of Rush to help. Certainly not something that should have me hyperventilating in the bathroom.

"Ugh." I buried my face in my hands, forcing air into my lungs. Then I pulled myself together and returned to the kitchen, walking in just as Dusty shook a batch of waffle fries from the fryer onto Rush's plate.

"Here you go, honey."

"Thanks." I swept it up and took it to the booth, braced for what I'd find this time.

Gloria was bent over her page, face hard in concentration as Rush watched.

When I set his plate on the table, he looked up and smiled. "Thanks."

"Thank you," I mouthed.

He winked.

The floor did a strange tilt and once more, my balance faltered, but this time, instead of running away, I took the seat beside my sister. And let my knee knock against Rush's beneath the table. "Do you want to have pancakes tomorrow night?"

He grinned as he picked up a fry. "Sure."

"What's with you guys and pancakes?" Gloria asked as she pushed her page across the table.

Not toward me to double-check her work.

But toward Rush.

CHAPTER FOURTEEN

RUSH

Gloria rifled through her backpack, taking out a piece of paper that had been shoved to the bottom of the bag. "I need you to sign my permission slip."

"Why is this wrinkled and folded?" Faye frowned as she took it from her sister, smoothing out the page as she splayed it on the table. "Put it in your binder. Take care of your stuff."

"Who cares? It's just a field trip form. And I was in a hurry when they handed it out."

Faye sighed, holding out a hand. "Pen."

Gloria produced a hot-pink pen from her backpack, smacking it into her sister's palm.

The permission slip needed the basic information. Name. Address. Phone number. Faye filled in every line without hesitation, like she'd done it a thousand times. She even completed the insurance information from memory. And for the emergency contact, she added herself.

Faye didn't act like Gloria's sibling. No, she acted like her mother.

Was she Gloria's legal guardian? How had I not known about Faye's sister yet? I'd been coming to the diner for weeks. Not once had Faye mentioned Gloria. Up until last night, I hadn't known she even existed.

I'd wanted to ask yesterday, but there hadn't been a chance. Gloria had stayed at the diner until the end of Faye's shift. So had I. After she'd clocked out, I'd walked them both outside to Faye's car.

When I'd come in tonight, ready for pancakes and a chance to actually talk to Faye, there'd been a bike chained up outside and Gloria had already been in my booth, a new algebra worksheet ready for me to review.

She'd had three of the twenty questions wrong. They were now correct and the worksheet stowed neatly—Faye's doing—in the binder.

"I'm going home." Gloria zipped up her bag.

"But you're not done with your homework. What about that English essay?"

"It's almost done. I'll finish it tomorrow morning on the bus."

Faye was on the inside of the booth's bench seat tonight so there was no stopping Gloria as she hopped to her feet and blew her sister a kiss.

"Text me when you get home," Faye said.

"Don't I always?" Gloria started to leave but stopped herself, taking a backward step until she was at the edge of my seat.

Faye seemed to get all of Gloria's sass. I'd mostly gotten glares tonight. Why? Not a damn clue. Either she didn't like that I was finding her math mistakes or she didn't like that I'd gotten Faye pregnant.

If she knew. Had Faye told her?

"Is Rush your real name?" she asked.

"Yes."

She looked me up and down. "You're hot."

"Thanks?" Okay, really didn't need Faye's little sister telling me I was hot.

"Most hot guys are dicks. Her ex is a dick. Though he's not as hot as you."

Faye didn't chime in to argue either point. Good to know I was better looking than the ex.

"Don't be a dick to my sister." Gloria pointed a finger at my nose.

I glanced at Faye. Her cheeks were flushed, her chin tucked. A lock of that silky hair covered part of her face.

"I'll do my best," I said. To them both.

Did that mean the ex had been a dick? Or maybe Faye had told Gloria about the incident weeks ago when I'd asked for that paternity test. Except Gloria didn't seem to know about the baby. Faye hadn't mentioned it, so I'd just keep my mouth shut.

Without another word, Gloria swept out of the diner. It wasn't until after the chime had faded that Faye finally looked up. Her gaze met mine only briefly before she turned to the glass.

"Thanks for helping with her math homework again."

"No problem."

She blew out a long breath, slumping into the seat. "Are you hungry? I can go tell Dusty to start our pancakes."

"Not yet."

Her eyes shifted to the table's surface. She spotted a fleck of pepper and raised a hand from her lap, brushing the black speck to the floor. "Gloria has a lot of attitude, but she's a good kid."

"Does she live with your mom?"

"No. She lives with her dad."

"Not your dad?"

She glanced up and gave me a sad smile. "I haven't seen my father since I was five."

So she'd been stuck with a piece-of-shit mother. That actually made me hate her father just as much for leaving her behind. Though maybe he was even worse.

"Gloria's dad is a good guy," Faye said. "She's lived with him full-time since I moved out of my mother's house."

When Faye had no longer been a buffer. Or a babysitter. Considering all I knew about Faye's mother was that she hadn't wanted her own kids, and the fact that Faye acted like Gloria's mother, it wasn't a stretch to assume she'd played the parent role. Probably for a long, long time.

"So if she lives with her dad, why are you filling out field trip permission slips?" I asked.

"Her dad is a truck driver, so he's on the road a lot of the time. He never went back to court to get full custody of Gloria. It was kind of this unspoken agreement that Mom didn't want kids in her house any longer, so when Gloria stopped going over to Mom's for weeks, Mom didn't say anything. But she still needs a parent when her dad is gone. I do my best to fill the gap."

"Where does she stay when he's traveling? Not alone?"

"No. Her grandmother lives with them. Their house isn't far from here, so she can ride her bike to the diner, and I'll help her with homework."

"I've been coming here for weeks. Did I just miss Gloria before?"

"She doesn't come when her dad is in town. They're close. When he's in town, they're together. He took some time off work to be around while she started the new school year."

"Ah." I nodded. "Makes sense. It's good of you to help."

She shrugged. "She's my sister."

Faye would be a good mom, wouldn't she? I'd had a good mom. Our child would have a good mom too.

"I'm getting hungry," she said, sliding out of the booth. Then she slipped away to the kitchen, returning with a backpack slung over a shoulder.

The reason I'd come tonight was to talk, not to study. But as she returned to her seat and opened her bag, I fished mine out from beneath the table and hauled out our playbook.

Faye glanced at it, then did a double take. "Football?"

"Yeah. I've got to review a few play changes before we take off for our game tomorrow."

"You're leaving?"

I nodded. "Away game. In Washington. Bus leaves tomorrow. Be back Sunday. Hopefully after a win."

"Are you winning?" There was hesitation in her question, like she wasn't sure if she was asking correctly.

"So far. It's been a good season. And I like Coach Ellis. This is his first year, and he's a good guy. A great coach."

Her eyebrows came together, like she was thinking hard about whatever it was on the tip of her tongue. "That argument on campus with Halsey. She said something about the NFL. I don't know much about football, but is that a possibility for you? To play professionally?"

"Maybe. Depends on how this season and the next go."

"But if you did that draft thing, you'd go?"

It should have been an easy answer. Play in the NFL? Hell yes. If all the stars aligned, and I was chosen, it should be an easy yes. Except it wasn't easy, not anymore.

The NFL would require me to move, potentially numerous times. If Faye was in Montana with our child, could I really leave Mission?

"The NFL was always the hope. It's what I've been working toward. At least a shot at going pro. But I'm having a hard time thinking much past the current minute."

"Same." She huffed a laugh, and it was nice to know that I wasn't the only one lost here. "I want to be a speech pathologist, except that seems impossible right now."

I didn't want her dreams to be impossible. Not when we were in this together. "We'll figure it out, right? We just have to rally."

"Rally." She arched her eyebrows. "You say that a lot."

"Do I? Well, I guess because it's true. We can rally. Figure this out, right?"

"I hope so," she murmured, returning her attention to her studies. Except I didn't want to lose her. I didn't want her to shut off the conversation, not yet.

"Why speech pathology? I've never heard anyone say that's what they wanted to do."

Her finger drew a circle on the table, then a swirl. Aimless wanderings and for a moment, I was blasted into the past. To a dark, drunken night when I'd been her canvas. When her finger had traced circles on my chest before we'd both passed out.

It was strange how moments from our night together seemed to come back in flashes. I hadn't forgotten anything, but I hadn't exactly remembered it all either.

Was it a blessing? Or a curse?

"When I was a kid, I had a lisp." Faye's voice ripped me out of the memory and back into the present. Into the booth where she kept tracing patterns onto a lucky table. "I struggled with my *l*s and *r*s or *s*s. In first grade, there was a boy who made fun of me. Marty Levens."

"The little shit," I said.

She scrunched up her nose in that subtle way I'd seen her do before. The Faye scrunch. "Pretty much. I sort of withdrew that year. I talked less and less. Didn't answer questions unless my teacher called on me. People just assumed I was quiet. I mean, I am quiet. But my third-grade teacher was the person who finally asked me why I never spoke up when I always had the right answer. I liked her and told her I didn't like how I talked. So she got me into speech therapy."

A teacher. Not her own mother. A teacher.

Really, really not looking forward to the day I met her mother. Keeping my mouth shut might not be easy. "And Marty Levens?"

"Moved away in fifth grade."

"Good riddance."

She laughed, a sound so soft and sweet it took me off guard. I'd heard her laugh before. Camping. The bachelorette party. This was different. It felt . . . intimate. Like maybe I was finally earning back some trust.

"Did you have a nemesis as a kid?" she asked.

"Candi Michaels." I chuckled. "It's been a long time since I've said that name."

"Why? Was she better at math than you?"

"She wishes," I teased. "I had the biggest crush on her my freshman year. The school held this spring dance every year, and I spent weeks mustering up the courage to ask her as my date. She was nice about turning me down. Told me she was just going to go with some of her friends. But then I overheard her talking at her locker about how my noodle arms creeped her out."

Faye pointed to my bicep. "Noodle arms? I'm not sure I believe that."

"I had a scrawny phase." I brought my arms forward, flexing the muscles of my forearms and triceps. "I was chubby as a little kid, then in middle school I shot straight up. I was strong but lanky until I started filling out again. Worked hard in the gym for football and basketball. Helped my dad on the ranch in the summers. By my junior year, the noodle arms were gone, but I never forgot hearing that from Candi."

To this day, I doubted she knew I'd overheard. I never really talked to her again. And that crush of mine died the moment I heart her laughing about me with her friends.

"Girls are mean," Faye said, giving me a kind smile. "Sorry."

"Don't be." I waved it off. "I haven't thought about that in ages. It sounds more melodramatic than it was. I grew up on a ranch about two hours from here outside of a small town. Small town means a small school. I graduated with seventy-two people, and in a school that size, you don't really get to have enemies. Candi wasn't my nemesis. She was just my least favorite classmate."

"Ah." Faye nodded.

"Can we talk about—"

The swish of the swinging door stopped my question.

Dusty emerged with two white plates, each heaped with pancakes and scrambled eggs. Mine had two sausage patties. A glass jar of maple syrup was dangled on a finger.

"Thanks," I said as she slid the plates onto the table.

Dusty smoothed her hands over her apron. "What else can I get you?"

"I can get it," Faye said. "Thank you."

"Welcome, babycakes." Dusty winked at her, then retreated to the kitchen.

Faye picked up her roll of silverware and fished out a fork, then she tore into the pancakes.

"No syrup?" I asked as I covered my own pancakes until it dripped off the edges of the stack.

She shook her head. "I don't like sauce."

"Syrup is sauce?"

"Yeah." She cut into her pancakes. "I don't really like condiments or gravy either."

"What about spaghetti?"

"I'll eat the noodles with some parmesan."

"Huh." I stared at her for a long moment. "Ranch? Salsa?"

"Meh. Not a fan of either."

"Mayo?"

That got me the nose scrunch.

I chuckled. "No sauce. Got it."

We ate in silence for a few moments, mostly because I was too busy shoveling food in my mouth to talk. The pancakes were the best I'd ever had, light and fluffy and sweet, like Dusty added vanilla to the batter.

"These are good," I told Faye.

"Best ever. These have been my favorite food since I started working here."

"When was that?"

"When I turned sixteen. I rode my bike out here after school on my birthday to fill out an application. I started work the next day."

"I'm surprised more people don't know about it."

Faye sighed. "Yeah. It's been slower than usual lately. I've put some flyers up around campus, just to see if I can spark some interest."

Maybe that was something I could help with. If the guys on the team knew about these pancakes or the cheeseburgers, they'd drive out in droves for a decent meal that didn't cost a fortune.

I'd be happy to give a plug for Dolly's later this year. Just not quite yet. I didn't want to step on her toes. And for now, Dolly's was mine. Ours. This was the only place where it seemed like we could escape the world.

My world.

The world of football and teammates and judgment and ex-girlfriends.

"About what you heard with Halsey," I said.

"You don't have to explain."

"Yeah, I do." I set my fork down, waiting until she did the same. "I didn't cheat."

It wasn't my reputation I was worried about. It was Faye's. I didn't want people to think that about her.

"I never thought you did, Rush."

"Thanks." It was faith I probably didn't deserve, but I'd take it. "On another topic, my parents are coming to the next home game. I'd like to tell them about . . . this."

Her shoulders curled in on themselves, but she nodded. "All right."

"You sure?"

"Yeah." She nodded. "I need to tell Gloria, but I'm not quite sure how yet. If you don't mind giving me some time to figure that out, I'd appreciate it."

"Take all the time you need."

Maybe once the people in our lives knew about the pregnancy, it would be easier to handle. Easier to contemplate. But I wasn't going to rush her into that conversation with her sister.

When we finished our meals, Faye slid out of the booth to clear the dishes, and when she returned, she collected her things and stowed them in her backpack.

"Done studying?" I asked.

A yawn tugged at her pretty lips. "I think so. I've just been really tired lately."

"But everything is okay, right?" Was being tired normal? Was there something wrong? Maybe she was working too much on top of school.

I stood from my seat, and before she could stop me, I snagged her backpack from the opposite bench and looped it over my shoulder.

"I can carry my backpack." She stood and reached to steal it back, but I shifted so the strap was out of reach.

"I've got it."

Faye's lips pursed in a line when she realized I wasn't going to budge on this. "I need to say goodbye to Dusty."

"I'll wait."

She didn't roll her eyes. I couldn't think of a time when I'd seen her roll her eyes. But the look on her face was the equivalent as she walked away.

I stowed the playbook in my bag, knowing I'd catch hell if I forgot it anywhere. Coaches didn't really like us taking them out of the fieldhouse, but I'd asked Coach Ellis for an exception. With a backpack on each shoulder, I walked to the door, waiting until Faye emerged with a white takeout container.

"More pancakes?" I asked.

Her lip curled. "Lasagna."

Which was made with marinara sauce.

"It's Dusty's favorite. She makes it once a month as a special." She lowered her voice, checking over her shoulder to make sure we were alone. "I don't have the heart to tell her I don't like it."

"But she knows you don't like sauce, right?"

She lifted a shoulder.

Meaning no.

Faye would take home this lasagna, and probably choke it down if I had to guess, simply because Dusty loved it and had given it to her as a gift.

"I love lasagna." I pushed the door open for her to walk outside and round the diner for her Explorer parked out back. "I also eat at least five times a day. Just sayin'."

She gave me a shy smile, and when I moved to take the takeout container from her hand, she didn't haul it back. "Thanks."

"Tell me something you like besides pancakes."

"Chicken strips. Mashed potatoes."

"No gravy."

"Definitely not."

"Butter?"

"I like butter."

"Jam?"

"Not raspberry. The seeds get stuck in my teeth."

I grinned, reaching my free hand past her to open the door to her car. Then I stretched past her to drop her backpack into the passenger seat. "No raspberry. Noted."

She tucked a lock of hair behind her ear, exposing her cheek to the fading evening light.

Nightfall would be soon, but the sun was still peeking

over the mountain horizon, casting the parking lot in rays of gold. The light brought out the copper strands in her hair, making them shimmer.

God, she was beautiful. It was impossible not to stare. My gaze roamed her face, from the blush of her cheeks to the freckles scattered across the bridge of her nose.

I moved on instinct, before my brain realized what I was doing enough to stop me. My lips brushed the smooth skin of her cheek, just an inch away from the corner of her mouth.

Her inhale was sharp, the sound one of surprise, not horror. "What was that for?"

"I don't know," I admitted. And I wasn't sorry.

She shook her head as she worried her bottom lip between her teeth. Her gaze dropped to my shirt, staring blankly at the gray cotton.

I was standing close. Too close. She was a magnet and I was metal, but before I kissed her again, this time on her mouth, I forced my feet back a step. "I plan everything."

Her caramel gaze was like liquid gold when she glanced up.

"Or I used to plan everything. I didn't plan that." I'd wanted to kiss her cheek, so I'd kissed her cheek. "Night, Faye."

I turned and retraced our steps, toward the corner of the building that would take me to the front lot.

"Rush?" she called before I could disappear.

"Yeah?"

Her fingers fluttered in a tiny wave. "Good luck at your game this weekend."

Something twisted in my chest. My heart, I guess. I'd never felt it twist like that before. Not a pinch. Not a spasm.

It twisted like it was two sizes too big and was turning upside down in an attempt to find more space.

Well, fuck. Given all that we had happening, I probably shouldn't have a crush on Faye Gannon.

CHAPTER FIFTEEN

RUSH

A s I walked into my parents' hotel room, Dad clapped me on the shoulder. "Good game, son."

"Thanks, Dad." My voice was hoarse. Probably because my fucking heart was in my fucking throat.

I'd been dreading this conversation for ten days. Well, longer actually. But since Faye had given me the go-ahead to tell my parents, it had been hard to think about much else.

"Hi, sweetheart." Mom opened her arms for a hug. "It's so good to see you."

"You too." I rested my chin on top of her head as she held tight. When she let me go, I sat at the small table in the corner of their room. My knees started to bounce the second my ass was on the chair's edge.

Somehow, during the game today, I'd managed to block this out. I'd managed to shut out the world and just think about football. But the minute the game had ended, the minute the Wildcats had declared victory, the rush of nerves had returned to turn me inside out.

How did I say this? Everything I'd rehearsed sounded

flat. They'd assume it was Halsey, just like Maverick had when I'd told him. Then I'd have to admit to a one-night stand and sex was not a topic I'd broached with my mother since I was thirteen.

But better here, in private, than anywhere else.

It would be hard enough to take the blow of their disappointment in private. I didn't need spectators while I devastated my parents.

Normally after a game, Mom and Dad would stick around the fieldhouse and wait for me to finish with the postgame meeting and a shower. Tonight, I'd told them not to wait and that I'd meet them here.

My hands were shaking as my knees kept bouncing.

Just do it. Say it. Get this over with.

Throw the ball. And see where it lands.

"Where should we go to dinner?" Mom asked as she dug into her purse, pulling out a tube of lipstick. "I don't know if I want to brave downtown. I'd rather go somewhere quiet so we can talk."

"Me too." Dad sat on the foot of their bed. "Maybe pizza?"

"I've got a place. A diner." I swallowed the lump in my throat. "But before we go, I need to talk to you about something."

"Is something wrong?" Mom put the cap on her lipstick. "School? Or football?"

"Neither." I leaned my elbows on my knees and stared at the abstract design of the denim-blue carpet.

Then, in a stream of words that barely made sense, I told my mom and dad they were going to be grandparents.

DAD'S TRUCK had been parked outside Dolly's Diner, engine off, for five minutes. We were still inside, sitting in silence, each still wearing our seat belts.

None of us moved to get out. None of us seemed to know what to say either.

So we just sat here, the three of us, reeling from my announcement.

It was real now. Not that it hadn't been real before, but now that my parents knew about the baby, about Faye, it was real.

I was going to be a dad.

And when I glanced to my own, the sting in my nostrils and burn in my throat were unbearable. I wasn't going to cry. But damn it, I kind of wanted to cry. I couldn't remember the last time I'd cried, but I'd been fighting it since we'd left the hotel.

"I'm sorry to disappoint you guys," I whispered.

"Oh, Rush." Mom sniffled from the back seat and reached forward to touch my shoulder. "Don't say that."

"We're so proud of you." Dad looked over with watery eyes. "This is just . . . a curveball."

Dad's favorite sport was baseball. He loved watching me play football, but baseball was his passion. In the hardest moments of my life, whenever Dad had something to teach me, baseball analogies were always part of the lesson.

And that curveball analogy was exactly what I'd needed to hear.

"I don't know what this means for the future," I said, twisting to talk to Mom.

She dabbed at the corners of her eyes with a wadded tissue. "It means that we'll have an excuse other than a football game to come visit."

"Faye is three months pregnant?" Dad asked, and God, I could hug the man for not stumbling over a single word in that question. Not pregnant. Not Faye's name.

"Yes. Three months."

"Then I think we're overdue for an introduction." He gave me a sure nod, then plucked the keys from the console and opened the door.

Fresh air flooded the truck's cab, crisp and cool. We'd sat in the hotel room for so long that night had crept over Mission. The mountain horizons were nearly black against the fading blue sky in the distance, and the last of the sun's rays had vanished on the drive to the diner.

I drew in a breath, held it in my lungs, then reached for the door's handle.

Maybe making the announcement and introducing them to Faye was too much for one night. Maybe I'd regret it come morning. But Mom and Dad didn't come to Mission often. And before they left, I wanted them to know Faye. I wanted them to see her face and maybe even that shy smile.

And maybe I wanted her to see them too.

She should know that I had good parents. Kind parents. People who were better than I was. People who'd support her too.

They hadn't asked me if I was sure about the pregnancy. They hadn't asked me if we'd gotten a paternity test.

Either they trusted me to be certain.

Or it hadn't crossed their minds. They'd already given Faye the benefit of the doubt.

"Dolly's." Mom scanned the front of the diner as she hopped out of the truck. "Oh my goodness."

"What?"

She looked over at Dad, held out a hand for him to clasp and laughed. "I kind of forgot about this place."

Dad chuckled. "Me too."

She smiled at him, then at me. "We used to come here. Ages ago. When we were in college. Not often, but sometimes for a big breakfast after a night at the bars downtown."

"Really?"

She nodded. "Yeah. I didn't even realize it was still open."

"Do you think the pancakes are the same?" Dad asked her.

"I bet so." Mom exhaled a breath so loud and full of relief I couldn't help but feel it too. She extended her other hand, taking mine. "In all our years coming to visit you, we never once thought to bring you out here for a breakfast. I'm taking Dolly's as a good sign. It's all going to be okay."

I hoped she was right.

As we reached the door, I held it open for them to go inside first. They took it all in, nostalgia widening their smiles.

Mom and Dad had met in Mission while they'd been in college, and their love for Treasure State was part of the reason I'd decided to come here for school. I'd had scholarship offers from bigger schools. I could have been part of a larger program with more media visibility and sponsorship opportunities. But I'd been a Wildcat since the day I was born.

This was my school as much as it was Mom and Dad's. And while the ranch was home, Mission would always be a close second for us all.

"It looks the same." Dad leaned down to speak in Mom's ear.

If they noticed the worn floor tiles or chipped tabletops, they didn't seem to care. Hell, maybe it really did look like it had twenty-something years ago.

There were more people in the dining room tonight than normal. Maybe this was a typical Saturday night? Dusty must make most of her money on the weekends because I'd never seen this many people at Dolly's. Nearly half of the tables were occupied.

The swinging door flew open and Faye walked out, her hands loaded with three plates each with an omelet beside golden hash browns.

Her caramel eyes flicked to me standing inside the doorway and an instant smile tugged at her mouth.

Usually when I walked in the door, I'd get a blush or tiny wave. But that smile?

That smile was a reason to come to Dolly's every chance I could get.

The twist in my chest was so hard I nearly choked.

Her gaze shifted to Mom and Dad, and the smile vanished as quickly as it had appeared.

I was the twenty-one-year-old version of my father. She knew immediately who I'd brought along tonight.

"Hey," I said as she rushed by, her cheeks flushed.

"Hey. Give me a minute."

As she continued on to a table in the center of the room, Mom leaned into my side. "That's her?"

"That's Faye."

"She's beautiful."

"Yeah. She is."

Mom's hand came to my back, rubbing up and down my spine like she used to do when I was a kid.

Faye served her customers, then went to check on a

booth. Her hair was in a high ponytail and the ends swished across her shoulder blades as she walked. When she finished taking an order, she seemed to pause for a moment, steeling her spine before facing us.

When she crossed the room, it was with a polite smile, but one that didn't reach her eyes.

"Hi," she said, holding out her hand to Mom. "I'm Faye."

"Hi, Faye." Mom clasped Faye with both her hands, and for a moment, I thought she'd pull her in for a hug. But Mom restrained herself. "I'm Macy. Rush's mom."

"Nice to meet you." Faye pulled her hand free and gave it to Dad.

"Ryan Ramsey. Glad to meet you."

Faye forced that smile wider. "Are you staying?"

"Yeah," I answered. "Thought we'd eat here tonight."

"Okay." She extended a hand toward the dining area. "Any seat you'd like. I'll bring over menus."

My parents both nodded, then headed toward an empty booth, giving me a minute alone with Faye.

"You told them?" she asked.

"Yes."

"And?" She worried her lip between her teeth.

"They were shocked at first. Pretty quiet. Then Mom asked to meet you. She thinks you're beautiful and will probably try to hug you before we leave. Dad asked if you've been to the doctor and if everyone was healthy."

"Oh." Faye's mouth parted, then she dropped her gaze to the floor, hiding whatever reaction she didn't want me to see.

"Hey." I hooked my finger under her chin, tipping up her face until I saw the tears swimming in her eyes. "What's wrong?"

"Nothing." She sniffled, waving it away. "I mean, you

said you were going to tell them. I guess I just didn't expect them to be . . . nice."

She didn't have enough nice people in her life.

Well, today, she'd earned two more.

I wanted to haul her into my arms. Hold her until those tears were gone. But I kept my distance and jerked my chin toward the booth where my parents were not even trying to hide their stares. "I'll grab menus for us."

"I can do it."

"So can I." I walked to the waitress station, plucking three laminated menus from their holder, then carried them to the booth. When I glanced back, Faye was gone and the swinging door was wagging on its hinges.

"Is she okay?" Mom asked.

"Yeah, Mom. She's good."

She took a menu, glancing toward the door a few more times, concern deepening the gentle creases in her forehead.

"She's all right." I chuckled. "This is a lot to deal with, especially for her."

"And you," Dad said with a small smile. Then he tapped the menu and tossed an arm over the back of the booth. "I'm getting pancakes, eggs and sausage links."

"Me too," I said.

"Me three." Mom collected our menus, stacking them together as the diner's front door blew open and a guy stormed inside.

He passed the waitress station and marched toward the kitchen. With both hands, he shoved the swinging door, pushing it so hard it clattered open. Then he was gone inside like he owned the damn place.

What the hell? Who was that?

The sound of something metal hitting the floor clanged.

Conversation in the dining room faded to a low murmur as people stared, ears strained.

I was on my feet, halfway there, when I heard Faye's voice.

"Justin, don't."

"Fuck you, Faye."

I lengthened my strides, walking into the kitchen just in time to see Dusty swipe a knife off a magnetic holder.

"Get the hell out." She pointed the blade's tip at the guy's nose from across the stainless-steel table that separated them. "Now."

Faye stood on the same side of the table as Dusty. Her arms were wrapped around her middle. Her gaze met mine for a split second before she aimed a glare at the guy.

Justin? So this was her ex?

He looked about our age. I didn't recognize him from campus but he was probably a student too. He stood a few inches shorter than me and his clothes were baggy on his lean frame. Without question, if he didn't heed Dusty's warning, I'd gladly toss his ass out the front door.

Without breaking a sweat.

"Your shit is out of the house. Tonight, Faye."

"You can't do that." Faye seethed, a fire raging to life in her eyes. "I already paid you rent for the month. You're not kicking me out."

"Either you empty your room tonight, or I'll throw everything outside myself." Justin pointed to her the same way Dusty still pointed to him with that knife. "You're gone. Locks are changed tomorrow."

Faye's nostrils flared. For a moment, she looked ready to tell him no. But then she flicked her wrist, dismissing him completely. "Fine. Leave."

Justin backed away a step, sneering as he looked her up and down. "Can't believe you."

"Out." Dusty pointed the tip of her knife toward the door.

Justin turned, realizing for the first time that I was standing in the kitchen. He glared for a moment and opened his mouth.

But the second he noticed my hands fisted, the fury radiating off my frame, he must have thought better of whatever he'd planned to say because without a word, he stomped past me and threw open the swinging door. A moment later, the front door's chime came next to tell us he was gone.

Dusty slapped the knife onto the holder, the blade sticking. "You okay?"

Faye shook her head. "So he cheats on me, yet I get kicked out of the house. Asshole."

Wait. He'd cheated on her?

Yeah, should have tossed him out myself.

"You know my couch is yours, honey. Bring everything over. We'll sort it from there."

I didn't ask why he'd kicked her out of her house. My guess was he'd learned she was pregnant, because while Treasure State wasn't a small school, it wasn't a big school either. And Faye being pregnant with my baby was campus gossip fodder.

"Goddamn it." Faye buried her face in her hands. Not to cry.

To scream.

The sound was muffled and ragged. It was raw frustration, the scream of a woman who'd had more than her fair share of unlucky breaks.

Dusty might as well have stabbed that knife into my heart.

"There's an extra room at my place," I said. "It's yours."

I wasn't going to have the mother of my child sleeping on a couch. Besides that, Dusty smoked. I doubted she went outside of her own home to have a cigarette.

Faye's hands dropped. "W-what?"

Dusty arched an eyebrow, then went back to cooking.

"After your shift, we'll go get your stuff."

"No. I can't . . . I appreciate the offer, Rush, but—"

"I wasn't asking, Faye."

Dusty glanced over her shoulder, giving me a once-over. "I like your boy, sugar."

Faye pinched the bridge of her nose. "He's not my boy."

No, I wasn't. But the way she said it, so dismissively, didn't sit right.

Was I really such a horrible option? Compared to fuckwit Justin, I was a goddamn prince.

"Your parents are visiting," Faye said. "I'll just spend tonight at Dusty's and then—"

The swinging door opened, and there were my parents. They didn't even try to hide the fact that they'd been eaves-dropping.

"We'll help get you moved," Mom said.

Dad nodded. "I've got my truck. We'll load everything in the back and have you out of there in no time."

Dusty laughed from the flattop. "Like I said. I like your boy, sugar."

CHAPTER SIXTEEN

FAYE

Rush's living room smelled like popcorn and clean-linen air freshener. It was quiet but the air still felt charged with the energy from the past two hours spent taking countless trips in and out of the front door, up and down the stairs to the guest bedroom—my bedroom.

Ryan and Macy had just left for their hotel after hauling in the last load of my things. One trip. That was all it had taken to clear my belongings out of Justin's house. Everything I owned had fit into my Explorer and Ryan's Ford Super Duty.

My lumpy twin-sized bed and TV-tray nightstand were upstairs along with my clothes, stuffed into my only suitcase and four garbage bags. My bedding we'd piled in a laundry basket. Everything else, books and toiletries and a few framed photos, had fit into the five boxes Dusty had given us when I'd finished my shift at the diner.

One trip. And now I lived with Rush.

The house was nice, with plain tan siding and a white

garage. There were a few brown shutters to give it character and tie into the wooden front door.

The open concept gave the house an airy feel. Beside the dining room was the living room with a massive, cushy beige sectional and huge TV. The kitchen was U-shaped, separated from the other spaces with a bar and three stools.

There were four bedrooms, two upstairs and two down.

Maverick had the primary suite on the first floor. Erik was on this level too. That left Rush and me upstairs, our bedrooms separated by a hallway and the bathroom we'd be sharing.

There were hardwood floors. The carpet in my bedroom was plush and soft. The bathrooms and kitchen had granite countertops.

It was one of the nicest homes I'd ever been inside.

What was I doing here? This wasn't *me*. Except when Rush had insisted, I sure as hell hadn't put up much of a fight.

I reached behind my back, feeling around to make sure my spine was still intact.

Yep, it was there. Bony and not quite as firm as I'd once believed it to be.

God, I was tired. Exhausted to my marrow. It didn't feel right, staying here. It didn't feel like this was the best choice for *me*.

But it was a choice for *now*. A choice for this baby. Crashing with Rush didn't have to be permanent, and since my pride had taken about all the hits it could endure tonight, I could bend.

The thud of footsteps on the stairs made me stand a little straighter as Rush jogged down the last few steps.

The sleeves of his quarter zip were pushed up his fore-arms and his hat was turned backward.

My mouth went dry.

He was gorgeous. Distractingly so. Every time he came into a room, my brain scrambled. Was that why I hadn't argued with him when he'd all but ordered me to move in here? Or was it just because I had no other option?

I loved Dusty, but sleeping on her couch was not a great option. Her house had a permanent cloud of smoke and she preferred her solitude. Would she smoke outside if I asked? Yes. Would she hide her two pet snakes? Yes, because she knew I was terrified of her boas. But that arrangement would only be temporary too.

Maybe I could have stayed with Gloria, but Chuck was on the road at the moment and that was something I'd have to run by him first.

So for now, I stood in Rush's living room, knowing exactly where I was on this earth and feeling more lost than ever.

My throat burned with the urge to cry or scream or both. *Don't cry. Not yet.*

Fucking Justin. I hated him for this. I hated him for making me out to be the villain.

"I made space for you in the bathroom," Rush said, crossing the room. "Entire right side of the vanity is yours."

"Thanks," I choked out.

"You okay?"

No. "Sure."

"Liar."

I lifted a shoulder. "This is fairly humiliating."

"For Justin. Yeah. He should be humiliated. But not you.

Never you." Rush lifted a hand to my face, his knuckles dragging along the line of my cheek.

Everything in my body came alive. Tingles broke out across my skin. Butterflies erupted in my stomach. My pulse quickened.

It was like I'd been dying of thirst and that single touch was a cool glass of water.

I should tell him to stop with the easy touches. I should have backed away the night he'd kissed me on the cheek. Except I liked it too much to say no.

"I'm sorry," he murmured, his body shifting closer.

"Me too." The scent of his cologne filled my nose, and for the first time all night, I took a full breath. Masculine spice mingled with soap.

"I take it he found out about us," he said.

"Yep. He's the reason I went camping that weekend. Remember how I told you about his best friend? He slept with her that weekend, so I broke it off. But we were living together, and I had my own room. It was cheap and there's not a lot open at the moment. So it's been easier to stay while I looked for an apartment."

"Makes sense. How'd he find out?"

"Apparently, he heard it around school. When I got to the diner this afternoon for my shift, I put my phone away. I checked it after he left tonight and found a bunch of texts from him. He found out I was pregnant and, well . . . you know what happened next."

Justin had heard a rumor on campus that Rush Ramsey had gotten a girl pregnant. *Me.* In Justin's initial text, he'd asked if it was true. Instead of waiting for me to reply, he'd taken it upon himself to ask around. Guess one of his friends had confirmed the truth.

His texts had changed after that.

fuck you faye

so much for getting back together

you're out of this house

you fucking whore

I'd never been called a whore before. Part of me wanted to tell Rush, just to get it off my chest. To maybe cry into his. But the more time I spent with him, the more I was learning that he was a protector.

He wouldn't let those texts go. So later, when I was alone, I'd delete them instead and block Justin's number. And someday, when this child of mine was old enough, I'd teach him or her, boy or girl, to never use the word whore.

"Thank you for letting me stay," I said. "I'm sorry for this. I'll start looking for a new place tomor—"

"Stay." Rush's finger landed on my lips.

Our gazes locked. I held the air in my lungs, afraid to exhale. Afraid that if I moved at all, even a blink, something between us would snap.

I didn't trust myself around Rush. I was seconds away from leaning into that finger or rising up on my toes to beg for a kiss when he cleared his throat.

His Adam's apple bobbed as he swallowed. He towered over me, eyes searching mine. "Say yes, Faye."

"Yes." My backbone might as well have been a wet noodle.

It was a whisper and my lips barely moved, but the friction against his finger was enough to send a fresh wave of tingles zinging down my spine.

I missed being touched. Being held. Being kissed. I missed feeling worshipped and craved. I missed Rush's large hands kneading my curves and the weight of his strong body pinning me to his bed.

I hadn't let myself replay that night, not for weeks. But here? In this house where it had all begun, how could I ignore it?

Ignore him?

Rush was charming and sexy and patient with exactly the right amount of pushy.

"Good." The corner of Rush's mouth turned up as he dropped his finger.

That should have been the end of it. We both should have broken apart, except he trailed that same finger across my cheek until it reached a tendril of hair that had escaped my ponytail. He twirled it around his knuckle.

Kiss me. I wanted him to kiss me so badly the words almost escaped my mouth.

Rush kept twirling the hair, tighter and tighter, like the coil in my lower belly, until I leaned into his touch.

He moved first. I moved first. Did it matter?

His face was an inch from mine and his gaze locked on my lips.

A kiss would be a horrible idea. Reckless and hasty and asking for more trouble than I was already in with this man.

But did I move?

Nope. Would it be as good as I remembered? A kiss from Rush Ramsey?

Part of me hoped it wasn't. Part of me hoped I'd built it up in my own head and reality would fall flat. How much easier would it be if that was the case?

Except the rational part of me knew it would probably be better than the first. And then I'd really be screwed.

There was only one way to find out.

His hand threaded into my hair, five fingers sliding through the roots until they reached the elastic tie and tugged it free. Rush's breath tickled my cheek.

My lips parted.

The front door flew open.

"Hey, whose car is parked on the stre—" A tall guy with brown hair came to a sudden stop on the entryway's mat when he spotted us.

Rush cleared his throat and took a step away.

My face flamed as I did the same. "It's, um, my car."

"Ah." The keys in his hand jingled as he tucked them into a jeans pocket. "You must be Faye?"

"Yes."

"Faye, this is Maverick Houston. Mav, this is Faye."

I lifted a hand to wave. "Nice to meet you."

"Same."

That sounded kind of like a lie. Maverick's expression was skeptical at best.

What had Rush told him about us? Did he know I was his new roommate? What about Erik? Had Rush texted them during the move? What were the chances I'd swapped one awkward home for another?

Whether Rush liked it or not, tomorrow's first item on my to-do list was more apartment hunting. Were there any places in Mission that wouldn't require a deposit? Because I didn't have one. Not with Justin taking all of this month's rent. That asshole.

"Give us a minute?" Rush asked me, then nodded to the stairs.

"Yeah. I'll, um . . . unpack."

I kept my eyes on the hardwood floor as I walked past the coffee table and couch. I was almost at the top of the staircase when Maverick spoke.

"Did she just say 'unpack'?"

I cringed and moved faster, practically running down the hall to my room. But even with its door closed, I could hear voices downstairs. I couldn't make out what they were saying, not that it mattered. The tone was enough.

Maverick was clearly pissed that Rush hadn't consulted with him on this first. Erik would probably feel the same.

I walked to the edge of the bed and plopped down on the bare mattress. With my knees hugged to my chest, I closed my eyes and listened to the deep rumble of voices until they stopped. And then a door slammed shut, the vibration carrying through the walls.

"I shouldn't have come here," I whispered to myself.

A soft knock came at my door. "Faye."

"Come in."

Rush stepped inside and strode to the bed, taking a seat beside me. Whatever had happened earlier, whatever kiss *might* have happened, was gone. He kept two feet between us as he leaned his elbows to his knees.

"I'm sorry," I said.

"Don't be. Erik is never around. He won't care. Mav is, well . . . don't worry about Mav."

"I think, in the long run, it's better that I find my own place."

Rush hummed.

Not a yes. Not a no. But it was so far from the way he'd asked me to stay earlier that I hugged my knees tighter.

Without a doubt, it had been a mistake to come here. To make such an impulsive decision.

Except I didn't have anywhere else to go, not really.

"I don't have any money," I blurted.

Whether Rush thought I should be humiliated or not didn't matter. This could be the most embarrassing situation of my life. I was poor. Pathetic. Exactly like my mother had told me so many times.

And mostly, I hated that his house was so nice and that he'd seen where I'd been living. In Justin's shitty trailer in a dodgy part of town.

"It's why I stayed with Justin. I'm broke. We didn't talk about rent. But this room is . . . well, you saw where I came from. I can't afford this."

I had no idea what the price was for this place, but without question, it was beyond my budget.

"You don't have to pay."

How had I known he'd say that? Did he realize that only made it worse? "I have to pay."

He hummed again.

"I can't be a freeloader. I don't want your pity."

"It's not pity."

"It feels like it to me." If all I had left right now was my pride, then I'd cling to it with all my might. "I was always going to leave Justin's once I had more money saved up, but I have no extra. Not right now."

Talking about money, or my lack thereof, felt like stripping off my clothes and standing naked in front of a stranger.

No one really knew how much I struggled to make ends meet. Dusty might have suspected, but money wasn't exactly something we discussed. Mostly because she didn't have much extra either.

I could swing three hundred dollars a month in rent.

Two fifty if I was being honest with myself. "How much do you pay?"

Rush stayed quiet.

"Tell me."

"Four hundred each."

Oh, God. I was officially mortified.

My pride—that beautiful, glorious pride—slipped from my grasp like drops of blood, splattering at my feet.

"Okay," I murmured. "Four hundred."

"You don't have to pay that much. This room has been empty all year."

"I have to pay." To make it fair, the rent would be three hundred. That was better than four hundred, but not by much. "All right."

Rush twisted, his gaze hot on my profile as I stared at an invisible spot on the floor. "Is it school? You work all the time. You're trying to pay for school, right?"

"Yes. And Gloria."

"Gloria?"

I nodded. "I give anything extra to my sister. Chuck, her dad, has a good job, but he's not loaded. She's not old enough to get a job yet, and when she is, I want her to concentrate on school."

She'd have to get a job. It would be good for her to get a job. But I didn't want her trying to work twenty-plus hours a week like I had at sixteen.

Granted, I doubted Chuck would make her pay for food like Mom had done for me. And Chuck would probably buy her a car.

"I never had extra when I was her age," I told Rush. "I didn't get nice jeans or name-brand shoes. I bought everything from thrift stores or the discount rack. High school kids are cruel. I don't want her to endure the judgment I did at her age. So I help where I can. I want her to come to the diner at night for homework, not to wait tables. But it means I make sacrifices. My budget can sometimes be stretched thin."

And it was about to be thinner.

It hung unspoken between us, the reality of our future.

Of mine.

Rush moved closer, the mattress shifting, until only an inch separated our shoulders. "You're not alone in this. Not anymore."

He had no idea. I *was* alone. Always alone. "I don't want—"

"Pity." He held up a hand. "I know. It's not pity. It's help. I'm offering. All you have to do is take it."

Wasn't that pity? What was the difference between it and help? "I'm not sure I know how."

He glanced over, his eyes shadowed by the brim of his hat. "You don't really know how to accept help, do you?"

I shrugged. "I guess it hasn't happened enough."

"You let me change the tire. So let me do this too. Stay here until the end of the month. Then we'll reassess."

Simple. Except it wasn't.

What happened if I got used to his help? What happened when he was gone, off to play in the NFL, and I was here, left behind?

"Hey." He nudged my elbow with his. "Is that a yes?"

Did I have another choice? "Yes."

"Thank you. I have a good feeling about this."

Well, that made one of us. My stomach was in a knot.

Rush bent and kissed my hair before he stood and left me alone, closing the door behind him.

I wasn't sure what it meant that he kept kissing me. That he might have kissed me earlier too. But whatever it meant, I doubted it would last.

Nothing good lasted. It would probably only muddle feelings and make it harder in the end.

Still, I liked it enough not to ask him to stop.

CHAPTER SEVENTEEN

RUSH

I opened my bedroom door just in time to hear Maverick's feral growl from downstairs.

"Give me that remote."

He and Faye were fighting. Again. *Fuck my life.*

"I'm not watching football," Faye said.

"It's Monday Night Football."

"So?"

"Unbelievable," Mav huffed as I started down the stairs.

Time to play referee. Again.

Yesterday, they'd gotten into an argument about how to load knives into the dishwasher. Mav liked blade up. Faye thought that was a great way to cause an accident that would require stitches.

Last week, Faye had used one of Maverick's Tide Pods for a load of laundry because I'd told her to use whatever was available, and I'd hit the store for more. Well, apparently Mav kept track of his detergent because that had led to a three-day cold war where neither would look or speak to the other.

And the week before that, Faye's first week in the house, had been so awkward that *I'd* been tempted to move. We'd tiptoed around each other. Faye had mostly hidden in her bedroom until I'd finally convinced her to come downstairs, telling her that if she kept avoiding all of us, it would only get worse.

I should have let her hide behind her closed door.

Putting her and Maverick in the same room was like asking oil to mix with water.

"What's so damn important that it can't wait until after the game?" he asked. The sound of the window shades dropping came next. "Can you stop opening the blinds? It puts a glare on the TV."

"I don't mind the glare," Faye said. "And I need to finish watching this documentary before class tomorrow."

"It can't wait until later?"

"No. I'm not going to wait until later. I'm not going to hand over the remote just because you demand it. You have a television in your room. I do not."

"Is your laptop broken?"

"Why should I have to use my laptop? I've been watching for thirty minutes. There's thirty left. Just let me finish. You can miss part of a football game."

"I shouldn't have to miss part of a football game I watch every fucking Monday just because you waited last minute to do an assignment for class."

I reached the bottom of the stairs as Faye shot off the couch, one hand in a death grip around the remote as the other balled into a fist.

Maverick stood with his hands planted on his hips, and if not for the coffee table separating them, I think she might have clocked him in the jaw.

"I'm almost done." She pointed the remote to the TV. "In the time you've been arguing with me, I could have been watching. Let. Me. Finish."

"This is bullshit." He threw his arms in the air. "This is my TV, and I'm paying for the fucking subscription you're using, so I'm going to watch whatever the hell I want."

Oh shit. That was the absolute last thing he should have said. The color drained from Faye's face.

I opened my mouth, about to tell him he'd crossed a line, when the remote flew through the air.

She launched it. He caught it.

"Mav," I warned as Faye stormed out of the living room for the kitchen.

"Don't." He shot a glare over his shoulder before plopping onto the couch to change the channel. "This is on you."

Because I'd invited Faye to move in without talking to him or Erik first.

Yeah, not my best decision. And Mav seemed hell-bent on making me pay for that mistake. At least Erik hadn't cared. Though over the past two weeks, he'd stayed even more at Kalindi's place. Either because they were absorbed in each other, or because he wanted to avoid the tension under this roof.

Damn it. I swallowed a groan.

This was supposed to be a good thing. Faye needed a decent place to live, and I didn't regret moving her here. But there was a reason I preferred to make plans.

Spontaneity usually bit me in the ass.

"Can you just . . . back off?" I asked Maverick. "Tonight's game isn't even going to be good. You can miss the first quarter. Let her finish the documentary."

"Of course you'd be on her side. Figures. Is this another Halsey situation?"

Was he always going to throw that in my face? "Mav, I'm not choosing sides. I'm trying to keep the peace."

"Should have thought about that before you moved her into the house," he muttered. "You have to pick a side."

What he was really saying? Pick *his* side.

Prove that I was more loyal to him than to a woman. First Halsey. Now Faye.

Hadn't we played this game enough?

I ground my molars together, keeping my mouth shut before I said something I'd regret. Then as the pregame announcer's voice blared through the TV's speakers, I went to the kitchen, where Faye was standing in front of the open refrigerator. "Hey."

Faye slammed the fridge closed so hard the condiments in the door rattled. "Where's my dinner?"

I blinked. "Huh?"

"My. Dinner. It was in a white container with my name on the top. Did you eat it?" She pointed toward the back of Maverick's head. "Or did he?"

We both knew it was Mav. And we both knew he was listening.

"Sorry. I didn't notice your name." I'd take the fall for Maverick if it meant the fighting would stop.

"Right." Faye crossed her arms over her chest, her jaw flexing.

"I'll make you something else for dinner." I raked a hand through my hair, moving to the fridge to reopen the door.

Options were sparse. I hadn't had a chance to hit the grocery store since before our game this weekend, and I'd had a full day of classes, so I hadn't had time to go in between school and practice.

"Turkey sandwich?" I asked, opening the drawer with lunch meat. Did we even have bread?

"I can't have lunch meat."

"Oh. Right." *Shit.* At her first appointment, the doctor had reviewed a long list of foods she couldn't eat. Sushi. Soft cheese. I'd forgotten about the deli meat.

I opened the freezer, shifting a bag of peas out of the way. "How about pizza? I could make this sausage pizza."

She shook her head. "Sausage gives me heartburn."

"It does?"

"Yes. Being pregnant apparently means heartburn is my body's new party trick. And I don't like the sauce."

Damn it. "What would you like?"

"The chicken and potatoes that 'you' ate." Her air quotes might as well have been two middle fingers to the guy in the living room.

"I'll go get you dinner."

"Forget it," she muttered. "I'll figure it out myself."

"No, I said I'd get you dinner."

Maverick chose that moment to turn up the volume. It clicked three times as the commentators talked about the Seahawks punter jogging onto the field.

"Mav, do you mind?"

He clicked it up twice more.

For fuck's sake. "Thanks, man."

"Welcome." He raised a hand and gave me a thumbs-up.

My nostrils flared, but I stayed rooted to my spot, refusing to let myself move for fear that I'd smack him upside the head.

"Anything else from the store?" I asked Faye. "Name it. I'm buying."

She flinched and her eyes blew wide. "Wow."

"What?" Was everything that came out of my mouth going to piss these two off at the moment? Probably.

Maverick clicked up the volume. Again.

"Are the reminders that I'm poor going to be an everyday thing?" she asked. "Or just for Mondays?"

"Whoa." I held up my hands. "I didn't mean anything by that."

"Sure," she deadpanned. "Just like you didn't mean anything when you told me the internet was on you. Just like you didn't mean anything when you left a twenty-dollar tip for a ten-dollar meal at the diner on Thursday. Just like you didn't mean anything when you recalculated rent and it's fifty dollars less a month. I told you, I didn't want your pity."

"It's not pity."

"No? Because it sure seems like it from here. Would you have said any of that, would you be offering to buy me whatever I want from the store, if I hadn't told you I was broke? Would you have made sure to fill Maverick in on my financial situation so he could throw it in my face every chance he gets?"

Christ. I hadn't expected Mav to be an asshole about the money. I'd just asked him not to nickel-and-dime Faye for her share. That I'd cover it. "Faye, I'm just trying—"

Maverick turned up the volume again, so loud the vibration pulsed against my skin.

"What the hell, Maverick!" I shouted at the same time Faye snapped, "Can you please turn it down?"

"Fine!" he shouted and shot off the couch. "The TV is yours."

He punched the off button on the remote. With a flick of his wrist, it went sailing into a couch cushion, hitting with a muffled thud as he stomped to his bedroom and slammed the door.

It took a moment for the noise to vanish. The silence that followed was unbearable.

"Damn it." I tilted my head to the ceiling, staring at a blank spot for a few heartbeats. "When did we start arguing so much?"

"When we moved in together."

My fault. This was my fault. "I'll get you some dinner."

"I'm not hungry anymore." Before I could stop her, before I could make it right, she walked away, through the living room and up the stairs. Faye didn't slam her door, but it closed loud enough for me to hear.

Well, even if she wasn't hungry now, when she was, I wanted her to have some dinner.

I swiped my keys off the counter and went outside, letting the cool night air chase away the fury and frustration burning beneath my skin. It took nearly the entire drive to the diner before I unclenched my jaw and relaxed my fingers on the steering wheel.

Was it really so bad for me to want to help Faye? I had a full-ride scholarship with a monthly stipend. There was a reason Maverick, Erik and I hadn't found a fourth roommate.

We didn't need the help on rent.

But the last thing I wanted was for Faye to feel . . . less.

I parked at the diner but didn't get out of the car. Dolly's had a lot of character, but it was old and rundown. I'd forgotten just how chipped the exterior paint was in the weeks I'd been coming to visit. I'd stopped noticing the faded colors and rough parking lot.

Mostly because when I came here, I wasn't looking at the building. I stared right through its filmy windows to the dining room, searching for Faye.

She worked harder than she should have to work. I wanted to help after she'd told me about her money problems, except my idea of helping had only made it worse.

Maybe I'd only dig myself even deeper by coming out here tonight, but I climbed out of the Yukon and walked into the restaurant. Dusty was at a table in the empty dining room with a newspaper open on its surface.

Besides her, the building was empty.

Was that why Faye didn't work on Mondays? Because there were no customers to serve? Why did Dusty even open? Did she really have to keep hours seven days a week?

"She's not here," Dusty said.

"Yeah." I walked over and pulled out the seat across from hers. The paper was open to the obituaries. "Light reading?"

"Something like that." She folded the paper in half, pushing it to the side. Then she leaned back in her chair, studying me while I studied her. "Did Faye ever tell you that it was me who sent you the text that she was pregnant?"

"No." But maybe I should have guessed. Dusty didn't seem like the type to pull punches. A short, frank text fit her personality much more than it did Faye's.

"She wasn't sure how to say it. So I said it for her."

"Okay," I drawled. "What else is Faye not sure how to say so you're going to say it for her?"

"She's terrified."

"That I did know."

Dusty scoffed. "Not of the baby, though that has her freaked. She's terrified of you. I doubt she even realizes it yet.

178

But she's not going to let herself get attached. She's too scared."

"That I'll hurt her?"

"Yes. That you'll hurt her like her mother. Or that you'll disappear like her father."

Fuck, Faye's parents sucked. In her position, maybe I'd be scared too. But I wouldn't leave her. I wouldn't leave my kid.

"When I'm playing football, I visualize plays. I see the field and the players and before I throw the ball, I see it in my head, where it's going. It's different with this. When I close my eyes, I can't picture what he or she looks like. The baby."

I couldn't imagine their laugh or hear their cry. The whole concept of fatherhood was still fuzzy.

"But I'm going to be there," I told Dusty. "I'm the guy who's going to teach him how to throw a ball. I'm the guy who's going to help him with math homework. The guy who will carry him on my shoulders so he can watch a parade."

The corner of Dusty's mouth turned up. "Him? You think it's a boy?"

"Oh. I, um . . . I guess. Or a girl." I hadn't meant to say *him*. I guess I hadn't even realized until this moment that I had been thinking of the baby as a boy.

Dusty sighed and leaned forward, her elbows to the table. "I think you see more than you realize. And I think maybe that's what scares Faye the most. That she can see you there too. She's never going to wish for something. She learned a long time ago that she's not the lucky type. This is not going to be easy for you, Boy Wonder."

I let the nickname slide. "I want to help. I'm trying to help. But she doesn't make it easy."

"No, she does not." Dusty grinned, like that made her proud.

Faye took after her in that regard, didn't she? Capable. Strong. Proud. Like a damn brick wall.

Maybe the only way through was with a sledgehammer. Or maybe I'd just lower my shoulder and push the whole thing over.

Starting with a dinner.

"I ate Faye's leftovers she brought home for dinner tonight."

Dusty frowned. "She eats about five things at the moment. You know how hard it is to cook for someone who doesn't like sauce?"

"You know she doesn't like sauce?"

"Of course I know."

"Then why do you send her home with lasagna?"

"Because my lasagna is damn good. I keep hoping she'll change her mind and give it a try."

I chuckled. "She won't. She's stubborn."

"Boy, do I know that too." Dusty stood from her chair and collected her newspaper. "Give me ten. I'll make you some pancakes to take home."

"Thanks."

Dusty disappeared to the kitchen, leaving me in the quiet restaurant. When she returned, the pancakes were wrapped in foil and she had a takeout box of scrambled eggs.

I raced home, and when I knocked on Faye's bedroom door, the food's container was still warm in my hand. "Faye?"

No answer.

I turned the knob and peeked inside.

The lights were on. The blinds were open. Her shoes

and backpack were set neatly beside the door. The air smelled like apples and soap, clean and fresh.

Faye was asleep on the bed, curled into a pillow on top of her covers.

I crossed the room without a sound, not wanting to wake her up as I set her food on the nightstand—it was a TV tray, not a nightstand, but I hadn't tried to get her anything better.

Other than the bed, that tray was the only furniture in the space. The two pieces had been enough to almost fill that closet of a room at her ex's trailer. But here, the room looked empty. Too empty. She needed a desk. Maybe a dresser. But unless she asked, I wasn't offering.

She looked so small as she hugged the pillow, her knees drawn into her chest.

I bent, about to touch her shoulder and wake her up, when I noticed her face.

Twin tear tracks had dried on her cheeks.

It knocked the wind from my lungs.

We couldn't keep doing this. Something had to give. But what?

I left the food on her nightstand. And closed the door on my way out.

CHAPTER EIGHTEEN

FAYE

My sweatshirt was pulled up beneath my breasts, and my jeans were unfastened. I turned sideways in the bathroom mirror, relaxing my belly before sucking it in flat.

Except it didn't suck in flat, not anymore.

I was almost halfway through this pregnancy. I was at seventeen weeks. And it was slowly starting to show.

The baggy sweatshirts and hoodies I'd taken to wearing every day hid most of the changes to my body, but in this bathroom, there was no concealing that my boobs and belly were bigger.

I ran a hand over the curve in my skin, feeling along my tummy as I stared at it in the mirror.

"Hi," I whispered.

It wasn't often and it was never loud, but it was getting easier to talk to the baby. Not that he or she could reply, but I wanted them to know my voice, even if it was quiet.

The door to the bathroom flew open.

"Rush," I snapped, pulling down my shirt. "Do you mind?"

"Shit. Sorry." He gulped, his gaze dropping to my stomach. "I, um . . . habit. I'm not used to sharing a bathroom."

I'd been here for nearly a month. Time for him to break that habit. "The door was closed. Try knocking."

"Sorry." He ran a hand over his jaw, his gaze returning to my belly.

I frowned and hiked up my jeans, zipping them up as far as they would go before taking the hair tie off my wrist and looping it through the button hole and over the button. I didn't have money to spend on maternity clothes, so I was hoping to keep these working for as long as possible.

"You okay?" he asked.

"Fine."

"You're, um . . ."

"Showing? Yeah."

It was normal to be showing at this stage, according to my research. I also had a hunch I'd be larger than estimated simply because Rush's genes meant I would probably birth a baby giant.

"Do you mind?" I glanced at the doorway.

"Yeah. Sorry. Again." He jerked into motion, taking a backward step into the hall before he turned and disappeared to his bedroom.

"Thanks for closing the door." I frowned and pulled it closed only to realize I was done in the bathroom. So I yanked it open again and marched for my room. "I'm done," I hollered and closed myself away.

God, this was awkward. When was it going to stop being awkward?

I plopped on the edge of my bed, reaching for my phone and the browser I'd pulled up earlier. There was a single rental in Mission that I could afford—barely—on my own. It was the worst trailer in the park where Justin lived.

The idea of being that close to him again made my stomach churn, but I couldn't stay here with Rush. If we weren't tiptoeing around each other, then we were bickering.

Add Maverick to the mix, and I avoided "home" more often than not.

I was contemplating Mav's murder daily at this point. That asshole seemed hell-bent on making my life miserable. And Rush playing Switzerland only seemed to make it worse.

He wasn't going to choose me. I didn't expect to be more important than his best friend. But I could be a little bit important, couldn't I?

It wouldn't matter if I was out of here. It wouldn't matter when I lived on my own.

My fingers flew over the screen as I typed a text to the trailer's owner.

Hello. Is your rental still available?

I waited a few moments, my breath catching when my phone dinged with a reply.

Sorry. It was just taken.

Of course it was. I wasn't lucky enough to get anywhere first.

"Damn it." I tossed my phone aside and snagged my laundry basket from the closet to carry downstairs.

The bathroom was empty and Rush's door open. I kept my eyes glued to the carpet, refusing to let myself glance inside to his bed.

A lifetime ago, I'd been in that bed. It was huge, fitting for the man who owned it. I hadn't noticed Rush's quilt the night we'd had sex. I'd been too busy tangled in his gray sheets to care about his bedding.

It was a patchwork quilt made of varying fabrics in an array of colors from rust to navy to hunter green. The edges were worn and corners slightly frayed, like he'd had that quilt for years.

Had Macy made it for him? During the frantic move out of Justin's trailer last month, she'd made a comment about sewing a blanket for the baby.

"That would be nice, wouldn't it?" I murmured as my free hand slid along my belly.

What would be his or her favorite color? Would they have my light brown eyes or Rush's chocolate?

He was in the kitchen when I made it to the main floor. He had his phone sandwiched between his ear and shoulder as he opened the fridge and bent to take out mustard and mayo and cheese and pickles.

I'd never met anyone who ate so often. Maverick too. These guys were always making something in the kitchen and eating it in the living room while they watched football. Always football.

So much football.

When he saw me walking through the living room, Rush smiled but kept talking. "What are you and Dad doing tonight?"

Macy. I'd also never met a guy who talked to his mom so often.

I eavesdropped on their conversations more than I should, but listening to Rush's phone calls with his mom was fascinating. He genuinely liked his parents. They spoke more like they were friends.

I hoped I had that. Boy or girl, I hoped my child *liked* me.

As he laughed at whatever Macy told him, I ducked down the hall for the laundry room. It was beside Maverick's room so I tried to come down whenever he was gone.

The moment I opened the door, I gagged. "Oh my God."

It smelled like sweaty feet, ammonia and rotten eggs. The stench burned my nostrils, and I covered my nose with a hand, breathing through the sleeve of my sweatshirt as I moved to the washing machine.

I opened the lid, about to dump my clothes in with a couple detergent pods, when I realized it was already full.

The smell was worse, making me dry heave.

My hamper landed with a plop as I bolted for the door, only breathing when I was back in the living room.

"Bye, Mom," Rush said, ending his call and setting his phone down. "Hey, sorry about barging in on you."

I pointed in the direction of the laundry. "Are your clothes still in the washer? It reeks in there."

"Oh, damn. I forgot to run it last night."

"Well, can you run it? Or take out your stuff so I can use the machine?"

"Yeah." He picked up his sandwich and chomped a huge bite.

I stared at him.

"Now?" he asked, cheeks bulging.

"Yes, now. Have you smelled it in there? It's disgusting."

He scowled as he chewed, swallowing the bite. "What do you want me to say? Sorry? I sweat when I'm playing football and work out twice a day. Can't exactly stop it."

"No, but you could not leave your sweaty stuff in the washing machine so it gets worse."

186

"I forgot. It was a fucking mistake, okay?"

"Fine." I held up my hands.

Fighting again. Fighting always. Every argument seemed to come out of nowhere. We were fine one moment, civil, and then boom. Now he was pissed, I was annoyed, and I didn't want to keep doing this.

Why couldn't we just get along like we had been weeks ago? Why was it like this? He'd stopped coming to the diner. I missed those days. We wouldn't talk much during his visits, but it would at least be pleasant.

He ate another bite of his sandwich, so big his cheeks bulged. With his mouth full, he couldn't really talk. We couldn't fight. Maybe that was the point. Maybe I should start eating more too.

He walked with angry strides from the kitchen, breezing past me for the laundry room. Then came the sound of the washer's lid slamming shut and running water. "Leave your stuff," he said when he returned. "I'll swap it out when mine is done in an hour."

"Okay." I sighed, going to the stairs. Except before I could disappear to my room, the front door opened and Maverick walked inside.

He wore a smile. It diminished the moment he spotted me in his house.

I was under no illusion that any part of this place was mine.

"Hi." His gaze shifted to the kitchen, and he jerked up his chin at Rush. "Hey."

"What's up?" Rush asked.

"Nothing. While you're both here, I need rent checks. I'm taking them to the office tomorrow. I got Erik's already."

"I'll write it tonight," Rush said.

"Can I give you cash?"

He shrugged and closed the door. "Cash works."

I walked to the dining room table and the backpack I'd left downstairs when I'd been studying earlier. As much as I wanted a desk in my room so I'd never have to spend a minute downstairs, I wasn't buying furniture until I knew where I was going to live.

My wallet was in the front pocket, so I took it out along with the money I'd gotten after cashing my paycheck last week. Taking out three hundred dollars, I held it out for Maverick. "Here you go."

He took it, fanning out the three bills, then blinked. "And the other seventy-five?"

Wait. The other seventy-five?

Rush had told me their rent before I'd moved in was four hundred apiece. That made it twelve hundred total. With me as a fourth roommate, that was three hundred each. That was how much I'd paid him for last month.

"Maverick," Rush clipped, "Faye's rent is three hundred. I told you that."

Faye's rent. Meaning mine was different.

In the kitchen, Rush's arms were crossed over his chest as he glared daggers at Mav.

"How much is rent, Maverick?" I asked him while keeping my gaze glued to Rush.

"Fifteen hundred a month total," Mav said.

I tore into my wallet and ripped out another hundred. "Here."

"Uh, I don't have change." Mav took the money.

"Keep it," I said, then turned and ran up the stairs, taking them two at a time.

"Damn it, Mav," Rush barked.

"I forgot, okay? Sorry."

"Sure you did," Rush said, and I felt more than heard his footsteps hustle through the house to follow me.

But I kept moving until I reached the threshold to my room. With one hand, I grabbed the door, flinging it backward and expecting it to slam. Except it bounced instead, off the towering man who was clearly faster than me.

"The rent is three hundred," Rush said.

I whirled, pointing to my chest. "My rent."

"Yes." He planted his fists on his hips. "Your rent is three hundred."

"And yours?"

His jaw worked but he stayed quiet.

"That's what I thought." I huffed. "All I asked was that you not give me special treatment. But we keep having this conversation over and over again."

"It's not charity."

"Bullshit."

"It's seventy-five bucks." He held out his hands. "So what? Let me help."

No. Never. I had to stand on my own two feet. Because in the end, it would always be me. And this baby.

His gaze locked with mine as we stared at each other. A crease formed between his eyebrows as his scowl hardened. His jaw clenched and the corners looked sharper than knives.

He had a great jaw. A night months ago, I'd had a great time fitting my palm to its edge to feel it flex beneath my skin.

The idea of all we'd done that night, of touching him, brought a flush to my face, and damn it, I broke first, dropping my eyes to the floor.

"Let me help, Faye." His voice was gentle. "Please."

I sighed. "Just let me pay rent."

When I dared meet his gaze again, there was disappointment in his chocolate-brown eyes, but he nodded. "Stubborn."

"So are you."

Rush scowled and spun away, leaving the door open on his way out.

"This sucks," I whispered as my hand splayed across my belly.

If only I could find a freaking place to rent. Every time I talked to a potential landlord, they told me I'd just missed the spot. I was perpetually too late.

A friend from class had suggested I try campus housing, but it was too expensive. They required residents buy a meal plan at food services, and even then, with record enrollment at Treasure State, the only vacancies meant sharing a cramped room. If I had to spend most of my time hiding in a room, at least this one was my own.

Since Chuck's mom had moved in with him and Gloria, they didn't have a spare room.

I was out of options until a rental came up.

Living with Maverick was bad, but living with him was better than living in my car.

Should I just move in with Dusty? The idea of her snakes made my skin crawl. So did the cigarette smell. Which was worse for me and the baby? Secondhand smoke? Or constant, stressful arguments?

Every day there was some sort of spat. It wasn't full-blown screaming and yelling, but the tension was crippling. I was tired of fighting. How much could one woman take?

I guess I'd find out. My only option tonight was to suck it

up and deal. And since I couldn't do my laundry like I'd planned, I'd finish studying for the night and go to bed early. Except my backpack was downstairs, the last place I wanted to go. "Grr."

I headed along the hallway, but at the top of the landing, Maverick's voice stopped me.

"Dude, this is not going well."

I blinked.

"No shit." Rush let out a dry laugh as the sound of a stool at the bar slid across the floor. "This is hard."

"What happens when all that hard work turns out to be for nothing because this isn't even your kid?"

I flinched, nearly falling backward. Was that Maverick's problem? He didn't believe me? My hands balled into fists.

"I'm not making her do a paternity test," Rush said. "For the last time, fucking drop it."

"I'm not going to drop it. This is your future, Rush. She's using you. It's already starting. Seventy-five bucks off rent. Takeout runs for dinner. What's next? That piece-of-shit car of hers gets replaced. She's using you. Everyone can see it but you."

I shut my eyes as the tears flooded. Angry, hot tears. Is that what the locker room talk was about these days? How I was trying to take Rush Ramsey for every penny?

Fuck these football players. I swallowed the lump in my throat and raised my chin. Then I walked downstairs and into the living room, refusing to pretend I hadn't been eaves-dropping.

Maverick's gaze flicked my direction.

Rush twisted to look over his shoulder.

"I'm getting the test," I ordered as I came to a stop beside the couch. "Then you'll know I'm not lying."

"I know you're not lying." Rush turned back to Maverick.

"Not you." I stabbed a finger at Mav. "Him."

Maverick had the decency to look sorry.

If he wasn't such an asshole, he'd actually be handsome. Not as good-looking as Rush, but Maverick was hot. Except his personality meant that his face did absolutely nothing for me.

I hurried to the table, grabbing my backpack, then, my heart racing, started for the stairs when Rush's voice made me stop.

"I'm not getting tested," he said. "You can go to the doctor if you want, but it's a waste of your time. I'm not doing it. And this is the last time I'm going to talk about it. Understood?"

Maverick's sigh filled the room. "Fine."

The tears came back. It was the hormones. I'd cried more in the last four months than I had in the past four years. Except I couldn't seem to stop. My eyes flooded fast, but I wouldn't let Maverick see me cry, so I kept my back to them, blinking furiously and breathing through my nose until the sting was gone.

Footsteps echoed at my back. Then they grew fainter down the hallway until a door shut. Maverick's door.

With him gone, silence settled, thick as fog.

"I hate how this is going," Rush said.

"Me too."

The stool slid across the floor, then came more footsteps. I felt the heat from his body before a hand landed on my shoulder. "Want to get out of here? Go to dinner or something?"

"You just ate a sandwich."

"So?"

I shook my head. "No, thanks. I went to the store yesterday. I'll just eat here."

"It's my treat. Dinner."

I closed my eyes and as much as I tried to hide it, the reaction was almost automatic. I tensed.

He felt it.

His hand dropped, and I missed the touch immediately.

"Don't take that as charity. I'm just offering to buy you dinner. Think of it as a date."

My heart trilled. Damn it. That shouldn't happen at the idea of a date. Maybe it was just hunger pangs.

I turned enough to look up at him over my shoulder. "You're asking me on a date?"

"No." He scoffed. "It's just dinner."

Ouch. Was the idea of dating me really so awful? "Don't sound so appalled. I wouldn't have accepted anyway."

He shook his head, his eyes narrowing. "Wait. What? I'm not appall—"

"Forget it." I walked away, refusing to look at him as I climbed the stairs.

Then like I did most nights, I curled into a ball on my bed and fell asleep with tears sliding down my face.

CHAPTER NINETEEN

RUSH

The house was quiet when I walked inside but the lights were on and the front door had been unlocked. My keys clattered as I tossed them on the console table.

"Faye?" I called without an answer.

Her Explorer wasn't parked on the street, and she was supposed to have a shift at Dolly's. She usually worked on Tuesdays.

"Hello?" Nothing.

I'd been the first to leave the house this morning, and someone, probably Mav, had forgotten to lock up. It wasn't the first time, and I doubted it would be the last. It hadn't bothered me before now, but with Faye living here, we couldn't leave the place unlocked. I'd have to talk to him about it when he got home from campus.

Tuesdays were our nights to study and rest. We'd only had a brief meeting for practice, and I'd gone in early this morning to work out. When I'd left the fieldhouse twenty minutes ago, Maverick and Erik had still been hunched over their textbooks in the study hall.

I walked to the dining room table, dropping my backpack onto a chair, then unzipped my coat and hung it on a hook before toeing off my shoes.

It was still early, only nine, but I was ready to crash. I hadn't slept much last night, not after that fight with Faye.

She thought I was appalled with her. What the hell?

Where had she gotten that idea? I'd asked her out to dinner, but when she'd asked me if it was a date, I hadn't wanted her to feel pressured. I mean, it could have been a date. I wanted it to be a date.

Maybe I should have just asked her out, put myself out there and gone for it.

Maybe she needed to know that I thought about her more than was healthy.

I constantly wondered what she was doing and how she was feeling. I woke up with a raging hard-on in the middle of the night and wrapped a hand around my dick, picturing her face when I came all over my stomach. I'd folded her laundry last night when it had been finished and contemplated putting it all in my closet so she'd have to step into my room again.

This thing—I wouldn't let myself call it what it really was, an obsession—wasn't because of the baby. The way she plagued my thoughts, the way she got under my skin, was all Faye.

And she thought I was appalled at the idea of a date.

What a cluster.

I scrubbed a hand over my face and yawned, then headed upstairs. On the drive home, I'd almost gone to Dolly's. It had been a while since I'd shown up at the diner. But with the way Faye and I snapped at each other these days, I wasn't sure how she'd take a visit. And I was too damn exhausted to fight tonight.

The door to my bedroom was cracked. I pushed it open, unbuttoning my jeans so I could crawl into bed, except my bed wasn't empty.

"What the fuck?" I roared at the same time the brunette on the mattress scrambled to drag a sheet over her naked body.

"Get out!" she screamed.

"You're in my fucking room."

"No, I'm—" She glanced around. "This is Maverick's room. We were talking earlier, and he said he had to finish studying, but that I could just come over and wait. He said his room had all the football stuff."

Both of our rooms had football stuff.

It had been a while since he'd pulled this stunt, but it wasn't the first time he'd given a girl from school a key to our house so she could be waiting in his bed for him when he got home.

Fucking Maverick.

The last time he'd done this had been our sophomore year. We'd walked inside, and when I'd asked him if he wanted to catch a game, he'd told me he couldn't because his bedroom was calling. It hadn't been until I'd heard his headboard pounding against the wall that I'd realized exactly what he'd meant.

Erik and I had both told him to stop giving his key to random jersey chasers. So much for his promise to stop.

"This isn't Maverick's room." I turned my back on the woman. "Get out."

"Which one is his?" The bed creaked as she moved.

I pointed to the floor.

"Okay. Sorry."

"Yeah." Now I'd have to wash my sheets before I went to bed.

The sound of fabric sliding on skin filled the room, then she tiptoed past me, wearing only a pair of lace panties with her clothes clutched to her naked chest.

Guess this encounter wasn't going to deter her from fucking Maverick.

"You're Rush Ramsey, aren't you?"

"Yes." Did that mean tomorrow she'd be going around campus telling everyone she'd been in my bed too?

She pulled in her lips to hide a smile. "It was an honest mistake. I swear."

"Sure." An honest mistake my ass. If she had actually looked around, she might have noticed the picture of me and my parents on my dresser.

She stepped into the hallway, and I was about to slam the door behind her, except a gasp stole my attention. My gaze shifted past the brunette to the other woman in the hallway.

Faye.

My stomach dropped.

She stood frozen, jaw slack, at the top of the staircase. She was dressed in her Dolly's T-shirt and a pair of jeans. Her hair was pulled up in a messy knot and her cheeks were still flushed from the cold night air.

"Can I just sneak by you?" The brunette inched closer to Faye.

The movement caused Faye to jerk out of her stupor. Her eyes met mine for a brief second, shock and hurt filling those caramel irises, before she spun around and jogged to her room, slamming the door so hard the brunette jumped.

"Jeez," she said.

"Please leave."

I meant the house, but it wasn't the front door that opened and closed. It was the door to Maverick's bedroom.

I'd give her points for tenacity.

Maverick wouldn't have sent her here on purpose, would he? Had he set this up to try and chase Faye out?

No. Mav was a lot of things, but he wasn't that cruel.

"Damn it." I stared at Faye's closed door.

Like all the others in the house, it was white with four inlaid panels. The rectangles at the top were longer than those at the bottom.

It was a standard, simple door. It might as well have been to a bank vault with the way Faye used it to shut me out.

Not today. We couldn't keep doing this, snapping and clawing at each other's throats. She couldn't keep closing herself away in a house that was hers too. This had to stop. Now.

I crossed the hallway and knocked. Hard. "Faye."

"Go away."

"It's not what you think."

She scoffed.

"It's not. I came home—" This fucking door. I tested the knob only to find it locked. "Damn it, would you open up and talk to me?"

"Go. Away."

"No. I'll stand out here all night if I have to. We both know you'll have to pee at some point."

There was a growl, then angry, muffled stomps before the lock clicked and the door flew open.

This time the flush in Faye's cheeks wasn't from the

chilly November air. It was rage and hurt. The tears welling in her eyes nearly sent me to my knees.

"She thought my room was Maverick's."

"Right." She crossed her arms over her chest. "That's why she was naked and your jeans are unbuttoned."

Oh, shit. I clasped the button. "I was going to go to bed. Alone."

"Why should I believe you?"

"Because I have never lied to you." Not once. Not even when it would have been easier to tell her I wasn't scared. That I had everything handled. Instead, I'd laid my fears and truths at her feet.

"Whatever," she muttered. "It's not my business anyway. Do whatever you want. Just wear a condom this time. It would be really strange if two of your hookups were pregnant at the same time."

This woman. I'd never met anyone who could cut my legs out from under me so quickly. It was like being tackled from my blind side and slammed into the turf.

"You did not say that to me."

"I did." She jutted up her chin. It quivered.

That little wobble, the crack in her iron shell, was the only reason I hadn't already walked away. "I'm not your asshole ex, okay? Stop getting us confused."

Faye swallowed hard.

"I didn't touch her."

"You can. Be with whoever you want."

You. I wanted Faye.

I wanted her so much I'd been turning myself inside out since the start. Since that damn gravel road and flat tire. Since a night of argyle socks and too many drinks. Since cheeseburgers and pancakes.

I was so fucking tired of pretending like this wasn't real. That I didn't crave her to the point of distraction.

"You," I whispered.

"What?"

"I want you."

"Rush." My name was a sharp inhale. But there was something else in her expression. Disbelief maybe.

I was foolish enough to hope she might want me the same way I wanted her.

We were already as complicated as it could get. We were already messy. Why not embrace it?

I stepped closer.

She didn't back away.

My hand lifted and closed around the back of her neck, my fingers squeezing against her pulse as my thumb drew a long line across her jaw.

"I didn't touch her, Faye. Say you believe me."

She sighed. "I believe you."

"Thank fuck." I bent low. "I'm going to kiss you now so you know exactly who I want."

Her eyes flared the moment before my lips captured hers.

It wasn't the hard, punishing kiss I wanted.

But it was the kiss she needed. That we both needed.

Something soft for a change. A truce.

I kissed along her bottom lip, moving from one corner to the other, keeping that hold on her neck. I waited to feel her tense, to pull back, but she didn't move, didn't breathe, until I hummed against her mouth.

Then she melted. One moment, she was stiff as a board, the next, she leaned into my touch, her eyelids finally fluttering closed as she kissed me back.

There she was. The spitfire who'd fight me for a moment before giving in. Completely.

My arms banded around her, hauling her close as I licked the seam of her mouth.

She parted for my tongue to slide inside and do a lazy swirl against hers.

Fuck, she tasted good. Better than I remembered. This mouth was heaven.

She whimpered as I tangled my tongue with hers, sinking deeper against my chest. She rose up on her toes as I folded around her.

It was gentle and sweet. It was hunger and pain. This kiss was likely going to bite me in the ass later, but I wasn't letting her go.

Her fingers snaked around my waist as she explored my mouth.

I nipped at her lips, letting the graze of my teeth draw out a mewl from her throat. Her scent surrounded me, clean, green apples and a hint of bacon from the diner. My body came alive, heat coursing through every vein as my heartbeat pounded for *more, more, more.*

Faye's hands trailed up my spine, her hands fisting the cotton of my T-shirt.

We molded to each other, holding tight as the soft, sweet kiss turned to something desperate and aching. We took weeks of frustration and tension and threw it at the other to swallow.

Her nails dug through the fabric of my shirt, scoring my flesh.

I held her so tight she'd never escape.

And damn, the feel of her in my arms. It was better than I remembered.

I needed a thousand nights to memorize every inch of her body. Every line. Every curve. A thousand nights to watch her change.

A thousand nights to make her mine.

I was seconds away from stripping her bare, of laying her on that tiny bed of hers just to see if we could both fit. But before I could pick her up off her feet, a door slammed in the distance.

The front door.

Maverick was home.

Faye flinched, like she'd awoken from a dreamless sleep. Her hands let go of my shirt and she dropped to her heels, wiggling out of my hold. Her eyes were wide, panicked, as she stared at me, raising a hand to touch her mouth. "You can't kiss me."

Because she didn't want me to kiss her? Or because she did?

Whatever the reason, that little declaration, that weak-ass line in the sand, pissed me right the fuck off.

"Well, I just did." I dragged a hand over my mouth. "You're still holding that fucking can of bear spray, Faye. What's it going to take to get you to put it down?"

She closed her eyes, her arms wrapping around her middle.

Fine. Shut down. Put that guard back up.

This time, I didn't let her slam the bedroom door. I did it for her as I stalked out.

I didn't feel like washing my sheets. I'd done enough laundry yesterday. So I stormed downstairs. And spent a sleepless night on the couch.

CHAPTER TWENTY

FAYE

Rush walked out of his bedroom at the same moment I stepped out of mine. It took all of my willpower not to slink away.

"Hey," he said.

"Hi."

He had a duffel bag slung over a shoulder, and he was dressed in a pair of royal-blue warm-ups with the Wildcat logo stitched into both the jacket and pants.

"Away game?" I asked.

"Yeah. We'll be back tomorrow night."

"Okay. Good luck."

He nodded. "Lock the doors, okay?"

"Of course."

He headed for the staircase, pausing at the top. "When I get back, we're going to talk, since you've been avoiding me for four days."

I didn't try to deny it. I'd done everything in my power to hide from Rush since that kiss. I should have stayed in my room this morning, but I'd thought he'd already left for the fieldhouse with Maverick. My mistake.

He'd told me I was still holding that can of bear spray. I wanted to argue.

Except he was right.

He disappeared down the stairs without another word.

I didn't move my feet until the front door opened and closed. Until the rumble of his Yukon's engine faded down the street.

The air rushed from my lungs as the quiet of the house seeped into my bones.

Well, maybe a weekend alone would give me a chance to breathe. I hadn't had much time alone lately. It was strange to always be around someone.

Maybe in this quiet house, I could think about *anything* other than that kiss. Though considering I caught hints of Rush's spicy scent with every inhale, I doubted there'd be much escaping him, even if he was in another town.

"Ugh." I unglued my feet and headed downstairs to make breakfast. Then I needed to get to campus for class.

My professors had been piling on the work over the last couple of weeks. They could keep that up for the rest of the semester as far as I was concerned. School was the only thing that kept my mind off Rush.

I wasn't sure what I'd do over winter break without studying and projects to distract me from the dumpster fire of my personal life. But that was a problem I'd deal with in December.

Maybe by then, I'd have my own place. The listings were still few and far between, but I'd kept looking. I could spend my free time setting up a nursery. I'd get a jump start on nesting.

Not that I'd have much in that nest. My budget couldn't swing an elaborate nursery. We'd be getting by with only the essentials for a while. A crib or bassinet. A few plastic drawers. Dusty was giving me a glider from her house that she didn't need, and hopefully, I could get out the cigarette smell.

A few of my friends knew I was pregnant. Hannah and a couple girls from her bachelorette party. She'd mentioned throwing me a baby shower, but I'd been stalling on picking a date.

I wanted my sister at a baby shower. And I still hadn't told her about the baby.

How much of a coward did that make me that I was terrified of a fifteen-year-old's reaction?

Gloria had come to the diner last night to do homework, and I'd been seconds away from spilling the truth, but I'd chickened out. She would judge. She was at the age where she knew everything.

I wasn't ready to suffer her disappointment. I had enough shit happening, I didn't need a lecture from my little sister.

Soon. I'd tell her soon. I had to tell her soon. If I waited too long, then she'd be pissed that I'd kept a secret. Maybe tonight at the diner when she came to study.

My phone rang in my back jeans pocket as I walked through the living room. *Gloria.* She must have known she was on my mind. "Hey. I was just thinking about you."

"I'm walking into school so I only have a minute."

"Everything all right?"

"Yeah, but can you call Mom?"

I stopped two feet short of the kitchen. "Um, what?"

"Mom. Our mother. Call her."

205

Not happening. Wait. Why was Gloria talking to her? "Why should I call her? Are *you* talking to her?"

Six months ago, Gloria had vowed never to speak to our mother again. They'd had some fight.

I'd always expected that the silence between them wouldn't last. Her relationship with Mom wasn't awful like mine. It wasn't great either, but they'd never gone longer than a few months without talking.

They'd fight. They'd forget. And the cycle would repeat on loop.

Me? I hadn't spoken to my mother since the beginning of my sophomore year at Treasure State. Two years ago. When I'd gone to my childhood home to pick up a few things I'd left behind only to find she'd thrown all of my belongings out.

My pictures from high school. The yearbooks I'd paid for with my own money. The silver necklace my father had given me when I was a little girl. It was a kid's piece of jewelry and hadn't fit, but I'd kept it in the heart-shaped pink velvet box.

What tiny pieces of my heart had remained, she'd shattered that day.

She'd thrown out my life because she'd wanted the bedroom as a place to keep her new puppy. A room where it couldn't ruin her things.

Gloria told me that the dog ran away a year later. That, or Mom had decided she didn't want a dog anymore.

My sister's vow to cut off all communication with Mom was flimsy. Mine? Iron.

"Why should I call her?" If Gloria was asking, there had to be a good reason.

"I can't get into it right now," she said. "Just do me a favor and call her."

Mom had my number. If she wanted to talk to me, she could call me herself. "No, thanks."

"Faye, don't be a brat about this." There was an eye roll attached to that sentence. Strange, how my mother used to slap me when I rolled my eyes. I'd learned never to do it from a young age. Gloria didn't roll her eyes around Mom. She'd learned that too. Instead, she saved them all for me.

"Just call her," she said.

"Go to school. I'll see you tonight at the diner."

She huffed. "You're not going to call her, are you?"

"Nope."

"Please? For me?"

There was a lot I'd do for my sister. Work myself to the bone so she had nice jeans and Nike gym shoes. Spend hours reviewing homework so she'd get good grades. Shuttle her all around Mission so she didn't have to walk or ride her bike across town.

But this? It was a betrayal. Shame on her for asking.

"I have to go," I said, and before she could stop me, I ended the call.

It took a moment for the wave of pain to pass. For me to remember that Gloria was only fifteen, and our mother hadn't left her with wounds quite so deep.

Not while I'd been there to act as Gloria's shield.

Still, she knew better than to ask. If anyone knew how much hurt I'd endured from Brynn Gannon, it was Gloria.

My heart was beating too fast as I made my way to the fridge. It took a moment, standing with the door open and the cold on my face, to shake off the call.

I refused to call my mother. Absolutely not.

Gloria would have to give me more of an explanation if she wanted me to change my mind. She wasn't guilting me into a conversation I didn't want to have.

When Gloria learned about the baby, would she tell Mom? When Mom learned I was pregnant, would she reach out? I wasn't sure what would be worse.

If she did.

Or didn't.

Someday, I hoped I wouldn't care. That the thought of talking to her wouldn't make me feel twitchy and nervous. That my palms wouldn't sweat.

But not today.

"Gah." I shook out my arms, like I could shake off the thought of my mother. Then I splayed a hand over my belly. "What are we hungry for today, Squish?"

The nickname had randomly popped up last week. I'd never heard it used before and now I couldn't stop saying it.

At least if I was home alone this weekend, I wouldn't have to worry about being caught calling my baby bump Squish.

Next week was my ultrasound, and we could find out if it was a boy or girl. Maybe the nickname would change at that point. Maybe not.

It all depended on if we learned the gender, and right now, I wasn't sure. Normally, I wasn't much for surprises, but part of me wanted to wait.

Dusty had asked me if I had a preference. The idea of a boy seemed exciting, if only for the reason that I'd been partially parenting Gloria for years. Maybe a boy wouldn't throw around quite as much sass. Or call me a brat because I didn't want to make a phone call.

"She's the brat," I muttered, hauling out a gallon of milk.

Did Rush want to find out? Did he want a girl or boy? We should be talking about these things. We should be making a list of supplies to get and names to consider. Instead, he was kissing me and scrambling my brain and making me want to scream and cry and throw up.

Boys were dumb.

Never mind. I didn't want a boy.

My generic bran flakes were entirely unappealing, but I snagged the box from the pantry and poured a bowl anyway. I opened the silverware drawer to grab a spoon just as a phone vibrated on the counter.

Not my phone. Mine was in my pocket.

It was Rush's phone that he'd left on the bar.

"Oh no."

He couldn't go away without his phone.

I picked it up, and before I could talk myself out of it, I put the milk away, grabbed my backpack and coat, then bolted out the door.

It was early enough that I got a decent parking spot on campus. With his phone in my pocket, I hurried across the lot at the fieldhouse, the cold sinking into the tip of my nose and cheeks.

There were two buses parked outside. Both had their engines running, white wisps of exhaust streaming into the air.

Were they already leaving? I started to jog. But when I got closer, the buses were empty. The drivers were standing outside talking. The storage compartments under the vehicles were open and the bins bare.

I nodded to a driver when he waved, then hustled inside, not exactly sure where to look for Rush, but hoping I'd find someone on the team who could give him his phone.

My tennis shoes tapped on the concrete floor as I speed walked along the hall.

I rounded a corner, scanning for a person to help, and came to a dead stop when I spotted Rush. He was talking to Millie, the assistant athletic director who'd broken up the fight I'd had with Rush in this very hallway last summer.

The fight when he'd asked me for that paternity test.

"Oh. Um, hi . . ." *Ugh.* I'd made a damn fool of myself that day, screaming at him in public. I hadn't been to the fieldhouse since. Mostly because I didn't have a reason to stop by. But also because I really didn't feel like bumping into Coach Ellis. Or Millie.

Why was it that embarrassment only seemed to expand over time? It had been bad enough in the moment, but facing her was like reliving it a thousand times over again.

"Millie," she said, like I could ever have forgotten her name.

"I remember." I nodded, then glanced at Rush, pulling his phone from my pocket. "Here. You forgot this on the counter."

"Shit." He shifted his duffel bag around to pat its front pocket. "Thanks for bringing it."

"Yeah." I handed it over, careful not to let our fingers touch.

Not that I didn't want to touch him. That was the problem.

I wanted Rush.

I liked Rush. I'd had a crush on him for longer than I wanted to admit.

He lifted a hand, reaching my way. It hung in midair for a moment.

My heart climbed into my throat, waiting to see what he'd do.

If he touched me, I'd cave. I'd probably collapse into his chest because fighting to keep these boundaries between us was so damn tiring.

God, I was tired.

Touch me. Please.

I needed him to make the move. Not that he hadn't already made the first move and the second and even the third. I needed him to do it again.

He wanted me to drop my guard. He wanted me to drop the bear spray. How?

I shifted on my feet, the nervous energy making it impossible for me to stand still.

He must have taken it as a rejection because his arm fell to his side.

My gaze crashed to the floor.

How did I do this? How did we get past this awkward, awful phase? Was it impossible?

"Better get on the bus," Rush muttered, before he walked away.

It wasn't until his footsteps faded that I finally looked up.

Millie's sad, pitying smile was waiting.

I hated pity. But today? I'd take it.

"How's it going?" she asked.

I shrugged, looking over my shoulder to make sure we were alone. "Kind of . . . bad."

Understatement of the year.

"Sorry."

"We moved in together," I blurted. "I was living with my ex-boyfriend, but when he found out about us, the baby, he kicked me out."

"Oof. Jerkface."

"Pretty much."

"How is living with Rush?"

I shrugged again. "Awkward? We argue a lot."

Why was I pouring my guts out to this woman? She didn't need to hear my sob story.

"You both have a lot to navigate," Millie said. "I'd say arguing is expected. Give it time."

"Yeah." Except it felt endless. It felt like if things didn't change, and soon, he'd hate me.

I wasn't sure I could live with Rush's hate.

"He told me not to get a paternity test. That he didn't need one." I straightened. Maybe Maverick still didn't believe me. But Rush did. And for some reason, I wanted Millie to believe me too. "I wouldn't lie about something like this."

"I believe you."

My frame deflated on an exhale. She had no idea how much I'd needed to hear that. To have someone impartial, someone on this campus, believe that I hadn't tricked Rush into this pregnancy.

"It's just temporary," I said. "Us living together."

"Does it have to be? Rush seems like a nice guy. I don't know him very well, but I get the impression he's trying to do the right thing."

"He is." Without a doubt. The one who was screwing it all up here was me. I wrapped my arms around my waist, my stomach knotting.

Yes, it would be easier to live with Rush. Logistically, it would be easier.

But what happened when he got tired of me too? What

happened when we imploded? Wouldn't it be better to have different addresses when it all fell apart?

Besides, I'd never had a place that was truly mine. Not my mother's house. Not the college dorms. Not the apartment where I'd lived my sophomore and junior year with three messy roommates who'd liked having me in the fourth bedroom because I wasn't afraid to clean. Not Justin's trailer.

Now I was in Rush's house.

"I don't think . . . It will be better if we keep some boundaries between us. Easier, I think."

"Okay." Millie looked disappointed in me.

Maybe I was a little bit disappointed in myself.

I took a step away. "I've got class."

"Bye, Faye."

"Bye."

I passed the first door I came to, following the hallway as it looped around to another exit. Two guys dressed in the same gear as Rush walked by on my way out, but I let the curtain of my hair hide my face until I was outside and hurrying toward my end of campus to start my day.

Concentration was futile. I was so lost in my own head I forgot to pin up the new, hot-pink flyers I'd made for Dolly's. Even my classes weren't enough of a distraction today.

Millie was right. Down to my bones, I knew she was right.

Rush was a good guy trying to do the right thing.

Why couldn't I just let him?

Justin had told me once that the reason he loved hanging with Alexa was because she was emotionally available.

Meaning, I was not.

I hadn't even been able to argue. He wasn't the first person to tell me I was closed off.

During my sophomore year, I'd taken a school counseling course that had required each student to spend six months seeing a counselor. It was the first time in my life I'd ever had someone neutral to talk to. Someone to hear about the shit with Mom and school and Gloria and just . . . everything.

Those six months had been eye-opening. I'd learned a lot about myself and how I interacted with others. My counselor had warned me that showing my vulnerabilities would always be a challenge, a fear to overcome.

Was that why everything with Rush was so hard? Because I was scared?

Without a doubt. I was terrified of that man. Rush had the power to destroy me like no other person in my life. And this baby would keep us linked forever.

I couldn't cut him out and refuse to speak to him for two years.

But I didn't know how to move past this. I didn't know how to let down my guard.

By the time I was finished with class for the day, my insides were twisted in a knot. And for the first time in a long time, I didn't feel like going to work, but my shift started at three and I couldn't afford to call in sick. So I walked through campus to my car and drove across town, finding Mike in the kitchen, slicing potatoes at the prep table.

I hadn't seen Mike in weeks.

"Where's Dusty?" I asked as I grabbed an apron.

"She's taking the night off."

My fingers froze on the apron's ties. "Really?" Dusty only stayed home if she was sick. "Is she feeling okay?"

"Yeah. I guess she's going out to dinner with her cousin."

My jaw hit the floor. "Seriously?"

"That's what she said."

When had she started talking to her cousin? After her aunt had died? That had to be the catalyst.

For Dusty's sake, I hoped the dinner went well.

"It's just you and me tonight, kiddo," Mike said.

I'd missed him lately. For however long it lasted, I was glad he'd come back. "Any customers?"

He shook his head. "Nah. It's quiet."

I glanced at the TV mounted in the corner. Dusty didn't turn it on often, but when Mike was here, he usually had it playing in the background.

Tonight, he'd tuned it to a sports channel. To a football game. I had no idea how the rules worked. I didn't know the teams playing.

There was an assignment due Monday in my capstone class that I wanted to get started on, but I left my backpack in Dusty's office, and instead of going to the dining room, I pulled up a stool beside the prep table.

"Hey, Mike?"

"Hey, Faye."

"Would you teach me about football?"

CHAPTER TWENTY-ONE

RUSH

W e lost.

We fucking lost.

I lost.

It wasn't the first time. Definitely wouldn't be the last. But something about our game today had felt off. This loss hit harder than others from the past couple of years.

Maybe because this was Coach Ellis's first year. We'd surpassed anyone's expectations for the team, and most of us were working our tails off not to let him down. The Wildcats were kicking ass and showing our fans and donors that we weren't defined by last spring's scandal.

We should have won today. We could have won against the Idaho Vandals. But we'd lost and that was on me.

I'd played like shit too. I'd thrown one pick-six and fumbled a snap. I'd been sacked twice. I should have been able to outrun both the linebacker and defensive end who'd tackled me, but I'd been slow in the pocket and unfocused. Like my head was in the clouds and my feet were running in sand. Everything had just been . . . delayed. Each time I made a decision, it was two seconds too late.

Granted, the Vandals had been on fire. They'd done everything right while we'd done everything wrong. Their defense against our secondary had shut down our passing game. The running game hadn't been much better. And our defense had run out of gas because they'd been on the field for too long.

I hadn't given them enough chances to rest by keeping the offense playing. I hadn't done my job.

Final score: twenty-one to three. We'd gotten our asses handed to us.

The flight home had been silent. No one had made eye contact. I hadn't been the only one who'd played like shit.

But by the time we'd landed and gotten on the buses to drive us back to the fieldhouse, some of the guys were talking. Voices were low but the mourning period was lifting.

Maybe for them.

"You want to talk?" Maverick asked in his seat beside mine.

I kept my gaze out the window, staring at the dark streets of Mission. "No."

He sighed, and before he'd even opened his mouth, I knew what was coming.

I didn't want to hear it.

"It's Faye."

My jaw clenched, my molars grinding. This was not the time or place to get into an argument with Mav.

I was still upset about that stunt he'd pulled with the brunette, giving her the key to our house. He'd apologized, so I'd dropped it, but that bullshit couldn't happen again.

Sooner rather than later, my kid was going to be in that house. We didn't need random strangers coming and going.

"Look, man, I know you've got a lot to sort out with her and the baby," he said. "All I'm saying is that you're distracted. Your focus is off. And it's been that way ever since you moved her into the house."

"Let it go."

"There's a lot of shit happening. Maybe you need some space from each—"

"Fucking drop it!" My voice was so loud that everyone on the bus turned toward my seat.

Coach Greely rose out of his seat in the front row, glancing toward us near the back. He arched his eyebrows, and I held up a hand to let him know it was all good.

"Sorry, Coach." I flipped the hood on my sweatshirt over my head and leaned against the window.

"I'm trying to be your friend, Rush."

"Right," I muttered.

The hell of it was, I believed him. He saw me spiraling because I *was* spiraling. I wasn't sure what was up or down, left or right. My personal life was impacting the game and that couldn't happen.

"She's in my life," I told him. "There's no changing that. I need her to be under the same roof. Until we can think this out, make a plan, I need her at the house. I feel helpless, and I don't want . . ."

My throat closed up. Because what I was about to say was about me, not Faye, yet I wasn't sure if Maverick would understand the nuance.

"What?" He nudged my elbow with his. "Talk to me."

Had he gone through any of this with his sister when she'd been pregnant? Had he witnessed her struggles?

The person I wanted to talk to about this was Mom, but I couldn't call her until later. Talking to Maverick was at least better than letting it fester inside.

"Faye's guarded." I sighed. "She's used to doing everything on her own. It's her body that's changing. It's her making the bigger sacrifices. I'm worried she's going to realize that she doesn't actually need me. I'm worried that I'm irrelevant."

His hum faded beneath the whir of tires on asphalt. "You're not irrelevant. And I don't think Faye believes that either. She won't cut you out, Rush. You'll be a good dad. We all know that. And she does too."

It was the first time he'd said anything decent about her. "Thanks."

"Welcome." He nodded as we pulled up to the field-house. "I'm not coming home tonight. I'm going to head over to Mom and Dad's place. Crash there. Mom hasn't been feeling great this week. Figured I'd hang with her tomorrow. Spend some time on the couch watching movies with her."

"All right. Tell her I hope she feels better soon."

There were days when I wanted to strangle Mav. When I thought he couldn't be more of a dickhead. But the guy loved his mom the way I loved mine. He was close with his dad, sister and nephew too. It was hard to stay annoyed with him because despite his complete lack of filter, his heart was usually in the right place.

We shuffled off the bus and went our separate ways. When I got home, the house was dark and quiet. It smelled like Faye. Crisp, green apples and fresh soap.

I toed off my shoes and hauled my bag upstairs, the exhaustion from the game and travel making my legs heavy and steps sluggish. The hallway was dark except for a sliver of yellow light coming from beneath Faye's door. The air felt humid and smelled like her shampoo. She liked to take showers when she got home from the diner, probably to wash out the smell of grease and food.

Go to bed, Rush. Just leave her alone and go to bed.

I set my bag down in my room.

Then went to Faye's.

Why was knocking on her door so damn hard? It took all of my strength to lift a hand and tap it against the white surface.

My heart hammered as I waited, four beats, five, six, seven, eight . . .

The knob turned on nine.

"Hi." She gave me a sad smile.

"Hey."

She was wearing a pair of oversized, navy sweats. Her hair was wet and matted in thick, uncombed ropes. There was a white towel in her hands. She shifted to the side and waved me inside. "Sorry about your game."

"You watched?" *Great.* I swallowed a grumble as I stepped into her room. She'd never mentioned a game before. Why was today's the one she'd decided to watch?

"Mike likes football. He had the game on today."

"Mike?"

"Dusty's boyfriend. Or sometimes boyfriend. Their relationship is strange. He comes in to cook sometimes and give her a break."

"Ah." I went to her bed and sat on the edge.

She came to sit beside me, reaching for the brush she'd left on the mattress.

Before she could pick it up, I snatched it out of her hand.

"What?" she asked.

I twirled the brush in the air. "Turn sideways."

"You're going to brush my hair?"

"Why not?"

She studied me for a long moment but finally turned, shifting sideways on the mattress. "If you must."

I started with the ends, gently pulling the brush through the strands until they were smooth against her back. "When I was eleven, I decided that I wanted to grow my hair out long. To this day I'm surprised my dad let it happen."

"Why?"

"Dad's pretty traditional. He gets a trim the second his hair starts to touch his ears. But when I was a kid, they were good about giving me some easy freedoms. If I wanted to wear shorts in the dead of winter, that was my choice. My hairstyle was my choice too."

She exhaled, her shoulders relaxing away from her ears as I worked the brush across her scalp.

"I grew it out until it touched my shoulders. Kept it that way until my junior year of high school."

"I can't picture you with long hair."

"I'll get Mom to text me a picture."

She breathed, her head lolling to the side as I kept brushing. Over and over and over again until that pretty reddish-blond hair was smooth and sleek. "I can't remember the last time anyone brushed my hair. My mother, I guess. When I was a little kid."

"What about when you go to the salon?"

"Salons are expensive. I just have Dusty take scissors to the ends when they get scraggly."

My mom lived for her hair appointments. She went

every three weeks to cover up her grays and because she loved being pampered by someone else.

If Faye would let me, I'd brush out her hair every night.

When I set the brush aside, she turned around, this time sitting sideways to face me. "Are you okay?"

"Today sucked." It was the game that I'd replay over and over and over again, regretting every move and every mistake for weeks.

"You don't like to lose," she said.

"Does anyone?"

"No, I guess not."

I leaned forward, elbows to knees. "I'm tired of fighting, Faye."

"Me too."

"I'm not sorry I kissed you."

She clasped her fingers in her lap. "Neither am I."

Well, that was something. "I don't know what to do."

"Rally, right? Isn't that what you said? We just need to rally."

"Yeah, sweets." I turned to face her and let myself drown in those caramel eyes. "We need to rally."

Today hadn't been the best day, but right now, just being with her, was a better end than I'd expected.

My gaze shifted down the line of her cute nose to her soft, peach lips. That mouth was a magnet and before I'd even realized I'd leaned in close, I was a breath away from another kiss.

"Rush?" she whispered.

I froze. "Faye?"

"Don't kiss me."

Damn. So much for turning this day around.

I leaned back, about to leave, when her hand shot out.

She fisted the fabric of my shirt, keeping me close as she shut her eyes.

"I want you to kiss me. But everything spins upside down when you do, and right now, I need to stand straight. Does that make sense?"

Perfect fucking sense. But that didn't mean I still wasn't disappointed.

"I've never initiated a kiss before." Her voice dropped so low it was almost hard to hear. Was she embarrassed about that? She didn't need to be. Any man in his right mind would want to kiss her. No one had probably ever given her a chance to take the lead.

Wait. That was it, wasn't it? She needed to take charge. She needed to be in control.

Fuck my life. I should have clued in to that ages ago. All I had to do was be there when she was ready.

"Kiss me anytime you want."

"Okay. Thanks." Pink colored her cheeks.

I brushed a knuckle over the blush. "Welcome."

She let go of my shirt, smoothing out the wrinkle with her fingers. "Rush?"

"Faye?"

"Thank you for brushing my hair."

I hauled her into my arms, resting my face on top of her head and breathing her in. She wrapped her arms around my waist as we sagged into each other.

We stayed like that, locked, for so long that her hair was halfway dry when I finally let go.

"We can do this, right?" she asked. "With Squish?"

"Squish?" I chuckled. That's what she called the baby? I liked it. A lot.

"Yep." A smile stretched across her mouth, blinding

white and so beautiful my heart stopped. Faye splayed both hands over her belly.

Fuck, I wanted to kiss her. Instead, I covered her hands with my own. "Hey, Squish."

CHAPTER TWENTY-TWO

FAYE

"Just call her," my sister snapped from across the table at the diner.

"Gloria." I matched her tone. "Enough."

She rolled her eyes. "You're being *so* dumb about this."

"If Mom wanted to talk to me, she could call."

"Maybe she doesn't feel comfortable reaching out since you haven't spoken to her for two years."

I scoffed. "So I have to make it comfortable for her?"

"It's a phone call." She crossed her arms over her chest and jutted up her chin. "It's not that big of a deal."

"And to reiterate my point, if it's not that big of a deal, then why can't Mom put forth the effort?"

"Fine." Gloria threw up her hands. "Then don't call her."

"Okay, I won't."

Her expression was half pout, half scowl. It was the same look she'd given me all month whenever we had this same, tired argument. "You care more about this diner and Dusty than you do our family."

I was beyond done with this topic. "*You* are my family. Dusty is my family. I love you both."

"You don't love Mom?"

"No." It wasn't something I'd ever admitted before. Not to Gloria. Not even myself.

"Faye." Gloria's expression was stricken as she gasped. "How can you say that? She's our mom."

Mom. That term felt a lot different now than it had months ago.

I was about to be a mom. And when my child came into this world and was placed in my arms, he or she would love me unconditionally.

I didn't have to make that baby love me. My job was not to screw it up.

Mom had lost my love. She'd done nothing to earn it back.

We were supposed to love our parents. It felt wrong admitting the truth. But I wasn't going to pretend, not where Mom was concerned. The sooner Gloria knew that bridge had been burned a long, long time ago, the better. Especially when I hadn't been the person holding the match.

It was time, wasn't it? Time to fess up?

Maybe if Gloria knew that my priorities had shifted, that I had a lot coming on the horizon, she'd realize why I wasn't going to open communication with Mom. Not when I wasn't just risking my own heart. I'd be risking my baby's too.

Over my dead body would I ever let her hurt him the way she'd hurt me.

I stretched a hand across the table, covering hers with mine. She tensed, like she was going to yank it away, but I gave it a squeeze. "I need to tell you something."

"What?"

I'm pregnant. I'm pregnant. "I'm pregnant."

Her jaw dropped.

"Rush and I are having a baby. In April."

The table hid my belly, but Gloria's gaze dropped, like she could see through the surface to my stomach. Her eyes lifted to mine, then dropped again. Up and down, up and down. She closed her mouth with a click, then ticked off fingers on her free hand.

"You're four months pregnant. And I'm just finding out?"

The hurt on her face sliced deep. "I'm sorry I didn't tell you sooner."

"So does everyone else know? Am I like the last person to find out?"

"No. Not many people know."

She tugged her other hand free from my grip. "Is this why you moved out of Justin's place?"

"Yes." When I'd told her I'd moved, she'd been so happy that I'd left Justin's trailer for good she hadn't asked why. And I hadn't had the guts to tell her he'd evicted me.

"Are you and Rush together?"

"No." Why was that the hardest part to admit? Maybe because deep down I didn't like the answer.

We weren't together. At all. One kiss weeks ago didn't count as a relationship. But there was . . . something. We were something.

The arguments had stopped so abruptly, for the first couple of weeks after he'd come home from that away game, the night he'd brushed my hair, I'd been on edge, expecting them to start again. But we'd found this peace.

It was easy again.

His football schedule was more demanding than ever, but he'd started coming back to the diner on the evenings when he was free. He stopped by my room at night to see how I was feeling. Monday night, when I'd been reading in my room, he'd come in and sat on the floor.

We'd talked for two hours about nothing and everything. About his childhood on the ranch and mine in Mission.

Maverick was still an asshole who couldn't seem to put knives in the dishwasher blade down or clean his crap off the laundry room floor, so it was easier to avoid him entirely. I still mostly hung out in my room.

Rush made it so I didn't have to hang out alone.

"This is . . . I don't even know what to say." Gloria's shoulders sagged. "You're really pregnant?"

"I'm really pregnant." I stood and lifted up my sweatshirt, turning sideways so she could see the slight swell of my belly. *Squish.*

"So that, like, makes me an aunt." Her face didn't change, but there was a spark in her eyes.

"You're an aunt."

She nodded as I righted my top. "Is it a boy or girl?"

"I don't know."

"Are you going to find out?"

"Maybe?"

We'd had my ultrasound a couple of weeks ago. There was a grainy, black and white photo on the nightstand in my bedroom. Rush had his own to keep and a copy he'd sent to his parents.

When the technician had asked if we wanted to know the gender, I'd told him I wasn't sure yet. Rush had shrugged, letting me make the decision, so the tech had sealed the results in an envelope for us to take home.

I hadn't seen the envelope since that day, but I had a hunch that Rush was keeping it close for when I made up my mind.

"Are you going to tell Mom?" Gloria asked.

What was this fixation on our mother? "I don't know. It's not a secret. But if you're asking if I was going to make an effort to share the news, then no."

"Well, you should." She scooted to the edge of the booth and stood too.

She hadn't brought her backpack along today. There was no homework to be done. She'd gotten out of school after lunch for Thanksgiving break, then come here to pester me about calling Mom.

"You're still coming over tomorrow, right?" she asked.

"Yeah. What time?"

"Six."

"Can I bring anything?"

"No, we've got it covered."

"Are *you* cooking?"

Chuck wasn't much of a cook. I wasn't sure Gloria knew how to make anything other than ramen and cold sandwiches. But she'd wanted to organize a Thanksgiving dinner tomorrow. Maybe her grandmother would be making a turkey. Not that I liked turkey.

She laughed. "Definitely not."

"Okay," I drawled. Should I ask what we'd be eating? To be safe, I'd probably have my own dinner before *the* dinner.

Gloria leaned in for a hug that was over before it even started. Then she turned and rushed for the door, skipping every other step like she was about to break into a run.

"Wait."

The last time she'd tried to make that fast of an exit was when she'd gotten her belly button pierced at some random guy's house who did underage piercings. She'd been touching her navel all evening, and when I'd asked her what was going on, she'd tried to run away.

It hadn't taken much to get a confession then. I doubted it would now.

She sighed, flailing her arms at her sides as she made a dramatic turn. "What?"

"You're hiding something." I crossed my arms over my chest.

"Nothing."

"Gloria."

She couldn't meet my gaze, instead looking at the floor as she mumbled, "Momiscomingovertoo."

I blinked. "Say that again?"

"Mom is coming over too." She gave me an exaggerated frown. "She's cooking."

And my sister was trying to trick me into a family reunion. She would have let me walk through the door without any warning. She would have put me face-to-face with a person I had no desire to see. The woman who'd made my childhood hell.

The pain in my chest was excruciating. It hurt so much I closed my eyes, breathing through the pain.

What had I done to earn her betrayal? Had I not given her enough time? Enough money? Enough love? How could she do this to me?

"I'm sorry, Faye. I just thought—"

"Goodbye, Gloria."

She stared at me for a long moment, her eyes watering as

her chin quivered.

It was the harshest I'd ever spoken to my sister. I'd never once dismissed her from this diner.

"Are you still coming tomorrow?"

Wow. "What do you think?"

The corners of her mouth turned down. She waited, like if she stood there long enough I'd cave, but I stayed frozen until finally she realized it was useless.

"I'm really sorry." Her voice shook as she started to cry. Then she walked out the door.

It took everything I had not to follow and call her back.

But she'd gone too far. This was a lesson she had to learn. Even if it broke me into pieces to teach it.

So much for Thanksgiving.

"Well, Squish." I walked through the dining room, hand splayed across my bump. "I guess we'll stay home and eat our own food."

At least the house would be quiet. Maverick had left yesterday to crash at his parents' house in town for the long weekend. Erik, who I'd only seen twice in all the time I'd been living at Rush's place, was with his girlfriend, Kalindi. And Rush had left this morning for the ranch.

When I walked through the swinging door, I figured I'd find Dusty at the prep table and Mike at the flattop, except the kitchen was empty.

Mike had been helping out a lot lately. He came with her to the diner most days. I wasn't sure what was going on with them, but I hoped this "on" period didn't eventually become another "off."

Dusty was happier when Mike was in her life. He was the only person who seemed to like her snakes too.

Eww.

They must have gone out back for a smoke, so I headed for the bathroom, wanting a minute to breathe and let the sting of Gloria's plan fade.

I turned the knob, swinging open the door, and shrieked, "Oh my God."

Dusty's chest was pressed up against the wall, her jeans pooled at her ankles. So were Mike's.

I let go of the door and slapped a hand over my eyes as it swung closed.

"Hell," Mike hissed.

"She's pregnant," Dusty said. "She knows about sex."

I spun away from the door and ran, not looking back as I passed the fridge with my fuzzy ultrasound photo taped to its silver face.

My entire body shivered as I pushed open the swinging door. No matter how hard I closed my eyes, I couldn't unsee Dusty and Mike going at it in the bathroom.

The door chimed and I jumped, smacking a hand over my heart as my eyes popped open.

Rush came inside with a blast of cold, November air. "Hey."

Now my heart was racing for an entirely different reason.

He looked perfect in a pair of faded jeans that molded around his thick thighs. His white, long-sleeved thermal was covered by a tan Carhartt coat that rested on broad shoulders. His hair was trapped beneath a faded navy Wildcats hat that seemed to accentuate that chiseled jaw.

He'd been gone for hours, and I'd missed him.

"What are you doing here?" In Mission. Here, at Dolly's. Why was he with me?

He stomped the snow off his boots and shrugged. "Drove

to the ranch. Hugged Mom. Spent an hour helping Dad. Realized I'd forgotten something at home."

"What?"

"You."

My heart. It was going to explode. I was going to die right here, in Dolly's Diner, because I didn't know what to do with all these . . . feelings.

Cry, apparently. That checked. Rush became a watery, blurry mess as I burst into tears.

"Sweets." His arms were around me in an instant, hauling me into the warmth of his chest and coat. It smelled like his cologne and laundry detergent and snow.

"Sorry." I sniffled, trying to suck it up. "Weird day."

"Want to make it weirder?"

"I don't think I can handle weirder."

He laughed and let me go.

It was after I wiped my eyes dry that I realized through the glass I couldn't see the street. Because parked alongside Dolly's was a massive RV. The same camper I'd seen this summer. "There's a camper attached to your truck."

"You're very observant." Rush slid an arm around my shoulders and walked me toward the nearest window. "Had an idea. Want to go camping?"

"It's winter."

"So? We'll stay inside."

Trapped in a camper with Rush. It was equally terrifying and enticing. "What about Thanksgiving?"

"You don't even like turkey."

No. No, I didn't. How did he know that? Probably because he'd been paying attention. "Camping. I've only ever been camping once."

"Yeah? How was it?"

"I got a flat tire and met this guy who changed it for me."

"Sounds like a decent guy."

I looked up at him, beautiful brown eyes waiting. "More than decent."

"So does that mean I can take you camping?"

I smiled. "If you must."

CHAPTER TWENTY-THREE

RUSH

F aye and I each smacked a card from our respective stacks onto the camper's table. Her ten beat my three, so she pulled both into her growing pile.

"I used to play this with Gloria when she was little," she said, putting another card down in our game of war. "I'd stack her deck with aces so she'd eventually win. Maybe that was my mistake. I protected her from losing too often."

"Maybe," I murmured. Or maybe Gloria's problem was that she was a brat who thought she could manipulate Faye.

It had been a few hours since she'd told me about the Thanksgiving fiasco, and I was still pissed. Probably would be for a while. Hopefully the anger would fizzle before I saw Gloria again. If not, she'd be receiving a lecture on how to treat her sister.

"You're mad at her," Faye said.

"Yep."

"I'm kind of mad at her too."

I gave her a sad smile, then turned over another card. Five. She beat it with a king.

After she swept them into her stack, she turned toward the window, staring out over the dark, snow-covered yard.

Our yard.

I hadn't wanted to risk a trip to the mountains where we could get stuck in the snow. Plus it was cold, not exactly great camping weather. So we'd gone camping in the driveway. If Faye decided it wasn't her thing, we could just go inside the house.

"How will the camper get back to your parents?" she asked.

"They're coming to our playoff game next weekend. They'll pick it up then."

"Ah." She nodded. "Playoffs are, what, exactly?"

I grinned as she turned over another card, both of us idly playing as I explained the difference between preseason and regular season and post season.

"So this playoff game is a big deal then," she said.

I chuckled. "It's a big deal."

Making the playoffs was huge. None of us had really expected to make it so far this season with a new head coach. But we'd surpassed everyone's expectations and won the conference championship in a victory over the University of Montana Grizzlies.

"The playoffs are about as big of a deal as beating the Grizzlies."

"Ah. Even I know beating the Griz is important."

During my time as a Wildcat player, we'd never lost that rivalry game. Whatever funk I'd been in had passed after that loss in Idaho. Clearing the air with Faye had cleared my head. Not that I'd ever admit that to Maverick.

But it wasn't just me who'd refocused. The whole team

and all of our coaches had shown up to the next practice with a newfound drive. No more losing. Especially to the Grizzlies. And I wanted to take us as far into the playoffs as we could make it.

"I hate the Grizzlies," I said.

"Hate? That's a strong word."

"Strong but true."

She hummed. "What if Squish wants to go to U of M someday?"

"Don't even put that into the universe."

She laughed and pretended to zip her lips closed.

That laugh was music to my ears. It was better than a stadium full of cheering fans. Better than the cannons that went off whenever the Wildcats scored a touchdown. Better than my name chanted over and over and over again in a parade.

"I like your laugh. I don't get to hear it enough."

Her cheeks flushed as she tucked a lock of hair behind her ear. "Thanks for this. Camping in the driveway. I needed it."

"Welcome." I flipped over a card. Queen. Hers was an ace. "I'm giving up. You win."

She laughed again as she collected the cards and organized them in a deck. "I never win. I'll take it."

It was only a joke, her never winning. But it was true, wasn't it?

Faye didn't win often enough.

Football had been my life for so long, winning had been such a priority and goal. I'd been lucky too. I won more often than not. If I was being honest with myself, I took most victories for granted. Some were hard-earned but most came easy.

Faye needed more wins.

Maybe I could help her with that.

Maybe if Faye and I stuck together, we could do this. All of it. We could have this baby and still chase our dreams.

We'd both win.

I relaxed into my seat, and since my legs were too long for this table, our knees knocked. They'd been touching on and off all day, and not once had Faye shied away.

"Do you have it?" she asked. "The envelope?"

"Yes."

Since her ultrasound, for weeks, I'd been carrying an unopened envelope in my pocket. It was wrinkled and folded in quarters, but I'd taken it with me everywhere in case Faye wanted to open it up. I'd even brought it to the camper.

She worried her bottom lip between her teeth. "Do you think we should open it?"

"Up to you."

It was killing me to know that the answer was in my pocket. That I'd had it with me for weeks. I was dying to know if we were having a boy or a girl. But I wanted Faye to make the call. If she decided to wait until Squish was born, then I'd wait.

"I think I want to know," she said.

I shifted in my seat, fishing it out of my pocket to lay on the table. "Do you want to open it?"

She shook her head. "You do it."

"Are you sure?"

"Yes?"

I chuckled. "Faye."

"Do it. Before I change my mind." She covered her face with her hands.

I wanted to find out so badly I wasn't going to give her the chance to change her mind. I tore into the envelope and tugged out the letter.

All the words blurred but one.

Boy.

"It's a boy."

Her hands dropped from her face to her belly. "A boy."

"A boy."

We stared at each other, both letting it sink in. Then a smile stretched across her face, a smile so beautiful I forgot how to breathe. "I guess we can start thinking of names."

I doubted my son would enjoy being called Squish in high school.

"How about Tyler?" The moment I said it I knew it was wrong. It didn't feel right.

Given the scrunch of her nose, it didn't to Faye either. "No. Mathias?"

"There's a Mathias on the team, and he's a douche. Cody?"

"No. Arlo," she suggested.

"Henry?"

"Meh. Owen."

At some point, we'd land on one that we both liked, right? Or at some point, we were going to run out of options.

We volleyed names back and forth for a few minutes until my phone dinged from the counter.

"Dinner." I slid out of my seat and held out a hand, helping Faye to her feet. Then we made the short trek from the camper to the house, our breaths billowing in the frozen air until we were inside, where it smelled like roasted chicken and potatoes and vegetables.

Other than a trip this morning to the grocery store to

pick up food, the camper had been our hangout spot. Normally on Thanksgiving, Dad and I would watch a football game or two, but I had no desire to turn on the TV. Instead, Faye and I had played games in the camper and when she'd started yawning, I'd sent her to the bedroom for a nap while I'd wasted an hour on my phone.

The only time we'd spent inside the house had been after the store, when we'd prepped the chicken and potatoes for the oven.

Spending a day with Faye had been as natural as breathing. I kept waiting for an awkward silence or for her to disappear to her room. But she hadn't once looked at the camper's door like she was ready to escape.

It was like hanging out with a friend.

If she thought of me as a friend? Well, that would suck. A lot.

She hadn't made a move to kiss me in the past month. I assumed it was because she wanted to take things slow. But did she see me as a friend?

No. Hell no.

I was not settling for friendship. Two people with this kind of chemistry were not just friends.

Faye took oven mitts out of a drawer, glancing at me as she opened the oven. "What's wrong?"

"We're not friends."

"Huh?" Her forehead furrowed, but the hot air escaping from the oven must have blasted her in the face because she frowned and took out the roasting pan, setting it on the stovetop. Then she tore off the oven mitts and faced me with hurt in those caramel eyes. "We're not friends?"

"No, we are friends. We're more than friends. We're roommates. We've got Squish. We have . . ."

A future.

We had a future.

It wasn't crystal clear. There were still big chunks missing from what tomorrow looked like. And on the edges, it was fuzzy at best. But there was one thing in focus.

Faye.

She was there, no matter what.

I wanted more days like this, again and again. If I did get drafted, if I went into the NFL, there was no way I could leave Faye behind in Mission.

"Would you go with me?" I asked.

"Go where? To a football game?"

"No. Go to wherever I get drafted. If I get drafted."

"Oh." Her eyebrows came together as she looked to the roasting pan. "I, um . . ."

Was she going to say no? She was going to say no. I could see it on her face. She was trying to find a way to let me down gently.

Had I read too much into us? Had I taken that kiss, the electricity, as something serious? Was this one-sided?

Fuck. My stomach dropped.

"Don't worry about it." I waved it off and went to the fridge, using the door as a barricade so she wouldn't see me grit my teeth.

"Rush," she said. "I didn't—"

"It's all right, Faye. That's a big ask for you to just wait around to see what happens. I get it."

"That's not—"

"Forget I asked."

"Would you listen to me?" She pushed the door, so hard the tray of condiments in the door almost hit me in the temple before I dodged out of the way. "I can't answer that question right now. I'm not going to make you a promise I can't guarantee I'll keep."

That was fair. And real. It just wasn't what I wanted to hear.

Because it meant she was still wary. She still had that bear spray. She still wasn't in this, not completely.

Damn, it was a blow. I'd never wanted a woman who might not want me back. It was sobering. Especially because I'd never wanted someone the way I wanted Faye.

"You're right." My shoulders sagged, my frame deflating on a loud exhale. "I don't know if I'll even go to the draft. I don't know why I'm even thinking that far ahead right now."

"You're a planner."

"Yeah, I am."

"I like making plans. But they usually fall apart."

Like moving out of her ex's place when she had money saved. Like dinner with her sister for Thanksgiving. Like going to graduate school.

Faye closed the distance between us, tilting up her face as I tilted down mine.

God, she was beautiful. Her ex was such an idiot. He'd had this beauty in his life, and he'd cheated on her. Dumb fuck. But at least he'd had her. I sure as hell couldn't call her mine.

"Michael," she said.

It was a truce. A name suggestion to keep us from getting into a fight on Thanksgiving.

I shook my head. "Tanner."

"Tommy."

"Eugene."

She scrunched up her nose. "Hard no."

I lifted a hand, about to brush the hair at her temples

with my fingertips. But her eyes clocked the movement, and I couldn't tell if it was wariness in her gaze or panic.

My arm crashed into my side. I was about to step away, to busy myself with setting places at the table, when her hand shot out toward my side, latching onto the fabric of my shirt.

She balled it into her fist and held tight. "Rush. We're not friends."

The air rushed from my lungs. "Thank fuck."

"You are petrifying," she whispered.

"I'm just me." I lifted the same arm, and this time I didn't stop until my fingers were in her hair.

"Just you?" She let out a dry laugh. "Rush Ramsey. Quarterback of the Wildcats football team. Smart. Funny. Gorgeous. Every girl's dream. Put yourself in my shoes. It's terrifying."

"Is that why you haven't kissed me? Because you're scared?"

She nodded. "I never want you to feel stuck with me. I never want you to feel trapped. If you go to the NFL, you'll have so many—"

"Don't say options."

She gave me a sad smile. "You're out of my league, Rush."

My league? Did she not think she was good enough?

All this time, I'd been trying to prove myself to her. To prove that I was loyal, despite my past mistakes. Prove that I would be around for her to lean on. But her mother, her ex and her epic losing streak really had done a number on her confidence.

"There is no league," I said.

"We both know that's not the type of world we live in. I

don't want to be the woman on the big screen and have spectators wonder what the hell you're doing with me."

It was the most raw, real confession I'd ever heard. It hit so hard that it rocked me on my heels. Not because it was right. Because she was so fucking wrong.

"If there wasn't a Squish, I would want you."

"Rush—"

"Just listen for a minute, okay?" I dropped my fingers from her hair to her mouth. "I don't know how to make you see what I see. I don't know how to convince you that you're the most beautiful, snarky, smart, caring, spitfire of a woman I've ever met."

Not a single one of those words sank in. I could practically see them bounce off her ears.

Practice. We needed practice. Until those words were as second nature to her as the plays in my playbook.

Dad had always taught me with baseball analogies. Faye was going to get football parallels instead.

"The NFL draft is all about picks. You're my pick."

All she had to do was pick me back.

Her eyes searched mine, maybe for permission. She wasn't used to doing anything for herself, was she? She'd bend over backward to give her sister cash or wait tables for Dusty or let me chase my dreams while she stayed behind.

She wrapped her hand around my wrist, tugging my fingers free from her lips. She swallowed hard.

Then she lifted up on her toes.

It was only an inch, but I got the message.

I bent, about to crush my mouth to hers.

Except the front door flew open and Maverick stormed inside.

Faye lowered to her heels and let go of my shirt.

Well, fuck. I dragged a hand over my face, leaving my palm over my mouth so I wouldn't scream. So close. And so far away. One step forward, two back.

Mav slammed the front door so hard Faye jumped.

"Maverick," I barked.

"Don't." He held up a hand as he marched through the house. He was supposed to be at his parents' place all weekend. The only reason he'd come here was if something bad had happened.

"What's wrong?" I asked.

"My mom has cancer." He dropped that bomb as he breezed past the kitchen, not sparing me or Faye a glance. Then he slammed the door to his bedroom too.

Faye gasped.

"Oh shit." I raked a hand through my hair.

His mom, Meredith, was one of the nicest people I'd ever met. He'd mentioned a while ago that she hadn't been feeling well, but I'd assumed it was just a cold or flu bug. Cancer?

"You should go check on him," Faye said.

"Yeah. Don't wait on me to eat."

"Okay."

So much for Thanksgiving.

By the time I left Maverick's room, hours had passed. He'd told me all about Meredith's diagnosis, that she wasn't just sick, but dying. And for the first time in my life, I'd watched my best friend cry.

I walked through the spotless kitchen and opened the fridge, finding the leftovers inside. Except my appetite was gone, so I shut off the lights and trudged upstairs.

Faye's room was dark too, so I went to my own and dug out my phone.

"Hey," Mom answered with a yawn on the third ring. "Everything okay?"

"I love you."

"Aww. I love you too. Happy Thanksgiving."

I swallowed past the lump in my throat. "Happy Thanksgiving."

CHAPTER TWENTY-FOUR

FAYE

In the past week, I'd lost Rush to football.

It was both fascinating and frustrating to watch an athlete's life from such a close vantage point.

Football had been a huge part of his routine before the playoffs, but now? Since Thanksgiving, he'd been utterly consumed.

I'd been desperate to talk to him, to pick up where we'd left off in the kitchen, but he'd been so busy that I hadn't pushed. He had plenty to worry about at the moment.

Every waking moment of his life seemed to be taken, either with football, class or mandatory study time at the fieldhouse.

Next week was dead week on campus as everyone crammed for finals, Rush included.

He left the house before I woke up each morning, and when I came home from the diner after my shifts, he'd already be asleep. Last night, I'd poked my head inside his room to see him snoring on top of his covers, still dressed in a hoodie and jeans. So I'd slipped a *good luck tomorrow* note under his door and left him to rest.

I'd spent a week observing from afar.

Until today.

The parking lots outside both the stadium and fieldhouse were full, and rather than spend an hour hunting for something close, I'd parked the Explorer by Williams Hall and hiked across campus for today's game. Even bundled in my thickest coat, hat and gloves, the cold was a shock, but the nervous energy was keeping me warm.

The lot that stretched from the fieldhouse to the stadium was chaos. Tents had been set up behind tailgates. Some people had brought in small campers, complete with portable firepits and barbecues. The scents of smoke and grilled meat filled the air.

A shirtless man wearing an enormous foam cowboy hat guzzled a beer, the liquid dribbling from the corners of his mouth and down his hairy belly. When it was gone, he crushed the can in a fist and yelled, "Go Big Blue!"

The other guys in his group cheered, and someone threw him another beer.

"Let's fucking go!" He popped the top and chugged.

I giggled and kept on walking. The crowd grew thicker and thicker as I approached the stadium until I had to weave past people to get to the entrance.

Was it like this all the time? Excitement and anticipation buzzed in the air like sparks.

Rush didn't know I was coming to today's game. He didn't know that I'd gotten up at five o'clock yesterday morning to come to campus and wait in line to get a student ticket—they'd sold out in ten minutes, and I'd been far from the first person in line.

He would have insisted on getting me a ticket himself. Maybe seating me beside his parents. It wasn't that I didn't want to see Ryan and Macy, but this was my first Wildcats football game. Maybe it was silly or sentimental, but today, I didn't want to be Rush Ramsey's roommate or friend or the woman having his child.

I wanted to be a student, just a normal student, here to cheer on her school's team in the freezing cold.

With my ticket clutched in my gloved hand, I shuffled into line with the other fans slowly filing into the stadium. I breezed through the metal detector and let the attendant scan my ticket. Then I wandered past the rows of concession booths below the stands.

I'd stuffed a stack of flyers in my pocket this morning, today's printed on electric-blue paper with the headline filling most of the half-page sheets.

SAVE DOLLY'S DINER

It was a new tactic, appealing to the sympathetic. Okay, so maybe it was over the top, but at this point, I was willing to try anything to lure customers to the diner.

Outside of the concession booths were tables with napkin dispensers and industrial ketchup and mustard pumps. I divided my stack and left piles on various tables until they were gone. Then I scanned the signs posted above the ramps leading outside and followed them toward my seat.

The student section was already packed, and clearly no one sat where they were assigned, but I managed to squeeze into an end seat on a bleacher five steps up from the railing on the front row.

People rushed around the sidelines on the field. Some wore orange vests. Others must be employees from the athletics department. And then there were the cameramen toting their equipment into position to record and capture the game.

The scoreboard flashed with different advertisements. Music blared from the stadium's sound system. It had been energetic in the parking lot, but by the time all of the seats were filled, this place was electric.

"Wow." I couldn't stop my smile.

"What?" the guy next to me asked, practically shouting over the noise.

"Nothing." I waved it off.

The stadium was huge from the outside, but the interior was bigger than I'd expected. Racks of massive lights stood on poles towering above the highest row of bleachers. The afternoon sun glinted off the windows of the skyboxes that overlooked the field. More and more fans were filtering in, filling up the empty spaces.

It was a sea of royal blue and silver, even with people wearing winter gear. I'd never been so grateful that my coat was gray. Not an intentional purchase, but at least I wouldn't stick out.

The only football game I'd ever been to had been in high school my freshman year. I'd gone with a few friends to watch the game, and afterward, we'd all decided to try out for the cheerleading team.

I'd mentioned it to Mom the next morning. She'd laughed in my face and told me I'd make a horrible cheerleader.

I'd skipped the tryouts. My friends had all been picked for the team, and then they'd stopped being my friends after that.

Was I a cheerleader? Probably not. I didn't smile enough

to be cheery. I wasn't loud or boisterous. Mom hadn't necessarily been wrong, she'd just been a bitch about the delivery.

Still, as I watched the Wildcat cheerleaders on the sidelines, clapping and laughing, a pang of envy twisted my side.

Who would I have become if I hadn't taken so much of my mother's criticisms to heart?

Maybe it was time to find out. Maybe it was time to stop believing I wasn't good enough.

The draft is all about picks. You're my pick.

Rush's words had played in my mind countless times this week.

It felt selfish to pick him. But I was going to all the same.

He was my pick.

Rush and Squish.

A flutter in my belly brought a smile to my lips. The baby had started moving a few days ago. It was slight, the feeling like bubbles in my tummy, but after an hour on Google, I'd learned all about *quickening*.

Soon, Rush would be able to feel it too.

More and more people arrived, fitting themselves into every available space until the clock on the enormous scoreboard ticked down to five minutes. My breath billowed in white puffs but the chill was tempered by the sea of warm bodies. The sun was a bright, white orb in the clear, blue sky.

I wiggled my toes in my boots, hoping the three pairs of socks I'd worn today would work. Most of the snow had been shoveled off the actual bench seats, but there was a layer of trampled ice beneath my soles.

The music cut out and the announcer's voice boomed through the sound system. "Welcome, Wildcats! It's a beautiful day for Treasure State football."

The crowd erupted, the noise deafening. It swallowed

my laugh. A new song started to play, the beat a low, steady thrum. Everyone around me started clapping and stomping to the rhythm.

The announcer kept talking, introducing the opposing team as they jogged onto their sideline. Then all attention turned to the tunnel across the field. A gleam of silver helmets came first as a line of players, arms linked, emerged.

Yards and yards separated us, but I knew the man in the center without seeing his face. I knew that walk, those shoulders, that stride.

Rush.

The camera zeroed in on him, projecting him to the big screen. Through the face mask, he stared out at the field, his expression hard and focused.

My heart skipped.

It was the same way he looked when I watched his games on television. He was nothing but steely determination. He was here to win, at all costs. It was intimidating and powerful and so freaking sexy.

My heart rate spiked, my pulse thundered.

Mine. That man was mine.

All eyes were glued on Rush. He commanded the attention of thousands of people as he walked to the sideline with the entire Wildcat team marching in formation at his back.

He owned this stadium.

And he was mine.

I was out of place in this mob of football fans. I was freeloading off Rush's insistence to help. I wasn't sure where exactly I belonged or what my future entailed.

But I did know exactly what I *wanted.*

Wants were risky. I wasn't used to letting myself want. But I wanted Rush enough to try.

My heart felt two sizes too big as the clock kept ticking down. Two minutes. One minute. It was wild to be this nervous for a game I wasn't playing in, but the emotions swelled so big I almost couldn't breathe. With only thirty seconds left until it started, I closed my eyes and tipped my head to the sky, letting the sunshine warm my face.

For the first time in my life, I was exactly where I was supposed to be.

The first quarter of the game was a blur. My football crash course from Mike helped some, but I still wasn't sure when to cheer and when to rage at a bad call from the referees, so I waited until the people around me reacted before I joined in with the same.

When Rush threw a touchdown pass, I screamed so loud my voice cracked.

He was in his element. He was larger than life. He threw the ball with precision, and when he tucked it beneath an arm to run it himself, he was almost unstoppable. He was a force.

The opposing team didn't stand a chance.

No matter what else happened on the field, I couldn't tear my eyes away from Rush.

He hadn't added the long sleeves beneath his jersey and pads like most of the other players. The roped muscle in his arms was on display every time the camera swung his direction. And the pants, oh my God, the pants. They accentuated the bulk of his thighs and the perfect curve of his ass.

The sweat at my temples and spine had nothing to do with my layers. There was a coil in my lower belly, twisting tighter and tighter with every play, every yard gained. By halftime, the Wildcats were ahead by fourteen points. By the end of the third quarter, twenty-one.

"We're going to fucking *winnnnn!*" The guy next to me pumped his arms back and forth like he was running in place, his entire body radiating the thrill. He cupped both hands to his mouth and screamed, "Rush Ramsey for President!"

Everyone around us laughed, and the people seated in the rows below us all turned.

There was a woman, a very beautiful woman, two rows below with dark hair trapped beneath a Wildcats beanie. The smile on her face dropped at the same time as mine.

Halsey.

We stared at each other for a long moment. She looked as stunned to see me as I was to see her. I'd been so focused on the game, on Rush, I hadn't spent much time looking around the student section.

Her shock faded before mine. Her eyes narrowed. Her nostrils flared. The girl beside her followed Halsey's line of vision, and when she spotted me, she sneered. When the friend leaned in to say something into Halsey's ear, there was no mistaking the word.

Slut.

It hurt more than I'd ever admit. No matter how much time passed, Halsey, her friends, would always think of me as a slut. A whore.

And there was nothing I could do but live with it.

Something happened on the field, a play I missed. When my eyes flicked back to the game, they were blurry with tears.

Now that I'd seen her, I couldn't stop from noticing every move Halsey made. She and her friends kept speaking in each other's ears. They'd glance back at me, standing alone, and snicker.

How many insults would I have to survive to have a thicker skin? Would it always hurt?

What would it take for people to just let me be? To let me live my life? I wasn't hurting anyone by breathing. I was just standing here.

Why did my very existence seem to cause so much anger for people?

The burn in my throat was unbearable as I kept blinking the tears away, doing my best to watch Rush on the field. To catch one more play.

He moved with such grace and agility. He was born to be out there, holding that ball. It was breathtaking. He launched it through the air, sending it flying with a perfect spin, into the arms of an open receiver. Erik.

He caught it and raced to the end zone for another Wildcat touchdown.

I let the cheers sink in deep, the chant for *Rush, Rush, Rush* soak into my bones. Maybe Squish could hear these people celebrating his father.

"Good game, Rush," I whispered, then slipped away, up the stairs and out the nearest exit.

I missed the end of my first Wildcats football game.

CHAPTER TWENTY-FIVE

RUSH

"Where are you going?" I asked Maverick because I doubted it was home.

He grinned as he walked to his truck, hitting the unlock button on the fob so the taillights flashed. "I met a girl at the bookstore yesterday. She gave me her number. Think I'll go to her place for a while."

As expected. He had a hookup preplanned.

"Have a good time." I waved and veered toward my Yukon.

He wagged his eyebrows. "That's the idea."

Since Thanksgiving, Maverick had yet to spend a night in his own bed. Even last night, when we'd been under curfew orders from the coaches to get some rest and not fuck around, he'd, well . . . fucked around. It was his way of escaping the shit going on with his mom. As far as I knew, he hadn't talked to her in over a week.

Considering Maverick was as tight with his parents as I was with mine, that was a long damn time to go without a phone call. Sooner rather than later, he'd have to face reality.

And sooner rather than later, he'd have to realize he couldn't waste a minute with Meredith.

But for now, he needed football and meaningless sex as a distraction. I'd save my lecture for later.

At least we'd won today. I wasn't sure how he'd react to a loss.

Fuck, it felt good to win. It was a high like no other. Adrenaline coursed through my veins. My heart still raced, even hours after the game. The whole team had been jittery during the postgame meeting. Most of the guys, like Maverick, had hurried through showers in the locker room so they could leave and burn off that excess energy with sex.

Since the only woman I wanted was Faye, that wasn't an option for me. Until she was ready, *if* she was ever ready, my fist was going to have to suffice like it had all season.

The sun had nearly set and the streetlights illuminated the roads as I drove through town toward an empty house.

My parents had stopped by after the game to say congratulations, but they hadn't wanted to wait around for dinner. There was a winter storm blowing in, so they'd loaded up the camper from my driveway and headed home to the ranch.

Faye would still be working at the diner. Part of me wanted to go to Dolly's, but since Thanksgiving, I hadn't spent much time with Faye.

I'd said what I'd needed to say.

I picked her. I wanted her.

The ball was hers. She had to make the next play.

The lights were on at home, both in the living room and upstairs in Faye's room. Her Explorer was parked on the street. Guess she hadn't worked late tonight. Maybe Dusty had sent her home in anticipation of the storm.

I took the spot in the driveway where the camper had been, a rectangle clear from the snow that had fallen earlier in the week. With my duffel slung over a shoulder, I made my way inside. It smelled like green apples and soap.

I flipped the lock on the door and shut off the lights in the living room before I hauled my stuff upstairs. A sliver of light escaped from beneath her door.

Her closed door.

I turned toward my room, about to go inside and crash, but then came the clunk of a handle turning and the swish of her door opening.

"Rush?"

I glanced back but refused to move my feet. "Hey."

"Hi." She stepped into the hallway, walking closer. "Good game."

"Thanks."

Her face was clean and fresh, the sprinkling of freckles across her nose on full display. Her hair was piled in a mess on top of her head. She looked beautiful with makeup and her long, sleek hair left down. But this was my favorite version of Faye.

I loved those freckles.

"It was fun to watch. Even if it was freezing."

Wait. My bag slipped off my shoulder as I spun to face her. "You came to the game?"

"Yeah." She gave me a sweet smile and shrugged. "I've never been to a game before. Thought I should do that before I graduate."

Well, damn.

She'd left the house early yesterday morning, but I hadn't thought much about it. Figured she was just heading to campus to get a jump start on studying, with finals coming up. But she must have gone to wait in line for tickets.

"I would have gotten you a ticket."

"It's okay."

"Is it the money? We get a few tickets for free. I wouldn't have had to pay."

"No, I just—"

"Didn't want me to know you were coming."

She blinked. "What?"

"Why?" Why hadn't she told me about the game? Why wouldn't she let me in? I would have looked for her in the stands. I could have shared today with her, even in some small way. Our victory would have been so much sweeter if I could have shared it with her.

Why would she cut me out? When would she stop putting this distance between us?

Did she not feel this pull? If she did, how could she be so strong to fight it? When she was in the room, every cell in my body screamed to get closer. The distance? It was killing me slowly.

"I wish I had known." I scrubbed both hands over my face. "It's been a long day. I think I'm going to crash."

"Rush—"

"Night, Faye." I snatched the bag off the floor and tossed it into my room, then followed it inside, kicking the door shut behind me. Then I walked to the bed and fell face down on the mattress. "Fuck."

She had me so keyed up that I couldn't even be polite.

I balled my hands into fists, slamming them into the bedding beside my ears. Then I sat up, about to retreat to the bathroom, when a knock came.

On a sigh, I climbed out of bed and opened the door.

Faye stood in the hallway, her shoulders pinned with her arms clasped behind her back. Poised and ready for a fight. Her rigid posture pulled the material of her tee taut across her belly.

She was the most stunning creature on this earth. And she was carrying my son.

"I should have locked you in my room that night so you couldn't sneak out," I said. "I should have tracked you down the next morning and brought you back."

Her eyes softened.

"I had this plan." The confession came on an exhale and my shoulders slumped. "It was all planned. One more season with the Wildcats. Play smart. Don't get injured. But play to win. Play hard. If I got drafted, no matter the round, no matter the team, give professional football a shot. If I didn't make it, then I'd find a job coaching. But football was my future."

"It can still be your future."

"Damn straight." My future didn't need to change. I'd been spinning my mental wheels for months, trying to find some traction. Turns out, it wasn't about a new direction. It was about making room in my plan for Faye. "Here's how this thing is going to go."

Her eyebrows arched as I crossed my arms over my chest.

"I don't want to take control away from you, Faye. The last thing I want is for you to feel trapped. But I'm hoping, if you're with me, if we do this together, that it's not my plan anymore. It's ours. It's *us*."

"Rush—"

I held up a hand. "Don't say anything yet. I'm not done."

She had to know it all, every detail. She needed to go into

this decision eyes wide open. She had to know the play, otherwise we'd fumble.

"We make it through this next year. I've got another season and two semesters of school. If you don't want to live in this house, we'll move. If you want to stay home with Squish for a year, then you can. If you want to keep working, we'll figure it out. If you want to jump into grad school, that's fine. Whatever you want, I'm here. One more year in Mission. Then we go."

She opened her mouth, but I wasn't done yet.

"If I don't get drafted, then we'll choose a school you want, and I'll find a coaching job, either at a college or high school. I'd like my parents to know Squish so if we can stick to the western half of the country, that would be great. And if I do get drafted, every city with a professional team will have a decent university, so we can get you into a speech pathology program. Ideally, I'd play for three to seven years. That should be enough time for you to get your master's. Then you pick where we land for good once I retire."

There. That was the whole plan. It was solid. It was a way for us both to chase dreams. Still, I sounded surer about it than I felt. My heart pounded, and I was breathless.

If she hated it, if she said no, I wasn't quite sure how I'd recover.

"Are you done now?" she asked.

"Yes."

"Good." She shifted, unclasping her hands from behind her back. And when she brought them forward, they weren't empty.

Clutched in a fist was a silver canister.

Her bear spray.

She looked at it, turning it sideways. "I came to the game

today because I wanted to see what it would have been like if I was just me, just another student watching the hottest guy on campus play a football game. I wanted to have that experience since so much of this year has been anything but normal."

"Oh." Well, damn. That made sense. And now I felt like an idiot for spewing my plan.

"I realized something in the fourth quarter," she said. "I'm not just me. I'm not just another student."

"Not to me."

She stared at the can for another moment, then she held it out between us. "I pick you too."

My heart left my chest. Gone. It floated past that can of bear spray and into her arms. Because it wasn't mine anymore.

It belonged to Faye.

This was what it felt like to fall in love, wasn't it? Misery and bliss.

She took a step forward, letting her arm drop to her side and the can slip from her grasp. It landed on the carpet with a muffled thud. Then she lifted on her toes as she pressed a hand over my chest, fisting my quarter zip to pull me closer.

She wasn't quite tall enough to reach my mouth, so I bent, hovering slightly out of reach. Every time she came close to a kiss, I pulled away.

"Rush." She tugged harder on my shirt. "Stop playing."

"Seems only fitting I torture you for a minute. You've been putting me through hell for months." I reached for the tie in her hair, pulling it loose until her hair tumbled down her shoulders. Then I threaded my fingers through the soft strands, leaning closer until our noses touched. "Do you have any idea how much I think about you?"

"More than football?"

"More than football."

"Good." She smiled. It was a smile so bright it lit up her entire face, like the white-gold rays of a Montana sunrise.

This time, when she tugged, I didn't fight back. I waited until her lips brushed mine, holding still while she initiated the kiss.

It was sweet and light. Knowing Faye, it was probably a test to see how long I could hold out.

I growled.

She giggled.

"Can I kiss you now?"

"If you must."

I sealed my lips over hers, my arms banding around her back as I lifted her off her feet.

Her tongue instantly tangled with mine, and *fuck*, she tasted good. Like honey and mint. A moan escaped her throat. Or maybe it came from mine.

We sank into each other, kissing without restraint or hesitation. Her arms looped around my shoulders and her fingers dove into my hair. She hooked one leg around my hip as I kicked that fucking bear spray into the hallway.

It clattered against a baseboard, ricocheting toward the stairs.

Good fucking riddance.

CHAPTER TWENTY-SIX

FAYE

Kissing Rush was like riding a roller coaster. Every time I felt steady he'd do something that made my stomach dip. The moment he carried me across the threshold and kicked the door shut, he spun me through his room. Two turns, then we were falling sideways into his bed.

We crashed into each other, tangling arms and legs and tongues. No matter how long I kissed him, it wasn't enough. I licked every corner of his mouth as he plundered mine.

My skin was on fire. The throb in my core was a punishing beat. I hooked a leg around his bulky thigh and ground against him, desperate for some friction.

Months and months and months of this push and pull with Rush. It was inevitable that we'd end up here, wasn't it? No matter how hard we'd resisted—*I'd* resisted—it had been futile. There was no extinguishing the fire between us. Every touch, every shift of his hands, and I melted.

He nipped at my bottom lip before slanting his mouth at a different angle. The slow slide of his tongue made me whimper. Then came the flutter that made my entire body tremble.

Damn, this man could kiss. If he kept it up, I might come from a kiss alone.

Rush stole his mouth away, leaning back to stare down at me with darkened eyes. His Adam's apple bobbed as he swallowed.

"What?" My voice was breathy and desperate.

"There's no going back from this. You're in my bed. From here on out. Be sure."

I'd been sure since the moment I'd left that football game. Since I'd come home and dug that can of bear spray out of my closet.

People like Halsey and her friends would always think Rush could do better than me. They'd always believe the only reason we were together was because of the baby.

I didn't care, not anymore. I was tired of fighting.

Rush was mine. Maybe we wouldn't have gotten here if I hadn't been pregnant. Or maybe we would have. Maybe that wild summer night had always been the beginning of us.

I cupped his jaw with my hand. "I'm sure."

He dropped his forehead to mine. "This is safe? For Squish?"

Rush couldn't make my last checkup appointment. It was the only doctor's visit he'd missed so far. It had been strange to be in the exam room without him. To stare at the empty chair where he'd sit quietly, spinning his hat back and forth, waiting until the doctor would let us listen to the baby's heartbeat.

Maybe it was because Rush had been gone that I'd had the courage to ask the doctor about sex. Not that I'd expected this to happen but since that kiss, maybe since the beginning, a part of me had hoped.

"Yes, it's safe."

He leaned away, a glint in those chocolate eyes. His hand lifted, starting at my temple and trailing along the line of my face to my chin. Tingles broke across my skin as he traced the column of my throat, his fingertip pressing into my pulse before dipping to my collarbone.

The tee I'd worn for bed was threadbare and thin. I hadn't bothered with a bra. It might as well have been nothing for the way his touch penetrated the fabric.

He trailed lower, over my heart and then to my breast. He circled my nipple three times before rolling it between his finger and thumb.

"Rush," I hissed, arching against him. The friction with the cotton of my shirt and the pinch of his fingers was delicious torment. I rocked my core against his leg, grinding against that rock-hard muscle.

"I've dreamed about these nipples." He bent and latched his mouth over my breast, sucking through the shirt.

"More." My eyes fluttered closed as I threaded my fingers into his hair. It was longer than it had been this summer. Long enough that it curled beneath the brim of his baseball hats.

When he sucked harder, I tugged at the strands, keeping him trapped against me.

His hand moved lower, skating along my ribs to the sliver of skin where my shirt had ridden up.

He slipped beneath the hem, and this time, there was nothing but that wide, strong hand cupping me, squeezing and kneading my breast as his mouth moved to my other nipple.

Oh, God, I was going to come apart. My heart was beating too hard, like it was knocking against my sternum. My breaths were ragged pants and my head was spinning.

He lifted up onto an elbow and before I even knew what was happening, he whipped the shirt over my head, forcing my arms up until they brushed the headboard. With a flick of his wrist, my tee went flying over his shoulder to the floor. Then his mouth, hot and wet, was on a nipple, and I bit my lip to keep from crying out.

Lightning zinged across my skin. Desire pooled between my legs.

Had it been like this before? I wanted to say yes. Our night together this summer had been the best sex of my life. But this? Tonight? It felt a thousand times better. Every touch was ecstasy. My pulse rocketed higher, its rhythm vibrating through every bone, every fiber, every cell.

I could fly. I could conquer the world. This was what people must feel like when they were high. I was drunk on Rush and never wanted this feeling to stop.

The heat from his body seeped into mine, and I sank into the burn, letting it wash over me, head to toe.

"Fuck, I missed you," he said, his mouth trailing over my breast before he shifted lower. His tongue darted out, leaving a wet trail on my skin as he kissed a path to my navel.

I lifted my head off the pillow and opened my eyes, watching as his hands molded to the curve of my belly. The bump still wasn't much, but the reverence in his eyes made my heart tumble.

Rush hadn't touched my belly often up to this point. I had a feeling that was going to change.

He planted a kiss to the swell, then met my gaze and

smirked. Like he was proud of himself for getting me pregnant.

That kind of arrogance shouldn't have been hot.

But it was. So. Freaking. Hot.

"Rush," I murmured.

The smirk vanished as a different expression transformed his features. Raw, unbridled hunger. "Faye."

"Kiss me."

His eyes became molten pools as he shifted, hovering over me, careful to keep his weight to my side. He bent, his mouth almost capturing mine, but he hesitated. He was so close that his breath feathered across my cheek. He brought his hand to my jaw, holding it in place. Holding my eyes in place.

The world disappeared. This universe was ours alone.

"I pick you," he said.

My heart doubled, tripled, until it felt too big. "I pick you."

It was barely out of my mouth before his lips collided against mine. The tender moment was gone with a sweep of his tongue. The raging inferno returned with a vengeance, and damn it, why were we wearing so many clothes?

I grappled with the hem of his shirt as our tongues dueled, doing my best to haul it up over his chest. But Rush was too big and unless he moved, there was no budging him.

"Off," I panted into his mouth.

He growled, the vibration shooting straight to my core. Then he was gone, and with a quick jackknife, he was off the bed, reaching behind his nape to haul his quarter zip and T-shirt over his head.

Before his shirt had even joined mine on the floor he was reaching for the waistband of my sweats.

"Later, we'll go slow," he said. "But not tonight."

I shook my head, lifting off my hips so he could strip me bare.

Dim light seeped from the window, casting Rush's room in shadow. Did he leave the blinds open because he'd noticed I never closed mine? Whatever the reason, I was grateful for that light. It caressed the granite features of his gorgeous face. It let me see the ridges and valleys of his delicious abs.

Rush stared at me, naked on his bed, and it took everything I had to stay still. Not to cover my breasts or cross my legs as his gaze roved over every inch of my body. His chest heaved, his stomach flexing with every ragged breath. He pressed a hand to his heart, fingers splayed wide.

"Faye." He was awestruck.

I'd never felt more beautiful in my life.

Rush shook his head, like he still couldn't believe this was happening. I wasn't sure it was either.

He inhaled, that broad chest expanding, then he hooked his thumbs in his pants and shoved them to the floor.

His cock bobbed, hard and thick.

Now it was my turn to stare, mouth watering. I'd forgotten how big he was. How nervous I'd been this summer at the sight of him.

Rush fisted his shaft, giving his erection a few hard strokes before he planted a knee on the bed and crawled on top of me. His elbows bracketed my face as he hovered, his nose running the length of mine. "Kiss me."

A shiver raced down my spine at the command in his voice. I leaned up and brushed my mouth against his. My tongue darted out to lick his bottom lip.

His knee nudged my legs apart.

As I spread them wide, he settled into the cradle of my

hips. His arms flexed, that incredible strength keeping us close but holding all of his weight.

He kissed the corner of my mouth, reaching between us. He dragged the tip of his arousal through my slit.

My heart climbed into my throat as I waited. Every second was agony. My arms and legs began to tremble as he lined up at my entrance and thrust inside.

"Oh, God." My hands came to his shoulders, my fingers pressing into muscle that might as well have been steel. The stretch was pain and pleasure as I molded around him.

"Fuck." He gritted his teeth as he plunged deep. He buried his face in my hair and groaned, the sound pure bliss. "You feel so good, Faye."

"More." I dug into his back, my short nails probably leaving marks. "Move, Rush."

I needed him to move, to fuck me and satisfy this ache.

He latched his mouth onto my neck and sucked hard enough to leave a mark. Then he eased out and rocked inside once more, hitting that spot where I needed him most.

My inner walls fluttered. My limbs trembled. He set a steady rhythm, rolling his hips with every thrust. The sound of our bodies coming together mingled with my short breaths.

"It's too much." It wasn't enough.

I was unraveling, stroke after stroke. He pistoned his hips faster, his mouth claiming mine. He kissed me until I cried out, desperately trying to breathe as my orgasm barreled closer, stealing the air from my lungs.

The edge was coming too fast. Too hard. I was going to combust and we'd barely even started. Except it kept building, higher and higher. So high I was terrified of what it was going to do to me.

Over and over he brought us together, until the room seemed to tilt sideways. Gravity vanished, and I was floating.

I clawed at Rush's back, writhing beneath him. "Rush, I can't—"

"Just let go, sweets." He bent to kiss my ear. "Just let go. I've got you."

I whimpered, a sound unlike any I'd made before. I sucked in a breath. I closed my eyes.

And shattered.

My body was in pieces. I lost all control, my muscles no longer my own. There were stars in my eyes and fireworks in my chest. Tears streamed down my temples, dripping into my hair.

"Faye." Rush wiped them away, peppering my face with kisses as he never slowed, never stopped.

He held onto my body, worshipping me, until I stopped floating and returned to reality as someone different.

His.

"Mine," Rush murmured.

When I opened my eyes, his were waiting. "Mine too."

He kissed me, slow and long, his tongue matching the pace of his cock.

After an orgasm like that, I should have been a puddle. I should have been comatose. But as he worked in and out, his tongue fluttering in my mouth, my heart rate spiked. My core pulsed around his length.

Rush groaned, the sound disappearing down my throat. Then he broke away, his own breath choppy. His jaw clenched. "Again, Faye."

It probably should have been impossible after that first orgasm, but I let the sensation sweep over me like a wave.

This release didn't rattle my bones or blank my mind,

but it was powerful in a different way. It was a claiming, his body to mine, in perfect unison as we came together.

Rush let out a low moan as he planted deep, then poured inside me, his massive frame quaking until he was spent. He collapsed, rolling to the side and hauling me into his arms. His heart hammered as I desperately sucked in air, my nose pressed to his chest to breathe him in.

My head was spinning so fast I was dizzy. A good dizzy.

Rush kissed my forehead, then eased us apart before hauling up the blankets we'd managed to kick on the floor.

The last thing I wanted was to leave the warmth of his arms, but the bathroom was calling, so I gathered my clothes and slipped away. When I emerged, I glanced at my room.

The light had been on earlier.

It was dark now.

Rush was in the hallway, dressed in only a pair of fitted black boxer briefs.

He held out a hand.

And made sure that when I fell asleep, it was in his bed, not mine.

———

SLUT. *Slut. Slut.*

My eyes popped open.

A dream. It was only a dream.

Ugh. I stared into the dark room, letting the dream fade from my mind.

Maybe it was the hormones, but ever since I'd gotten pregnant, my dreams had been so real. In tonight's, I'd relived the football game, but instead of Halsey whispering the insult to her friend, she'd screamed it in my face. Then the crowd had started chanting *slut* instead of Rush's name.

I really hated his ex. Not only was that word stuck in my head, now there'd be no going back to sleep. I was fully awake. Freaking great.

Rush was passed out beside me, his face buried in a pillow with one arm draped over my hips to make sure I didn't escape.

I shifted, inching toward the edge of the bed. He didn't budge.

So I slid out from beneath him and tiptoed to the door, easing silently into the hall before going to my room.

I snagged a sweatshirt from the closet, pulling it on before climbing into bed to scroll aimlessly on my phone. Well, not aimlessly. I opened Instagram and, like a fool, went to Rush's profile. He hadn't posted anything in months. But I wasn't looking for his photos. I clicked on his followers and found her name in the list.

halseyray

She had five thousand followers. She even had the little blue check mark beside her name.

I had twenty-something followers. Granted, my account was private, and I hated posting pictures of myself, so most of mine were of Gloria or Dusty or the diner. Still, it was just another reminder that she was bright and shiny, while I was, well . . . me.

I scrolled through her feed, mostly finding selfies and photos with her friends. But there were a few videos with Rush. Wasn't it a rule or something to remove posts of your ex after a breakup?

He wasn't hers anymore.

Rush was mine.

I scowled at her face, wishing I could find a flaw. But she was as gorgeous on social media as she was in real life. Did her five thousand followers know that she was a mean girl?

Was she even a mean girl?

She'd been in love with Rush, and he'd broken it off. Then she'd found out I was pregnant, and if I was in her position, I'd probably consider me a slut too.

It was hard to hate someone when you could empathize with their feelings.

I lay down on my pillow, curling my legs in as I slipped under the covers. Then I kept scrolling, my envy growing a little bit more with every picture.

How long had they dated? How many nights had she slept down the hall in his bed? Why did my brain come up with questions that I really, *really* didn't need to be thinking about at 2:39 in the morning?

I set my phone on the nightstand, screen down, and hugged my pillow to my chest as I closed my eyes.

Slut. Slut. Slut.

"This is ridiculous."

"Agreed." The light flipped on and I yelped, smacking a hand over my heart as I sat up straight.

Rush scowled from the doorway as he crossed his arms over his chest. "Care to explain why I woke up alone? Again?"

"I can't sleep." My shoulders slumped. "I didn't want to wake you up."

He sighed and flipped off the light, padding to the bed to crawl in behind me. He moved beneath the covers, curling against me as he used my one and only pillow and I used his arm as a headrest.

"What's going on in here?" He touched my temple.

"It's nothing."

"Is it about earlier? You and me?"

"No. I had a bad dream. They're very vivid lately. I'm blaming Squish. It was about, um . . . Halsey."

He stiffened. "Halsey?"

"Yeah. I saw her at the game. She was in my dream." And since I was a tiny bit sleep-deprived and delirious, I kept the confession coming. "I dreamed that she called me a slut and then the whole stadium started chanting *slut, slut, slut.*"

His chest started to shake.

"Don't laugh." I elbowed him in the stomach, and he turned his face into the pillow, muffling the sound. "It's not funny."

"It's not funny." He held me tighter, his nose in my hair. I didn't need to see his face to know he was still grinning.

"Anyway," I drawled, "I was looking at her Instagram. She's very pretty."

"Meh."

I scoffed. "Meh?"

"It's all staged, sweets. It's not real. Your beauty? It's real. And it's a thousand times prettier than anything Halsey posts online."

"Rush," I whispered. There was a lot to unpack in that statement. Maybe, for a change, I didn't have to analyze it at all. I could just . . . believe him. "Thank you."

"Welcome."

"I like it when you call me sweets."

"Good." He kissed my hair, then snuggled deeper, holding me as he relaxed.

"Rush?"

"Faye?"

275

"I'm jealous that she had you first. That she spent so many nights in your bed." I had to be delirious. That was not something I ever would have admitted otherwise. It had to be the sex. He'd scrambled my brain.

"*You* could be spending the night in my bed," he teased.

"You know what I mean."

He held me closer. "Yeah. I know. I'm not crazy about the idea of you living with fuckwad Justin."

My nose scrunched at his name. It had been surprisingly easy to forget about him.

"If it makes you feel better, Halsey didn't sleep here."

I lifted up on an elbow to twist and look at him. "Really?"

"We stayed at her place. Like Erik does with Kalindi."

"Let me guess. Maverick?"

"Something like that." He yawned. "Can we save that story for daylight hours?"

"Yeah." I lay down again, trying to relax and shut off my brain.

Slut. Slut. Slut.

"Rush?"

"Faye?" he murmured.

"This bed is too small."

Rush moved his hand beneath my hoodie, pressing his palm against my belly. "Go to sleep."

He wasn't talking to Squish.

So I snuggled deeper, certain there was no way I'd crash.

But when I woke up, there was sun streaming through my windows. Rush's body was curled around mine. And for as clear as it had been in the middle of the night, I'd forgotten all about that silly dream.

CHAPTER TWENTY-SEVEN

RUSH

Faye did a double take when she came through the swinging door at the diner and saw me standing beside the *Please Seat Yourself* sign. Her cheeks pinkened. "Hi."

"Hey, sweets."

She carried a platter in each hand, both plates loaded with hash browns and chicken-fried steak smothered in country gravy.

My stomach growled.

"Be right back," she said, taking the food to one of the booths along the window.

Dolly's was busy. Well, busier than it was in the evenings. About half of the tables were occupied by Sunday-morning patrons and each of the front-row spaces in the snow-covered parking lot were full.

Faye delivered the food, smiling at the customers. She snagged a coffee pot from the warmer in the beverage station, then made the rounds, refilling ceramic mugs before putting it away and joining me beside the door.

There was a shy smile on her face. It was the same

adorable smile she'd had when we'd woken up in her tiny bed this morning. The same smile she'd had when she'd left the house for her shift and I'd gone to campus to work out and meet with the team.

I really loved that smile.

This girl. She was it for me. She was the real deal.

"I thought you were at the fieldhouse all day," she said.

"Changed my mind. Coaches told us to take the rest of the day to study and review plays. Thought I'd do that here."

I bent and kissed her cheek. How long had I wanted to do that? To come in here and let a restaurant full of people know she was mine? Too long. Fuck, it felt good to stop pretending like we were nothing.

Her smile brightened. "Want something to eat?"

"Surprise me."

"Breakfast or lunch?"

"Breakfast." It was noon, but Dusty's all-day breakfast never got old. "Has it been busy?"

Faye sighed, taking in the dining room. "Not really. It's been normal for a Sunday morning."

"Sorry."

She shrugged. "I'm not giving up."

"That's my girl." I hauled her into a hug, pressing my lips to the top of her hair. Then I let her go so she could get back to work, and I could do the same.

It was impossible to corral my focus when Faye was in the room. Every time she walked by or I heard her voice, my attention would shift away from the playbook spread in front of me. There was a reason the coaches made us stay on campus this time of year. That we'd study as a team.

But today, I didn't want so much distance between us.

Not after last night. I didn't want her to have a chance to disappear behind those walls.

Though considering that when I looked at her, more often than not she was already staring at me, maybe there was nothing to worry about.

She disappeared into the kitchen, and I concentrated on the open page in front of me. It was a play we'd run for years, one I knew like the back of my hand. I studied it anyway, closing my eyes and visualizing it in my head.

Twins right, special.

It was one of the simpler plays, but it gave me a chance to run the ball if my running back wasn't open to receive a pass. Some quarterbacks didn't like the risk it put us in for injury, but I wasn't afraid to get hit, and if it meant yards gained, I'd run.

I'd just turned to the next page in the book when a plate slid across the table. Chicken-fried steak and hash browns.

"I saw you drooling over it when you came in," Faye said.

"Maybe I was drooling over you."

She smiled and took a seat on the opposite side of the booth. "How's it going?"

I lifted a shoulder, unwrapping the silverware from the rolled napkin. "It's all right."

"What's this?" She motioned to my book.

"Playbook. It's my constant companion this week."

"And your next game is Saturday?"

I nodded. "Yep. Because of our record, we'll have another weekend of playing at home."

"Are you nervous?" she asked.

"Yes." Any other person, even my parents, I probably would have lied. I would have said no. But not with Faye.

"Can I help? Quiz you or something?"

"I've got this." I tapped the corner of the book. "But yeah, you can do something. Come to the game."

She dropped her gaze to her fingers clasped on the table. It would be cold and the forecast was predicting more snow. She was probably scheduled to work too.

The worst she could say was no.

And I was going to make her tell me no. That's how badly I wanted her at the game.

"Okay."

My heart soared. "I'll get you a ticket to sit with my parents."

Relief flashed across her face. "Thank you."

The only dream I wanted her to have after Saturday's game was about me. I didn't need Halsey's bullshit messing with her head.

"I've been thinking," I said, shifting the book out of the way so I could cut up my steak. "We should move in together."

"Didn't we already do that?"

"No, I mean just the three of us. You, me and Squish."

Faye's pretty eyes softened in that tender way they always did when I called the baby Squish. "We really need to come up with a different name, or he's going to hate us once he starts school."

I grinned and took a bite. Damn, it was good food. I swallowed and took a drink from the water glass she'd brought earlier. "Henry."

"You said that one already."

"Trying it again."

"It's a maybe. How about Brock?"

"Nah. Rylie?"

"Liam."

"Carson," I said, even though the moment it was out of my mouth I knew it wasn't right.

Thankfully, she shook her head. "Maverick."

My fork and knife stilled. "You'd want to name him Maverick?"

"Not even a little bit." She grimaced. "No, I'm wondering if Maverick is the reason you want to move."

I set my utensils on the edge of the plate. "Yes and no. I want us to have some privacy, but there's history with Maverick too."

"Is it the same reason why you and Halsey always stayed at her place?"

This wasn't exactly where I'd thought we'd have this conversation, but maybe it was better here. Dolly's was Faye's safe place, and in a way, it had become mine too. It had become ours.

I leaned back in the booth, glancing around. While I'd been reviewing plays, most of the tables had cleared out. There were a couple of guys visiting in a table on the far end of the room, but their napkins were balled up on their plates and Faye had already dropped off their check.

"Mav and I have known each other since freshman year. He was my roommate in the dorms."

"Oh. I didn't realize you'd been living together that long."

"He's a good roommate."

She arched her eyebrows.

"To me." I held up a hand. "He's been a good roommate to me. And he's been a good friend, even when I haven't deserved it."

"What do you mean?" Her eyebrows came together.

Where did I even start? "Mav and I met freshman year. We both were known for, well . . . screwing around."

Her nose scrunched. "Maybe I don't want to know."

I didn't want to know about her past lovers either, but if she wanted to know the truth about my friendship with Mav, it was part of the past.

"Maverick met Halsey first. It was toward the end of freshman year. We were at a friend's house, and she showed up with some other friends. They hooked up and kept hooking up for a few months."

"Oh." Faye blinked. "Wow."

"It was never serious. They weren't dating. But Halsey didn't like that he was screwing around with other women too."

"She wanted it to be exclusive."

"I guess. There wasn't really anything to break off, but she came over one night to do it anyway. Except he was gone. Out with someone else. I wasn't."

"And you got together."

I nodded. "Yeah. They might not have been together, but I crossed a line. Not my finest moment. I should have sent her home."

"But you started dating instead."

"We did. About a month later. Maverick wasn't in it for a relationship. He swears he never cared, but our friendship changed after that. I guess, I've been trying to prove my loyalty. Prove that I was sorry. Prove that he could still trust me as a teammate and friend."

Prove that I wasn't an asshole who'd slept with his roommate's hookup when she'd come knocking on his door, even though that's exactly what I'd done.

It was why hearing Halsey call me a cheater had cut so deep. She knew how we'd started. She knew how much I hated our beginning.

"Mav would have been right to be angry, but he wasn't. He never really cared for Halsey. It was his idea that we get a place together sophomore year, even though Hals and I were dating. I was afraid if I said no, it would cause drama and ruin our friendship."

And ever since, I'd been walking on eggshells. Part of that was keeping him and Halsey apart, which was why I'd never had her sleep over. Not that she'd cared. It would have been awkward for her too.

"I knew a while ago that Halsey and I weren't end game. But I stayed with her, I dragged it out, when I should have walked away."

"To prove that it wasn't a mistake," Faye guessed. "To Maverick? Or yourself?"

I gave her a sad smile. "Both."

She reached across the table, holding out her hand. "For the record, I think you're a good friend. Even if you made a mistake."

"Thanks." I covered her hand with my own, my palm flat against hers. "I let Mav get away with more shit than I should."

"Maybe he knows that."

I drew a circle on her inner wrist with my finger. "Maybe."

"Your food is getting cold."

"I don't care."

The door chimed behind me and Faye pulled her hand away before I was ready to let her go. Her eyes drifted over my shoulder, hardening at whoever had come inside.

I twisted. Gloria stomped her shoes on the entryway mat.

She searched the space, looking for Faye. When she spotted us, Gloria trudged to the edge of our booth and stuck out her lower lip in a dramatic pout. "I hate it when you're mad at me."

"Then don't lie to me." Faye crossed her arms over her chest.

"I'm sorry," Gloria said.

I believed her. And from the way Faye's gaze gentled, she believed her too.

"I just wanted you to talk to Mom."

"Why?" Faye asked.

"Because. She's our mom."

Faye stood from the booth and put a hand on Gloria's shoulder. "That's not enough of a reason."

"Then do it for me. Please," Gloria whispered. "She's been different lately."

Faye sighed. "I'll think about it."

"Thank you." Gloria pulled her into a hug, then let her go, taking her place in the booth across from me. For the first time, she seemed to even notice I was here. "Hey."

"Hey." I picked up my fork for a mouthful of hash browns.

"So you got my sister pregnant."

I stopped chewing. "Yeah."

She narrowed her eyes. "If you break her heart, I'll break every bone in your body. Twice."

"Gloria," Faye snapped.

I burst out laughing, nearly choking on my food. I pounded a fist against my chest as I swallowed, then gulped some water to clear my throat. When I looked up again, Gloria's glare was harder than ever.

"Don't worry, G." I held up both hands. "Her heart is safe with me."

CHAPTER TWENTY-EIGHT

FAYE

"They're going to lose." Macy's arm looped through mine.

"Yeah." The Wildcats were going to lose. Rush was going to lose.

When I looked to the scoreboard, the crack in my heart got a little bit wider.

"I don't know if I'm cut out for this." I swallowed the lump in my throat, sniffling away the sting in my nose.

"I wish I could say it gets easier." Ryan put his arm around my shoulders, hauling me into his side. "But it doesn't."

As much as I wanted to blame the tears in my eyes on hormones, it had nothing to do with being pregnant. I was about to lose my shit over a football game.

Over the man on the field who wasn't giving up.

There were only sixteen seconds left in the fourth quarter and the Wildcats were down two touchdowns. They had time for one more play. But even if they scored, it wouldn't be enough. Yet Rush wasn't giving up.

He took his position behind the center, hands at the ready to receive the football. He looked down the line, to his left and then his right. On his command, the center snapped the ball. Rush dropped back three steps, searching for a receiver.

Erik raced down the field, his legs pumping as he did his best to outrun the defender on his heels. He raised an arm in the air, still sprinting.

Rush launched the ball, sending it spiraling through the winter air.

Catch it. I stared unblinking as the ball sailed straight into Erik's hand.

"Yes." I jumped as a cheer broke through the stadium.

Erik tucked the ball and ran, ignoring the guy giving chase. He ran hard, every step taking him closer to the end zone. Except right before he reached the line, the defender surged and tackled Erik to the turf.

The clock ticked to zero.

"Ouch," I murmured.

Rush's strong frame deflated, and that crack in my heart split it in half. He tore off his helmet, steam rising from his sweaty hair, and dropped his gaze to his feet.

"Damn." Ryan hugged me tighter.

Macy's hold on my arm didn't loosen as she sniffed.

My mouth turned down, my chin wobbling as I fought the urge to cry.

Around us, Wildcat fans were making their way down the stairs toward the exits. It was eerily quiet compared to how it had been earlier today. When excitement had been crackling in the air. Even when the score had been tied at the end of the first quarter.

But once we'd fallen behind, the atmosphere had

changed. Frustration had settled like a rain cloud. Anticipation had morphed to anxiety. One guy a few rows back had started yelling at the referees, blaming everything on the officials.

On the field, the guys circled, a couple of them clapping Rush on the shoulder. With his helmet in a hand, dangling at his side, he started toward the tunneled exit, congratulating a few of the other team's players as they crossed paths.

But before he disappeared from sight, he turned to the stands, searching us out.

When he found us, exactly where we'd been since the beginning of the game, he raised an arm.

Ryan nodded. Macy waved back.

And I hoped that all he could see was my wobbly smile, not the tear sliding down my cheek.

He was swept up with the rest of the team, leaving the field with the coaches.

We waited until the line at the stairs had dwindled before finally breaking apart to collect our things.

Ryan and Macy had brought collapsible seats that fit to the metal benches. They'd brought one for me too, though we'd barely sat the entire game. We'd been on our feet for hours, not just because the game had been too tense to sit, but because it was warmer to keep moving.

The high had only reached ten degrees today, and while the sky was clear, the sun blindingly bright, it was cold as hell.

"Thank you for this." I folded one of the blankets Macy had brought that I'd kept wrapped around my shoulders.

"Of course." She folded her own blanket as Ryan bent and collected our empty hot cocoa cups.

Three empty cups.

They'd brought three of everything. When Ryan had gone to the concessions stand, he'd returned with three of everything too.

"We're so glad you could sit with us today," Macy said.

"Me too."

"Did Rush talk to you about Christmas?"

"Um, no."

Rush and I hadn't really talked about much. The past week had been a jumbled blur.

Between last-minute studying and final exams, the limited time we'd spent together had either been hunched over textbooks at the diner or tangled together in Rush's bed.

"I suppose he's been busy with school and football," Ryan said. "We'd love to have you come out to the ranch, if you can get away from work. We've always reserved Christmas for family only, so it'll be fairly laid back. Just the four of us."

The four of us. Family.

"I—" They considered me family?

Usually, I spent the day with Gloria and her dad and grandmother. Except she'd already warned me this week that Mom would be joining them. Dusty was closing the diner for a week to leave with Mike to visit his family in Idaho.

My family wasn't an option.

Would Rush mind if I borrowed his for Christmas? Probably not.

Ryan and Macy stared at me, waiting for an answer.

"Y-yes." I nodded. "Thank you. I'd love to come."

"Wonderful." Macy blew out a heavy breath, like she'd been braced for a rejection.

Ryan beamed, his smile so similar to Rush's that all I could do was smile back.

I had no idea what I'd get them as gifts, maybe a couple of Dolly's Diner mugs that Dusty had stowed somewhere in her office. I still hadn't figured out what to get Rush either.

"Shall we?" Ryan gestured toward the end of our row, and we filed out in a single line, making our way down the stairs and ramp, then beneath the stands and through the gate that led to where people were tearing down tents and trailers.

"Whenever Rush lost a game in high school, which was rare, he'd pout for days and days." Macy laughed as we headed for their truck. "Something tells me he'll be okay after this one."

"He won't have to pout alone," I told her.

She laughed again as we weaved through the tailgates. We loaded into their vehicle, giving it a few minutes to warm up in the cold before they drove me home so I could change and head in for work.

Dusty had offered to give me another Saturday night off, but I'd already shorted myself on hours for finals week. I couldn't afford to miss too many hours, especially with two more people who now needed Christmas gifts.

So while Ryan and Macy hung out at our house, relaxing in the living room, I drove to the diner, arriving at four to start my shift until close.

"Hey," I told Dusty as I walked into the kitchen, grabbing an apron to tie low beneath my growing belly.

"Hi, sugar." She blew me a kiss from the prep table.

"Was it busy today?"

She scoffed.

Damn. I'd left another stack of flyers at the stadium today. They were the same graphic—*SAVE DOLLY'S*

DINER—but printed on neon-yellow paper rather than electric blue.

"Do you need help with anything in here?" I asked.

"I'm good, babycakes. I just took a load of clean silverware to the dining room."

"Okay. I'll go roll it up."

She winked as I walked by the table, leaning closer to see what she was mixing in her bowl. Macaroni salad. The curved noodles were mixed with sliced green onions and bits of celery. She'd tossed in bacon bits, then coated it all in creamy mayonnaise.

It looked . . . good. I hated macaroni salad but that looked delicious.

"What?" Dusty stopped stirring.

"Can I have a bowl of that?"

"This?" She pointed to the mixture with her wooden spoon. "It's got mayo."

"I can have mayo if it's made with pasteurized eggs."

"I made it without eggs."

"Oh." Even better.

"You hate mayo."

I nodded. "I do hate mayo. But I really want to eat that."

"Maybe this baby will cure you of your aversion to sauce," she said, walking over to the rack of dishes for a bowl.

I shrugged. "Maybe."

"Maybe I'll finally get you to eat lasagna. Though I suspect Rush won't like that since he's been eating it for you."

"How did you know—never mind." Either he'd complimented her on the lasagna—something he'd never ordered here—or she'd just assumed I'd given him the takeout.

Dusty scooped me a spoonful of the salad and went back to mixing as I headed for the dining room.

I tentatively ate the first bite of macaroni, waiting for the cringe that normally came with mayo. But it was incredible, so I inhaled the rest, then washed my hands and got to work rolling silverware.

Two older men wearing winter coats and scotch caps over their white hair came in at a quarter to five for dinner. By five thirty, six tables were full. Two groups were decked out in Wildcats gear.

Maybe, just maybe, those flyers had worked.

The door's bell chimed as I cleared away the dishes from the two older men. Ryan and Macy stood at the hostess station, their cheeks flushed from the dark, cold evening.

The door had just closed when it swung open again, eliciting another chime.

Rush walked in, and I nearly dropped a plate when my knees buckled.

His hair was still damp from a shower. He was in a button-down plaid shirt and a pair of Wrangler jeans that draped to scuffed, brown boots. All he was missing was the hat and he'd be the sexiest cowboy to walk the face of the earth.

My ovaries exploded.

"Wow."

Getting pregnant from that man had always been inevitable, hadn't it? From the day he'd changed my tire.

He searched the room, and when our eyes locked, that pout on his face faded a little.

I set the plates down to clear later and crossed the diner. I walked straight into his open arms and buried my nose in his chest. "Hi."

"Hey." He dropped his mouth to my hair.

"Sorry about the game."

"Me too."

"Are you okay?"

"Yeah," he muttered. "I don't like to lose."

I slid my hands into the back pockets of his jeans and leaned away to meet his gaze. "I didn't realize you guys were coming here for dinner."

His forehead furrowed. "Where else would we go?"

If the only person I'd turned into a regular Dolly's patron was Rush, I guess my mission to save this diner hadn't entirely been a failure.

I slipped my hands free of his pockets and grabbed three menus, not that Rush needed one. He'd memorized it by now. "Dusty made macaroni salad. It's pretty good."

Rush's eyebrows lifted. "You ate macaroni salad? The kind with mayonnaise as the sauce?"

"Weird, right?"

"Huh." He nodded to my belly. "Must be Squish."

"Squish?" Macy asked, horror clouding her expression. "Rush. Please tell me that you are not naming my grandson Squish."

Rush grinned, shooting me a wink.

He teased her for almost an hour before finally admitting it was only a nickname.

And like Macy had predicted, the sadness over his loss didn't last long.

———

THE HOUSE WAS dark when we pulled into the driveway, but there was a strange car parked on the street out front. One step through the front door, and I knew exactly who it belonged to.

Well, sort of. I had no idea who the woman was in Maverick's bed, just that he was definitely not in there alone.

His headboard slammed against the wall, a steady *thump, thump, thump* resonating through the house.

Rush closed the door as he came inside behind me. He heard the sound and groaned.

At least his parents weren't here to hear this. Macy and Ryan had left the diner shortly after eating to drive home to the ranch. And since Rush had ridden with them to Dolly's, he'd waited until the end of my shift so we could come home together.

"Okay," I told him.

"Okay, what?"

"Okay, let's move in together."

He stepped closer, taking my face in his hands. "Are you sure?"

It had only been a week since he'd asked. A week didn't seem like enough time to make this big of a decision.

Part of me wanted to prove to myself that I could live alone. That I didn't need anyone's help.

Maybe I didn't *need* it.

But what if I *wanted* help? That was the scariest part of it all. Wanting to lean on someone. Wanting to give up that control. Wanting to stop doing everything myself for once.

I wanted Rush's plan to be my plan. Squish and school and speech pathology. Football and a future. "Kiss me before I change my mind."

He was on me in a flash, his mouth slamming over mine. He kept my face in his hands, holding me to him as he licked the seam of my lips, coaxing them open. I expected him to delve inside, to plunder and devour until I was breathless.

But Rush fluttered his tongue against the tip of mine, that quick flick enough to earn a whimper before he pulled away.

"Faye, I—"

Thump. Thump. "Oh, Maverick! Harder!"

"Eww." I cringed.

Rush growled as he clasped his hand over mine, pulling me toward the stairs. "We're moving."

"Yep." I probably wasn't going to change my mind.

The thumping faded by the time we made it upstairs. Rush didn't take me to his bedroom, but to the bathroom instead, reaching into the shower to turn on the spray. The water's noise drowned out anything beyond the closed door.

Rush went to work on the buttons of his shirt. Two undone revealed the coarse, dark hair that dusted his chest. He loosened a third and there came the abs.

"Clothes off, sweets." He shifted closer, reaching for the hem of my tee. He pulled it off my torso slowly, inch by inch, as my fingers found their way to his rippled stomach.

It was impossible not to touch him. Now that we'd started this, I'd never be able to stop. When he was close, my hands were on his body, in his pockets or on his arms. If we were sitting, I'd have a hand on his thigh. I'd never been like this with another man, but as in all things, Rush was the exception.

My hands lifted higher, dragging up his chest until I reached his shoulders and pushed at his shirt.

He shook it off his arms, letting it fall to the floor. Then he closed his eyes and bent low until his forehead was pressed to mine. His entire body relaxed as his grip settled on my hips. "I liked looking into the stands and finding you there today."

"I liked being there."

He stood tall and brought his fingers to my hair, pulling out the tie that I'd had in at work. When the strands tumbled free, he took it all in his fist, wrapping it once around the width of his hand. Then he tugged, forcing my head back so he could claim my mouth.

He licked and sucked, constantly changing the pace from slow to fast. Hard to soft. It meant I was always a beat behind. He was in control, and I was at his mercy.

It was freeing, giving in. Letting go.

He hummed against my lips, then broke away, loosening my hair as he spun me toward the mirror. As he kissed my neck, I stared at our reflection framed in the fogged edges of the glass.

My cheeks were flushed, my mouth wet. Rush's body surrounded mine, tall and broad and strong and perfect.

When he looked up, his eyes finding mine, my heart trilled.

We were beautiful, the two of us together. Somehow, we fit. His strength and size complemented my petite frame and soft curves.

A slight smile ghosted his lips as he reached around my belly to pull off the elastic tie keeping my jeans fastened. Then after tugging the zipper down, he slid the denim off my legs, taking my panties too while I unclasped my bra.

When he stood, wrapping his arms around my shoulders, his arousal pressed hard against my hip.

I spun in his hold, my hands reaching for his neck to pull him down. Then it was my turn to lead for a moment.

He let me nip at his lip while I reached between us and

worked on his jeans until they were on the tile with mine and his cock was throbbing in my hand.

"I need you inside," I murmured into his mouth.

He thrust his hips forward, pushing fast into my grip as I stroked. His palms settled on my ass and he kneaded my flesh, digging hard. Then he hoisted me onto the counter, the marble cold against my naked skin.

Rush took my knees, pressing them apart before he dragged a finger through my slit. "Are you wet for me?"

"Soaked."

He brought his finger to my mouth, pushing it past my lips until I tasted myself on his skin. It was a first. Firsts usually came with hesitation or embarrassment, but the flash of heat in his gaze was erotic. I licked his finger, sucking it deeper, as his Adam's apple bobbed.

"Fuck, Faye." He eased his finger away so his mouth could take its place. "Do you have any idea what you do to me?"

"Rush." I inched toward the edge of the counter, hooking a leg around his hip to pull him closer.

He kissed me and thrust forward, filling me entirely.

I cried against his mouth as my body stretched around his length. "Yes."

"You feel so fucking good."

"More." I braced my hands on the counter as he took hold of my thighs, keeping me in place as he started to move, in and out, until I was a trembling mess.

My moans mingled with the sound of the shower's water. Steam billowed, coating my skin with a sheen.

Rush hit that spot inside, over and over, with every roll of his hips.

Every time he planted deep, there was a moment when

297

he stayed rooted. Every stroke was deliberate, like there was an underlying message in his movements.

Like he wanted to say something.

My inner walls began to flutter around him, my body racing faster and faster toward the edge. He reached between us and found my clit with his finger.

One circle against the bundle of nerves and I exploded. Every muscle tensed and quaked as I pulsed around him, clenching and squeezing as my toes curled.

"Fuck," he cursed through gritted teeth, his hands tightening on my thighs. Then he tilted his head to the ceiling and roared through his own release until we were both utterly spent.

I fell forward, collapsing against his chest as he wrapped me in his arms. We clung to each other, breathing hard, until finally my heart rate slowed and I cracked my eyes open.

Rush smiled at me, planting a sweet kiss on my nose before he carried me into the shower.

He washed my hair. I washed his body. And when the water ran cold, we dried off and went to his bed to crash, not bothering with clothes as we curled together beneath the sheets.

"I'm sorry about your game," I said, my nose nuzzled into his throat.

He brushed his lips against my temple. "What game?"

CHAPTER TWENTY-NINE

RUSH

My feet were kicked up on the coffee table. ESPN was playing on the TV, the volume muted. And Faye was curled into my side on the couch, asleep and drooling on my shirt.

This had become our Monday evening routine. We'd cook dinner, then spend the rest of the night curled together, either reading or studying or watching TV until Faye crashed, and I'd carry her upstairs to bed.

She'd been asleep for nearly an hour already, but I wasn't ready to move her yet. Not until I felt another kick. At least, I thought it had been a kick.

My hand was splayed across her belly, and there'd been a ripple of movement about thirty minutes ago. If I had to wait all night to feel it again, I'd stay right here on this couch.

The front door opened and Maverick stepped inside.

He opened his mouth, but before he could speak, I pressed a finger to my lips and mouthed, "Shush."

He rolled his eyes. *Shithead.*

His shoes dumped clumps of snow on the mat in the

entryway and a rush of cold air flew inside before he closed the door. Then he set his backpack on the floor with a plop and unzipped his coat.

We hadn't talked much in the past few weeks. He'd spent most of Christmas break at his parents' house, hanging with his mom. And Faye and I had gone to the ranch for the holiday.

Mom and Dad had spent seven days smothering her with affection. It had been almost sad to watch at first. Not because she didn't deserve the love, but because she'd been so shocked by it.

She'd never had parents spoil her with gifts or special meals. Even after the week was over, the hugs from my parents seemed to take her by surprise.

But she'd get used to it in time.

That's what we needed. Time.

Three more months and Squish would be here. Three more months of just us.

And Maverick. For now.

Middle of the school year, there weren't many rentals available, especially in Faye's price range. She hadn't mentioned a budget, but I'd noticed the tension in her face every time we found a listing she couldn't afford.

So for now, we'd decided to wait and keep looking. Hopefully toward the end of the semester, we'd have more options. Worst-case scenario, we'd turn her bedroom into the nursery for a few months.

Faye was sure Maverick would hate living with a newborn and was hoping he'd move out before the baby was born.

Maybe she was right. But Mav also loved kids, and I had a hunch he might surprise her.

Maverick crossed the room and took a seat on the opposite end of the sectional. He spun his hat backward and turned his attention to the TV.

When he realized the volume was off, he stretched for the remote resting on the cushion beside me, but before he could touch it, I swatted his hand.

"Seriously," he muttered.

"Read the captions."

Since school had started again, Faye had been putting in long hours on campus and at Dolly's. She needed the sleep more than he needed to listen to an announcer talk about weekend sports highlights.

"You've changed," he said.

"Not really."

His jaw flexed. "I've hardly even seen you lately."

I'd seen him at both practice and weight training today.

"Every waking minute you're with her," he said.

"Yeah."

"You weren't like that with Halsey. You always put your friends, your team, first."

Faye's body tensed, a sign that she was now awake, but she didn't move or open her eyes.

Or maybe she didn't realize I knew she was listening.

If Mav wanted to have this conversation, if she wanted to be here for it, then that was fine by me.

"Faye is my team, Mav. She comes first, always. No, I wasn't like that with Halsey. Because Halsey isn't Faye."

Maverick and I had talked about Halsey, about everything that had happened, more times than I could remember over the years. It was usually a snide comment on his part, an apology on mine. He'd wave it off, tell me it didn't matter, and I'd make sure the two of them were always kept at a distance.

We'd had the conversations, but we hadn't solved anything.

It was time to talk about it again. For the last time.

"I'm sorry about what happened with Halsey. I'm sorry that I broke your trust."

"It's fine," he said.

"No, it's not. I regret it. That's not the kind of man I am."

He sighed, taking off his hat to run his hands through his hair. "It's not a big deal. We weren't together, and it was a long time ago."

"Then stop testing my loyalty."

"What?"

"You never said it, but you expected me to choose between you and Halsey. And for the most part, I chose you."

How many times had I canceled plans with Halsey to hang with Maverick? How many times had I blown her off because he'd wanted to watch a game? How many times had I used football as the reason to put off a date when really, Maverick had made a comment that had gotten under my skin?

All those months ago, when I'd listened to Halsey's irate voicemail messages when I'd been camping, I'd brushed them off as angry and dramatic. But she hadn't been entirely wrong. Blaming our breakup on Halsey wasn't fair. I'd never put her first, truly first.

Even if I had, we wouldn't have lasted. I realized that now.

Halsey wasn't Faye.

"I will always choose Faye. Always. You're my best friend, Mav. But she's my team."

Maverick's gaze dropped to her face, his eyebrows coming together. "I get it. You're having a kid and—"

"It's not the baby."

"Rush." He scoffed. "You're telling me you'd be together if she wasn't pregnant?"

"Yeah, I am."

It was an alternate reality. I wasn't sure how or when we would have gotten together, but in my bones, I knew I would have found the path to Faye.

He shook his head, dropping his gaze to his lap.

I wasn't sure what it would take for him to believe me. There was a chance he never would. But that was his problem, not mine.

"I'm going to take her to bed." I grabbed the remote and threw it across the couch. Now he could listen to the volume as loud as he wanted.

Except as I made a move to sit straighter, a wobble rolled through Faye's side, right beneath my palm.

Her eyes popped open and her hand flew to cover mine. "Did you feel that?"

"Hey, Squish." I smiled so wide it hurt.

Faye didn't move, barely breathing, as we waited for it to happen again. Except he must have been done twirling around because her belly went back to its normal stillness. She looked up and frowned. "Dang it."

I kissed her forehead. "He'll do it again."

She pushed off my chest, shifting to the edge of the couch. Then she stared at Maverick, her head cocking to the side. "Why don't you like me?"

Mav, the asshole, didn't deny it. "He's my best friend."

"And you think I'm going to screw him over or something? Or is it just because you think I got pregnant on purpose?"

"He's got greatness in him. More than anyone I've ever met. He's going somewhere, and that means fame and fortune. I'm just looking out."

Faye hummed, her hand absently running up and down her side as I watched the two of them stare at each other. "If I were in your position, I'd be suspicious too. That's fair."

"Really?"

"He does have greatness in him." She looked up at me and smiled. "But you're not the only one looking out."

Did Faye have any idea how special she was? Probably not. But from the look on Maverick's face, he was starting to realize it too.

Faye shrugged and stood. "Believe what you want, Maverick. I actually like the way you're protective of Rush. We have that in common. But if he really is your best friend, then stop being such a dick."

I couldn't stop the laugh that escaped.

With a saccharine smile, Faye sidestepped the coffee table and started for the stairs. Except before she made it out of the living room, Mav shot to his feet.

"Wait."

She turned, giving him a bored stare. "Yeah?"

He looked at me, studying my face for a long moment. If he thought I'd jump in the middle, then he was wrong. Faye didn't need me to play mediator. She could handle herself.

Mav let out a strangled breath, then held out his hand toward Faye. "Truce?"

She stared at it, eyes narrowing like it was a trap.

"I've kind of been a dick lately."

"Kind of?" I scoffed.

"I'm sorry," he said. "I don't want you guys to move out. I don't want to move, and I sure as hell don't want to find new roommates. So let's call a truce and be done with it."

The corner of Faye's mouth turned up as she took his hand. "Fine. A truce."

He nodded, opening his grip to let her go, but she held firm.

"If you ever eat my food again, I'll have my boss bring over one of her pet snakes and leave it in your bed."

· "Fuck." He pulled his hand free from hers like she'd stung him as I burst out laughing.

Faye giggled, shooting me an evil smile. If Maverick didn't believe that threat, he'd be a fool.

"For such a small person, you're actually kind of terrifying," he said. "Glad I'm not the guy sleeping beside you at night."

"Someday, I hope the woman you fall for twists you up so tight you won't know up from down. And I hope I get a front-row seat to witness it."

"Ha." His laugh was short and dry. "Never happening."

"Never say never." Faye's warning lingered as she disappeared upstairs.

"Huh." Mav rubbed his jaw when she was gone. "She's feisty."

"That she is."

He faced me with a frown. "All right. Fine. I get it. I can see the appeal. She's beautiful. And yeah . . . I don't believe anymore that she got knocked up on purpose."

Was that approval in his voice? If so, it didn't really matter. But I'd take it. I'd take their truce if it would cut back the stress on Faye.

"Are you seriously going to move out?" he asked.

"Depends on you." I stood from the couch. "Be. Fucking. Nice."

He held up his hands. "Okay. Shit. Sorry. Message received."

"Thanks." I followed Faye's path around the coffee table, walking toward the stairs.

"Rush?" Mav stopped me before I could climb. "On Thanksgiving, when you sat with me. I never said thanks."

"No need, man. I'm here. Whatever you need."

He swallowed hard. "Appreciate it."

With a sad smile, I headed upstairs, finding Faye in my room. She was sitting on the edge of the bed, typing on her phone.

"Gloria?" I asked.

She nodded. "She sent me a list of baby names. They were my mother's suggestions."

"Oh."

Gloria, like Faye, was stubborn to a fault. No matter how often Faye told her to back off about their mom, Gloria wouldn't stop.

If she wasn't careful, if Gloria kept pushing, she'd shove Faye right out of her life.

"Whatever." Faye set her phone on the nightstand. "They were all names we've vetoed already."

"Want me to take your mind off it?" I closed the door and crossed the room, bending until my face was in hers.

"Yes." She smiled against my mouth as I pressed her into the mattress, her gorgeous hair spilling in silky waves around her face.

It looked more golden than red in tonight's light. There

were a couple features I hoped like hell my boy would inherit from Faye. Her caramel eyes. And this hair.

With my hands threaded into the strands, I kissed her until we were breathless and tearing at each other's clothes.

It had been over a month since we'd started sleeping together, but every night, I had to remind myself this was real.

Stripping her bare had become my favorite part of the day. I stretched out beside her on the bed and let my hands wander, exploring every inch of her creamy, smooth skin and the swell of her belly.

She reached for my cock, taking it in her hand.

That first stroke was sheer bliss. A bead formed at the tip, and she swiped it with her thumb before bringing her finger to her mouth.

"You want more?" I asked, trailing my fingers to her core. Then I spread her folds apart and eased my middle finger inside. "You want me to fill your mouth or this?"

"Rush." Her pussy fluttered, her knees opening wider as her grip on my dick tightened. "Fuck me."

I shifted between her legs, kneeling above her. Then I hauled her ass onto my thighs so I could tilt up her hips as I positioned myself at her entrance.

Another night, I'd fill her mouth like I'd done last night in the shower. Tomorrow, I'd have her taste on my tongue. But tonight, I wanted to see my come dripping out of her body after I fucked her to sleep.

So I thrust home, closing my eyes as she cried out.

It started slow and steady, my hold on her hips forcing her to keep still and take every stroke. But as a flush crept into her chest, spreading across those pretty breasts and turning her nipples a rosy red, she propped up on an elbow and reached for me.

With our mouths fused, we moved in tandem, two bodies in perfect unison.

"Rush." Her hands clawed into my shoulders as she panted. "Harder."

I fucked her harder. Faster.

"Oh, God." She arched her back, her body writhing as her orgasm hit, pulsing around me like a vise.

Her release triggered my own and we came together in a tangle of tongues and limbs.

"Faye." I groaned her name over and over as I poured into her body.

It got better, every single time. How was that possible? How was this real?

Spent and boneless, I sagged against her, shifting my weight to her side and off her belly. She was halfway asleep before I even pulled out.

"Sleep." I kissed her forehead and tucked her beneath the covers, then headed for the bathroom.

She was out when I returned, but her eyes fluttered open as I pressed the warm washcloth against her flesh to clean her up. "Rush?"

"Sweets?"

She waited until I met her gaze. "Do you ever feel like this is too good to be true?"

Yeah. Every damn day.

"It's not," I promised, hoping like hell that pit in my stomach, the dread that something was going to come along and screw this up, was just a figment of my imagination.

CHAPTER THIRTY

FAYE

The diner's door chimed as Rush walked inside, his hair full of stark white snowflakes.

It was early March, and for a blissful week, it had almost looked like spring. Green grass had started sprouting amidst the brown. But we'd woken up this morning to gray skies and ominous clouds. It had started snowing during my eleven o'clock class and hadn't stopped since.

"Hey," Rush said, ruffling his dark hair. "Sorry I'm late."

"It's okay."

He unzipped his coat and tossed it over the back of the nearest booth. "The roads are shit. I think we'd better leave your car here tonight, and we'll come get it tomorrow after the plows have had a chance to catch up."

"Okay." I didn't like being without a car, having that freedom taken away. But I didn't want to drive on bad roads either, especially now that it was getting more and more uncomfortable to sit behind the wheel.

My belly was enormous. In the past two months, it had grown so fast that I hardly recognized myself in the mirror every morning. At my appointment last week, the doctor had predicted Squish was going to be a nine-pound baby. This was the problem with having a child with a human giant.

"How was the team meeting?" I asked.

"Fine." He shrugged. "I stayed late to talk to Coach Ellis. He wanted to check and see how things were going."

With the baby. With me.

I was a little bit jealous that Rush had his coaches. From everything he'd told me, they'd all taken an active interest in this pregnancy. They knew that my doctor's appointments were a priority and if they conflicted with workout or practice schedules, his coaches excused him from the mandatory requirement. They genuinely cared about him and his future.

They were a team.

Rush had told Maverick two months ago that I was his team. I hadn't really understood at the time why he'd used that word. But the more time we spent together, the more I realized just how important a *team* was in his life.

There weren't many pregnant students on campus. It was fairly common knowledge around campus that we were having a baby. There was just no hiding my bump, even behind my winter coats and thick, warm layers. I was a small person and it looked like I'd swallowed a watermelon whole.

I did my best to ignore the strange looks and focus on school, which was drowning me at the moment.

Rush came to the table where I was sitting, pulling out the chair next to mine. He kissed my hair and draped his arm around my shoulders. "You okay?"

"Stressed." I nodded to the textbooks and papers scattered across the table.

This last semester should have been the easiest. I didn't

have a huge class load, except what other seniors were doing in four months, I was cramming into three. My professors had given me an accelerated schedule so that I'd take my final exams two weeks before my due date.

I only hoped that my two-week buffer was enough. If Squish came early, well . . . I couldn't even think about that right now.

We didn't have the nursery set up. Rush kept asking me to move my things into his closet but I'd been so busy I hadn't made it a priority. I didn't have baby clothes or diapers or a crib. We needed to go shopping, but I couldn't afford much. Rush would buy whatever we needed, but I was . . . running out of time.

Soon, everything would be different.

It was good right now. So, so good. Life was better than it had ever been. I wasn't ready for different.

I wasn't ready for the good to end.

"Maybe this weekend we should go shopping." The words felt thick and heavy as they came out.

"All right. My mom wants to buy the crib. How about we split the rest?"

"Sure." I gave him a sad smile, grateful that he hadn't offered to just buy it himself.

Someday, if this worked out between us, I'd have to learn how to take his money, wouldn't I? The idea made my skin crawl, but in time, I hoped it wouldn't feel like I was leaching. Like I was giving up my independence. And it wasn't like I wouldn't work. I would always contribute.

But if he went to the NFL . . . well, that was a level of wealth I couldn't really comprehend.

And now was not the time to try.

I shook away the thought, getting way too far ahead of

myself. We still had another year to survive first with a newborn baby.

Without school expenses, I was hoping to save more of my paychecks. Unless daycare turned out to be more expensive than I'd researched. But maybe I could work during the hours Rush was home to stay with the baby.

The logistics were fuzzy and my head began to throb.

I hadn't spoken to Dusty about a maternity leave. I was only planning on taking a couple weeks away, but what if I needed more?

There were too many questions, too many unknowns. Why hadn't I figured these things out by now? How could I be six weeks away from my due date and have no plan?

Most parents probably had these things sorted by now. This urgency to figure it out, figure it out *now*, had been plaguing me for days.

"Sweets."

I jerked at Rush's voice. "Yeah?"

"You're in your head."

Yes. Yes, I was. "It's overwhelming."

"Break it down. One thing at a time."

"Okay." I glanced around the diner. "How long should I take off after he's born?"

"Couple months?"

My eyes bugged out. "I can't take off two months."

"Why not?"

Money. That was the real answer. Except I knew what he'd say to that. He'd tell me we had money, so I gave him a different answer. "Dusty. She needs my help."

He kept his eyes trained on mine, his mouth shut.

We were alone in an empty diner.

Dusty didn't need my help, not really. Since she and

Mike had gotten back together, he was here with her more often than not. Last night, I'd overheard them talking about getting a third snake. A python. *Eww.*

If they really were serious this time, she could wait on tables while he cooked in the kitchen.

"Talk to her," Rush said. "See what she's thinking."

I nodded, staring blankly at the book open in front of me.

"What else do you need to do here tonight?" he asked.

"Not much. Turn up the chairs and mop the floors."

"I'll help. Maybe Dusty will close early. I doubt anyone is going to come in with this weather." He stood, holding out a hand to help me to my feet.

We'd just started on the chairs, picking them up to put on the tables, when the swinging door to the kitchen opened.

Dusty stormed into the dining room, her face red and her mouth pursed in a scowl. The only other time I'd seen her this angry was when a customer had called me a little bitch three years ago when I'd accidentally spilled a water glass on his table.

"What's wrong?"

She lifted a hand and, in it, a neon-yellow flyer. The paper and its headline—*SAVE DOLLY'S DINER*—was crumpled, like she'd balled it into a fist, then flattened it out. "A friend of Mike's who works on campus gave it to him today. What the hell is this?"

"Um, marketing?" *Shit.*

Rush's heat hit my back as he hovered close, like he was going to leap in front of me if Dusty took another step closer.

I would have told him he was being ridiculous, but she was livid. At me.

She'd never been mad at me before.

Okay, so maybe *SAVE DOLLY'S DINER* was a slap in

the face. I hadn't meant to humiliate her, I'd simply been trying to snag attention. If people came out of pity, they'd stay for her food. We just needed to get them through the door.

"Dusty." I held up both hands. "I was only trying to spread the word about the diner."

"Don't," she snapped and my entire body flinched.

Tears welled in my eyes as she stared at me, her entire body vibrating with rage. Then it all stopped. One blink, she was furious. The next, her shoulders curled inward and that flyer in her hand floated to the floor.

"I am so fucking tired of this restaurant, Faye. I hate this place. Most days, I wish I could burn it to the ground."

My mouth opened, but I had no idea what to say.

Dolly's was her life. Her legacy. She hated it here? Since when?

"I can't sell it," Dusty said. "My mother would roll over in her grave. My family . . ."

Her family hated her for getting this restaurant. They'd despise her if she sold it. She'd never told me about that dinner with her cousin. I'd assumed it had gone well, though as far as I knew, they hadn't met again.

"Doesn't matter." She flicked a hand in the air. "It doesn't fucking matter. I can't sell it because it doesn't make any money. No one wants an old diner that's slowly going bankrupt."

"I-I'm sorry."

Dusty dropped her chin, staring at the floor as she planted her hands on her hips. For a minute, I thought she might cry.

I'd never seen Dusty cry. She was tough as steel. As solid as stone.

"I'm trapped here." When she looked up, the emotion was gone from her face. She stared at me with a blank look that was even more unnerving than the anger. "I get to face my failures each and every day."

"But Dolly's doesn't have to fail. That's why I made—"

She held up a hand, stopping me short. "The only way I'm free of this place is if it fails."

I shook my head. "You want it to fail?"

"It's not if, sugar. It's when." The hopelessness in Dusty's voice stabbed me straight through the heart.

Even if she had the chance to save Dolly's Diner, she wouldn't take it, would she? Was it spite for her family keeping her here? Or loyalty to her mother's wishes? Both? It made no sense that she wouldn't sell this place and walk away. That she'd sacrifice her pride and go down with a sinking ship.

How much money had she dumped into this restaurant? How long would she let it bleed her dry?

Until the end. Until she had no other choice.

Stubborn. She was so freaking stubborn.

"I don't want you tied to this diner," she said. "Not like me."

"All right." I wasn't tied to this place. Yes, I loved it here. Dolly's had been such a big part of my life, it had become a piece of my heart. But I'd always known someday I would walk away.

"You're fired."

I staggered, my shoulders crashing into Rush's body. "W-what?"

"You're fired."

"You're firing me?" Was this a joke? She was firing me because of some silly flyers?

"Yep."

My jaw dropped. "But I need this job."

"I'm cutting you loose. You're too attached, babycakes."

"Attached to my paycheck? Yes." My voice was too loud with a panicked edge. "You can't fire me."

No one was going to hire me, not this pregnant.

Dusty's gaze dropped to my belly, like she was realizing that if she fired me, I'd truly be screwed. "You've got until that baby is born. Then you're done."

"Dusty—"

"I'm not gentle, you know this."

No. She wasn't gentle. But she wasn't cruel.

This was cruel.

She bent and picked up that flyer, wadding it into a tight paper ball. "It's for your own good, sugar."

"You actually believe that," I whispered.

"I do." She nodded once, then spun around and disappeared into the kitchen.

When the door stopped swinging, a heartbreaking silence filled the room. My heart ached with every beat.

Fired. She'd just fired me. She'd taken away my livelihood without so much as a pause. She'd taken this from my child.

So she'd stay here out of loyalty to her mother, stay here so her asshole family members couldn't say she'd quit, all the while losing business in the hopes that it would fail because that was an outcome they could accept.

What the fuck sense did that make?

How could her loyalty not extend my direction? After all these years, this was how my time at Dolly's would end?

A part of me never wanted to set foot in this restaurant again. To leave her tonight and never look back. But I needed this job. I needed the money for rent and baby clothes and diapers. My own pride would bring me back here tomorrow afternoon for my regular shift.

I was just as trapped in this building as Dusty.

"It's okay." Rush wrapped his arms around my shoulders, pulling me against his body. "Give her some time."

I swallowed the lump in my throat as more tears welled. "She won't change her mind."

"She's just mad."

He didn't know Dusty, not the way I knew her. The decision was made. She wouldn't waver.

"I want to go home," I said, walking out of Rush's hold. "I'll be fine to drive."

"Faye—"

"I don't want to leave my car here." I went to the table with my books and began stuffing them into my backpack. I'd just zipped it up when the door's chime had my face lifting to the door.

"Sorry, we're closing up," Rush said.

He didn't realize that the woman in the entryway wasn't here for a meal.

She was frail and thin. Too thin. Her cheeks were sallow and her skin gray. She brushed snowflakes from her head scarf. The fabric was the same strawberry-blond color as my hair. The same color as hers should have been.

Except she had no hair.

When her caramel eyes met mine, they were dull and muted, but she forced a smile. "Hi, Faye."

Where was her hair? "Hi, Mom."

CHAPTER THIRTY-ONE

RUSH

It was heartbreaking to watch someone you loved shut down. Shut you out. Heartbreaking and wholly frustrating.

Faye had withdrawn so far within herself that she was like a walking ghost.

She moved silently through the house and had barely spoken a word in the past two days.

Ever since Dusty had "fired" her. Ever since her mother had shown up at the diner.

She'd become Zombie Faye.

"Where are you going?" I asked from the kitchen as she pulled on her coat. It was Friday morning. There was no reason for her to go to campus this early, not when her only class today didn't start until one. And she wasn't working at the diner until three.

She swallowed hard but didn't answer. Though her silence was answer enough.

"I'm going with you." I abandoned the piece of toast I'd

been buttering, leaving it on a plate as I crossed the living room for my own jacket.

"I need to go alone."

I pulled on my boots.

"Rush—"

"I'm going with you, Faye." No arguments. If she was going to go and see her mother, I'd be there too.

"You have class," she said.

"Then I'll miss it."

After Wednesday night, I wasn't letting Faye anywhere near Brynn without my company.

Not because Brynn had been rude or cruel. But because she was dying.

Faye might have a difficult relationship with her mother, but Brynn was still her mother nonetheless. The way she'd retreated, pulled away, was terrifying me.

I knew my girl's heart. It was big and open and more vulnerable than she'd ever admit.

Whether she was close to Brynn or not, her death would hit Faye. Hard. And when that hit came, I'd be there to make sure she didn't take it alone.

"I don't . . ." Faye shook her head and a sheen of tears glistened in her eyes. It was the first real emotion I'd seen from her in two days.

I hated to see her in pain, but anything was better than Zombie Faye.

"Don't what?" I stood in front of her and pushed my fingers into her hair. At least she didn't shy away from my touch. She might have gone quiet, but at least she let me touch her. And at night, she let me hold her close.

"I don't want you to see where I lived," she whispered.

I kissed her forehead. "You either let me go with you now, or I'll get the address from Dusty."

"She won't tell you."

"No, but Gloria will."

Her eyes lifted to mine, narrowing. I'd suffer that tiny glare a thousand times. It was only a hint of the spitfire who had my heart. "You don't have Gloria's number."

I pulled my phone from my pocket, scrolling through the contacts until I hit her sister's number. Then I held it up so she could see. "I'm going with you."

"Fine." She sighed.

That was easier than I'd thought it would be. Either because she knew there was no winning this argument, or because deep down, she was shredded. She knew how hard this visit was going to be.

When she had boots on her own feet, she grabbed her backpack from the dining room table, then followed me outside.

"I'll drive," I told her, unlocking the Yukon.

She wordlessly opened the passenger side door, climbed inside and fastened her seat belt.

The storm from earlier in the week had passed and the sky was clear and blue. The sun had already chased away the morning chill and was working to melt the snow. Water dripped from the gutters and the roads were covered in slush.

Faye gave me directions as we weaved through town, and as the homes became older, rougher, her hands stroked nervously at her belly. "It's not a nice place."

"So?" I reached over and took her hand, lacing our fingers together. "I don't care where you lived. All I care about is where you live now."

She nodded, pulling her bottom lip between her teeth as she pointed with her free hand for me to turn left. Then her grip on my hand tightened as she stared through the windshield, down the narrow lane.

Old cars and rundown homes filled the block. We passed a house with every window and door boarded with plywood. Someone had sprayed DO NOT ENTER in orange on the front wall. There was yellow caution tape lining the yard.

It was what the authorities did for meth houses that would need to be demolished and the land itself treated for harmful chemicals.

"That one. Brown." Faye nodded to the place right beside the meth house.

I schooled my features, hiding any reaction, so that my face stayed impassive. But fuck. This was where she'd grown up?

The home was small, about half the size of our place. It was two stories with siding falling off in some areas. The overhang on the porch looked one more heavy snow away from collapse. The roof upstairs was caving in on a corner, and like its neighbor, a few of the windows were covered in plywood.

I parked on the street, glancing around to the other homes.

Brynn's seemed to be in worse shape than most. A few had newer cars parked outside. One looked to be in the middle of a remodel.

Faye got out of the car and walked down the unshoveled sidewalk.

I followed, hands ready to catch her in case she slipped, but she took it slow. Was that because of the ice? Or because she didn't want to go inside?

She stopped at the mouth of the driveway, staring at the house with a blank expression. Then she pointed to the boarded-up window. "That was my room. The window broke when I was in eighth grade. She had that board put up instead of getting new glass."

Was that why she never wanted the blinds closed? *Damn.*

What did I say? How did I make this easier?

"I didn't think I'd be back here," she said, more to herself than to me.

My hand clasped hers.

There were two cars crammed into the driveway. One was covered in this week's snow and looked like it hadn't moved in months. The other was a dry, navy minivan with *Mission Hospice* written in white on the sliding door.

It was the same van that had brought Brynn to the diner on Wednesday.

"Does she know you're coming?" I asked.

Faye shook her head. "I didn't want to promise."

Even if it was to a woman who'd been a monster to her daughter, Faye wouldn't make a promise she might break.

I loved her.

More and more every day.

Faye inhaled sharply, then squared her shoulders and walked to the porch.

I gave the sagging roof a wary glance as I stepped up beside her while she knocked.

Brynn hadn't told her much on Wednesday. Only that she was sick. No, dying. She'd been specific in her word choice. She was dying.

Gloria knew about the cancer. It was the reason she'd been pressuring Faye to call their mother. But Brynn had made Gloria promise not to tell Faye the truth. Brynn didn't want Faye calling her out of guilt.

She must have realized that Faye wasn't going to speak to her again. That if she wanted to see her oldest daughter, she'd have to take that step. So she'd come to the diner on Wednesday in the middle of a snowstorm, driven by her hospice nurse, to extend an invitation.

If Faye was willing, Brynn wanted the chance to talk.

The door swung open with a sharp squeak. A heavyset nurse with short, white hair dressed in rose scrubs gave us a warm smile. "Hello. You're Faye."

Faye nodded. "I am."

"Your mom talks about you all the time. You're as pretty as she says."

Faye's hand twitched in mine, a moment of shock at the notion of a compliment from her mother, no doubt.

Gloria had promised Faye that Brynn had changed. Maybe it was true.

"Come on in." The nurse waved us inside.

We shuffled in, Faye's hand slipping free of mine as we followed the nurse down the short entryway to a living room. There was a candle burning on the coffee table, the scents of vanilla and sugar filling the room.

"She's in her bedroom," the nurse said. "Let me tell her you're here."

Faye spun in a slow circle as she took in the space. "It's clean. It never used to be clean."

I kept my gaze locked on her, searching for a hint of what was going on in her head, but she was blank. Zombie Faye was back.

"Come on back," the nurse hollered.

Faye wrapped her arms above her belly, hands clutching

elbows, and walked through the house, down a skinny hall that passed a staircase.

The nurse nodded, gesturing us into Brynn's bedroom.

"Hi." Brynn was lying in bed, blankets tucked around her body. Her pale face lit up at the sight of her daughter. "I didn't think you'd come."

"I, um . . ." Faye gulped and rubbed at the tip of her nose. "I didn't have class this morning."

It smelled like antiseptic and medicine and death. The scents burned my nostrils as I stepped past the threshold behind Faye.

The room, like the rest of the house, was clean and tidy.

"Would you like to sit?" Brynn nodded toward an empty chair in the corner. "Forgive me for not getting up. I'm wiped today. After treatments, they give me a good steroid. Those days, it's easier to move around. But when it wears off, I'm not much use to anyone."

She must have had a treatment on Wednesday then, because she'd looked awful that evening, yet ten times better than she did now.

I'd never seen someone dying before, but without question, Brynn was not long for this world.

Was this what Maverick had in store with his mom? Would he get to sit bedside and watch Meredith wither to skin and bones?

Faye didn't move. She simply stared at her mother, frozen in the space between the door and the bed.

"Please." Brynn tried to smile again, but it barely turned up her mouth. "Sit with me."

There was a plea in her voice, like she knew that if Faye walked out of here, it would be the last time she saw her daughter.

I put my hand on Faye's lower back, not pushing, not pulling. Just a touch so she'd know I was here.

She leaned against me for a moment, stealing whatever she needed, then walked to the chair and sat on its edge.

I shifted toward the wall, standing beside a five-drawer dresser. There was a framed photo on top, the picture faded and aged with yellow.

The woman was laughing into the camera. I didn't do a double take, thinking for a moment it was Faye. But it was of Brynn, young and healthy from years past.

Faye looked so much like her mother it was uncanny.

"Gloria told me about the baby." Brynn's tired eyes flicked toward Faye's belly—her frame was mostly hidden by her coat, but there was no mistaking she was pregnant. "A boy?"

"Yes." Faye nodded.

"I hope he gets your hair. You have such pretty hair."

Faye stared at a spot on the old carpet.

"Thank you for coming." The crack in Brynn's voice came with a wash of tears. Then came the coughing, so hard and loud it seemed to tear her body in two.

The nurse rushed in, moving to Brynn's side until the fit was over. Then she gave her a sip of water, helping her rest once more against the pillows.

"It's hard for her to talk much," the nurse said.

As in, make this short.

"I'm okay." Brynn's tone was ragged and rough.

The nurse gave her a sad smile, then eased out of the room.

"I'm sorry, Faye." Brynn breathed hard, like every inhale was a labor.

It probably was, considering she had lung cancer. Terminal lung cancer.

Her treatments were simply to draw this out, but there was nothing they could do. She'd told us on Wednesday that she'd waited too long.

"I just wanted to say that to you." Tears slipped down Brynn's face. "While I can."

Faye's chin quivered as she bit her bottom lip, fighting tears of her own.

I walked to her side and held out my hand.

She took it without hesitation, squeezing it so hard that my knuckles cracked.

"Do you have names?" Brynn seemed desperate for conversation. For any reply from her daughter.

But Faye stayed quiet, so I answered for her.

"Not yet," I said. "We're still tossing around ideas."

"I texted Gloria a list. Did she send it over?"

I gave her a sad smile. "Yeah, she sent it."

"You don't have to use them." Brynn wheezed, the noise in her chest so loud and miserable it filled the room.

"Harry?" Faye looked up, her hand still clutching mine.

"No. Jason?"

She shook her head.

"What about Gannon?" Brynn said. "Use your last name? Maybe not as his first, but it's a good middle name. Kind of unique."

Faye's gaze shifted to her mother. The blankness faded. And my girl, my strong fucking Faye, gave her mother grace. Whether Brynn deserved it or not, Faye's heart was big enough for them both.

"Good idea, Mom."

"Thanks." Brynn hummed, her eyes fluttering closed. "I like it too."

CHAPTER THIRTY-TWO

FAYE

"Hey." Maverick came into the kitchen with an empty glass.

"Hi." I took the last of the forks and spoons from the dishwasher's basket to put away in the silverware drawer.

"Rush told me about your mom. I'm sorry."

I stacked utensils in their respective slots and murmured, "Thanks."

My mother had died.

It had been three weeks since Rush and I had gone to visit her at my childhood home. Since, I'd gone another four times, each with Gloria. We'd sat with Mom in her cramped bedroom, listening to her wheeze and cough and attempt conversation. We'd listened to her apologize for the wrongs she'd desperately tried to right in her final days.

I'd planned to see her a fifth time, to go alone. Except Friday, the day I'd planned to visit, I'd received a call from the hospice nurse instead.

Mom had died in her sleep.

She hadn't wanted a funeral, so two days ago, Gloria, her dad and I had gone to the mountains outside of Mission to scatter Mom's ashes.

Chuck had said a few words while he'd wept.

Gloria had cried so hard she'd been unable to speak.

And I'd stared at the gray cloud of her remains until it vanished on the wind.

It was Wednesday. She'd been gone for five days, and I had yet to shed a tear.

That wasn't normal. I was extremely pregnant and my body was swimming in excess hormones. I should be a blubbering, frantic mess. What was wrong with me that I couldn't cry?

"I, um . . ." Maverick dragged a hand over his face. "I get it. Kind of. If you want to talk."

No, I didn't want to talk. "Maybe some other time."

"Yeah. No worries."

I finished with the dishes, closing the washer, and slipped past him for the living room, more than ready to disappear upstairs to the shower where I could wash my hair, change into pajamas and go to sleep.

Except before I could leave, Mav called my name. "Faye?"

This guy. Couldn't he just pretend I didn't exist? We'd spent weeks mostly avoiding each other. It had been the easiest way to maintain our truce. I only turned because of the truce. Because I didn't have the energy to fight. "Yeah?"

Mav cleared his throat, hesitating for so long it was like he'd forgotten what he wanted to say. Then he walked to his backpack at the kitchen table, unzipping the top to pull out a plain blue gift bag. The corners were crumpled and the sides wrinkled, like it had been in a fight with his textbooks and lost.

"I got this for you." He ran a hand over the white, ribbon handle. "I wasn't sure when I should give it to you after your mom and . . . anyway. Here."

He crossed the room, holding out the bag until I took it from his grasp.

After shifting a piece of blue tissue paper aside, I pulled out a navy onesie with the Treasure State Wildcats logo on the chest.

It wasn't the first gift we'd gotten for the baby, but it might be the most precious.

Rush had told me Mav loved kids, and I hadn't believed him. It was going to be impossible to keep hating Maverick Houston if he loved my son.

"Thank you." With a smile, I stowed the onesie and started for the stairs again.

"Faye? I'm really sorry. About your mom." The crack in his voice might as well have been a sledgehammer pounding into my chest.

The emotion swelled so fast it was hard to breathe. Tears flooded as the sting in my nose became unbearable. I'd managed five days without crying. Five whole days. My time must be up. Maybe I wasn't broken after all.

How was it that Maverick, a huge pain in my ass, was the guy who'd finally made me crack? I'd held my composure when I'd received the call from the nurse. I'd kept my shit together every time Gloria had broken down and cried in my arms. But watching Maverick fight his own tears might be my undoing.

He really loved his mother, didn't he? Her illness had rocked his world.

I wished, for his sake, I had some advice to give about how to say goodbye. But I'd drifted apart from my mother a long time ago. And I hadn't said goodbye.

On my last visit, Mom had fallen asleep while Gloria had been telling her about a boy at school. We'd left her to rest, and I'd planned to say what I needed to say on the next visit.

Except there hadn't been a next visit, and now everything that had been unsaid was clawing at my throat. The words that I'd mentally rehearsed over and over again were shouting in my head, begging to be set free.

Only the person they were meant for was gone.

It was a blessing. I was glad she couldn't hear them because they hadn't been entirely kind. Honest, but real. And my reality with Mom had been painful.

My silence had been her mercy.

I think it might have broken her, and in the end, she'd been broken enough.

He stared at a wall as he wiped beneath his eyes. "I mean it. I'm here if you want to talk."

"All right." I swallowed the lump in my throat. Then, not wanting to cry in front of Maverick, I trudged upstairs, the weight of my heart as heavy as the weight of my belly.

When I reached the last step, I looked at the open bathroom door. The idea of a shower suddenly seemed like too much work, so I shuffled into Rush's room, sinking to the edge of his bed.

I waited, my breath lodged in my throat, for the tears to come. For the body-wracking sobs of a daughter grieving her mother. Except that brief swell of emotion from downstairs had died somewhere between the first floor and second.

Now there was only fog in my brain and numbness in my chest.

I wasn't sure how long I sat there, staring into the nothingness, waiting to feel *anything*. But my lower back was aching by the time Rush's rugged voice cut through the haze.

"Hey." He leaned against the door, dressed in the jeans and long-sleeved T-shirt he'd pulled on this morning.

"Hi."

He came into the room, closing the door at his back, then he knelt in front of me, untying my shoes. He'd tied them for me today before he'd left for campus because I couldn't reach my feet.

"My mother didn't teach me to tie my shoes," I said. "Did I ever tell you that?"

"No."

"It was my fourth-grade teacher. She noticed one day that I poked my laces into my shoes rather than tie them and so she taught me how during recesses. I taught Gloria when she was eight."

He massaged my calves, his large hands kneading my tense muscles and swollen ankles. Rush never said much whenever I talked about my mother, probably because there wasn't much to say. He wasn't her biggest fan.

Neither was Dusty.

Was that why I was struggling to cry? Because I'd already used up my tears where Brynn Gannon was concerned? I'd used them all up in the last twenty-one years?

"Why can't I cry?" My throat felt like it was being scraped with sandpaper. My eyes were watery, but three blinks and they were dry again. "I'm almost nine months pregnant and exhausted and enormous, and I should be crying over my dead mother, but I can't. What's wrong with me?"

"Nothing." He rose up, his forehead to mine as he took my face in his hands. "There's nothing wrong with you."

I sniffled, not even trying to pull the emotions off the surface. They just slunk down deep, crawling into their hole where they'd eventually vanish. "I think I'm going to take a shower."

"Don't." Rush's thumb traced a line across my cheek. "Stay with me."

I searched his eyes, that gorgeous, unguarded face. Rush was a fairly approachable man, but when it was just the two of us, he dropped all pretenses. He was utterly vulnerable. It was the kind of openness you gave the person who held your heart in their hands.

"I used to feel alone. Every day." I put my hand on his cheek. "I don't feel alone anymore."

"You're not."

"It scares me." Being alone, there wasn't much to lose. Now? "If this is too good to be true, if this falls apart, I'll never recover."

"Then I guess we can't let it fall apart."

I stared into his eyes. "Promise me."

"I promise you." He leaned forward, pressing his lips to mine in a soft, sweet kiss. Then when I collapsed forward, his arms were waiting, hauling me close until my face was burrowed in his throat and I breathed in the scent of his skin.

"I don't know if anything would be different if I had called her months ago when Gloria told me to call her. I think if we had had more time, we would have hashed out too much. We would have relived all the hurt. I don't know what to think. I forgive her. I can't carry it around forever."

"Good," he murmured.

"I don't miss her. At the same time, I do."

There was a lot of heartache for me to process. It was something we weren't going to solve tonight, not entirely. But Rush would be here, no matter how long it took, ready to listen when I was ready to talk.

"Did I ever tell you that she hated sauce too?"

He shook his head. "No."

"She's the only person I've ever known like me. Or maybe I was like her."

And there it was. The biggest fear of them all. The one I knew soul-deep but hadn't had the courage to voice.

I leaned away, searching Rush's eyes. "What if I'm like her? What if I mess him up? What if I die and he can't cry because he hates me?"

Not that I hated my mother. Not really. I just wasn't sure how to grieve her yet. And I suspected this grief wouldn't be the kind with a river of tears. It would be a quiet sadness in my heart that I'd likely carry for decades.

"He won't hate you," Rush said.

"He might."

Rush shook his head. "He will love you the way I love you. With everything I have."

He loved me. It wasn't a surprise, not really. "You love me?"

"I love you." His thumb brushed across my cheek. It came away wet with a tear. My tear.

The relief was staggering, and I fell into his arms, letting him hold me as the first sob escaped. "I love you too."

I loved him so much it hurt.

He pulled me away, taking my face in his hands, and he kissed me as tears dripped down my face.

My hands fisted his shirt, keeping him close until we were both breathless. When we finally broke apart, my face was wet and a half sob, half laugh escaped my throat. "Say it again."

"I love you."

Rush Ramsey, quarterback extraordinaire, Wildcat football hero, honors student and fixer of flat tires, loved me.

Maybe I was lucky after all.

CHAPTER THIRTY-THREE

RUSH

April twenty-fourth.

Draft day. Faye's due date.

I'd planned to watch the draft tonight, but instead, I drove across town to the diner, checking my phone for the hundredth time. I'd expected a text or call hours ago, but I hadn't heard a word from Faye since she'd left for her shift this afternoon.

She'd had a rough night last night, barely sleeping because she was so uncomfortable. Then her lower back had started to hurt. She'd called the doctor who'd told her it could be early signs of labor and to call if her contractions started.

She was supposed to check in. Why the hell hadn't she checked in?

I raced down the road, driving well over the speed limit on the rough road to Dolly's. When its green siding came into view, Faye's Explorer parked at the back door, the air rushed from my lungs.

My foot came off the gas as I slowed to turn into the parking lot.

The oddly crowded parking lot.

"What the hell?"

The only open space was in the third row. I took it and parked, hopping out to scan the extra vehicles.

Three cars had Treasure State stickers in their rear windows. There were a couple out-of-town license plates. And, wait . . .

Was that Maverick's truck?

I hustled across the lot to the front door, peering inside the windows. The dining room was packed with people.

Students, actually. Other than one table with a couple of older regulars I'd seen a few times at Dolly's, all of the other tables were taken with people my age.

The door's chime was familiar, but the noise and bustle of the restaurant swallowed it whole. It didn't linger like it did normally.

"Rush." Maverick slid out of a booth—my booth—and walked over, hand extended. "Hey, man."

"Hi." I shook his hand. "What are you doing here?"

"You never told me Faye worked here."

"Okay," I drawled. "So you came to see her?"

"No. I just said I didn't know she worked here."

"Then what are you doing here?"

"Eating dinner with Erik." He gestured toward the booth. "Kalindi and one of her friends are on their way too."

Erik twisted in his seat, lifting a hand to wave.

I jerked up my chin. "Oh. How'd you find out about Dolly's?"

"Well, not because of you or Faye." He rolled his eyes. "I found a flyer advertising this place on campus. It said 'Save Dolly's,' so I thought I'd check it out. I was telling Erik about it while we were in the weight room. He told

Kalindi. Some of the other guys overheard and decided to try it too."

Faye's flyer had worked. I'll be damned. I grinned as pride swelled.

Now that I was inside, I recognized most of the faces. Some were younger guys on the football team. Others were athletes from different sports.

Months ago, I'd planned to spread the word about Dolly's. Tell guys from the team so they'd give it a chance. We'd had so much happen, I hadn't mentioned it.

Damn, I was glad I'd kept my mouth shut.

This victory was Faye's.

"Huh." I shook my head, still not sure what to make of a Dolly's Diner that was crammed with customers.

"Take it you're here to see Faye?"

"Yeah." I nodded, rubbing my jaw.

"She's in the kitchen. Want to sit with us?"

"Uh, sure." I took a step, about to follow him down the aisle, when the door opened at my back.

Two girls from the volleyball team stepped inside. One was Jennsyn Bell, the star who'd transferred to Treasure State last summer and absolutely dominated on the court. The other was Stevie Adair.

Stevie took one look at Maverick and the smile she'd been wearing turned to a scowl. "Maverick."

"Stevie," he sneered.

It was a rare sight to see a woman glare at Mav. Well, a woman other than Faye.

While Maverick didn't talk much about Stevie, I'd known of their mutual hate since freshman year.

Maverick's parents and Stevie's parents were best friends. They'd grown up together, here in Mission. Their childhood friendship had ended ages ago. According to Mav, Stevie had decided to hate him for some unknown reason.

So of course, he had to hate her back.

Someday, I'd like to hear Stevie's side of that story. I had a hunch it was very, very different than Maverick's tale.

"Cool diner," Stevie said. "Even if they let *anyone* in the door."

Maverick scoffed. "Nice, Adair. Always so good to see you."

"You can rot, Houston." Stevie shot him a glare, then followed Jennsyn toward the last empty table.

Yeah. I'd definitely like the other side of that story.

The swinging door to the kitchen flew open and Faye walked out carrying three plates loaded with burgers and fries. "Hey."

"Hey, sweets."

Dusty emerged next, her plates full of pancakes, omelets, bacon and toast.

"I'm helping," I told Dusty. Not a chance I was going to sit while Faye waited on all of these people.

"Damn straight." Dusty nodded for the kitchen. "You're on dishes. Mike's busy cooking."

I clapped Mav on the shoulder, then headed for the back, hanging my coat on a hook beside Faye's, then hauling off my sweatshirt until I was in jeans and a T-shirt, standing at the sink to start on a stack of dirty plates.

Five were rinsed and loaded into the dishwasher's tray when Dusty stormed into the kitchen with Faye close to follow.

"You didn't stop with your flyers, did you?" Dusty whirled on Faye, hands planted on hips.

"Nope."

"What the hell are you thinking?" Dusty flung out a hand. "Did you not hear a word I said?"

"Yes, I heard you." Faye jutted up her chin. "And I decided it was utter bullshit. If you don't want to be trapped in Dolly's, then sell it. Who gives a damn what the assholes in your family think? It's not like they're speaking to you anyway."

"Baby girl," Dusty held up a finger in warning, "watch yourself."

"Please." Faye rolled her eyes.

It was the first and only time I'd ever seen her roll her eyes, and for a moment, she was every bit Gloria's older sister.

"You have no problem being blunt when it comes to my life," she said. "So don't act so offended when you finally get a taste of your own attitude. Sell Dolly's. Start a snake farm with Mike. Move to Mexico. I don't care what you do as long as you're happy. And if Dolly's doesn't make you happy, then let it go. But your best shot at attracting a buyer is by filling empty seats."

Mike, standing by the flattop, ducked his chin, but not before I caught the hint of a smile he was trying damn hard to hide as he inspected his shoes.

"You're a pain in my ass," Dusty said. "And you're still fired."

"No, I'm not." Faye crossed her arms over her chest.

My spitfire.

Good for her. She was going to fight for her happiness. She was going to fight and win.

I loved her. God, I fucking loved her.

"You're not firing me. I'll quit when we move. Until then, you're stuck with me until you sell this place."

Dusty opened her mouth, like she was about to snap, but then confusion replaced her anger as her forehead furrowed. "What do you mean, move? Where the hell are you going?"

Faye opened her mouth, except before she could answer, her eyes bulged. Her hands flew to the sides of her belly. "Um."

"What?" I was at her side in a second, my wet hands covering hers. "What's wrong?"

Her nose scrunched. "I think my water just broke."

Dusty flew into action, running to get Faye's coat. She threw it at my head. "Don't just stand there, Rush. You need to drive us to the hospital."

Us. Faye's eyes welled with tears.

She'd lost a mother this year. But she still had one too.

"Mike?" Dusty called, jogging to her office.

"I've got the diner, honey," he shouted. "Get outta here."

My heart climbed into my throat as I met Faye's gaze.

Time was up. But we'd had enough. Thank fuck, we'd made it here. Together.

"Ready?" I asked.

She nodded. "Yeah. I think I am."

I kissed her forehead. "Me too."

THERE WAS a baby in my arms.

My son.

The faint rays of dawn lit the windows of our hospital room. Faye was resting in bed, her face turned toward the glass. But her eyes were on us in the chair in the corner.

Dusty had left an hour ago to get a few hours of sleep now that we were settled in our room for a couple of days.

341

But before she'd left, she'd kissed Faye's forehead and told her she'd be back before lunch with decent food and not to even think about ordering from the hospital's cafeteria.

My parents were nearly to Mission from the ranch. They'd be staying until we went home.

But for now, we had a few quiet moments of us. The three of us.

"Squish," I murmured, dropping a kiss to the blue knit cap over his head. Then I looked at Faye. "I love you."

"I love you too." Her eyes were heavy from a long, sleepless night of labor to deliver a nine-pound, three-ounce baby boy.

Without a doubt, she was the strongest person I'd ever met.

"We did it," she murmured.

"*You* did it."

She shook her head. "*We.* We just had to rally."

I stared at my son's face, peaceful in sleep. *Rally.* "Rally Ramsey," I murmured, trying it out to see how it sounded.

"Huh?" Faye asked.

"What if we named him Rally?"

She hummed. "Rally Gannon Ramsey."

It clicked. Instantly. "That's his name."

"That's his name." Faye smiled, letting out a quiet laugh. "I guess we have to stop calling him Squish."

"Nah." I touched the tip of his nose. "Not yet."

EPILOGUE
FAYE

Six years later . . .

"Mommy, is this where I was born?" Rally asked from the second row of our Cadillac SUV. With every word, his legs kicked the back of my seat.

I'd given up telling him to stop an hour ago and just let him squirm in his booster seat. We were all restless and ready to get out of the car. Today had been a long haul from Salt Lake, our halfway stopping point, to Mission.

But we'd made it. Finally. We were home.

"Yep, this is where you were born." It wasn't his first trip back to Montana, but usually when we visited, we went straight to the ranch. And in the summers, we always spent a week camping with Ryan and Macy at Gray Rock Lake. Rally hadn't been to Mission since Gloria's high school graduation, when he was still too young to remember.

"But not Mila," he said.

"No, not Mila. She was born in Phoenix."

"Oh." He let out a big sigh. "How much longer, Daddy?"

343

"We're here, Squish. Ten more minutes to the house." Rush glanced over his shoulder from his seat behind the wheel and winked at our son. Then he stretched a hand across the console for mine, clasping it tight.

He always held my hand through the big moments. When Rally had been born. When he'd been drafted. When we'd gotten married at the courthouse in Mission the day before we'd moved to Arizona. When we'd had Mila.

Together was how we'd gone into all of our adventures.

"It feels right," he said.

"Yeah." I smiled. "It does."

He brought my hand to his mouth, kissing my knuckles, then he let me go to point out the Wildcats stadium in the distance as we drove past campus. "See that, Rally? That's where I used to play football. And that's where I'll be working now."

Rally shifted, stretching his little body to peer through the windows. "It's not very big."

Rush chuckled. "No, I guess it's not."

Not compared to the Arizona Cardinals stadium where Rally was used to watching Rush play.

"This is where Mommy and Daddy both went to college," I told him.

"I thought you went to college at home?"

Home, for Rally, was still Phoenix. But soon, I hoped he'd consider home to be Montana.

"I went to *two* colleges. One in Phoenix. And the other here, in Mission."

After Rush had been drafted, the spring after his last year playing for Treasure State, we'd moved to Phoenix so he could play for the Cardinals.

We'd hired a nanny to watch Rally, and I'd enrolled in grad school. After two years, I'd graduated, then spent another two in a clinical fellowship. From there, the plan had been for me to get a job and gain some experience. I'd hoped to be hired at a school or healthcare facility.

Except then I'd gotten pregnant with Mila, so after completing my fellowship, I'd put the job hunt on hold to stay home with her after she was born, like I'd done with Rally. I hadn't wanted her to be with a nanny while she was a baby.

It had taken me a while to get comfortable seeing Rush's income as *our* income, no matter how often he reminded me that we were a team. The first year after Rally was born, I'd been so damn stubborn, refusing to quit my job at the diner just so I could pay rent.

I regretted how much time Rally had spent with babysitters. Though considering usually he'd been with Rush or Maverick, it hadn't been too bad.

Rush's last year at Treasure State, we'd stayed in that house with Maverick and Erik. We'd decided not to move after all. There hadn't been another rental that we'd desperately wanted for our home, and Maverick, well . . . that last year, he'd been nearly as scarce as Erik.

When he had been home, he'd doted on Rally.

Back then, if someone had told me Maverick Houston was good with babies, I would have laughed in their face.

Maverick was still living here, in Mission, and while Rush had made friends on the Cardinals team, those friendships hadn't been the same. Both were excited to be closer again.

I peered out my window, soaking it all in as we turned

onto a side street, navigating the quieter roads of town. Where there'd once been fields, there was now a subdivision of homes.

Mission had grown, but not so much that it was unrecognizable.

"See that school with the big playground, Rally?" I pointed out my window.

"Yeah?"

"That's where I'm going to work. And that's your new school too."

"But not Mila's."

Rush shook his head, grinning as we shared a glance.

Now that Mila was eighteen months, walking and old enough to start playing with her older brother's toys, Rally had become a bit territorial. He always wanted to know what was his and what was hers. He'd share, albeit reluctantly, as long as ownership was clearly defined.

"No, that's not Mila's school."

She'd be going to a local daycare for the first time while I started as the new speech therapist at Mountain View Elementary.

Rush would be joining the Treasure State Wildcats coaching staff, working for Coach Ford Ellis, a man who'd remained connected to our lives, even after all these years. A man my husband would always consider a hero.

It was a dream, for us both, to be back in Montana.

Ryan and Macy were ecstatic that we'd be closer so they could spoil their grandchildren, though I think Rush's dad was secretly disappointed he hadn't wanted to take over the ranch.

It wasn't entirely out of the question. That might be where we landed someday. Just not yet.

There was no work for me in their small town, and before we made that big of a lifestyle change, we wanted to give Mission another try.

My phone rang in my lap, Gloria's name on the screen. "Hey," I answered, putting it on speaker.

"Did you make it?"

"Just got to town," I said. "We're almost at the house."

We'd broken the trip into two legs, but both had been miserably long. Rally had gotten bored watching movies, and Mila was so over being trapped in her car seat that she'd screamed herself to sleep a half hour ago.

"How's my Rally man?" she asked.

"Here. I'll let you talk to him." I handed the phone to him so he wouldn't have to shout.

"Hi, Aunt Glory."

"Hey, bud. How was the trip?"

"Looong," he groaned. "I watched all my movies two times."

"Yikes. I miss you."

"I miss you too." He pouted. Rally loved his aunt Glory and Gloria loved her Rally man.

"I'm going to come visit," she said. "Soon."

" 'Kay." He stretched the phone forward, apparently done talking to Gloria. "Here, Mommy."

I took it off speaker and pressed it to my ear. "You okay?"

"This sucks."

After Gloria had graduated high school, she'd decided Montana winters weren't her style, so she'd moved to Phoenix for college. She'd come over for dinner at least three times a week and spent the night at our house whenever Rush was gone for an away game. She'd been my date to the Super Bowl game two years ago when the Cardinals had beaten the Steelers and Rush had earned himself a ring. And the night of Rush's last concussion, she'd watched the kids while I'd been at the hospital with my husband.

Gloria was not at all happy about this move.

Rush suspected it wouldn't take her long to be back on Montana soil, especially now that the guy she'd been dating for a couple years had just broken her heart. Her ties to Arizona were loose at best.

"Love you," I said.

"Love you too." She had as much pout as my six-year-old. "Bye."

I hung up and glanced at Rush, a smirk toying on his lips.

"Bet she's living here within the year."

"I'm not taking that bet," I muttered, earning a quiet laugh.

He slowed for one last turn into our new neighborhood, easing through the gates of the country club.

Lush, green grass sprawled between rustic homes with wooden siding and gleaming windows. The houses were all situated around Mission's best golf course, exclusive to members of the club. Not a home here was less than five thousand square feet. The clubhouse had a pool and fitness center.

A few miles away, on the opposite end of town, was a small, rundown house that was somehow still standing. I hadn't been to my childhood home since the day Gloria and I had packed the last of Mom's things and put them into storage. Since we'd sold the house to a man intent on flipping it.

It felt like another life. Another place. Maybe I'd drive by one of these days, if curiosity got the best of me. Or maybe I'd let the past stay tucked away, replacing old memories with new.

Rush slowed and pulled into the driveway of our new house. "We're here."

The minute the wheels stopped, Rally unclicked his seat belt. "Can I get out?"

"Yep." Rush shut off the engine, snagged the keys and climbed out to catch up to our son as he raced for the front door.

A whimper sounded from the back, so I rescued Mila from her car seat. "Hey, baby girl. Did you have a good nap?"

She rubbed a chubby fist into her eye, then sagged against my shoulder as I carried her into the house.

It was empty except for a bouquet of flowers left on the kitchen island, a gift from our real estate agent. The rest of our things, including my car, would be arriving tomorrow on the moving truck.

Racing footsteps thudded down the hall.

"Rally is picking his room," Rush said, taking Mila from my arms.

She burrowed into his strong chest, still half asleep. Her dark hair curled at the ends as she popped a thumb into her mouth.

Rally had inherited my strawberry-blond hair, but otherwise, he was a miniature version of Rush, with brown eyes and the same nose and mouth. He'd been taller than any other kid in his kindergarten class in Phoenix, something I suspected would be the case here too. And he had Rush's natural athleticism, always wanting to play catch or kick a soccer ball.

Mila, other than her brown hair, was mine. Caramel eyes. Tiny frame. Big attitude.

I walked to Rush's side, both of us staring through sliding

glass doors that overlooked the backyard and golf course beyond. Two men raced by in a golf cart.

"I love you." I leaned into Rush's side.

His arm slid around my shoulders, holding me close. "Love you too, sweets."

There were people who thought Rush was a fool for retiring after such a short time in the NFL. Sportscasters and spectators alike had questioned his decision countless times.

But they hadn't been in that hospital room in January. They hadn't listened to the doctors warn us about the risks of multiple concussions.

Rush had taken a hard hit during his last game and been knocked out cold. It had been his third major concussion and had scared us both.

He wanted to be the man who helped our kids with their math homework. He wanted to live his life without chronic headaches or memory loss. Brain damage? Not worth the risk. So he'd retired and walked away from professional football. And after a call to Ford Ellis, we'd made a new plan.

"Are we sleeping here?" Rally blew into the living area, his voice bouncing through the empty space.

"Not tonight," Rush said. "We will tomorrow, after our stuff gets here."

Rally's shoulders slumped. "I'm hungry."

"Let's get dinner. Then we can go to the hotel and you can swim."

"We get to swim? Yes." He pumped his fist, then ran for the front door.

"Dow." *Down.* Mila kicked her legs until Rush set her on her feet, then she chased after her brother.

Rush and I took another moment to soak in our house,

then we loaded up the kids, and without needing to ask where I wanted to eat, he drove us across town.

To Dolly's Diner.

It looked exactly the same. Weathered, green siding. Red and teal neon sign. Those white block letters perched on the roof. Windows that needed to be cleaned and a parking lot in dire need of repaving.

It was beautiful.

Dusty hadn't sold the restaurant after all. During Rush's last year at Treasure State, Dolly's had become a popular hangout with students from campus. Apparently, all Dusty had needed to revive her love of her mother's restaurant was a steady stream of young customers who gushed over her cooking and left tips.

With the influx of income, she could afford a line cook to cover the nights she didn't feel like working. She had a dishwasher and regular waitress. Her staff made it possible for her and Mike to take vacations too. They'd visited us twice a year, every year, after we'd moved to Phoenix.

I wouldn't have blamed her if she'd wanted to sell the business or close its doors, but Mission wouldn't be home without Dolly's.

Without Dusty.

She didn't know we were coming into town today. I'd tried her three times last week, but she was notoriously awful at returning calls. If she bitched at me for this surprise, well . . . she'd probably bitch.

With the kids in tow, we headed inside. The door's chime was the sound of my youth, tinny and tired. I smiled, standing beside the hostess station.

"Be right with you," a waitress called from the drink station.

Rush drew in a long breath. The diner's scents of bacon and cheeseburgers and french fries would stick to my hair. "I missed that smell."

"Me too."

He bent to brush a kiss to my lips, and for a moment, it was years ago. I was a waitress, pregnant and panicked, falling in love with the guy of my dreams.

The kitchen's swinging door flew open.

Dusty marched out, her hair, grayer than it had been during her last visit, was twisted into a knot and secured with two yellow pencils. She had a paper pad in one hand and a pen in the other. She froze when she spotted us, blinking twice.

"Nana!" Rally raced for her, crashing into Dusty's legs.

She wrapped him up tight and buried her nose in the top of his hair. When she looked up, it wasn't with tears, but a glare. Aimed at me. "I hate surprises. You know this."

"Then answer your phone."

She scoffed, shifting Rally to a side so she could pick up Mila and kiss her cheek. "Does this mean you live here now?"

"Yep." Rush nodded.

"Well, it's about time." She kissed both kids again, then set them down and waved toward the booths. "Find a seat. I assume you haven't had dinner."

"No, and I'm starving, Nana." Rally groaned, clutching his stomach like he hadn't eaten in a week. Then he took Mila's hand, holding it tight, as he walked to a booth, helping her into the seat.

He loved his baby sister, even if he wasn't all about sharing.

Dusty walked over to me and Rush, standing in front of

me. Her eyes raked over my body, head to toe, like she was making sure I really was here, in the flesh. Her hand came to my cheek, her eyes softening for a moment. Then she hauled me into a hug that was a little too hard and a lot too short, before nudging me along to join my children.

"What are we having?" she asked.

"Pancakes," Rush and I said in unison.

Rally held up a finger. "With no syrup."

BONUS EPILOGUE
RUSH

"Oh no, my shoe is untied again." Faye feigned a sad face. "These laces just won't stay tight. You'd better play without me. I'd hate to drag down the game by always having to fix my shoes."

I chuckled, gathering her in my arms and picking her up off the turf. "Nice try, sweets. You're playing."

"Rush." She squirmed, but I didn't let her down. Not until she stopped wiggling and let me kiss her mouth.

"Come on. It's tradition."

Today was the third annual Wildcats coaches' game. Coach Ford Ellis's End Zoners versus Coach Toren Greely's Grid Irons.

The sun was shining bright in the big, blue Montana sky. The air smelled like pine trees and summer. The kids chased each other around the stadium's field, their peals of laughter ringing through the stands.

It was the perfect day for a game of flag football.

Every coach on the staff was here today and everyone had brought along their families. As we had for the past three summers, we'd play football for a couple hours, then break for a barbecue.

Most of the wives played each year, but there were usually one or two who sat on the sidelines and watched. Faye had always been in that group. But this year, I'd convinced her to play.

Well, I'd thought I'd convinced her to play. All had been going according to plan up until twenty minutes ago when we'd been driving to the stadium, and she'd gotten cold feet.

"I don't know how to play," she said, her voice low. "Everyone is going to know I don't know much about football, and I'll embarrass you."

"Never." I took her face in my hands, then dropped another kiss. "You won't embarrass me. Besides, we have a deal."

I wanted her to play. And in turn, she'd get something she wanted. It was a win-win.

My guess was she'd use this opportunity to convince me to get a cat. I wanted a dog, but her heart was set on a cat.

So we'd get a cat, whether she played today or not.

Her lip curled. "I have regrets."

"You'll be fine." I tucked her into my side and led us toward the others on the fifty-yard line.

A lifetime ago, I'd spent a long night lying on that line, freaking the fuck out about my life.

Turns out, I hadn't needed to worry. Everything had turned out better than I could have dreamed.

"Did they actually pay to have logos designed for the shirts this year?" Faye asked, her voice low.

Ford and Toren both stood beside boxes of T-shirts, each printed with their respective team's name. "Probably."

Ford and Toren took this game seriously. Maybe a little too seriously. Not that I'd ever admit that to Faye.

Faye tried to shift away. I kept her close—if I let her go, she'd run away and hide—as I stopped in the space between Ford and Toren.

They'd each won a game in the past, and Toren had current bragging rights. He'd told me at work yesterday he wanted to keep them for another year.

Faye stood on her toes, peering past bodies to find our daughter playing on the opposite end of the field.

Mila was dressed in her favorite Wildcats cheerleading uniform, wearing a pair of pink, heart-shaped sunglasses as she danced to the music playing through the stadium's sound system.

Ford and his wife, Millie, had arranged for a few students from the golf and tennis teams to babysit. Then we'd asked a handful of guys from the team to be our referees.

Thomas, our quarterback and a kid I'd felt fortunate to coach this year, was playing catch with Rally.

My son caught a long running pass and grinned. Then he took three steps back and launched the ball through the air. "Go long!"

It spiraled and whatever conversation had been happening between the adults drifted to silence.

My kid could fucking throw.

He was nine.

Thomas sprinted hard, arm stretched to catch the ball. When he stopped running, his jaw dropped. The other guys all cheered, one of them running over to Rally to clap him on the back.

"Damn." Ford rubbed his jaw.

Toren shook his head in disbelief. "How old is he again?"

"Nine," I said.

"We'll never get him to play for the Wildcats, will we?" Ford sighed. "A big school is going to scoop him up."

"He's only nine, guys," Faye said.

"Exactly." I chuckled. "We've got nine more years to brainwash him that the only college on earth is Treasure State."

She elbowed me in the ribs as Ford and Toren laughed. "You know that's not what I meant."

No, it wasn't. And I didn't want football to be Rally's only focus. But it was fun to tease my beautiful wife. Anything to get that flash of fire in her caramel eyes.

Ford and Toren shared a look. A look that said they weren't so against that early brainwashing. It was the same look I'd seen them share when we were in recruiting meetings. An unspoken conversation passed between the two of them.

They'd played together in college. They were coworkers and friends.

Across the field, Maverick walked through the gate with the two bags of ice Toren had asked him to pick up for the coolers.

Mav was a special teams coach, which meant just like Ford and Toren, we got to hang out almost every day.

"All right." Ford clapped. "Now that everyone is here, let's do this. We'll flip a coin to see who gets to pick first."

Toren pulled a quarter from his pocket and flicked it in the air. "Tails."

It landed heads.

Ford grinned, cupped his hands to his mouth, and hollered, "Rally! Want to be my QB?"

My son's face was sheer joy as he nodded wildly, running over to join the adults.

Faye met my eyes and the beaming smile that spread across her face made my whole day.

She was happy if the kids were happy. If I was happy.

And all I really needed to be happy was her.

Love you, I mouthed.

She snaked her arms around my waist. "Love you too."

We had to break apart as the teams were picked. She landed on Ford and Rally's team. Toren picked me third after snagging his wife, Jennsyn, and Ford's Millie.

It was one of the best afternoons of the year, playing a game I adored with the people I loved most. When it was over, Ford's team had beaten us by a touchdown, but not a person on the field was upset.

"Congratulations," I told Faye.

"Thanks." She laughed. "Now that I played, I get what I want."

"A cat?"

"Nope." She crooked her finger, luring me in until only I could hear her voice. "One more baby."

"For real?"

She nodded.

"Fuck yes." I sealed my mouth over hers, kissing her as the people around us whooped and cheered. Then I hauled her over my shoulder.

"Rush!" she screamed, laughing as I jogged along the sideline, pretending like I was going to whisk her away to the car. She smacked my ass, laughing so loud and carefree it made a good day great. "Put me down."

I did as ordered, then kissed her again, losing myself in

the woman I'd never expected. The woman who had become my entire world.

My Faye.

———

SHE DIDN'T PLAY the fourth annual Wildcats coaches' game. She got to sit on the sideline, on a blanket beneath a huge umbrella.

With Reece, our newborn baby boy.

ACKNOWLEDGMENTS

Thank you for reading *Rally*! It's always such a joy to write in the world of the Treasure State Wildcats, and I hope you enjoyed Faye and Rush's story.

I am so lucky to get to work with an incredible team. My editor, Elizabeth Nover. My proofreaders, Julie Deaton and Judy Zweifel. My cover designer, Sarah Hansen. My agent and publicist, Georgana Grinstead. And my assistant, Logan Chisholm. From the bottom of my heart, thank you!

Also a massive thanks to the influencers who read and promote my books. I am so grateful for your support. And lastly, to my friends and family, thank you for your endless love. I could not do this without you.

ABOUT THE AUTHOR

Devney Perry is a *Wall Street Journal* and *USA Today* bestselling author of over forty romance novels. After working in the technology industry for a decade, she abandoned conference calls and project schedules to pursue her passion for writing. She was born and raised in Montana and now lives in Washington with her husband and two sons.

Don't miss out on the latest book news.
Subscribe to her newsletter!
www.devneyperry.com

Made in United States
Orlando, FL
06 August 2024

50027382R00225